Entwined Publishing books by Kiera McKenna

Eldritch Curiosities
The Dragon's Harp

Eldritch Curiosities

THE DRAGON'S HARP

KIERA MCKENNA

ENTWINED PUBLISHING

The Dragon's Harp
ISBN # 978-1-80250-265-7
©Copyright Kiera McKenna 2025
Cover Art by Kelly Martin ©Copyright September 2025
Interior text design by Entwined Publishing
Published by Enchant, an Entwined Publishing imprint

Published in 2025 by Entwined Publishing, United Kingdom.

Entwined Publishing is a division of Totally Entwined Group Limited.

THE DRAGON'S HARP

Dedication

For every reader who has ever felt the call of something wild and ancient, who has gazed at ruined castles and wondered what secrets they keep, who believes that the most dangerous adventures are always worth the risk.
And for those brave enough to choose their own legend — may you find your fire, claim your dragons and never apologize for the magic that burns within you.

Chapter One

When Scotland breathed, the land exhaled mist and memory. It curled over the damp stone, clung to the air like something half-forgotten, waiting to be remembered. The wind whispered against Isobel Rhode's skin, tasting her, testing her, like an unseen presence brushing the edges of her soul.

She shivered, but not from the cold.

The moment the plane set down on Scottish soil, she felt it—something older than history itself. Not just in the weight of the air or the scent of the sea threading through the cracks in the world, but in the hum beneath her skin. A low, thrumming awareness.

Magic.

It had taken her weeks to admit it, even after Margaret Alden had handed her that whiskey, looked her straight in the eye and said, *"Dragons are real, Izzie."*

She hadn't believed it, not at first. But belief would stop mattering when the truth stood right in front of her. Her new boss had promised her that.

Now here she was, standing in a quiet pocket of Glasgow Airport, her boots damp from the rain-slicked floor, her heart pounding like she had just stepped off the edge of the world.

Because maybe she had.

She adjusted the strap of her shoulder bag, fingers brushing the envelope inside—her instructions, her mission, the reason she was really here. But the weight of it was insignificant compared to the deeper truth pressing in from all sides.

This was not just a new country. Not just a job.

She was walking into a story older than the stones beneath her feet. A story of dragons and relics, of power buried beneath time itself.

And whether she wanted to be or not, she was now a part of it.

The scent of rain curled through the airport's automatic doors, cool and sharp against the recycled air. It was different here—thicker, richer, wet stone and brine, like the breath of something ancient stirring beneath the earth.

Izzie inhaled, the weight of the air settling deep in her lungs.

Scotland.

The word unfurled in her mind, reverent and disbelieving all at once. She was really here. Not just in some daydream fueled by too many late-night history documentaries or reading about it in a leather-bound book beneath the dim lights of Eldritch Curiosities antiquities shop.

The hum of the terminal barely registered— murmured conversations, the rhythmic thud of luggage wheels, the clipped, efficient tones of intercom announcements. It all faded beneath the pulse in her ears, a steady, insistent rhythm that had started the moment she stepped off the plane.

Something was different.

She exhaled slowly, Margaret's words echoing in her mind. *"Everything here has been a test. And you passed spectacularly."*

Her pulse skipped. She didn't feel like she'd passed anything — more like she'd been shoved through a door she hadn't meant to open. A month ago, she'd been cataloging dusty grimoires and debating whether she could afford the subway fare home. Now she was standing in a foreign country with a dossier full of classified information in her bag and a sinking feeling in her gut. This wasn't just a new job. It was a gamble with her entire life.

And she still wasn't sure if she was playing the right hand.

She stepped deeper into the terminal, slipping into the crowd, but the feeling didn't fade. That wrongness... Like the air itself was different here, charged with something invisible. It prickled over her skin, humming in her blood.

Izzie swallowed hard.

She'd read the files, pored over every page until her vision blurred, but nothing — nothing — had prepared her for this.

Dragons are real.

The words still didn't fit in her head properly. They sat there like a stone dropped into deep water, sinking, sinking, waiting to hit the bottom.

She hadn't believed it. Not at first. Not even after Margaret had slid the photos across the table, each one impossible — men caught mid-shift, golden eyes reflecting light that shouldn't be there, the blurred stretch of wings too large for human frames.

Not even after reading the classified reports, the historical accounts that felt too detailed to be myth.

Not even after the moment she knew, deep in her gut, that Margaret wasn't lying.

But here, now, in this place where the air felt too full, too thick, where something unseen curled at the edge of her senses —

She believed.

And she didn't know if that was a good thing.

A voice crackled over the intercom, breaking the spell. Izzie sucked in a breath, the weight in her chest loosening just enough to move again.

She had a mission. A relic to find. A ferry to catch.

And no time for the ghosts of forgotten myths pressing against her skin.

* * * *

The road stretched before her, a winding ribbon of damp asphalt cutting through a landscape too vast to hold in a single glance. Scotland unfolded in pieces — mist-laced hills, glens tucked between shadowed ridges, the occasional flicker of a ruined castle on a distant rise. Rain smeared across the windshield in lazy streaks, the wipers thudding a steady rhythm against the glass.

It should have felt like any other drive. But it didn't.

Izzie gripped the wheel tighter, shifting in her seat as the thoughts she'd been avoiding began circling back, relentless as the tide. Things she'd rather not think about, now that she was here.

Dragons didn't just mate with human women. They claimed them.

The word alone made her stomach knot.

Margaret had been clinical about it, laying out the facts like a doctor explaining an unavoidable procedure. It was a matter of survival. A biological imperative—a solution to a crisis centuries in the making.

Izzie had nodded, taken notes, kept her expression neutral. But inside, something had twisted.

Because it wasn't just one dragon. It was never just one.

A woman who bonded with a dragon bonded with all his brothers. An entire clutch—born of the same egg season, tied together by something deeper than blood. Brothers-of-the-egg, they were called. And once she conceived, the father of the clutch of eggs she carried became her true mate, whether he was the one she'd fallen in love with or not.

Permanently. Unbreakably.

She exhaled sharply, fingers flexing against the wheel.

It was archaic. It was insane. And it had absolutely nothing to do with her.

She was here for the Harp.

The ancient relic that could lull dragons into sleep, strip them of their defenses, make them vulnerable in a way they rarely were. That was what mattered. That was what she needed to focus on.

Not the way her skin prickled when she thought of them. Of him.

Her stomach clenched.

She didn't even know who he was. Only that Margaret had said she'd be working with a specific clutch—the ones overseeing this part of the territory. And they would decide how much they trusted her.

By the time she pulled into the ferry lot, the sun had begun its slow descent, barely visible through the mist rolling in from the water. The ferry bobbed against the dock, white paint weathered by salt and time.

And still, that feeling lingered — a slow press of awareness settling against her skin.

She tightened her grip on the wheel and drove onto the ferry, the weight of unseen eyes trailing her every move.

Chapter Two

Izzie's car rumbled along the winding, narrow road that led to the B and B on the isle of Arran as the sun began its descent behind the hills. The landscape was breathtaking, with the jagged cliffs of the Arran coastline visible just over the trees, and the faint scent of the sea salt hanging in the air. The stone house ahead stood out against the lush green of the surrounding fields, its aged exterior covered in ivy and moss. Despite its beauty, there was an undeniable aura of something older, something not quite right about the place. But it was exactly the kind of eerie charm Izzie had been craving.

She parked her rental car, its engine giving a final sputter before falling silent. The B and B's large oak door creaked open as she approached, and a woman in her fifties stepped out to greet her, her silhouette bathed in the golden light of the setting sun.

"Welcome, dear," Moira said, her voice soft yet firm, the faintest trace of a smile curling on her lips. "I'm Moira. So glad to have you with us."

Izzie forced a smile, giving a small wave as she retrieved her bags. Moira's appearance was just as much a part of the house as the stone walls. Her silvered red hair was pulled back into a neat bun, her clothing simple but elegant — a long skirt and a shawl over her shoulders. There was an undeniable calm about her, but there was also something a little too keen in her eyes, which made Izzie feel like she was under constant observation.

"Lovely place you've got here," Izzie commented as they walked into the house together. The inside was as charming as the exterior — wooden beams crisscrossed the ceiling, and a large stone fireplace flickered with the remnants of a fire. Old paintings and intricate tapestries adorned the walls, and the smell of burning wood mixed with the scent of something floral and herbal, familiar yet unplaceable.

"Thank you, dear. It's been in my family for generations," Moira replied. She paused for a moment, studying Izzie with an intensity that felt just a little too much. "Are you visiting Arran for business or pleasure?" she asked, her voice light but laced with curiosity.

Izzie hesitated for a split second before answering, unsure why she felt the need to be guarded. "Just a bit of both, I suppose. Needed a break, and I've heard good things about this part of the world."

Moira smiled warmly but didn't respond further, as if she knew the answer already.

After a quiet, simple dinner — vegetables roasted with herbs and a delicate fish dish served alongside a glass of red wine — Moira led Izzie to her room. The old wooden staircase creaked beneath their feet, the house whispering its secrets with each step. When they reached the door, Moira bade her a pleasant goodnight, then disappeared down the hallway.

Izzie closed the door behind her, taking a moment to survey her surroundings. The room was spacious yet cozy, decorated with heavy antique furnishings. A large, four-poster bed sat against one wall, draped in a floral-patterned quilt. Wooden shutters, wide and imposing, were closed over the windows, and the thick curtains added a layer of seclusion to the already isolated feeling of the place.

She dropped her bags by the door and walked to the window, pulling the heavy shutters open with a slight groan. The night air was cool against her skin, refreshing after her long journey. She took a deep breath, the scent of the sea mingling with the earthy fragrance of the surrounding forest.

The sound of the wind rustling the trees outside the window was calming, and after a moment of enjoying the quiet, Izzie stripped off her clothes and headed for the cramped en-suite bathroom. She let the hot water from the tiny shower wash over her, steam rising around her as the tension from the day's travel melted away. The water was soothing, like a gentle embrace, and she allowed herself to linger under the spray, enjoying the solitude.

When she stepped out, her skin flushed from the warmth of the shower, she slipped into the silk nightgown Margaret Alden had insisted on packing for her — light, delicate, and feeling luxurious against her skin. As she stood in front of the mirror, adjusting the straps of the gown, a strange sense of anticipation crept over her, though she couldn't say why.

The bedroom was warm, almost too warm, so she cracked the window open a bit further, letting the cool night air slip in. The moon hung high in the sky now, its light casting a pale glow across the room, making the shadows of the furniture stretch long and mysterious. Izzie crawled onto the bed, the silk of her nightgown rustling softly against the comforter. She closed her eyes for a moment, savoring the stillness, the weight of the day's journey settling around her.

But as her mind quieted, her hands began to move of their own accord. The softness of the fabric, the warmth of the bed, the stillness of the room—it all conspired to ease her into a state of relaxed vulnerability. She shifted on top of the bed, her body responding as her fingers explored her skin, brushing against the delicate lace of her nightgown.

Within minutes, she was biting the white pillowcase to stifle her cries as she climaxed atop the comforter, her silk nightgown bunched around her waist so that the cool night breeze wafted over her spread legs.

What Izzie didn't know, what she couldn't possibly have imagined, was that outside the room, on the rooftop of the B and B, something was watching her as she masturbated.

Someone…

Hidden in the shadows of the tall chimneys, a dragon perched—its large, leathery wings folded against its back. Its scales shimmered in the moonlight, red, orange, gold. The creature's eyes glowed like amber as it peered through the window, its attention fixed on Izzie. On her legs spread wide for him. Its nostrils flared, the air thick with its ancient presence, the weight of its gaze felt even from the distance.

Unseen and unheard, the dragon watched her, its interest unwavering.

Inside, Izzie's body tensed for a moment, as if she felt the presence of something—or someone—else. But the feeling passed as quickly as it came, and she drifted further into the night, unaware of the silent observer perched above her, waiting in the dark as she pleasured herself.

The dragon remained, vigilant and patient, its eyes locked on her every movement.

Chapter Three

The stillness of the night was shattered by a faint sound — heavy and deliberate. Was that a tree branch scraping the roof? Izzie stirred in her bed, her heart suddenly racing as the noise continued. It was subtle, like the scratching of claws against stone, the creak of something too heavy for its frame. The sound traveled down the walls of the old house, echoing through the silence of the B and B. She held her breath, straining to listen, but there was nothing else — just the rhythmic thumping, like something pacing above her head.

Izzie's pulse quickened as she slipped from the warmth of the bed, her feet landing on the cold wooden floor. Moonlight through the open window illuminated the room in eerie shades of silver, casting long shadows across the antique furniture. She moved to the window, her bare feet making no sound as she pushed the shutters wider. Cool night air rushed in, and she leaned forward, her gaze searching the roof opposite her room in the L-shaped building, her breath catching in her throat as she peered into the darkness.

For a moment, the world outside was impossibly still, dense fog rolling in thick blankets across the landscape beyond the parking area. But then, just at the edge of her vision, a massive shadow flickered — too large to be a bird, too swift to be a person. It vanished into the fog with unnatural speed, melting into the mists like a phantom.

Izzie stepped back from the window, her heart pounding. Had she imagined it? Could it have been a very large bird? Or was it something else entirely? Was it one of the dragons she'd been sent here to work with? Her mind spun, trying to make sense of what she had seen — or thought she'd seen. She shook her head, trying to calm the racing thoughts in her mind. The night seemed to grow colder, more oppressive, as she pulled the shutters closed, locking them with the small brass latch and crawling back into bed. But sleep was elusive, and she lay awake, her thoughts tangled in the mystery of what she had glimpsed outside her window.

* * * *

The morning light, pale and diffused through the mist, felt both comforting and unsettling as it filtered into the room. Izzie sat up, her muscles stiff from a restless night, and rubbed her eyes. She'd locked the shutters closed last night, but they were spread wide now, open to the fresh morning air. Had Moira come in and opened them without waking her? She tried to shake off the unease, but it lingered, nagging at the back of her mind. She dressed quickly in a comfortable sweater and jeans, trying to shake off the remnants of her strange experience. The quiet of the house seemed even more oppressive in the daylight, as though the walls were still holding the secrets of the night.

Downstairs, the smell of freshly brewed coffee and warm bread greeted her as she entered the dining room. Moira was already preparing breakfast, her movements graceful. But this morning, there was something different in the air — a shift in the way Moira looked at Izzie. Her gaze lingered on Izzie a moment longer than usual, a knowing glint in her eyes that made Izzie's skin prickle.

"Good morning, dear," Moira said, her voice soft, as she set down a plate of eggs and bacon in front of Izzie. "Sleep well?"

Izzie forced a smile, trying to push away the lingering discomfort. "Not the best night's sleep," she admitted, pushing her food around on her plate. "I think I heard something outside, like something was moving on the roof."

Moira's expression didn't change, but Izzie noticed the brief flicker of something in her eyes — a glimmer of recognition, perhaps? "The roof is quite old," Moira said, her voice calm. "The wind can make strange sounds, especially when the fog rolls in. You'll get used to it."

Izzie nodded, but the unease didn't leave her. She couldn't shake the feeling that Moira knew more than she was letting on.

Before Izzie could speak again, the front door creaked open, spilling a breath of cool, damp air into the warmth of the inn. A man stepped inside, shaking the mist from his broad shoulders, his presence commanding yet unhurried. He carried himself with the quiet assurance of one who had spent years braving the wild, his storm-gray eyes scanning the room before settling, unerringly, on her.

Dark hair, streaked with silver at the temples, framed his angular face, the sharp lines softened only by the hint of a smile playing at the corner of his lips. A large hiking pack hung from one shoulder, his clothes worn by travel yet carrying a certain rugged elegance.

"I'm Callum," he said, his voice deep and smooth, like the hush of waves over polished stone. "Callum Sìol Dòmhnaill. I've been hiking the island for days now—didn't realize there was a place to stay here."

Moira greeted him with the warmth of someone accustomed to welcoming wanderers. "Aye, and you're in luck. I've a room if you're needin' rest."

He nodded, setting his pack down. "That'd be grand. A real bed sounds better than I care to admit."

"I'll fetch the key once breakfast is done," Moira assured him. "But for now, why don't you sit? Have something to eat with Miss Rhodes here."

His gaze flickered toward Izzie once more, unreadable yet intent. He pulled out a chair across from her, the scrape of wood against the floor the only sound between them for a moment. "Mind if I join you?"

Izzie hesitated, her fingers tightening around the porcelain of her teacup. Last night's unease still clung to her like the lingering chill of a half-remembered dream. But there was something disarming about him, something steady, as though the world itself quieted in his presence.

"No, not at all," she murmured, though her voice lacked its usual certainty.

Callum studied her, not unkindly. "You all right, then? You seem a wee bit unsettled."

She exhaled slowly, torn between brushing it off and admitting the truth. Finally, she chose the latter. "I didn't sleep well. Thought I heard something outside last night." She let out a soft, self-conscious laugh. "Probably just the wind."

Callum tipped his head, considering. "The wind, aye? Or somethin' else?"

Izzie shrugged, feeling foolish now in the light of day. "It was late. I was probably imagining things."

He reached for the teapot, pouring himself a cup, his movements slow and deliberate. "Well," he said, a glint of something unreadable in his expression, "if there is anything lurking out there, you've no need to worry. I'm a fair enough hand at keeping the night's shadows at bay."

His voice, laced with quiet amusement, coaxed a small smile from her despite herself. The tension in her shoulders eased, just a fraction.

"I'll hold you to that if the noises come back tonight," she said, the words lighter now.

He grinned, raising his cup in an easy toast. "Then here's to a quiet night ahead — and a fine breakfast in the meantime."

A quiet laugh escaped her, and she tapped her teacup against his, warmth beginning to bloom where unease had lingered. "I'll drink to that."

Izzie definitely noticed the way Callum Sìol Dòmhnaill's eyes lingered on her as he dug into the bowl of oatmeal Moira set before him. There was something in his gaze — something intense, like he was studying her, sizing her up. She fumbled with her fork, trying to spear a bite of her omelet, his deep gaze making her nervous. It was as though he was trying to figure out something about her, something he hadn't asked yet.

Callum flashed her another smile, his teeth white against his tan. "You're the only guest here?" he asked, his voice smooth, but the question seemed to hang in the air too long.

"I'm the only one for now," Izzie replied, her voice betraying none of the discomfort she felt. "Until you arrived." She took a sip of her coffee, trying to ignore the unsettling weight of his gaze.

Moira, apparently sensing the awkwardness, filled the silence with a few questions about his hike, but Izzie found herself distracted, her thoughts still clinging to the strange vision from the night before. Every time she looked at Callum, she had the distinct feeling that he knew something—about her, or about the island—that he wasn't saying. His eyes never strayed too far from her, as if he were waiting for her to speak, to give him some sort of signal. But she remained silent, keeping her thoughts to herself.

After breakfast, Izzie excused herself, eager to get out of the house and away from the strange energy that had settled in the air. She made her way upstairs to gather her things, but as she reached her door, she noticed a small, folded piece of paper on the ground. It had been slipped under her door sometime during the night. Her heart skipped a beat as she knelt to pick it up, her hands trembling slightly as she unfolded the note.

Be careful who you trust. You're not alone.

The words were simple, but their meaning was anything but. Her stomach tightened, and the air in the room felt suddenly thick, as if she were being watched. She scanned the hallway quickly, but there was no one in sight. Her mind raced—who could have left this note? And why now?

The cryptic warning echoed in her mind as she tucked the note into her pocket, her senses heightened. Whatever had been on the roof last night, and whatever

Callum's eyes were saying, it was clear that something more than a simple hiking trip was happening here on the island. And Izzie was tangled in it—whether she liked it or not.

As she left the B and B and headed out to explore the island, the fog still hung thick in the air, hiding the rocky cliffs and twisting paths. She couldn't shake the feeling that she was being drawn into something larger, something that had been waiting for her, watching from the shadows. The question now was whether she would be able to uncover the truth before it was too late.

Chapter Four

Scotland's island fog hung heavy around Izzie as she walked across the dense peat, her boots crunching on the soft earth beneath her feet. The air was damp and cool, a fine mist swirling around her legs as she made her way up a narrow path leading to an ancient broch. The ruins were rumored to be the birthplace of the Harp's legend, a story that had captivated Izzie's imagination since she had first learned of it. According to the island's folklore, the legend spoke of a harp with the power to control dragons, to put them under a spell that allowed the Harp's player to manipulate them. It was said to have been created long ago by an enigmatic figure, a sorcerer, who had disappeared into the mist.

As Izzie drew closer to the broch, the towering stone structure emerged from the fog like a ghost, its jagged edges rising from the overgrown ground. The remnants of the round walls stood at odd angles, their stones weathered by centuries of exposure to the harsh winds and salt of the sea. She felt a rush of awe as she stepped closer, placing her hand on the cool, ancient stone. There was an energy here—something she couldn't quite place, but it felt old, potent, as though the broch itself was holding onto secrets long forgotten.

Izzie spent a few moments exploring the area, brushing her fingers along the intricate carvings that decorated the stones. Some of the markings looked like symbols, others like a language she couldn't understand. The air seemed to hum with an unfamiliar energy as she took in her surroundings, and for a fleeting moment, she felt as though she wasn't entirely alone. The sensation of being watched returned, prickling at the back of her neck. It was subtle at first— just the faintest shift in the air, the quiet rustle of leaves in the wind, but it was enough to make her heart beat a little faster.

She paused, turning slowly, scanning the misty landscape. The fog had thickened, blurring her vision, but there was something—someone—there, standing just beyond sight. A shadow, a figure, almost indistinguishable from the mist itself.

Then, through the haze, a man stepped forward.

His silhouette emerged from the shifting fog, tall and imposing, the faint outline of his features barely visible through the mist. His face was sharp, his jawline strong, but it was his eyes that drew Izzie's attention. They were an unnatural gold, glowing faintly in the dim light, like twin orbs of molten amber. His gaze locked onto hers, and for a moment, a shiver crawled up Izzie's spine. There was something deeply unsettling about him, yet something compelling, magnetic that drew her in despite the warning bells going off in her mind.

He took a few steps closer, the mist swirling around him as though he were part of it. His movement was fluid, effortless, like he wasn't quite bound to the world in the way she was. He stopped a few paces away from her, his golden eyes never leaving hers.

"You need to leave." His voice was deep, low and filled with an authority that sent a chill through her. The sound of it reverberated in the air, making the fog seem even thicker, more suffocating. "Before nightfall."

Izzie's pulse quickened at the weight of his words. There was a strange energy around him. It made her skin prickle and her breath come in shallow bursts. She felt his presence like a weight on her chest, but even more so, she felt the pull of his words. He was a warning, a messenger. But from what? And why?

"Leave?" Izzie repeated, trying to mask the unease creeping into her voice. "I'm not going anywhere."

The man's lips twitched slightly, as if he was amused by her defiance. "You don't understand," he said, his voice softer now, but still carrying an undeniable weight. "Arran is no place for someone like you. You've already come too far. The fog is not the only thing that hides here. You don't know what you've uncovered."

Izzie's curiosity flared. This was the most anyone had said about the island since she arrived, and it only made her more determined to find out what he was talking about. "What do you mean? I haven't uncovered anything yet. I'm just walking. Exploring." She took a step toward him, her eyes narrowing. She refused to let fear dictate her actions, not when there were answers just out of reach.

The man's expression darkened, his golden eyes flickering as though something stirred beneath the surface of them. "You're meddling with forces you don't understand," he said, his tone no longer a suggestion, but a command. "The island is ancient. It's steeped in power — power that has been dormant for centuries. The Harp of Ceòthach Glen, the legend — it's not just a story. It's a warning."

A sudden gust of wind swept through the area, sending the fog swirling and the trees shuddering with the force of it. The man's form wavered as though the mist were swallowing him whole, his presence slipping in and out of the fog like a phantom.

Izzie's breath hitched as the wind howled through the glen, rattling the trees, the mist curling thick around them. The man stood firm, unaffected by the chill that raised goosebumps along her arms. There was something unnatural in the way he moved — or rather, how he barely seemed to move at all, his presence as unshakable as the rocks beneath their feet.

"I've been watching," he said at last, his voice a low murmur, nearly lost to the wind.

Izzie stiffened. "Watching?"

His golden eyes held hers, dark and knowing. "Aye. Last night."

A cold dread slid through her veins, mingling with something warmer, something illicit that she couldn't name. She swallowed hard, shaking her head. "That's not possible. No one was there."

A slow smile, the kind that sent heat licking down her spine. "You think locked doors and drawn curtains keep out the things that haunt this island?" He tilted his head, studying her as though she were the thing out of place. "I saw you."

Her stomach twisted as mortified realization crashed over her. *Oh God.* The heat of shame rose in her cheeks, scalding. She had been alone in her bed, tangled in the sheets, her body humming with restless energy. The weight of the island's strange magic had lingered in her bones, in her blood, pushing her toward pleasure.

And he had seen.

"You—" Her voice cracked, breathless. "You were spying on me?"

His gaze darkened, though there was no apology in his expression. Only certainty. "I was watching. There's a difference."

The words should have repulsed her, should have sent her running, but instead, they settled into something deep, something dangerous. Her pulse thrummed wildly against her throat, a traitorous heat pooling low in her belly.

She should deny it, should tell him he was sick, twisted—but the words wouldn't come. Because beneath her embarrassment, beneath the pulse of fear, was something else. Something raw and electric, a charge that crackled between them like a coming storm.

"You shouldn't be here," she whispered, though even as she said it, she knew it was a lie.

His lips parted, and for a moment, she thought he might move closer. "Neither should you."

The wind howled, rattling the branches above them, but Izzie barely heard it over the wild pounding of her own heart. The stranger took a step forward, slow, deliberate. Instinct made her retreat a pace.

He followed, a step of his to a step of hers, measured as a hunter closing in on prey.

Izzie's breath came fast, sharp little exhales that did nothing to steady her racing pulse. The fog coiled around them, thick and shifting, blurring the world beyond the two of them. She should turn, should run—but she didn't. She couldn't.

The man's golden eyes held her captive, glinting with something unreadable in the dim light. Another step, another retreat, until her shoulders met cool stone. The ancient broch rose behind her, its weathered surface solid, unyielding. There was nowhere left to go.

He loomed above her, close enough that she could see the faint stubble along his jaw, the way the mist clung to his dark hair. Close enough that his body heat brushed against her skin, despite the chill.

"Izzie," he murmured, and she shivered at the way her name shaped itself in his mouth, low and rich.

His hands reached for her waist, cradled her hips.

She swallowed hard, pressing her palms to the cold wall behind her. "You—" Her voice wavered, caught between fear and something darker, something she didn't want to name. "You need to back off."

He didn't. One hand moved, lower… Lower…

It covered her mound through the heavy fabric of her jeans. His fingers began a rhythmic seeking, sliding back and forth along her lips, as she began to get wet at the stimulation. He had been outside her window. He had watched her masturbate.

And now he was doing to her what she had done to herself.

She groaned, but her hands came up to his chest. Tried to push him away. "No. Stop."

Instead, he lifted a hand, pressing his palm flat against the stone beside her head, caging her. The movement made her breath hitch, her whole body taut with awareness.

"I saw you," he repeated, his voice softer now, more intimate. "Saw the way you moved on top of the covers. The way you ached."

Heat flooded her face. "Stop."

"Ached for a man to touch you," he went on. "Ached for a man inside you."

He inhaled slowly, like he could taste her embarrassment, her unease...her curiosity.

"Stop," she said again, her voice weak.

"But you don't want me to stop," he said, the words barely above a whisper.

Izzie sucked in a sharp breath, the denial on her tongue—except she couldn't force it past her lips. Because some terrible part of her didn't want him to stop. Some terrible part of her was burning under his gaze, unraveling with every moment he stood so close, every syllable that rolled from his tongue in that dark, knowing way.

She clenched her jaw, her nails biting into her palms. "Who are you?" she asked, voice hoarse.

His gaze flickered, something unreadable crossing his face. "A man who knows what this island is. And what it does to people like you."

She swallowed against the thickness in her throat. "People like me?"

He leaned in, his mouth inches from hers, his breath warm in the cold air.

"People who don't belong," he murmured. "I've warned you," he said, his voice a mere whisper now, almost lost to the wind. "Leave before the nightfall. Or the island will take what it's owed."

Before Izzie could respond, before she could demand answers or ask him what he meant, the man's figure dissolved into the mist, vanishing as swiftly as he had appeared. The fog seemed to close in around her, swallowing him up and leaving only the faintest echo of his words behind.

She stood frozen for a moment, her heart pounding in her chest, the weight of his warning settling over her like a heavy blanket. The island? The Harp? What was he talking about?

But she couldn't shake the feeling that he had been right—she was tangled in something far larger than she had anticipated. The unease from before had returned, now stronger than ever, and it gnawed at her. She had come to Arran seeking answers, but now she wasn't so sure she was ready for the truth.

Izzie took a deep breath, trying to steady her nerves, and glanced around at the ancient broch. The stones seemed more imposing now, their secrets buried even deeper beneath the weight of history. Whatever this man had been warning her about, she was already too far in to turn back.

With one last glance at the fog that seemed to pulse with something unseen, Izzie turned toward the path and started back toward the B and B, her mind racing with questions that had no answers yet. The man in the mist had left her with more confusion than clarity, but one thing was certain—Arran had more to reveal, and she wasn't about to leave without discovering what that was.

Chapter Five

The evening air had turned cold, biting through Izzie's jacket as she walked along the cobbled streets of Brodick, the island's charming small village. The glow of the street lamps cast long, flickering shadows on the ground, and the sound of her boots tapping against cement echoed in the quiet night. She'd hoped that a walk through the village would clear her head, to shake off the unease that had settled like a weight on her chest after her encounter in the mist. But, as with everything on Arran, nothing was as simple as it seemed.

She passed by the small shops, now closed for the night, the pub alive with quiet chatter spilling out into the streets. It was peaceful, almost idyllic, but a strange tension lingered in the air. The strange warning the man had given her echoed in her mind, along with the cryptic words he had left her with— "The island will take what it's owed." She had to admit, she didn't know what that meant, but something deep inside told her she needed to figure it out. Now more than ever, she needed answers.

Turning a corner, she found herself by the harbor. The soft sound of the waves lapping at the shore soothed her momentarily, but as she walked past the row of low stone buildings, she stopped abruptly. There, standing under the flickering glow of a streetlamp, was the man—the one with the golden eyes.

Her heart skipped a beat, but she didn't move, choosing instead to watch from a distance. He stood with another man, a familiar figure that took her a moment to recognize. It was Callum, the ruggedly handsome guest who had arrived at the B and B earlier that day. He was leaning in toward the man with the golden eyes, his posture tense, his expression intent. Izzie could feel the distance between them, the coldness in the air around them, even though she was standing several paces away.

The man with the golden eyes was speaking to Callum, his voice low and measured, and though Izzie couldn't hear the words, she could see the subtle shift in Callum's body language. He nodded occasionally, his brow furrowed, and there was a flicker of something—recognition? Unease? Izzie couldn't tell for certain. What was going on here? Why was Callum talking to the man she'd seen in the mist? And how did they know each other?

As she stood there, hidden in the shadows, the man turned his head, and his gaze swept across the street. For a moment, their eyes locked—golden eyes meeting her startled gaze, even though she was hidden in the shadows. A chill ran through her, her breath catching in her throat. There was no mistaking it. He knew she was watching. And he wasn't surprised.

The moment stretched, then, as if he had grown bored with the conversation, the man with the golden eyes gave Callum one last look. He turned sharply, disappearing into the night, his silhouette swallowed up by the darkness as though he had never been there.

Callum stood still for a moment, looking after the man, a frown pulling at his lips. Then, as though snapping out of a trance, he turned and walked in the opposite direction, heading toward the main street, away from where Izzie was watching.

Izzie stood frozen in place, her thoughts racing. What was that about? Why was Callum talking to the man she had seen in the mist? Was there some kind of connection between them? And why did it feel as though she had just witnessed something she shouldn't have?

The answer, she realized, was simple—she didn't know. She didn't know what was going on, but she needed to find out. And fast.

After a few more minutes of walking through the quiet streets, Izzie made her way back to the B and B. The fog had begun to roll in again, thick and oppressive, but she barely noticed. Her mind was too consumed with what she had just witnessed. She couldn't shake the feeling that she was being pulled deeper into something she wasn't prepared for.

When she returned to her room, Izzie's first instinct was to make a hot cup of tea, but something stopped her. The door creaked softly as she pushed it open, and she froze in the doorway.

Her room was different.

Her blood ran cold. She got the unmistakable feeling that someone had been here—someone who hadn't been invited. Her heart began to race as she stepped inside, scanning the room with wide eyes. The antique furniture, the heavy shutters, the thick curtains—they all seemed unchanged. But her mind couldn't focus on the details. No, her gaze was drawn to the small desk by the window. The drawer was open.

She rushed over, her breath catching in her throat as she peered inside. Papers, journals, and a collection of old letters lay scattered across the surface of the desk. But it wasn't the disorganization of the papers that made her stomach churn. It was the distinct feeling that the room had been rifled through—searched. But why? She hadn't left anything of real importance behind. Had she?

A quick glance at her suitcase confirmed what she feared. It was still locked, still intact. Nothing appeared to be missing, but the sense of violation was undeniable. Her new silk lingerie was tossed in a mess, when she had left everything carefully folded. Someone had been here. Someone had been looking for something.

She turned to the bed, her mind racing, but nothing seemed out of place there. Then, she noticed something on the floor beside the bed—a scrap of paper.

Cautiously, she bent down to pick it up. As her fingers brushed against the edge of the paper, a shiver ran through her. It wasn't a note. No writing on it, just a symbol—a crescent moon with three jagged lines drawn through the center, as though the moon were being struck by some unseen force.

Izzie stared at the symbol for a long moment, the weight of its presence sinking in. It was familiar, but she couldn't place it. She was certain it was important—though why, she had no idea. Could this be connected to the man she had seen in the mist? Or Callum? Or both?

She stood in the middle of the room, the disarray swirling around her like the fog outside. A creeping suspicion began to take root in her mind, and she realized one thing with undeniable clarity—whatever was going on, whatever dangerous web she had stumbled into on Arran, it was much bigger than she had anticipated. And she was now a part of it.

Izzie knew one thing for sure—she couldn't ignore the warnings any longer. Whatever secrets the island held, they were coming for her—whether she was ready or not.

The storm arrived with little warning.

One moment, the night was eerily still, the air thick with the lingering unease of Izzie's discovery. The next, wind howled through the trees like a living thing, rattling the windowpanes and sending rain lashing against the old stone walls of the B and B. The power flickered once, then again, before finally holding, casting long shadows in the dimly lit hall as Izzie dragged her luggage toward the door.

She had to leave.

Her hands trembled as she adjusted the strap of her bag, her pulse still hammering from the violation of her room. Someone had been inside. Someone had gone through her things. That note—the crescent moon slashed through with three jagged lines—was burned into her mind, as was the realization that she was no longer just stumbling into something strange on Arran.

She was being watched. She was being stalked.

She reached for the front door knob just as a gust of wind slammed against the house, rattling the entire frame. She hesitated, peering out through the narrow window by the entrance. The rain had thickened into a solid sheet, and beyond the dim glow of the streetlamps, she could see nothing but darkness and swirling mist.

Damn it.

She exhaled sharply, leaning against the doorframe. There was no way she was going out in that. She had planned to book another B and B in town, somewhere less isolated, somewhere she wouldn't have to look over her shoulder every second. But the storm had other ideas. If she stepped outside now, she'd be soaked to the bone in seconds, and she doubted she'd make it far before the roads turned to rivers of mud.

Reluctantly, she turned back.

The common area of the B and B was warm, the flickering light of the fireplace casting a golden glow over the worn wooden furniture. The scent of burning peat mingled with the crisp tang of whiskey, the firelight dancing along the glass in Callum's hand as he leaned against the mantle.

She stopped short.

He was watching her.

"I figured you'd be back by now," he said, voice smooth as he lifted his glass to his lips, his gray eyes never leaving hers. "I saw you out in the village…in the dark. Storm came in fast. You won't be going anywhere tonight."

His gaze lingered, the unspoken implication hanging between them like a weight, and Izzie's heart skipped a beat. She wasn't sure whether it was the cool night air or something darker in his voice that made her shiver.

Izzie set her bag down with more force than necessary. "Convenient."

Callum arched a brow. "You think I control the weather now?"

She folded her arms, the heat of frustration burning through the lingering chill in her bones. "I think someone broke into my room tonight, and I have a feeling you might know something about it."

For a moment, he said nothing, simply swirling the amber liquid in his glass. Then, with a slow, unreadable smile, he tilted his head toward the armchair opposite him. "Why don't you sit down, have a drink, and we'll talk?"

Izzie hesitated.

He was magnetic—there was no denying that. But trusting him? That was another matter entirely.

* * * *

The fire had burned low by the time Izzie finally made her way upstairs.

Her head buzzed faintly from the whiskey, but her mind was still sharp—sharper than Callum probably expected. He had been smooth, careful, dodging her questions with ease. Every time she pressed him about the man in the mist, the man he was speaking with in the village, or about why someone had searched her room, he had redirected the conversation, pouring another drink, flashing that roguish smile.

And damn it, she had felt the pull of him. The heat in his gaze. The way his voice dipped when he said her name.

But desire didn't erase suspicion.

She closed her bedroom door behind her, locking it firmly. The storm still raged outside, wind battering against the shutters, rain streaking down the old glass panes. She let out a breath, running a hand through her hair.

Nothing made sense.

The man in the mist, warning her off, then putting his hands on her, touching her, kissing her. The way his presence made her burn for more. Much more. The symbol left in her room. The way Callum had looked at her like he knew exactly why she was here — why she had been drawn to this particular place, even if she didn't fully understand it herself.

She changed into a soft chemise and clean panties, exhaustion pulling at her limbs as she climbed into bed. The mattress was firm, the sheets cool against her skin, and despite everything, her body ached for rest. She closed her eyes, trying to let the sound of the rain lull her to sleep.

Then —

A sound.

A scrape.

Her eyes snapped open, pulse spiking.

It came again — a dragging noise, slow, deliberate, just outside the window.

Izzie sat up, the blankets pooling around her waist. The shutters were closed, but the thin wooden slats let in just enough moonlight to see shadows shifting beyond the glass.

She held her breath.

Another scrape. Claws.

Heart hammering, she swung her legs out of bed and crossed the room in three quick strides. Her fingers trembled as she reached for the latch, hesitating for only a moment before she threw the shutters open.

The storm roared in. Wind howled, sending a spray of rain against her skin, dampening her chemise. But outside, beyond the weather, there was — nothing.

Just the rolling dark of the storm. The silhouette of trees twisting in the wind.

Then —

A sound. A deep, rhythmic beating, barely audible over the storm.

Wings.

Something massive moved in the distance, a shadow against the blackened sky, disappearing into the rain.

Izzie staggered back, her breath coming in quick gasps. She slammed the shutters closed, securing the latch, pressing her back against the wood as she tried to steady her racing pulse.

She didn't sleep after that.

Instead, she lay awake, eyes locked on the window, listening for the sound of wings.

When morning finally came, she hesitated before approaching the window again.

Slowly, she unlatched the shutters and pushed them open.

Claw marks.

Four deep, jagged grooves carved into the wooden frame. Fresh. Splintered.

Not a dream. Not her imagination.

Something had been here.

And now, there was no denying it — whatever it was, it wanted her to know.

Chapter Six

Izzie had barely slept.

The memory of the claw marks burned in her mind, a lingering imprint of something impossible. The wind had howled through the night, but no storm could explain what she had seen — or what she had heard.

And Callum knew.

She was certain of it now. The way he had dodged her questions, the way his gaze had lingered on her with something between warning and regret — he was hiding the truth. By the time she stepped into the dining room for breakfast, she had made up her mind. She would get answers.

The scent of fried eggs and fresh-baked bannocks filled the air. The B and B's small dining room was cozy, its wooden beams low, the windows still streaked with last night's rain. A few other recently arrived guests sat at their tables, murmuring quietly over their morning tea.

And there, at the farthest table, sat Callum.

He looked up as she entered, his expression unreadable. His dark hair was slightly damp, as if he'd been outside already, and his broad shoulders were tense beneath his woolen sweater.

Izzie didn't hesitate. She crossed the room and sat down across from him, fixing him with a steady look.

"You knew this would happen," she said.

Callum sighed, setting down his fork. "Good morning to you, too, Izzie."

"Don't do that." She leaned forward, keeping her voice low. "Something was outside my window last night. And don't tell me it was a trick of the wind, because I heard it. I saw it."

His jaw tightened. "Then you should leave."

She let out a short, humorless laugh. "Right. Because that's not suspicious at all."

"I'm not joking." His voice was quiet but firm. "You don't belong here."

She bristled. "Actually, I think I do."

Callum exhaled, rubbing a hand over his face. For the first time since she met him, he looked — tired. Worn down by something far older than last night's storm.

"You're looking for something dangerous," he said finally. "And you're not ready for what you'll find. We protect our...treasures."

Izzie studied him. He wasn't trying to scare her off — at least, not for the sake of it. There was something in his voice that almost sounded like...concern.

"I'm not leaving, Callum." She crossed her arms over her chest. "I have a job to do here."

A muscle twitched in his jaw. He held her gaze for a long moment, then gave a single nod.

"Then you'll need to be careful," he said.

She would have pushed for more, but just then, Moira bustled in with a plate of eggs and toast, giving them both a knowing look before setting the food down.

Izzie ate quickly, the tension still thick between her and Callum. When she finished, she grabbed her coat, slung her backpack over her shoulders, and walked out into the cold morning air.

She had a destination in mind — the stone circle of Machrie Moor, a place older than legend itself.

And this time, she wouldn't leave without answers.

* * * *

The wind howled across Machrie Moor, carrying the scent of damp earth and salt from the nearby sea. Izzie pulled her coat tighter around her body, her boots crunching against the sodden grass as she navigated the ancient stone circle. The ruins here were older than memory, standing like silent sentinels against the shifting mist.

Somewhere among these stones, she felt certain, lay a clue. Something connecting the legend of the Harp of Ceòthach Glen to the strange happenings on Arran.

But once again, she wasn't alone.

The sensation of being watched prickled against her skin. It wasn't the distant murmurs of tourists or the occasional hiker passing through — it was something else. Something deeper.

Then, a flicker of movement caught her eye.

A figure stood among the stones, half-shrouded by mist. Tall, broad-shouldered, clad in dark clothing that rippled in the wind.

Golden eyes burned through the haze.

Izzie's breath caught in her throat. It was him—the man she had seen in the ruins before. The one who had vanished like a ghost.

Only this time, he didn't disappear.

He stepped forward, his gaze fixed on hers. The air between them grew heavy, charged with an energy she couldn't explain. He was magnetic, powerful—and utterly inhuman.

"You should have left," he said, his voice low, resonant.

Izzie swallowed, forcing herself to stand her ground. "Who are you?"

He didn't answer. Instead, his body tensed, his hands clenching at his sides. A strange shimmer passed over his skin, like heat rippling off stone in the summer sun.

Then—he changed.

It happened in the space of a heartbeat. One moment, a man. The next, something more.

Scales rippled over his arms, spreading like liquid gold. His spine elongated, muscles shifting beneath his clothing as it tore away. Massive wings unfurled from his back with a deafening snap.

A dragon.

Not the shadow she had glimpsed in the fog, not some imagined nightmare. A living, breathing, impossible creature. Izzie staggered back, heart hammering against her ribs.

The golden-eyed dragon regarded her with unsettling focus, his scales shimmering red and orange like fire caught in amber, his head tilting slightly, as if weighing something in his mind.

Then—a roar split the air.

Izzie turned just in time. Another form was rising on the moors beyond the stone circle.

This one was darker, larger, its scales the color of storm clouds. Midnight blue and silver. Wings spread wide, catching the wind as it bellowed a challenge.

The red and orange dragon before her let out a deep, warning growl.

Izzie stood frozen between them, caught in the crossfire of forces far beyond her understanding.

One dragon had revealed itself to her.

And the other had come to claim her.

Chapter Seven

The roar of the storm-colored dragon echoed across the moor, shaking the very ground beneath Izzie's feet. The red dragon in front of her tensed, wings flaring in warning, then leaped into the sky above the moor. The air crackled with energy, ancient and primal, pressing against her chest until it was hard to breathe.

This couldn't be real.

It couldn't be.

Her first encounter with dragons in the real world. In the wild.

Yet—there they were. Two dragons, one red and orange like firelight, the other dark midnight blue and silver, as if he was an approaching storm, their gazes locked in a silent battle of wills.

The second dragon, deep midnight blue with silver streaks, landed within the stone circle in front of her, with a force that sent tremors through the ground. Izzie couldn't tear her eyes away. That dragon...she knew it. She felt it. It was Callum.

As the dust settled, Callum's form shifted—his massive dragon body contracting as his scales faded into flesh. The transformation was nothing short of mesmerizing, the sound of bones and muscles reshaping filling the air before Callum stood before her, now fully human. His storm-gray eyes locked onto hers, tension and wariness written on his face.

Izzie opened her mouth to speak, but the words caught in her throat as her suspicions were confirmed. She looked at Callum, her voice barely above a whisper. "You…you're a dragon, too."

Callum didn't flinch, but there was a trace of regret in his eyes. "Aye. I am."

Izzie's heart was racing, the reality of it settling over her like a cold wave. "Why didn't you tell me?" she demanded, her voice shaking with frustration and confusion. "I—everything—this…this whole time, you've been hiding this from me?"

Callum sighed deeply, his expression softening with something that bordered on guilt. "I didn't want to drag you into this. But it's too late now. You're already part of it, whether you understand it or not."

Before Izzie could respond, the red dragon growled—a low, dangerous rumble that vibrated through the air. Izzie instinctively turned to see the massive form of the red dragon land next to Callum and begin shifting once again, its body rippling with energy as it returned to its human shape.

The man who stepped forward was tall, broad-shouldered, with striking auburn hair and eyes that gleamed like burning embers. He met Izzie's gaze with a smirk that bordered on smugness.

Callum tensed at his side, his jaw tight. "I should've warned you. This is Rhys. My brother."

Izzie's gaze darted between Callum and Rhys, the pieces of the puzzle finally clicking into place. Her heart raced with the realization. "Rhys..." she murmured, her voice thick with disbelief. "So...you're both—"

"Dragons," Rhys finished for her, his voice deep and rich with a playful lilt. He took a step closer, his amber eyes flickering over her with a look that seemed both intense and oddly amused. "Aye. Callum and I are dragons. And you, lass, seem to have caught our attention." He stepped closer, leering at her. "And dragons are always hungry for a bit of..." he leaned in and inhaled loudly. "A bit of human flesh."

Izzie shook it off, her thoughts spinning. "But why? Why didn't you just tell me? Why all the secrecy?"

Callum's gaze softened, but his expression was still serious. "We had our reasons. But right now, that's not important." He looked back at Rhys, his posture tense. "What's important is what you're doing here, Rhys. And why you're still after her."

Rhys chuckled darkly, stepping back with a shrug. "It was never my intention, brother. To take her for my own. Our own. But she's after the Harp, you know. And I can't stand by while this succulent bit of human flesh tries to destroy us all."

"I don't smell that on her," Callum objected. "But I do smell you—"

Rhys grinned. "Well, as for that, brother," he said, his face darkening, "she offered herself to me. She spread her legs in full view of my own—" Rhys grabbed the front of his trousers and lifted what was there, as if Izzie could see through the fabric to his cock and balls. "—and pleasured herself repeatedly. How can a shifter refuse such an invitation? I felt her, just a wee bit. And I'll do more—"

Izzie could feel the tension between them like a physical force, but she was too overwhelmed to process it fully. "What the hell is going on?" she demanded. "I don't understand any of this. Why are you both here? What do you want from me?"

Callum's storm-gray eyes softened with something like regret. "I wish I could tell you everything, Izzie. But some things...you're not ready to hear yet."

Rhys tilted his head, his lips curling into a sly grin. "Maybe, maybe not. But we're both in this now, aren't we? Together. And trust me, lass—this is only the beginning."

"Keep it in your pants, Rhys," Callum warned, then turned back to Izzie. As his eyes met hers, he exhaled slowly. "Rhys and I...we were raised with a purpose. A duty passed down for centuries." His voice was steady, but there was something behind it—something weighted with history.

Izzie narrowed her eyes. "What kind of duty?"

Callum met her gaze, solemn and unwavering.

"We're sworn to protect the Harp."

Izzie's pulse pounded in her ears, her mind racing to catch up with the words Callum had just spoken.

Sworn to protect the Harp. The same Harp she was supposed to find and bring back to Margaret.

The pieces clicked into place with horrifying clarity. Margaret had warned her. Warned all of them. "Dragons are possessive and dangerous, especially when more than one sets their sights on a woman."

Her stomach twisted.

"So that's why you're here?" she asked, her voice barely above a whisper. "Because of the Harp?"

Callum hesitated, then gave a slow nod. "Aye."

Izzie let out a bitter laugh, shaking her head. "Of course. That's what this is all about, isn't it? You're not some wandering hiker, and this isn't some chance meeting. You were watching me from the start." She folded her arms, glaring at him. "What? Were you planning to take it from me? Use me to find it?"

Callum's expression tightened. "It's not like that."

"No?" She scoffed. "Then what is it like?"

Before he could answer, a deep, rumbling voice carried through the mist.

"She's cleverer than you gave her credit for, brother."

Izzie shivered.

Rhys stepped closer, his gaze flicking over her before settling on Callum. "You should've told her sooner. She might have been gone days ago. And then I wouldn't have gotten her scent."

Callum let out a low growl, stepping protectively between them. "Stay out of this, Rhys."

"Oh, come now." Rhys smirked, tilting his head as he regarded Izzie. "She's part of this now, whether you like it or not."

Izzie swallowed, torn between the instinct to run and the strange, magnetic pull she felt toward them both.

Rhys turned his golden gaze back to her. "You feel it, don't you?" His voice was softer now, almost coaxing. "The connection."

Izzie took a step back, her heart hammering. No. No, no, no.

She couldn't. She wouldn't.

And yet—she did.

51

It wasn't just Callum. There was something about Rhys, too, something that called to her in a way she didn't understand. It made no sense. It went against every instinct she had.

And yet, her body didn't lie.

"Enough." Callum's voice was low and dangerous. "She's not part of this."

Rhys only smiled. "Are you sure about that, brother?"

Izzie's breath hitched as he reached out, tracing one finger lightly under her chin, then ran that finger down her cleavage, over her belly, and between her legs. A teasing touch. A test.

And gods help her — she didn't pull away.

Chapter Eight

The tension between the two brothers crackled like a storm about to break. Callum's shoulders were rigid, his stance protective, while Rhys stood tall and unyielding, a smirk curling at the edge of his lips.

"You've put her in harm's way," Rhys said, voice smooth but edged with accusation. "You should've sent her off the island the moment you realized what she was looking for."

Callum scoffed. "You think I led her into danger? She was already searching for the Harp long before I met her. She doesn't need me for that."

Izzie's frustration boiled over. "I am standing right here," she snapped, stepping between them. "And I'd appreciate it if you two would stop talking about me like I'm not."

Rhys raised an eyebrow, but Callum had the decency to look sheepish.

"Now," Izzie continued, folding her arms, "I'd really like some actual answers. Why are you both so desperate to keep me from finding the Harp? I'm trying to make sure it's protected. Isn't that what you want?"

Callum let out a slow breath, but it was Rhys who spoke first.

"The Harp of Ceòthach Glen is not just a relic, Izzie," he said, his golden gaze locking onto hers. "It was used once before to bring dragons to their knees. An enchanted sleep, deep and unbreakable, leaving them defenseless. Their enemies came in the night and slaughtered them."

Izzie swallowed. Margaret told us this story...

Rhys took a step closer, lowering his voice. "If the Harp is found again, it will be weaponized. You might not intend for that to happen, but humans rarely control the consequences of their own greed."

She bristled. "That's not fair. I have no intention of using it against anyone. I just want to make sure it doesn't fall into the wrong hands."

"And how do you propose to do that?" Rhys asked, arching a brow.

"I can take it to the Draconic Council's vaults," Izzie said without hesitation. "They can secure it. No one will be able to get to it there—not humans, not even dragons."

Rhys laughed, a low and dangerous sound. "You're naïve if you think the Council would let you simply hand it over. They have their own agendas, lass."

Callum, however, looked thoughtful. "It might not be the worst idea," he admitted. "The Council vaults are secure."

Rhys shot him a sharp glare. "You're actually considering this?"

Callum met his brother's gaze evenly. "Do you have a better plan?"

For a long moment, Rhys said nothing. The wind howled through the ruins around them, mist swirling at their feet like restless spirits.

Then, with a slow, dangerous smile, Rhys turned back to Izzie. "Fine," he said. "Let's make a deal."

Callum's expression darkened as the wind picked up around them, carrying the scent of rain and salt from the sea. "You don't understand what you're getting yourself into," he said, his voice rough with warning. "If you find the Harp, you will never leave Scotland alive."

A shiver traced its way down Izzie's spine, but she lifted her chin. "You think I'm just going to walk away now?" she shot back. "After everything I've learned? After coming this far?"

Callum exhaled sharply, raking a hand through his dark hair. "Damn it, Izzie, this isn't a game."

"No," she agreed, staring him down. "It's a job. It's my job, to find the Harp. It's what I was hired and trained for. And I have to find it or lose my job."

Rhys, however, took a different approach. He studied her with an unreadable expression, then smirked. "You're determined — I'll give you that. But if you insist on finding the Harp, you won't be doing it alone."

Izzie frowned. "And what exactly does that mean?"

"It means we're coming with you," Rhys said smoothly. "You let us accompany you, we help you find it, and we make sure it doesn't fall into the wrong hands."

Izzie hesitated, glancing between the two of them. Callum still looked tense, his mouth set in a grim line. And Rhys...she wouldn't trust him alone in the dark. Or in broad daylight, for that matter. "And if I say no?"

Rhys shrugged. "Then I suppose we'll have to stop you by other means."

A spike of irritation flared in her chest. "So those are my options? Accept your help or be hunted down?"

"I wouldn't phrase it quite so harshly," Rhys said, flashing a wicked smile.

Callum, however, wasn't smiling. "Izzie, listen to me," he said, stepping closer. His voice was low, urgent. "If you do this, there's no turning back. The moment you get too close to the Harp, forces far worse than us will come looking for you."

Izzie swallowed hard, but she refused to let fear dictate her actions. "That's a risk I'm willing to take."

Rhys grinned. "That's what I was hoping you'd say."

Callum cursed under his breath but said nothing.

The mist thickened around them, curling over the ruins like ghostly fingers. Izzie let out a slow breath, her heart hammering. She didn't trust Rhys, and Callum's warning lingered in her mind like an echo, but she had no choice. She couldn't turn back now.

"Fine," she said at last. "You can come with me. But make no mistake—I'm doing this my way."

Rhys' golden eyes gleamed. "Of course, lass." He seemed to loom over her, partly an illusion, a trick of the light. And partly—she was certain—his dragon magic. "And we'll do you our way."

Callum muttered something under his breath, shaking his head.

Izzie wasn't fooled. She had just made a deal with two dragons, and if she wasn't careful, she might not live long enough to regret it.

Chapter Nine

The road narrowed as they ascended into the wild, untamed Highlands, the landscape shifting from rolling fields to jagged peaks shrouded in mist. The air carried the scent of damp earth and pine, thick with the promise of rain. Izzie sat in the back seat of the rugged Land Rover, arms crossed, her nerves coiled as tightly as the storm clouds above them. She'd turned her rental car back in as soon as they'd taken the ferry back onto the mainland, having agreed to stay with the brothers. The loss of freedom irked her, but in reality there was no reason to drive in two cars when they were going to the same place.

Wherever that was.

Callum drove in brooding silence, his knuckles white on the steering wheel. Rhys, in the passenger seat, seemed perfectly at ease, drumming his fingers along his thigh. The tension between them had been thick since their agreement, but now, as they ventured further from civilization, it had reached a boiling point.

"How much farther?" Izzie finally asked, unable to stand the quiet any longer.

"Not long," Callum muttered, eyes fixed on the winding road.

"We're nearly there, love," Rhys added, flashing her a knowing smile. "Getting cold feet?"

Izzie scoffed. "You wish."

As they ventured deeper into the Highlands, the road grew narrower and more treacherous. The Land Rover's engine roared as Callum navigated the sharp turns and steep inclines. Suddenly, Rhys spoke up, his voice barely audible over the sound of the engine.

"Callum, pull over for a minute. I need to take a piss."

Callum nodded, slowing the car to a stop on the side of the road. Rhys stepped out, disappearing into the dense forest that lined the road. Izzie watched as he vanished into the shadows.

As the minutes ticked by, Callum turned to Izzie, his eyes gleaming with a predatory hunger. "You know, lass, you're playing a dangerous game, hunting for that harp. The Highlands are full of secrets, and not all of them are pleasant."

Izzie leaned forward, resting a hand on the back of the driver's seat. She met his gaze, her eyes flashing with defiance. "I'm not afraid of danger, Callum. I may be new at this kind of thing, but I've some tricks up my sleeve."

Callum chuckled, a low, rumbling sound that sent shivers down her spine. "Is that so? Well, we'll just have to see about that."

He lifted his hand, slow and deliberate, his fingertips grazing over her wrist before slipping beneath her sleeve. A single calloused finger traced along the sensitive skin inside, a teasing stroke that sent a sharp tremor through her. Izzie sucked in a breath, but she didn't pull away. If anything, her pulse quickened.

Callum smirked. "Seems I'm not the only one playing with fire."

Izzie narrowed her eyes, covering her reaction with a smirk of her own. "Oh, I don't just play with fire — I know how to wield it."

Callum's gaze darkened, the playfulness in his expression shifting into something deeper, more assessing. "You say that like you've experience handling dragons."

Izzie leaned in just a little more, her voice dropping to a conspiratorial murmur. "Handling? Oh, I've done more than that." She let the words hang, enjoying the way his grip tightened ever so slightly, betraying his interest. "You think you're the first dragon shifter I've crossed paths with?"

Something flickered in Callum's eyes — curiosity, suspicion. Maybe even a sliver of possessiveness. "Is that so?" His voice was quieter now, measured.

"Oh, aye." Izzie tilted her head, watching him carefully. "You Scottish dragons think you're so mysterious, so dangerous." She dragged a slow finger along the seam of the seat, her touch mimicking his own teasing caress. "But I've met your kind before. And let's just say...I held my own."

Callum stilled, nostrils flaring. "Who?"

Izzie's smirk deepened. "Let's just say that back in the States, there was a gathering at Eldritch Curiosities. A rather intimate evening with some rather impressive men." She let the words sink in, watching as realization dawned in his gaze. "Men who didn't need to warn me about the dangers of dragons, because, well...I got up close and personal with them."

Callum's grip on her wrist tightened, and he dragged his thumb along the inside of her sleeve in a slow, possessive sweep. "And by 'personal,' you mean...?"

Izzie gave a slow, deliberate shrug, her pulse thrumming beneath his touch. "Oh, I think you can figure that one out for yourself, dragon."

For a second, Callum said nothing, his gaze locked onto hers, heavy and unreadable. Then, with a sharp breath, he exhaled through his nose, shaking his head. "You really are a menace, lass."

Izzie grinned, unbothered by the warning. "And don't you forget it."

"Playing with fire..." Callum whispered, his eyes locking onto hers.

Before Izzie could respond, Rhys emerged from the forest, his zipper still undone. He slid into the backseat beside Izzie, his thigh pressing against hers. She couldn't avoid noticing that his penis was rather...impressive, even in its current state. "Sorry about that, love. Nature calls, you know?"

Izzie shifted in discomfort, acutely aware of Rhys' proximity. Callum put the car in gear, and they set off once more, the Land Rover's engine purring like a contented cat.

As they drove, Rhys traced lazy circles on Izzie's thigh with his fingers. Izzie stiffened initially, her heart pounding in her chest. "Rhys, what are you doing?"

"Just helping you relax, love. You're wound tighter than a spring."

Callum's gaze flicked to the rearview mirror, a knowing look passing between the brothers. "Careful,

Rhys. Our lass has experience with dragons, remember?"

Rhys' touch grew more confident, sliding his hand higher up Izzie's thigh. "Is that so? Then she knows what she's getting into."

Izzie hesitated for a moment, then deliberately relaxed into his touch. If she was going to maintain any control in this situation, she needed to show them she wasn't some innocent they could overwhelm. She'd been trained for this at Eldritch Curiosities—dealing with sexually dominant supernatural beings required confidence, not cowering. His fingers found the hem of her shirt, and instead of pulling away, she let her breath catch audibly. "I suppose I do," she murmured, her nipples hardening beneath her bra as arousal began to replace her initial wariness.

The Land Rover's headlights carved twin beams through the encroaching dusk, illuminating the winding single-track road that cut through the Highlands like a scar. The mountains loomed in the distance, their jagged silhouettes dark against the fading sky. Mist curled low over the heather-strewn moors, whispering around the tires as Callum guided the vehicle through the remote landscape.

In the back seat, Izzie watched the road in brooding silence, her arms folded across her chest, blocking any further attempt from Rhys to put his hands on her. Beside her, Rhys lounged with infuriating ease, one boot propped up against the door, idly toying with the hilt of a blade he'd produced from somewhere.

"We're losing the light," Callum murmured, eyes scanning the road ahead. He gestured toward a narrow track veering off to the right. "There. That'll do."

Izzie glanced at him. "That's not a road. That's barely a suggestion of a path."

Callum gave her a look in the rearview mirror. "You want to keep driving 'til we drop, or do you want to get some rest?"

With a sigh, she watched him take the turn, the Land Rover bouncing over the uneven ground. The track wound through a dense thicket of pines before opening into a small clearing. The air smelled of damp earth and woodsmoke, though there was no sign of a fire—just the remnants of an old stone ring, moss creeping over its edges.

Callum had been there before. Maybe he'd even planned this, to get Izzie far away from any help...if she called for help.

Callum killed the engine, and silence crashed around them, thick and heavy.

"So." She exhaled, rubbing a hand over her face. "I don't suppose either of you had the foresight to bring a tent?"

Rhys chuckled from the back. "What, and miss the chance to suffer a little? Where's the fun in that?"

Izzie climbed out, stretching her stiff limbs as the brothers rearranged the space. Callum shot his brother a look before flipping the lever to collapse the back seats. "We'll make do."

When she opened the rear compartment, she found a single wool blanket shoved beneath a spare tire.

She held it up. "One blanket? That's it?"

Callum shrugged, unbothered. "You expected luxury?" he said as he pulled out their assortment of luggage and crammed it into the front seats.

Rhys smirked. "I think she expected a bit of chivalry. I'd offer to sleep outside, lass, but then who'd keep you warm?"

Izzie rolled her eyes but said nothing, sudden heat curling low in her stomach.

Inside the Land Rover, the space was cramped — tighter than she'd expected once they were all lying down. Izzie found herself wedged between them, Callum's solid warmth at her back, Rhys' powerful frame pressing lightly against her front. The blanket stretched across them, though it didn't quite reach all the way, forcing them even closer.

For a while, none of them spoke. The only sound was the rhythmic rise and fall of their breathing, the rustling of fabric as they shifted, trying — and failing — to find a comfortable position.

Then Callum exhaled, a low, frustrated sound. "This is ridiculous."

"Speak for yourself," Rhys murmured, voice thick with amusement. "I'm quite comfortable." His hand found Izzie's beneath the blanket, fingers intertwining with hers before he lifted their joined hands to brush against her breast through her shirt. "What about you, dove? Comfortable?"

Izzie's breath hitched. She could pull away — should pull away. But her training at Eldritch Curiosities had taught her that showing fear or uncertainty with dominant supernatural beings only put her at a disadvantage. Instead, she let herself lean into his touch, a soft sigh escaping her lips. "Getting warmer," she admitted, her voice barely above a whisper.

Izzie bit her lip. Every slight movement sent a ripple of awareness through her — Callum's heat against her spine, the steady rise and fall of his chest. Rhys, barely inches away, his breath warm against her hair.

She swallowed. "This is...cozy."

Rhys chuckled, a soft rumble. "Aye, it is." He brushed his hand against hers, the touch featherlight but deliberate.

Izzie's breath hitched.

Callum shifted behind her, whether on purpose or accident, she wasn't sure—but suddenly his fingers ghosted along her hip beneath the blanket. A slow, lingering touch.

A charge crackled through the air, electric and undeniable.

In the moonlight through the vehicle's windows, Callum snaked an arm around Izzie, reaching up to touch her cheek. "You're a lovely woman, Izzie. It's a shame to see you waste your time on a foolish quest."

Izzie pulled back, her eyes flashing with anger. But in the confines of the back of the Land Rover, there really was nowhere to go. "Finding the Harp is my job, Callum. No, it's more than that. It's a sacred charge. Whether I can find it will determine the entire course of my future. I won't be deterred by the likes of you."

Callum chuckled, a low, dangerous sound. "'The likes of me,' huh? We'll see about that, lass. We'll see about that."

The night wore on, Izzie sandwiched between the two brothers, the full lengths of their bodies pressed against hers. When she finally drifted off, it was a light sleep—the kind where every sensation filtered through her awareness. She felt Rhys' hand find her breast again, his fingers gentle this time, exploring rather than demanding. Callum's hand slid between her legs, his touch featherlight against her most sensitive spot.

For a moment, she lay still, letting the sensations wash over her. Her experience with dragon shifters had taught her that they could sense arousal, could smell desire. There was no point in pretending she wasn't affected. When Callum's fingers began unbuttoning her jeans with careful precision, she shifted slightly, making it easier for him.

"Awake, are we?" Callum murmured against her ear, his tongue finding the sensitive whorls before nipping gently at her earlobe.

Rhys chuckled softly, his breath warm against her face. "I could tell she wasn't really sleeping." He moved closer until his lips hovered just above hers. "Dragon shifters have excellent hearing, love. Your heartbeat gave you away."

She opened her eyes to meet his gaze in the moonlight. "Maybe I wanted you to know I was awake," she whispered back, her training kicking in. Control the situation. Show confidence. Don't let them think they're overwhelming you.

When Rhys captured her breast more firmly, she arched deliberately into his touch, a soft moan escaping her lips. She knew she should maintain some boundaries, but the heat building between them was intoxicating. Her body knew what it wanted, and her training had taught her that confidence was power, even in surrender. As the brothers' hands and mouths began exploring her body more thoroughly, she made a conscious choice to let herself feel everything, to embrace the moment instead of fighting it.

Izzie's heart raced with anticipation as she gazed up at the star-studded sky beyond the windows of the Land Rover. The cool night air caressed her neck and shoulders, a stark contrast to the heat building within her. Rhys leaned in, capturing her lips in a passionate kiss, his tongue delving into her mouth, tasting her, claiming her. Callum tangled his fingers in her hair, tilting her head back as he trailed hot kisses along her neck, his teeth grazing her sensitive skin.

Izzie moaned, embracing the sensation of being worshipped by two strong, powerful men. Rhys threw back the blanket to reveal that he had stripped to the waist while Izzie slept, and now he knelt on the floor of the car beside her. In the moonlight, he raised the hem of her shirt to cup both her breasts, his thumbs circling her hardening nipples through the thin lace of her bra. Callum helped remove her shirt, tugging it from her shoulders and tossing it aside to free her torso to his touch, to his mouth. His lips moved lower, down her neck, the curve of her shoulder, his tongue flicking out to taste the swell of her breasts as Rhys deftly unclasped her bra, freeing them from their confines.

The cool night air puckered Izzie's nipples, but the brothers' hot mouths quickly warmed them, licking and sucking, their teeth grazing the sensitive peaks. Izzie arched into their touch, her hands fisting in their hair, urging them on. They worked in tandem, Rhys lavishing attention on one breast while Callum focused on the other, driving Izzie wild with need.

As if reading her mind, Rhys slid his hand lower, dipping beneath the waistband of her panties to cup her mound. He groaned against her breast as he felt the damp heat of her arousal beneath her panties. Callum's hand joined his, both men stroking and teasing her through the thin fabric, their fingers slipping beneath to tease her slick folds. They looked at each other then, both grinning in agreement as they worked Izzie's jeans over her hips and down her legs, leaving just her panties to cover her. And those panties were already soaked through with her juices.

Izzie bucked against their touch, desperate for more. "Please," she gasped, her voice thick with need. "I want you both."

Callum laughed softly. "And here I thought you just wanted to sleep?"

"N—no! Not sleep," Izzie whispered, still embarrassed by her own intense reaction. She had never felt like this—every nerve in her body tingling with need—when she'd fucked her college boyfriends. "I need...I need... Oh, by all the gods! Fuck me, please!"

Rhys and Callum exchanged a heated glance before nodding in unison. They quickly divested Izzie of her remaining clothes, their own following suit until they were all naked in the rear of the vehicle. Rhys settled between Izzie's thighs, his hard length pressing against her entrance as Callum positioned himself at her side, his own erection jutting proudly against her hip. In one swift thrust Rhys was inside her wet cunt, filling her completely.

Izzie reached for Callum, wrapping her hand around his thick shaft and stroking him in time with Rhys' thrusts. The brothers groaned in unison, their hips bucking into her touch. Rhys surged forward, sheathing himself fully inside Izzie's tight heat. She cried out at the sudden fullness, her muscles contracting around him.

Callum captured her lips in a searing kiss, swallowing her moans as Rhys began to move faster, his thrusts deep and powerful. Izzie lost herself in the sensation, the slick slide of Rhys' cock inside her, the rough texture of Callum's against her palm, the taste of him on her tongue. It was overwhelming, yet not enough.

As if sensing her need, Callum shifted, positioning himself at her lips. Izzie eagerly took him into her mouth, her tongue swirling around the head of his cock. Rhys' thrusts grew more urgent, gripping her hips as he pounded into her. Izzie moaned around Callum's length, the vibrations making him groan.

The brothers set a relentless pace, fucking Izzie in tandem, their bodies moving in perfect sync. Izzie felt the coil of pleasure tightening in her belly, her muscles clenching around Rhys' cock as he drove into her. Callum tangled his fingers in her hair, guiding her movements as he fucked her mouth, his cock hitting the back of her throat.

Izzie's orgasm crashed over her like a tidal wave, her body convulsing as wave after wave of pleasure washed through her. Rhys followed suit, his thrusts growing erratic before he buried himself deep and came with a roar, his hot seed spilling inside her. Callum was not far behind, his cock pulsing as he spilled his load down Izzie's throat, his fingers tightening in her hair.

They collapsed together, a tangle of sweat-slicked limbs and heaving chests. Izzie lay sandwiched between the brothers, their bodies pressed against hers, their heartbeats syncing as they caught their breath. The night was still, the only sounds the gentle rustling of the leaves and the soft sighs of contentment from the trio.

But Izzie knew this was far from over. The brothers had awoken a hunger in her that could not be sated with a single encounter. She rolled onto her side, facing Callum, her hand trailing down his chest to wrap around his already hardening cock. Rhys pressed against her back, his lips finding the sensitive spot on her neck that made her shiver.

They moved together again, their bodies merging in a dance as old as time. Rhys delved his fingers between Izzie's thighs, stroking her slick folds, teasing her clit. Callum's mouth found her breasts, his tongue swirling around her nipples, drawing them into his mouth. Izzie gasped, her hips bucking against Rhys' touch, seeking more.

This time, it was Callum who took her, his cock sliding into her tight heat as Rhys positioned himself at her rear entrance. Izzie tensed for a moment, unsure, but Callum's soothing words and Rhys' gentle caresses soon had her relaxing. Rhys coated his fingers with her own arousal before slowly pressing inside, stretching her, preparing her.

When he finally replaced his fingers with the head of his cock, Izzie cried out, the dual penetration sending shockwaves of pleasure through her body. The brothers moved in tandem, their thrusts slow and deep, allowing Izzie to adjust to the new sensations. But soon, the pace quickened, their hips snapping forward, driving into her with increasing urgency.

Izzie was lost in a haze of pleasure, her body trembling with the force of her impending orgasm. Callum found her clit, rubbing tight circles around the sensitive nub, pushing her closer to the edge. Rhys' teeth grazed her shoulder, his breath hot against her skin as he pounded into her ass.

With a final, powerful thrust, Izzie came undone, her body convulsing between the brothers as her orgasm crashed over her. They followed suit, their cocks pulsing inside her, filling her with their hot seed.

They collapsed together, their bodies slick with sweat and other fluids, their chests heaving as they struggled to catch their breath.

But even as they lay there, sated and spent, Izzie knew this was not the end. The night was young, and the Highland air held a promise of more to come. She smiled to herself, nestling between the brothers, their arms wrapping around her, their heartbeats a soothing lullaby.

If this was what it was like to fuck a dragon, she was all in. Her experience back in Wilmington had nothing on this. Callum and Rhys...they were meant to fuck her.

For just a moment she considered asking...

Then she gathered her courage and took the plunge. "Do you..." Her voice was soft at first, but dragons have very good hearing. "Do you have...other brothers?"

Callum was the one who answered, raising himself on one elbow to gaze down into her face. "And if we do, lass? Are you asking—"

Rhys wasn't so reticent. "There are three more of us back home on Skye," he answered Izzie's question. "All with big cocks, like most dragons. Not as big or as strong as mine, now," he said with a chuckle. "But if you want to be with us all, I bet they'd enjoy fucking your brains out."

"Don't push her, Rhys," Callum chided. "She's new to all of this. She gets to make her own choice."

Rhys chuckled again. "I'm just saying," he began, "that she'd find all of us Sìol Dòmhnaill brothers quite attentive to her...needs."

As the stars wheeled overhead and the moon cast its silvery light upon the forest, Izzie drifted off to sleep, dreaming of dragons and the wild, untamed passion they had unleashed within her. The night was theirs, and they'd made the most of it, exploring the depths of their desire and the boundaries of their pleasure.

And she was sure it wouldn't be the last time.

Chapter Ten

Truthfully, Izzie wasn't sure if it was fear or excitement thrumming through her veins. The knowledge that she was traveling with two dragons — two possessive, powerful beings who seemed equally determined to keep her close — was unsettling. And yet, she couldn't deny the way her pulse quickened when she caught Callum's steady, intense gaze or when Rhys' teasing remarks sent an unwelcome flush to her cheeks.

The cabin appeared suddenly, nestled in a clearing at the edge of a dark forest. It was nothing like the B and B, but that was precisely the point. Izzie hadn't planned on staying in one place for long — she was chasing the Harp, and it hadn't been on Arran. Now that she was tangled up with two dragon brothers, lingering in a quaint guesthouse with thin walls had felt like a mistake waiting to happen. Especially given how dragons roared their pleasure.

The lodge before them was an old hunting retreat, built from weathered stone and thick wooden beams, the kind of place that had endured countless winters and kept its share of whispered secrets. Smoke curled lazily from the chimney, and a single lantern flickered by the door, casting long shadows against the worn threshold. It wasn't cozy, not in the way the B and B had been, but it was isolated. Private. And for now, that was all that mattered.

"This is where we're staying?" Izzie asked, stepping out of the vehicle.

"It's remote," Callum said. "Safe."

Rhys stretched, rolling his shoulders. "And cozy," he added, throwing her a wink.

Izzie ignored him and grabbed her luggage. As she stepped inside, the scent of burning peat and aged wood surrounded her. The interior was simple—a large stone fireplace crackled in the corner, casting shadows along the rough wooden walls. A couch sat in front of it, a sturdy table in the center of the room, and beyond that, a single door led to what she assumed was the bedroom.

"Someone's been here," she said. "The lantern, the fire—"

Rhys grinned wickedly. "Dragon magic," he said, tracing a sigil in the air.

Izzie copied his movements. "That's the sign for starting a fire and turning on the lights?"

Rhys' grin deepened. "No, love. That's the sigil for getting a wee bit of a lass to strip out of her clothes."

She turned, narrowing her eyes at the brothers. "Tell me there's more than one bed."

Silence.

Callum rubbed the back of his neck. Rhys grinned.

"I'll take the couch," Izzie declared.

Rhys made a tsking sound. "That hardly seems fair. You're the only lady here. Shouldn't one of us be the gentleman?"

She shot him a look. "I wouldn't trust either of you to be gentlemen."

Rhys laughed, Callum sighed, and Izzie steeled herself for a long night. But she wasn't going to let either one of them get too used to fucking her. This entire thing was going to happen on her terms or not at all.

* * * *

The familiar weight of the situation settled over her, bringing back memories of her first week at Eldritch Curiosities. Margaret had been blunt about what the job would entail.

"You'll be dealing with dragon shifters," Margaret had said, sitting across from her in the sterile conference room. "They're sexually dominant, possessive, and they respond to strength, not submission. If you can't handle intimate encounters with supernatural beings, this isn't the position for you."

Izzie had thought she was prepared. She'd thought wrong.

The training evening had been held in a specially prepared room on the third floor — one she'd never seen before and suspected existed solely for this purpose. When Margaret led her inside, Izzie's first impression was of controlled chaos. The bed dominated the space, its covers already rumpled and twisted. Candles flickered on every surface, casting dancing shadows that made the room feel both intimate and clinical.

They don't even change the sheets, she'd thought, a mix of disgust and nervous anticipation twisting in her stomach. The evidence of previous "exercises" was obvious, and yet Margaret spoke about it with the same detached professionalism she used to discuss artifact authentication.

Three dragon shifters had been waiting—all American, all devastatingly attractive in that otherworldly way that marked their kind. The tallest had introduced himself as Kaian, his voice carrying the slight growl that identified him as an Alpha. The other two flanked him with the easy confidence of predators who knew they held all the advantages.

"This is about proving you can maintain professional boundaries," Margaret had explained, her voice cutting through the charged atmosphere. "Dragon shifters will test you. They'll push every limit you have. If you can't handle this controlled environment, you'll never survive in the field."

Izzie had felt the weight of their gazes, assessing her like she was prey. Her instincts screamed at her to run, but she'd worked too hard to get this position. She thought about her student loans, her tiny apartment, the career she'd dreamed of since she was a child fascinated by ancient artifacts.

If this is what it takes...

The decision had been surprisingly easy once she made it. She met Kaian's predatory stare with one of her own, straightening her shoulders. She wouldn't let them see weakness. She wouldn't give them that satisfaction.

"I understand the exercise," she'd said, her voice steadier than she felt. "What do you need me to do?"

Kaian had smiled then, slow and dangerous. "Just be yourself, sweetheart. We'll handle the rest."

What followed challenged every assumption she'd had about intimacy and control. She'd never been with multiple partners before — hell, she'd barely been with anyone who could match the raw magnetism these three projected. But as they moved closer, as hands began to explore and clothes became obstacles to be removed, she'd discovered something surprising about herself.

She could do this. More than that — she could maintain her sense of self even as they guided her toward the rumpled bed, even as the clinical nature of the exercise gave way to something far more primal.

The details blurred in her memory now, but the lesson remained crystal clear — power wasn't about who was on top. It was about who decided to surrender, and why.

When it was over, when she lay catching her breath between bodies that radiated supernatural heat, Margaret's words echoed in her mind — *"Yours, not theirs."*

She'd passed the test. More importantly, she'd learned that she could handle whatever the job threw at her.

* * * *

That night, heat surrounded her in her dreams — scales and fire, rough hands on her skin. She woke breathless, aching, tangled in the blankets, the scent of smoke and something primal lingering in the air.

Izzie swallowed hard, her throat dry, her pulse pounding. The remnants of her dream clung to her skin, leaving her flushed and restless. The cabin was too warm, too small, and the air was thick with something unspoken.

Callum sat in the armchair by the fire, one arm draped lazily over the backrest, a glass of whiskey in his hand. The flickering flames cast sharp shadows across his face, but his smirk was unmistakable.

"Restless night?" he asked, his voice like dark velvet, curling around her like smoke.

Izzie stiffened, fingers clenching the fabric of her oversized sleep shirt. "Just a dream," she murmured, though even as she said it, she wasn't sure if it was a lie.

When she turned, she felt the heat of another body behind her before she saw him. Rhys stood close — too close — his golden eyes glowing like embers in the dim light.

"Not just any dream, I'd wager," Rhys said, voice low, edged with something wicked. "You reek of fire and need, lass."

She shivered, her breath catching. Her instincts screamed at her to step away, to break the dangerous spell settling between them. But instead of running, she stepped closer.

Callum's smirk faltered, his gaze darkening. Rhys exhaled sharply, his lips parting as if she'd surprised him.

"You should be careful, Izzie," Callum murmured, setting his glass down with a soft clink. "You have no idea what you're playing with."

She tilted her chin up in defiance. "Then tell me. Show me."

The silence that followed crackled like the air before a storm. Rhys chuckled, low and husky. "Brave little thing, aren't you?"

Callum ran a hand over his jaw, exhaling slowly, as if trying to rein himself in. "You don't understand, Izzie. This isn't just a game. You're standing between two dragons, in the middle of nowhere, with no one to stop us if—"

"If what?" she interrupted, pulse hammering. "If I say yes?"

Rhys let out a sharp breath, his nostrils flaring. Callum flexed his hands on the armrests.

"You have no idea what you're inviting," Callum said, voice taut.

Izzie swallowed, her resolve wavering for the first time. But she forced herself to meet their gazes, to stand her ground.

"I know what Margaret told me," she said. "She warned me that dragons are possessive. That when more than one sets their sights on a woman, it can be dangerous."

Callum's jaw tightened. Rhys' smirk deepened.

"She wasn't wrong," Rhys murmured, reaching out, his fingers barely grazing the fabric of her sleeve. The touch was light, but it sent a shiver straight through her.

A gust of wind howled against the cabin, rattling the windowpanes. The fire popped, embers scattering in the hearth.

Izzie's breath hitched. She was playing with fire— two of them. And for the first time, she wasn't sure if she wanted to escape the burn.

The memories of her training flooded back— Margaret's warnings, the clinical exercise with the

American dragons, the lesson about maintaining control. But this felt different. More personal. More dangerous.

And infinitely more tempting.

Chapter Eleven

The heat in the secluded cabin was unbearable, the air thick with tension. Izzie could barely breathe, every inch of her skin hypersensitive to the closeness of the two dragon shifters.

Callum's eyes bored into hers, his usual smile replaced by something far more dangerous. "I'm warning you, Izzie," he said, voice dark, low. "Dragons don't share. And once you step into our world, there's no going back. There will be no more 'intimate encounters' with other dragons."

The words settled heavily between them, but Izzie couldn't ignore the raw magnetism pulling at her. She stepped closer, her heart pounding, unable to tear her gaze away from him.

"I'm not asking you to share," she teased, her voice a little breathless, a challenge in her tone. "I'm willing to be faithful, as long as we are together. You, me and…Rhys?"

A knowing, almost predatory look passed between Callum and Rhys, one that sent a thrill through her. Her pulse skipped. Her breath caught.

Rhys chuckled, the sound sending a shiver down her spine. "Careful, lass. You're playing a dangerous game." His golden eyes gleamed in the dim light, a predatory gleam that made her stomach tighten.

The fire crackled behind them, throwing dancing shadows across the rough wooden walls. Outside, the wind had picked up, rattling the windows and making the old cabin creak like a ship in a storm. The isolation pressed in around them—no neighbors for miles, no one to hear if she screamed. The thought should have terrified her. Instead, it sent a forbidden thrill racing through her veins.

Callum moved closer, his presence filling the small space between them. She could smell the scent of him— pine and leather and something uniquely male that made her mouth go dry. "You think you understand what you're offering," he murmured, his voice rough with barely leashed control. "But you have no idea what dragons are capable of when we claim what's ours."

"Then show me," Izzie whispered, the words tumbling out before she could stop them.

The silence that followed was deafening, broken only by the snap and hiss of the fire. Rhys straightened slowly, like a predator sensing weakness in its prey. Callum's jaw clenched, the muscles in his throat working as if he was fighting some internal battle.

"You don't know what you're asking for," Callum said, his voice strained. "We've been holding back, trying to give you space, trying to be—"

"Gentlemen?" Izzie interrupted with a breathless laugh. "I never asked you to be gentlemen."

Rhys was suddenly there, stepping forward so quickly that she didn't have time to react. He cupped her cheek gently — almost tenderly — before his other hand pressed against the wall behind her, caging her in. His golden eyes smoldered with an intensity that stole her breath.

"You don't get to play coy with us, Izzie," Rhys whispered, his voice low and filled with promise. "You've already crossed the line, and now you'll pay for it."

Her breath hitched as he leaned in, his lips brushing the shell of her ear. "You're treading dangerously close to the edge, and if you push me, I won't be able to hold back."

The heat radiating from his body was impossible to ignore. Dragon shifters ran hotter than humans — she'd learned that during her training — but being this close to one, feeling that supernatural warmth seeping through her clothes, was intoxicating. She could feel her resolve crumbling, her professional detachment dissolving under the weight of pure want.

Izzie's heart thundered in her chest, her mind reeling with a rush of conflicting emotions. Every instinct screamed at her to pull away, to flee from the fire building between them, but her body betrayed her. The heat in the room was suffocating, the air thick with desire and something darker, more primal.

"Maybe," she said, her voice barely above a whisper, "I want to see what happens when you stop holding back."

The words hung in the air like a challenge, and she watched as something shifted in both their faces.

Callum's careful control slipped for just a moment, revealing the hunger beneath. Rhys' fingers tightened against the wall, his knuckles going white with the effort of restraining himself.

"Izzie." Callum's voice was a warning, but she could hear the want beneath it. "You need to be sure. Once we start down this path —"

"There's no going back," she finished for him. "You've said that already."

She shifted against the wall, deliberately letting her body brush against Rhys'. The contact sent electricity shooting through her, and she saw his pupils dilate in response. Behind them, she could feel Callum's gaze like a brand on her skin.

"If dragons are so powerful," she breathed, her voice trembling, "why are you hesitating?" Her words hung in the air, daring them to act, to prove their claims.

Callum's mouth curved into a smirk, but there was something tight about it, as though he was controlling himself with great effort. "You think you can push us into action, Izzie?" His voice was a low growl, laced with a warning. "You don't know what you're playing with."

Rhys, on the other hand, seemed to shift with barely contained hunger. He stepped even closer, the heat from his body radiating off him in waves, pressing her back against the rough wall of the cabin. The length of his body crushed her into the wall, his arousal evident between them. "You've awakened something you can't control. We're giving you a choice, Izzie. A chance to step back before it's too late."

The rational part of her mind — the part that had been trained to handle supernatural encounters professionally — was screaming warnings. This was exactly what Margaret had cautioned against. Getting personally involved. Losing objectivity. Becoming prey instead of predator.

But another part of her, a part that had been awakened during that training exercise with the American dragons, reveled in the danger. In the knowledge that she was dancing on the edge of something that could consume her completely.

"You're both so powerful," she said, her voice a mix of breathless temptation and challenge. "But you're hesitating. What are you so afraid of?"

The question hit its mark. She saw Callum's jaw clench, saw Rhys' nostrils flare. They weren't used to being questioned, especially not by a human. The power dynamic had shifted, and for a moment, she held the advantage.

"Afraid?" Rhys' voice was silk over steel. "Lass, you have no idea—"

The words were barely out of his mouth when a noise broke the thick silence, shattering the fragile moment of intimacy.

A twig snapped sharply outside the cabin, followed by the softest rustle of movement—like someone or something had shifted in the shadows. Izzie's heart stuttered in her chest, and she instinctively stiffened. The blood in her veins turned cold.

The transformation in both men was instantaneous. The sexual tension evaporated, replaced by something far more dangerous. Callum's eyes flicked toward the window, his body going still, every muscle coiled for action. Rhys stepped away from her immediately, his golden eyes scanning the darkness beyond the cabin window with predatory focus.

"Someone's out there," Rhys muttered, his voice taut with suspicion. His gaze never left the window as he took slow, deliberate steps toward the door, his muscles rippling beneath the surface of his shirt.

Izzie pressed herself against the wall, still breathless and confused by the abrupt shift in mood. The brothers were no longer lovers — they were hunters, alert and focused, as though everything had changed in an instant.

"What is it?" she whispered, her heart still racing from the intensity of the moment, but now overtaken by a flicker of fear. "Who's out there?"

The cabin felt smaller now, the isolation that had seemed exciting moments before now feeling like a trap. They were miles from anywhere, surrounded by dark forest and Highland moors. If someone had found them here…

Rhys didn't answer immediately. Instead, he reached for the door handle, his body tense with readiness. "I'm going to check," he said, his voice low, barely more than a whisper. "Stay inside."

Before she could respond, he threw open the door, and his figure was swallowed by the darkness of the night. The wind howled outside, sending a chill through the cabin. Callum, his jaw set, followed Rhys' lead but paused long enough to cast one last glance at Izzie.

"Stay here," Callum warned, his voice fierce and commanding. "Lock the door."

Izzie nodded, but her gaze stayed fixed on the darkened doorway. Her pulse pounded in her neck and a sense of dread pooled in her stomach. The threat outside wasn't just unknown — it was real. Something, or someone, had followed them here.

The moment they disappeared into the darkness, the cabin felt vast and empty. Every creak of the old wood, every whisper of wind against the windows, made her jump. She moved to the door and turned the heavy deadbolt, the metallic click unnaturally loud in the silence.

Through the window, she could see nothing but inky blackness. The brothers had vanished completely, swallowed by the Highland night. She strained her ears for any sound — voices, footsteps, anything to indicate what was happening out there.

But there was only silence.

And in that silence, Izzie realized that whatever game she'd been playing with Callum and Rhys had just become deadly serious.

Chapter Twelve

The night's silence hung thick, as if the world itself were holding its breath. The immediate threat outside — the soft shuffle of an unseen presence in the shadows — had faded into the dark, but the tension inside the cabin had only sharpened.

Callum and Rhys had rushed out, their dragon instincts thrumming beneath their skin, but whoever had been lurking was already gone. No trace left behind, no tracks in the damp earth, nothing but the lingering sense of being watched. When they returned, the firelight cast long shadows over their sharp features, their bodies still taut with vigilance.

"It's clear." Callum's narrowed eyes contradicted his words as he shut the door behind him, sliding the heavy bolt home. "For now."

Rhys leaned against the stone hearth, arms crossed. "We warned you, lass. The closer you get to the Harp, the more dangerous this will become."

Izzie nodded, but her gaze stayed fixed on the darkened doorway. The night stretched beyond it, thick with shadows that shifted in the wind, yet she knew — someone waited there. Watching. Her pulse hammered at the base of her throat, unease curling deep in her stomach. The threat outside wasn't just imagined. It was real. Someone had followed them.

And they weren't done yet.

But the fear twisting inside her wasn't only for the stranger in the dark. It was for what stirred within herself.

She turned toward Callum and Rhys, their presence solid, unyielding, each movement deliberate, as if they already knew what hunted them. Dragons — creatures born of legend, older than anything she could comprehend. They were dangerous. She knew that. She should have been afraid of them.

Perhaps she was.

Yet she wanted to be near them. She wanted them.

Her pulse quickened, not just with fear, but with something just as reckless, just as dangerous. She wanted to understand them — the fire that burned in their veins, the sharp edge of their power. She wanted to know if the same heat that could destroy could also protect. Could she trust them to keep her safe? Or would she have to protect herself from them as well?

Their gazes pinned her, unreadable yet searing. A silent challenge.

Could she survive the storm that came with them? Or worse — did she even want to?

She shifted slightly, turning toward the fire. The flames flickered and danced, casting shadows that seemed to echo her inner turmoil. What was it about them? What was it about this moment that had her feeling both alive and afraid in equal measure?

Her mind drifted back to Margaret's warnings, to the danger that came when dragons set their sights on a woman. But there was something deeper at play here, something that called to her on a level she couldn't ignore, no matter how much she tried.

Izzie stepped closer to them, drawn in by the heat of their presence, the quiet tension simmering beneath their calm exteriors. Callum's sharp eyes tracked her every movement, but he didn't reach out, didn't act. He was waiting, testing, holding back. The weight of that restraint was almost too much to bear.

"You know, dragons don't hesitate. Or so I thought." The words hung in the air, daring them to challenge her.

Callum's lips twitched — a flicker of amusement, or perhaps something darker. "It's not hesitation. It's caution." His voice rumbled like distant thunder, full of authority. "This isn't about desire, Izzie. It's about control. Power. And what we're capable of."

Rhys shifted closer. His presence pressed against her senses, a wildfire sweeping over her, untamed and inevitable. His breath skimmed her ear. "You think you can play this game without consequences?"

A flicker of uncertainty stirred within her. She wasn't even sure what game she was playing anymore. Part of her wanted to understand them — to unravel the pull they had on her, why she was drawn to both in ways she'd never felt before. But another part feared what it meant. The power they wielded. The darkness running beneath their skin.

"I'm not afraid of you." Her voice faltered only slightly.

The moment stretched between them, balanced on the edge of something dangerous. She wasn't sure what she wanted — not truly. But she knew she couldn't leave. Not yet. Not when so much remained unanswered and the stakes had never been higher.

Her heartbeat thundered — not with fear, but something raw, unfiltered.

What began as slow-burning tension — the exchanged glances, the subtle shifts of weight — ignited into something far more intense. A wild current pulled her under, her instincts screaming to run. But she didn't. Instead, she stepped closer, heat licking at her skin as their focus burned into her.

The air thickened, laden with unspoken promises and secrets too dangerous to name. Her pulse quickened, her mind fraying with each breath. She felt them — Callum's quiet command, Rhys' insatiable hunger — wrapping around her like a force she couldn't escape.

It was possessive, inescapable. A feeling of being wanted — not just for who she was, but for what they believed they could claim. Her mind fought against it, but her body betrayed her, responding to a force she couldn't control. It was everything Margaret had warned her about — the danger of dragons, the way they took what they desired. And yet, in that moment, she didn't know how to resist.

She didn't want to resist.

There was no space for hesitation, no room for anything but what was happening between them. Her thoughts blurred, surrendering to the overwhelming force of their desire.

Izzie's breath hitched as the space between them vanished, Callum in front of her, Rhys behind, their bodies close, caging her in a heat that coiled around her like smoke. Their presence was overwhelming, suffocating in a way that didn't make her want to run—but surrender.

Callum's fingers traced the curve of her jaw, tilting her chin up so she had no choice but to meet his gaze. His eyes burned, molten and wild, his dragon nature barely restrained beneath the surface. Behind her, Rhys' hands settled on her shoulders, thumbs pressing into the tension she hadn't realized she was holding. A shiver worked through her, the sensation too much and not enough all at once.

"You feel this." Callum's breath warmed against her lips. Not a question. A fact.

She swallowed hard.

Rhys' lips found the side of her neck, a slow, deliberate drag of heat against her pulse. She gasped, her fingers clutching at Callum's shirt, but his grip tightened around her waist, steadying her as if sensing she might collapse.

"Let go." Rhys whispered against her ear, his teeth grazing her earlobe before he sucked it into the heat of his mouth.

She didn't know if he meant her thoughts or her fears or something else entirely. Callum kissed her then—no hesitation, no pretense of restraint. His mouth claimed hers, firm and possessive, his tongue sweeping over hers with a hunger that sent a sharp thrill straight through her core. She melted into him, into Rhys, her body caught between them, every sense sharpened, every nerve ending alive.

She had been a fool to think she could resist them, not after what she had experienced in the back of the Land Rover the night before. Rhys' hands slid down her arms, caressing the sensitive skin of her forearms, her wrists, before ghosting back up, tracing the curve of her shoulders. His mouth was at her throat now, pressing open-mouthed kisses along the fragile line of her pulse. She could feel the quiet growl that rumbled in his chest, an animalistic need barely held in check.

The air around them felt charged, thick with something ancient, something dangerous.

Izzie could sense it — the shift beneath their skin, the way their dragons stirred, demanding more, demanding everything. The power of them, of what they were, should have terrified her.

Instead, she burned for it.

Her head fell back against Rhys' shoulder, her lips parting in a soft gasp as Callum's mouth left hers only to trail fire along her jaw, down her throat. She could feel them both — their heat, their strength, the inescapable force of their desire pressing into her from all sides.

She had never felt safer.

She had never felt more at risk of losing herself.

Then — impatient as any feral animal would be — Callum ripped her sleep shirt from neck to hem, Rhys seizing the open edges from behind and tearing it from her body.

"Mmm, you're so beautiful, Izzie." Callum's fingers traced the curve of her breast as he unclasped her bra. Her nipples hardened in the cool air, begging to be touched.

Callum's mouth and hands seized her breasts, sucking her nipples into his mouth, one, then the other, and back again.

"Oooh! By all the gods!" Izzie's legs almost collapsed out from under her.

Callum raised his head again, his lips finding hers as his hands continued to cup her breasts. Rhys' hands tightened around her waist, pulling her closer, pulling her back into him, and she could feel his hardened length pressing into the curve of her ass —

And she realized something else —

She didn't care that she had no say in what they were doing to her. For her.

Rhys slid his hands down her sides, hooking his fingers into the waistband of her panties. "And all ours for the night." His fingers pulled the flimsy fabric down her legs.

Naked and exposed, Izzie felt a surge of excitement course through her veins. The thought of being filled by both Callum and Rhys once again sent waves of desire crashing over her.

Callum captured her lips in a searing kiss, his tongue delving into her mouth as Rhys' hands massaged her ass. She moaned into the kiss, her hips pressing forward, seeking friction against Callum's growing erection.

Breaking the kiss, Callum leaned back, allowing Rhys to take his place. Rhys turned her head, her face tilted up to his. Tonight, his lips were softer, his kisses more tender as he explored her mouth. His hands roamed her body, caressing every inch of her smooth skin.

Even the fire dragon had a softer side, once his initial lust for her had been sated.

Callum moved lower, trailing kisses down her neck and across her collarbone. He paused to lavish attention on her breasts once more, his tongue swirling around one nipple while his fingers pinched and tugged at the other.

Izzie gasped, her head falling back against Rhys' chest. The dual sensations of Rhys' passionate kisses and Callum's expert mouth on her breasts were driving her wild with desire. Rhys slid his hand between her thighs, his fingers parting her wet folds. "Fuck me, lassie, you're so wet." His fingers circled her clit.

Izzie bucked her hips, desperate for more. "Please." Her voice was heavy with need.

Callum moved lower, his tongue leaving a trail of fire down her stomach. He knelt on the floor at her feet, his mouth pausing at the juncture of her thighs, his breath hot against her sensitive flesh.

Rhys captured her mouth once more, his tongue tangling with hers as Callum's mouth descended on her pussy. His tongue delved deep, flicking at her clit and running along her lips, then lapping at her juices as his fingers continued to tease the sensitive nub of flesh.

Izzie cried out, her hips grinding against Callum's face. The pleasure was overwhelming, her body trembling with the force of her impending orgasm.

As if sensing her approaching release, Callum pulled back, denying her the satisfaction she craved. Rhys broke the kiss, his lips trailing down her neck as he positioned himself between her legs from behind, holding her hips firmly against him.

She could feel the entire hard length of him between them, the head throbbing against her.

"I need to be inside you." Rhys' cock pressed against her entrance.

Izzie nodded. "Yes." She breathed, her body aching to be filled. "Please!"

Rhys thrust forward, his cock sliding deep into her tight heat. Izzie gasped, her nails digging into his forearms as he began to move.

Callum rose from the floor in front of her, his cock hard and throbbing. "Suck me." He grabbed her shoulders and bent her forward until her face was at the level of his hips. Rhys' thrusts grew stronger, this new position offering him an easier route into her cunt. Izzie opened her mouth, wrapping her lips around Callum's thick shaft. She bobbed her head, taking him deep into her mouth as Rhys continued to pound into her from behind.

The sensation of being filled at both ends was unlike anything Izzie had ever experienced. Just the freedom of being naked in the cabin with her two dragon lovers was amazing, even after having them both inside her in the car the night before. Her body was on fire, her nerves raw with pleasure.

Rhys' thrusts became harder, more urgent. "Fuck, I'm close." His fingers dug into her hips.

Izzie could feel her own orgasm building, her body tensing as she teetered on the edge. She sucked harder on Callum's cock, her hand stroking what she couldn't fit in her mouth.

With a final thrust, Rhys buried himself deep inside her, his cock pulsing as he came. The feeling of his hot seed filling her pushed Izzie over the edge, her own orgasm crashing over her in waves.

Callum followed suit, his cock exploding in her mouth. Izzie swallowed every drop, her throat working to take him all in.

As the three of them came down from their high, Rhys picked her up and carried her into the bedroom, the sheets already tangled from the brothers' earlier attempts at sleep. He laid her down and crawled up beside her, Callum joining them in a tangle of limbs and sweat-slicked skin.

"That was incredible." A satisfied smile played across Izzie's lips.

Callum chuckled, his hand stroking her hair. "We're not done yet, sweetheart. The night is young, and we have so much more of you to explore."

Rhys grinned, his hand sliding down to cup her breast. "And we're going to take our time with you, Izzie. We're going to worship every inch of your body until you're screaming our names."

The room was thick with dragon heat, the air laced with the scent of them — embers and sea salt, wildness and sweat. Izzie lay sprawled between them, her body boneless, her skin still humming where their hands and mouths had claimed her. Callum lay on one side, propped up on an elbow, his fingers idly tracing the curve of her breasts. On the other, Rhys stretched out, watching her with that dark, unreadable intensity, his arm draped possessively over her mound.

She should have felt overwhelmed. Should have felt anything other than this bone-deep satisfaction and the slow, deep ache that came from being loved by them both.

Callum broke the silence first, his voice husky, roughened by the echoes of what they'd just done. "So, what's it like? Making love to two dragon men?"

Izzie let out a breathless laugh, shaking her head. "Is that really what you want to know right now?"

Rhys smirked, his fingers brushing up the inside of her wrist, feeling the faint flutter of her pulse. "We want to know if it's something you can handle." His voice was quieter, threaded with something deeper. Not doubt, exactly. But concern. "In the long term."

Callum's hand settled low on her hip. "We're not like human men, Izzie. You know that. We love harder.

We need more. And once we've claimed something..."
His grip tightened, just a little. "We don't easily let go."

Her heart stumbled at that, a flicker of fear twisting inside her pleasure-enhanced haze. Not fear of them, exactly, but fear of what this meant. What she had just allowed. What she was quickly becoming.

She swallowed, shifting slightly so she could look back and forth at them both. "And what does that mean? For us? If I say yes, if I say I can handle it—what happens then?"

Rhys' fingers slid into her hair, tilting her face toward him. His golden eyes burned in the dim light. "It means you're ours."

Callum kissed the curve of her shoulder, his breath warm against her damp skin. "It means there's no turning back."

"And remember, lass"—Rhys traced the line of her jaw with a long finger—"there are three more of us."

Izzie inhaled slowly, trying to make sense of the chaos inside her. There was fear. There was uncertainty. But beneath it all, there was something else—something fierce and undeniable, something that had already bound her to them, whether she admitted it or not.

Could she handle this? The sheer force of their lovemaking, the inhuman nature of their desire, the knowledge that she was tethering herself to creatures who did not live, or love, the way mortals did?

She should have hesitated.

But instead, she reached up, cupping Callum's jaw with one hand, threading the other through Rhys' dark hair.

"I think I was yours before I even knew who you were."

Izzie shivered with anticipation, her body already humming with renewed desire. She knew this night was going to be one she would never forget.

As the hours ticked by, Izzie found herself lost in a haze of pleasure. Callum and Rhys took turns fucking her, their cocks sliding in and out of her pussy and ass as they switched positions.

They brought her to orgasm after orgasm, their mouths and hands never ceasing in their exploration of her body. Izzie had never felt so desired, so cherished.

At one point, she found herself on her hands and knees, Callum's cock buried deep in her pussy as Rhys fucked her ass. The dual sensation was overwhelming, her body shaking with the force of her climax.

They tried every position imaginable, their bodies moving in perfect synchronization. Izzie felt like a goddess, her pleasure the sole focus of their attention.

When it ended, silence filled the room, heavy with the weight of what had transpired. Izzie lay between them, tangled in their warmth, her chest rising and falling, her mind foggy. She had crossed a line she could never return from. And yet, a small voice in her head whispered — had she ever truly had a choice?

The aftermath settled deep, something more than just physical satisfaction. A sense of possession. Of being marked. Of belonging. She hadn't asked for it, hadn't understood it, but it was there, lingering in the quiet of the night.

As sleep pulled at her, still pressed between them, a cold thought took root in her mind, sinking like a stone in her chest.

If dragons mated for life...what did this mean for her?

The question shadowed her thoughts, dragging her into restless dreams. The weight of her decision pressed against her, heavier than ever.

Even as exhaustion claimed her, she knew — she might have just become part of something she could never escape. Something far greater than herself. Something beyond her control.

And the worst part?

She wasn't sure if she wanted to be bound so tightly to a world she was barely beginning to understand.

Chapter Thirteen

Early morning mist settled over the water, cloaking the island ahead in a pale, ghostly veil as the ferry cut through the calm waves. The steady hum of the boat's engine was the only sound breaking the silence, a sound that seemed too loud in contrast to the stillness of the world around them. Izzie stood at the bow, her gaze fixed on the horizon, the Isle of Mull drawing nearer with each passing moment.

For three days, they had wandered the Highlands, tracing the whispers of history through the narrow streets of tiny villages and the hushed corridors of ancient libraries. Izzie had pored over crumbling manuscripts in old manor houses, her fingers tracing faded ink as she pieced together fragments of the Harp's legend. Callum and Rhys had watched her with quiet intensity, their presence both protective and possessive, as if the weight of their newfound bond tethered them together as much as the mystery they pursued.

Nights had been spent wrapped in firelight and each other, the cabin becoming their sanctuary—until the search for answers pulled them back into the world.

After hours of travel, they had arrived in the seacoast port of Oban. The town was a welcome break from their search, offering a brief moment of respite in a cozy bed and breakfast where the crackling fire and soft beds allowed them to briefly let down their guards. But even here, their bond—their connection—remained, coiling around them like an invisible thread. There was an undeniable sense of something shifting, growing between them, something Izzie found both thrilling and terrifying.

This morning, the ferry to Craignure had been their first step toward something larger. As the boat cut through the mist-filled waters toward the Isle of Mull, Izzie sensed a growing anticipation, the weight of the quest pressing against her chest like the notebook she clutched tightly. Each wave that passed brought them another step toward unraveling the mystery that had begun with a simple mission, a song that now echoed through her thoughts constantly, refusing to be ignored.

She had tucked her notebook tightly against her chest, the pages filled with scribbled notes, sketches, and fragments of her thoughts from the previous days. The Harp of Ceòthach Glen—the mysterious artifact that had consumed her mind since she had received her assignment back in Wilmington—was what had drawn them here, to the heart of the Hebrides. She couldn't shake the feeling that they were getting closer to something—something that would change everything.

Izzie shifted her gaze briefly to Callum and Rhys, who stood a few paces behind her. Their presence was a constant reminder of the strange, magnetic pull they had on her, the unspoken connection that had only grown more complicated since her first nights in the Highlands. But now, as the boat churned through the water, their tension was palpable. Callum leaned against the railing, arms folded, scanning the water as if he could sense something lurking just beneath the surface. Rhys was no better — his gaze flickered from the darkening shoreline to the open sea, his jaw clenched as if he were holding something back.

Izzie had grown accustomed to their watchful eyes, but today, there was a new sense of unease in the air — an unspoken tension that made the already chill morning colder.

"You're both on edge." Her voice was low, her words more a statement than a question. "What's going on?"

Callum's mouth tightened into a thin line, his expression unreadable. "It's nothing." The way his eyes narrowed told Izzie it was far from nothing. "Just a feeling. We've been in strange territory lately."

Izzie frowned, glancing between the two of them. "What kind of feeling?"

Rhys and Callum exchanged a look, the kind that spoke of things long unsaid. The tension in their posture wasn't just unease — it was something deeper, something old. Callum exhaled sharply, pushing off the railing as if shaking off an invisible weight.

"There's a family of sea dragons nesting nearby." Rhys kept his gaze on the water, as if expecting something to rise from the depths at any moment. "They've lived in the sea caves along this coastline for centuries."

Izzie's breath hitched, her fingers tightening around the notebook pressed to her chest. "Sea dragons." She tasted the words, trying to imagine creatures even older and more mysterious than the men beside her. "You mean actual dragons? Like you?"

Callum shook his head. "Not like us. They're different—more creature than man, their blood tied to the tides in ways ours isn't." He glanced toward the mist-covered horizon, his mouth set in a grim line. "Our families haven't always been on the best of terms."

A chill that had nothing to do with the cold morning air settled in Izzie's bones. "Why?"

Rhys' jaw tightened. "The Sìol Dòmhnaill and the clan of Na Firghean Mara—those who walk the sea—have a long history. Some would call it a feud, others an uneasy truce. We've fought alongside them, and against them. Our kinds were never meant to coexist peacefully, and yet..." He trailed off, his eyes dark with something unspoken.

Izzie swallowed, her heart pounding. The thought of dragons beneath the sea, watching from the hidden depths, sent a shiver down her spine. "Are they dangerous?"

Callum gave a short, humorless laugh. "To us? Sometimes. To humans?" He met her gaze, the amber in his eyes flickering like firelight. "Let's just say they don't take kindly to outsiders."

A slow unease crept over her. The world was bigger—darker—than she had ever imagined, and every step she took deeper into it pressed against the edges of something ancient and waiting.

The ferry cut through the mist, the Isle of Mull looming closer. Izzie had the distinct feeling they weren't just being watched by the past, but by something very present.

She shook off the thought, forcing her attention back to the task at hand. The archives in Mull were her next step. There, she would dig deeper into old family records, first-person accounts, and any forgotten mentions of the Harp that might have slipped through the cracks of time. She needed to find something — anything — that could bring them closer to unlocking the secrets of Ceòthach Glen.

"We'll head to the inn as soon as we dock." She spoke more to herself than to the others. "You two stay sharp."

Callum's gaze softened ever so slightly, a flicker of concern in his eyes before he masked it. "We'll be watching."

Izzie nodded, but even as she spoke, the weight of their unease settled over her like a cloud. Something was waiting for them on Mull, and whatever it was, it wasn't going to make their search easy.

* * * *

The town of Craignure, the gateway to the Isle of Mull, was quiet as they disembarked. The mist still lingered in the air, curling around the streets in tendrils, obscuring the distant hills. The smell of the sea mixed with the scent of damp earth and pine. Izzie adjusted the strap of her bag, feeling the weight of her purpose — her mission — bearing down on her. She was here for the records, the history that might contain a hidden reference to the Harp of Ceòthach Glen. But she couldn't shake the feeling that this was about more than just the Harp. There was something in the air —

something older, more ancient—that tugged at her like an unseen current.

Callum guided the Land Rover up the narrow lane, its tires crunching over loose gravel as the inn came into view. The building was small but sturdy, its weathered stone walls draped in ivy, the green tendrils creeping up like whispers of the past. A wooden sign, faded by years of wind and rain, swayed gently from iron brackets above the entrance.

He cut the engine, and for a moment, the three of them sat in silence. Outside, the village stirred with quiet life—muted voices carrying on the damp air, the distant clang of a shop bell, the occasional echo of footsteps on cobblestones.

Rhys was the first to move, pushing open the door. "Let's get this done."

Inside, the inn was warm, the scent of burning peat curling in the air. A low fire crackled in the hearth, its glow casting flickering shadows against the dark wooden beams. The innkeeper, an elderly man with silver-threaded hair and a gaze as sharp as cut glass, greeted them with a nod, his assessing gaze flicking over Izzie before landing on the two men at her side.

Callum spoke first, his voice easy, measured. "Three rooms, if you've got them."

The innkeeper's brows lifted a fraction, but he said nothing as he reached for the keys. Here in the islands, among humans, traditions ran deep. A single woman traveling with two men—unmarried, at that—was enough to stir talk if they weren't careful. Discretion was the price of keeping the peace.

Izzie accepted her key with a polite smile, though she could feel the heat of Callum's gaze as she turned toward the stairs. Separate rooms might be necessary for appearances, but they all knew it wouldn't keep them apart. Out in the open countryside, beneath wide skies and hidden among the wild heather, there would be ways to steal time for themselves.

They settled their bags in their respective rooms — small, tidy spaces with iron-framed beds and windows fogged with the sea air. There was no time to linger. The library awaited.

Leaving the Land Rover behind, they set out on foot, the mist-thickened air clinging to their skin as they moved through the twisting streets. Callum and Rhys walked ahead, their gazes flicking over every alleyway, every passerby. Their silence was not unusual, but Izzie knew what it meant. They were on edge, attuned to something she could not sense.

The library was nestled between two shops, its modest stone façade nearly swallowed by climbing vines. A single window, its glass wavy with age, reflected the gray sky. The door, painted a peeling shade of blue, creaked softly as Izzie pushed it open.

"I'll wait out here." Callum's voice was low. Rhys gave a curt nod, his hands tucked into his pockets, his stance deceptively casual.

Izzie hesitated, glancing between them. "You're acting like I'm walking into a lion's den."

Rhys smirked, but it didn't quite reach his eyes. "Just a precaution, love. I'll come with." He continued. "In case you need an interpreter."

With a sigh, Izzie stepped inside with Rhys at her heels, the door clicking shut behind them. The scent of old books enveloped her, a comforting contrast to the unease lingering just beyond the threshold.

The hours slipped by as Izzie combed through old documents. The papers were yellowed with age, brittle at the edges, and covered in the intricate scrawl of old Gaelic, many of them indecipherable to her. Rhys did an excellent job of reading aloud the pertinent scraps and pages, between sliding his hands beneath her bra or between her legs. She had to work at concentrating, squinting at the pages, searching for any mention of the Harp, but the deeper she dug, the more it seemed like she was chasing shadows.

By the time she pushed the last of the texts aside, her stomach was protesting. Rhys checked the time and suggested they find something to eat before heading back to the inn. The evening air was crisp as they stepped out of the library and found Callum waiting across the way, the scent of the sea threading through the narrow streets. They found a small shop still open, its windows aglow with soft light, and bought food to take back—a thick broth, fresh bread, and wedges of sharp cheese wrapped in waxed paper.

Back at the inn, they settled in the public lounge, their meal spread across a wooden table near the fire. Other travelers sat scattered about, speaking in low tones, nursing pints of ale. It was a cozy, almost domestic moment, but underlying tension buzzed beneath the surface. Callum and Rhys kept an easy posture, but their gazes flicked to the door, to the windows, ever watchful.

When the meal was finished, they climbed the stairs to their rooms, the hallway dimly lit by sconces. Outside her door, Izzie turned to say goodnight, but Rhys leaned in, his breath warm against her ear.

"Leave it unlocked for me."

She arched a brow. "I thought we agreed to be discreet."

"I will be discreet." His lips grazed her earlobe. "I'll make sure no one hears your moans when I have you writhing beneath me."

Callum huffed a quiet laugh. "There wouldn't be room in that little bed for all of us anyway. And it wouldn't be fair to leave me out."

Izzie placed her hands against both their chests and gently pushed them back. "Get some rest. Alone." She smirked, stepping into her room. "I'm locking my door."

She shut it firmly behind her, ignoring the low chuckle from the other side.

Just inside the threshold, something caught her eye — a folded sheet of paper, stark against the wooden floor. Unlike the brittle pages she'd been poring over all evening, this was crisp, the inn's letterhead printed neatly across the top.

A chill prickled down her spine as she bent to pick it up. The handwriting was sharp and deliberate, each stroke carved onto the page like a warning —

We know what you're looking for. What have you found out about the Harp's location? Be ready to share — soon. Or face the consequences.

No signature. No sign of who had left it. Just the weight of the threat hanging in the air.

Izzie swallowed hard, her pulse hammering. Someone was watching them. Someone knew what she was searching for.

Her fingers tightened around the note as a deeper unease settled in her chest. The warning wasn't just about the Harp — it was about her. About what she had uncovered, what she had yet to discover.

Her mind flickered back to the Highland cabin, to the noise outside in the dark. Was it the same person?

Had they followed her here, waiting for the right moment to make their move?

She flicked the door lock into place, but it did nothing to ease the sense that she was no longer just searching for the Harp.

Someone was following her. And they knew why she was in Scotland.

Chapter Fourteen

Izzie wandered through the narrow streets of Craignure, the crisp scent of the sea lingering in the air. The town was quiet in the early afternoon, the occasional chatter of locals drifting from small cafés and souvenir shops that lined the main road. She wrapped her scarf tighter around her neck, feeling the absence of Callum and Rhys more acutely now that she was alone. They had been called away to handle a family matter, assuring her that she would be fine for a few hours. There had been no sign of trouble since that first night at the Highland cabin, but still she couldn't shake the sense that she was being watched.

She stepped into a small shop displaying handwoven tartans and intricately carved wooden trinkets. A bell jingled softly as she entered, and the warmth inside was a welcome contrast to the brisk breeze outside. She ran her fingers over a soft woolen shawl, admiring the deep blues and greens of the pattern. It reminded her of the landscape surrounding the town — wild, untamed, and steeped in history.

As she moved to a display of silver jewelry, a voice interrupted her thoughts.

"Miss Rhodes, isn't it?"

Izzie stiffened at the sound of her name. She turned to see a man standing a few feet away, examining a row of Celtic pendants as though they held his genuine interest. He was tall, well-dressed in a dark coat, with the kind of face that was easy to overlook in a crowd — swarthy, but unremarkable. Yet there was something about him that set her on edge.

"Do I know you?" Her voice remained neutral despite the chill racing down her spine.

He smiled, but it didn't reach his eyes. "No, but I know you. More importantly, I know what you're looking for."

Izzie's stomach tightened. She had been careful, discreet. But someone had still taken notice. "I don't know what you're talking about."

"Come now." He selected a pendant and turned it over in his fingers with deliberate care. "There's no need for pretense. You're searching for the Harp, aren't you? The same one that so many before you have tried and failed to find."

He must be the person who had slipped that note under her door. Her pulse pounded in her ears. "I don't know who you are, but you have the wrong person."

The man's laugh was soft, condescending. "No, I don't. And I think you'll want to hear what I have to say." He placed the pendant back on the rack with deliberate care before turning his full attention to her.

"Who are you?" Izzie demanded.

His smile widened, though it remained cold. "Who I am doesn't matter. You can just call me 'The Fixer' for now."

"What do you want from me? Is it you who's been following me?"

He took a step closer, narrowing the distance between them. "I represent someone with a great deal of interest in rare and valuable artifacts. Someone who believes the Harp belongs in the hands of a true connoisseur, not left to decay in some forgotten ruin."

Izzie swallowed hard, keeping her expression composed. "And what does this collector want from me?"

His smile widened, though it remained cold. "Only your cooperation. If you help us locate the Harp, I can assure you that you will be well compensated. Money, security — anything you desire." He took a step closer, lowering his voice. "Or, you can continue your little treasure hunt alone and risk attracting the attention of far less agreeable parties."

The weight of his words settled over her like a storm cloud. She had known this search would be dangerous, but this was the first real proof that she wasn't the only one looking. And whoever this man worked for, they had resources — enough to know her name, her whereabouts, and exactly what she was after.

"Think about it, Miss Rhodes." His voice turned smooth, oily. "But don't think too long. Opportunities like this don't last forever."

With that, he turned and strode out of the shop, leaving Izzie standing amidst the souvenirs and trinkets, her heart hammering against her ribs.

The game had changed. And she was no longer playing it alone.

* * * *

Callum and Rhys returned that evening, carrying takeout bags filled with dinner. Once again, they ate in the inn's public lounge, the low murmur of other guests around them adding a dull hum to the atmosphere. Izzie didn't speak of the man in the souvenir shop, though his shadow clung to her, never quite fading from her mind. His words had lingered long after he'd gone — "We want what you're looking for."

She pushed the thought away, forcing herself to focus on the warmth of the fire crackling in the hearth, the heat from the flames a small comfort against the cold gnawing at her chest. But it was no use. Worry twisted like a vine around her heart. Who had he been? How had he been so certain of her purpose?

It was almost as if he'd known why she was in Scotland before she had.

Rhys, unaware of her growing unease, grinned as he leaned in closer. "While we were handling family business, I heard a rumor about an old chapel near the shore, some ruins a few miles from here. Supposedly, there's a clue to the Harp's location there."

Izzie frowned, though she masked it quickly. "How reliable is this lead?"

Callum shrugged, casual as ever. "Reliable enough to check it out. We'll head there in the morning."

The thought of wandering through ruins stirred something uneasy in her, a sense of vulnerability she couldn't shake. Too many eyes seemed to be on them already, and the idea of searching for a clue to the Harp — in ruins — felt like an invitation to disaster.

As they finished their meal, the lounge began to empty, the other guests retiring to their rooms for the night. The fire's crackle softened, leaving them in a quiet cocoon. The three of them lingered, sipping whiskey, their conversation lowering to a quieter hum. Rhys, emboldened by the drink, slid his hand along Izzie's thigh beneath the table. She stiffened instinctively, her nerves still raw from earlier in the day.

He tilted his head, a question in his eyes. She forced a smile, thin and unconvincing.

"I'll leave my door unlocked." The words slipped from her lips before she could stop them.

Rhys grinned, a gleam in his eye, but Callum caught the exchange. He watched her closely, his expression unreadable.

* * * *

Later, in her room, she stood by the window, staring out into the village as darkness settled. The wind off the sea howled through the narrow streets, rattling the inn's old windows. Sleep seemed a distant prospect, her mind a swirling mess of unease, anticipation, and fragments of the encounter in the shop.

Her door creaked open, and her pulse quickened. She turned sharply to find Rhys slipping inside with the ease of someone who had done this many times before. He said nothing, merely watching her with that familiar hunger. Izzie braced herself, expecting him to move toward her, but before he could, the door opened again.

Callum followed, silent and measured, moving as quietly as Rhys. Their gazes met, and something passed between them—something she couldn't name. She didn't object, though the air in the room thickened, charged with unspoken tension.

Callum closed the door behind him, and the space between them shrank, drawing them closer with every breath. The three of them stood still, the weight of the moment settling over them like a fog.

The dragon shifters stood there, their eyes dark with wanting her. "We couldn't help but notice you." Rhys' voice was soft, pretending they were all strangers. "We were hoping we could come in and keep you company."

Izzie bit her lip, playfully considering their request. She didn't make them wait long. She stepped aside and waved them further in, whispering theatrically, "But we have to be quiet. If the innkeeper finds out, he'll throw us all out."

Callum and Rhys both grinned, their eyes roaming over her body, taking in the sheer nightgown she wore. If this went anything like previous nights, she'd soon be out of nightgowns. And there probably wasn't anywhere to get decent replacements in the Islands. She'd have to place an emergency call to Margaret for a special delivery. Rhys reached out and traced a finger along her collarbone, sending a shiver through her. "We can be very quiet."

They moved closer, their hands exploring her body through the thin silk. Izzie's breath caught in her throat as they kissed her, their lips soft and insistent. Callum's hands slid down to cup her ass, pulling her to him so she could feel his hardness pressing against her.

Rhys motioned to the bed, a question in his eyes. Callum shook his head.

"Too noisy."

Rhys pointed to the floor. Callum considered, then stepped away from Izzie, tearing the covers off her bed and tossing them down on the carpet. They guided her to the floor, laying her down on a nest they built from the many pillows the inn provided its guests. Rhys knelt between her legs, pushing her nightgown up to expose her thighs. He ran his hands along her smooth skin, his touch sending electricity through her body. Callum leaned down, pushing aside the silk bodice of her gown and capturing her nipple in his mouth, sucking and nibbling gently.

Izzie bit her lip to stifle a moan as Rhys' fingers found her wetness, sliding easily through her folds. He circled her clit with his thumb, applying just the right amount of pressure to make her hips buck against his hand.

Meanwhile, Callum released her nipple and kissed his way up her neck, his long hair tickling her skin. He whispered in her ear, "You're so beautiful, so perfect. We're going to make you feel so good."

Izzie could only nod, lost in the sensations they were creating in her body. Rhys continued to stroke her clit, his fingers dipping inside her, stretching her, preparing her for what was to come.

Suddenly, he withdrew his hand and moved up her body, positioning himself at her entrance. He pushed inside her slowly, filling her completely. Izzie had to bite her lip hard to keep from crying out at the intensity of him filling her.

Callum leaned down and took her nipple back into his mouth, sucking harder this time, his teeth grazing the sensitive bud. His hand snaked down between their bodies, finding her clit and rubbing in time with his brother's thrusts.

They moved together in perfect synchronization, their bodies creating a rhythm that was both silent and powerful. Rhys' cock plunged in and out of her, hitting that spot inside her that made her see stars. Callum's fingers and mouth worked in tandem, driving her closer and closer to the edge.

Just as Izzie felt herself teetering on the brink of orgasm, Rhys pulled out, leaving her empty and aching. He moved aside, allowing Callum to take his place. He entered her in one smooth thrust, his thickness stretching her deliciously.

Rhys moved to her head, his cock brushing against her lips. Izzie opened her mouth, taking him in, sucking him deep into her throat. The three of them moved together, a silent dance of pleasure and desire.

Callum's thrusts grew harder, faster, his fingers still working her clit. Izzie could feel her orgasm building, coiling tighter and tighter in her core. Rhys' cock twitched in her mouth, and she knew he was close, too.

With a final, powerful thrust, Callum pushed her over the edge. Her body convulsed with pleasure, her inner walls contracting around him as she came, her lips tight against his shoulder to stifle her cries. He followed shortly after, his hot seed spilling deep inside her.

Rhys pulled out of her mouth, stroking his cock a few more times before he came, his essence painting her breasts and neck. They collapsed together on the floor, their bodies intertwined, basking in the afterglow of their silent passion.

But their night was far from over. As they caught their breath, Izzie's dragon shifters began to touch her again, their hands roaming over her body, reigniting the fire within her.

They took turns fucking her, switching positions, exploring every inch of her body with their hands and mouths. They brought her to orgasm again and again, their own releases painting her skin and filling her up.

Through it all, they remained silent, their moans and cries of pleasure trapped in the quiet of the night. Only the soft rustle of the sheets and the creak of the floorboards beneath them betrayed their activities.

As dawn began to break, the men dressed and slipped out of her room, leaving Izzie spent and satisfied. She knew she would never forget this night, this silent surrender to pleasure in the most unexpected of places.

Izzie exhaled slowly, her breath shaky. For the moment, she let go of the questions, of the unease that clung to her like a second skin. She would focus on this — on them. The rest could wait. The search could wait.

Chapter Fifteen

Dario Tejedor sat in the dim light of a blacked-out van parked a discreet distance from the inn, its dark windows reflecting the faint glow of streetlights. His face was illuminated by the cold blue light of his tablet screen, where Maximilian Thorne's face appeared, sharp and calculating, his eyes fixed intently on his Fixer. The vehicle's engine hummed in the background, but everything else outside the confines of the van was quiet — stillness hanging in the cool night air.

The Fixer shifted in his seat, adjusting his position for better comfort, but his attention never wavered from the tablet. He cleared his throat before speaking.

"She's getting close, sir." His voice was low but steady, betraying no hint of unease despite the gravity of his words. "Miss Rhodes. She's getting closer to uncovering the location of the Harp."

Thorne's face remained unreadable, but his gaze sharpened, his eyes narrowing as he leaned forward. His surroundings were impeccably neat, the luxury of a high-rise penthouse surrounding him. Soft lighting framed a tall bookshelf behind him, filled with rare volumes and personal artifacts that spoke to a wealth of taste and experience. A painting on the wall beside him depicted a storm-swept sea, a powerful visual metaphor for his ever-churning ambitions.

"Explain." Thorne's voice cut through the silence like a blade.

The Fixer took a breath before continuing, knowing Thorne wasn't one for unnecessary details. "She's on the trail of the Harp. She's already uncovered more than she should have been able to — documents, old records. I've been monitoring her movements, but she's unpredictable. She's persistent, intelligent. She's digging, Thorne. Places your people never discovered."

The Fixer paused, his eyes flicking momentarily to the side window, his mind alert to every shift in the night. The shadows seemed darker here than they should be. Maybe it was paranoia, maybe not. Either way, he kept his focus on the conversation.

Thorne's expression remained cold, his fingers steepled before him, his jaw clenched ever so tight. He sat in his chair, motionless but for a slight turn of his head as he processed the information. His fingers brushed against the smooth surface of his desk, the sound faint but deliberate as if testing the silence of the room. The high-rise penthouse was a symbol of control, a place where he conducted his affairs with precision. Behind him, the muted lights of the city skyline sprawled across the window, a glittering reminder of the power he wielded.

"I was told she could be an asset." Thorne's tone was almost bored, but ice ran beneath the words. "But I underestimated how far she could go."

The Fixer's brow furrowed at the words. "What should I do now, sir?"

Thorne's lips curled into a slight, almost imperceptible smile. It was a smile devoid of warmth, like a wolf considering its next move. "You've let her know that we want the Harp? I need you to keep pushing. Tell her there will be serious compensation for the artifact, if she guides it into my keeping. But remember that if she gets too close to the Harp, it'll be harder to control her. You understand?"

The Fixer nodded, though Thorne couldn't see the gesture through the screen. "Understood, sir. Play on her greed. I'll escalate my efforts. She won't slip through my fingers."

Thorne remained silent for a moment, his eyes never leaving Dario's. The tension was palpable, as if the very air between them was thick with the weight of what was at stake.

"Good." His voice cut through the silence. "Make sure of it. I don't want to hear that she's made another move without you knowing. If that Harp ends up in the Draconic Council's vaults, you won't live long enough to tell me how you failed."

As the call ended, the screen went dark. The Fixer stared at it for a long moment, his thoughts churning. There was no room for failure now.

* * * *

Maximilian Thorne's eyes never wavered as the video call ended, the screen flickering to black. He remained seated in his high-backed chair for a moment longer, his fingers drumming against the sleek surface of his desk. He had no patience for incompetence, and any failure on Dario's part would not go unpunished.

His voice, cold and sharp, echoed in the silence of his sprawling penthouse office above Los Angeles. "He better not disappoint me." The words were spoken to himself, but carried the weight of a promise. "If he lets her slip through his fingers, there will be consequences. Dire consequences."

He paused, his thoughts turning dark as he imagined his Fixer's failure—a failure he would not tolerate.

With a swift motion, he pushed himself from his desk and strode toward the massive windows that spanned the walls of his office, overlooking the city below. His gaze swept over the glittering lights of Los Angeles, a city that reflected his own ambitions—shiny, hollow and ultimately beneath him. No, he didn't need this city. He needed what lay below. He needed what his ancestors had coveted for centuries.

He turned on his heel, his polished shoes clicking against the floor as he made his way toward the back of the office. With one finger, he pressed a hidden button on the wall, and a section of the floor opened with a low, grinding hum. A secret elevator, the kind known only to those who were meant to know, slid into place.

As the elevator descended, Thorne's mind raced. The Fixer had one job, and if he couldn't handle it, Thorne would find someone who could. But for now, the hunt for the Harp was too critical. Once he had it, nothing in this world would stop him from gaining the power he sought.

The elevator halted with a soft chime, and Thorne stepped out into a dimly lit hallway. The walls were lined with vault-like doors, reinforced steel that gleamed under the low, artificial light. He walked with purpose, each step echoing in the silence, until he reached a large reinforced door at the end of the hallway. With a flick of his wrist, a keypad appeared, and Thorne entered a series of codes with precision, his fingers moving like a maestro conducting an orchestra. The door slid open with a hiss.

Inside the vault, the air was thick with the scent of polished wood and metal. Display cases lined the walls, each one housing a different dragon artifact, some of them gleaming with an almost unnatural glow. His fingers brushed across the glass of one case, his lips curling into a smile that bordered on lust. There was power here — raw, untapped, dangerous power.

He stepped closer, his eyes tracing the contours of the artifacts as if each piece held a part of his soul. But it wasn't enough. Not nearly enough.

Thorne's gaze shifted to the empty display cases in the back. Ten of them, waiting for something, or rather, someone, to fill them. He had a plan — a grand one. The Eldritch Curiosities, a group of relic hunters who had scattered themselves across the globe, were searching for the last of the dragon relics. And Thorne was going to take them. He would use these artifacts to destroy the dragons once and for all.

His thoughts were interrupted as he walked past a large oil painting hanging on the far wall. Beneath it was a brass plaque with a single name engraved — *Mia Thorne.*

The painting depicted a young woman, her eyes filled with innocence, but with something darker lurking behind them. Thorne stared at it for a long moment, his fists tightening at his sides. Mia had been his only daughter, and she had betrayed him. She had mated with a dragon in Scotland, and never returned home.

It had taken years, but he had discovered the truth — Mia had borne a clutch of dragon eggs, a legacy of her union with an ancient shifter family. Thorne's lips curled into a bitter smile. His revenge on dragonkind would be as brutal as it was inevitable.

His phone buzzed in his pocket, and he answered without hesitation. "Emily! How is Scotland?" His voice, despite its calm exterior, carried a thread of excitement. This was it. His plans were finally falling into place.

Chapter Sixteen

The wind howled over the cliffs as Izzie, Callum, and Rhys approached the abandoned chapel. Its crumbling stone walls loomed against the grey sky, a forgotten relic of a time long past. The overgrown ivy and moss covering its exterior added to the eerie atmosphere, giving the chapel a sense of being swallowed by nature itself.

Izzie's heart raced with anticipation. This was it — the next clue in their search for the Harp of Ceòthach Glen. The lead had been vague, but something about the chapel felt right. The air around them thrummed with the same energy that had drawn them to this desolate place on the west coast of Mull.

Callum was the first to step through the rotting wooden door, scanning the interior for any sign of danger. Rhys followed close behind, his posture tense, always on the lookout. Izzie lingered for a moment, staring at the chapel's crumbling beauty, a part of her reluctant to enter. She couldn't shake the feeling that they were being watched even here, but she pushed the thought aside. She had come too far to turn back now.

The interior of the chapel was even more desolate than the outside. Dust and cobwebs clung to the high ceilings, and broken stained-glass windows cast fragmented patches of color on the stone floor. The altar at the far end of the room was bare, save for a few forgotten relics and old candles. Yet there was something about the space that felt...*off*.

"I don't like this." Rhys' voice was low. "It's too quiet."

Izzie nodded, though she didn't share his sense of unease. As they moved deeper into the chapel, her gaze fell on a section of the rotted floor behind the altar. Something about the way it was positioned didn't seem quite right, the color or texture seeming wrong.

"I think it's a trapdoor. There's something under here." Her voice was barely above a whisper.

Callum looked over at her, his sharp gaze assessing. "Are you sure?"

She nodded, crouching down and running her fingers along the edges of the wooden trapdoor. Grit scraped against her skin as she searched for a grip, then braced herself and pulled. The trapdoor didn't budge. She tried again, straining with all her strength, but it was impossibly heavy, wedged in as solid as the earth itself.

A quiet chuckle sounded behind her. Before she could snap at them, Callum and Rhys stepped forward. Without a word, they set their hands against the slab, muscles tensing as they heaved together. The stone groaned in protest, then lifted, sliding just enough to reveal a narrow stairway vanishing into darkness.

Izzie shot them both a glare — equal parts gratitude and irritation — as they shifted the slab aside with ease. Of course, they had to step in, all muscle and brute strength, like she was some helpless damsel. She wasn't a child, unable to manage things herself, despite her cotton candy hair. She wasn't. Just because she lacked their dragon-forged power didn't mean she couldn't manage on her own. Huffing, she slipped past them and descended into the unknown.

With each step, the air grew colder, wrapping around her like damp silk. The scent of mildew and earth thickened, clinging to her nostrils. Shadows crowded close, pressing in from all sides, but thin slivers of light knifed through the ceiling — narrow cracks between the warped floorboards above. Dust swirled in their pale glow, shifting as she moved. At the bottom, the narrow stairway opened into a small, hidden chamber, its silence thick and expectant, the faint shafts of light doing little to chase away the gloom.

Shelves lined the walls, many empty, others holding dust-coated artifacts. A wooden table stood at the room's center, littered with old books. Izzie moved toward it, her fingers trailing over the cracked leather spine of one volume. It felt important, its weight solid in her hands, its history humming beneath her fingertips.

She opened it carefully. The pages, brittle with age, crackled under her touch. She squinted, straining to make out the faded inscriptions in the dim light, but the symbols and words blurred together in the darkness. Frustration curled in her stomach — she needed light.

Turning, she moved back to the stairs, stopping where the faintest sliver of light flowed down the stairs from the opening above. There, in that thin pool of illumination, she angled the book just right, and at last, the inked letters sharpened into focus. Her breath caught as a name emerged from the text, scrawled again and again in the margins — *Ceòthach Glen.*

Her pulse quickened. She had found something important, something that could bring them closer to the Harp. She glanced up at Callum and Rhys, who had followed her down into the chamber. They were both watching her closely, their expressions unreadable.

"This...this is it." Her voice was barely a whisper. "This may be the information we need."

But just as she spoke, a faint noise echoed from above — a soft creak of wood, the shuffle of movement. Someone — or something — was upstairs.

Before Izzie could react, the first tendrils of smoke slithered down the hidden staircase, curling through the air like grasping fingers. Then it hit them all at once — a wall of thick, acrid heat. It clawed at their throats, burned their eyes, filled their lungs with something sharp and bitter. The air turned suffocating, heavy with the unmistakable stench of gasoline.

Rhys swore, eyes darting to the staircase. "We have to move. Now."

Callum didn't hesitate. He grabbed Izzie's arm, yanking her toward the steps. They stumbled upward, half-blinded, the smoke thickening by the second. Coughing, Izzie clutched the book to her chest and forced herself to move, even as her lungs screamed for air. The walls of the basement seemed to contract behind them, the heat pressing against their skin.

The stairway was narrow, the air hotter with each step they climbed. Splinters scraped Izzie's palms as she pulled herself up, gasping for breath. Above them, flickering orange filled the chapel, casting shifting shadows along the walls.

Flames devoured the wooden pews, crackling and snapping as they climbed the crumbling walls, their glow turning the smoke-choked air an eerie orange. Embers spiraled down like burning snowflakes, hissing where they met flesh. The acrid stench of gasoline cut through the thick, suffocating haze, each breath a struggle against the heat.

Above, the skeletal remains of the ceiling trembled. A massive beam groaned, splitting with a deafening crack before plummeting to the floor in an explosion of embers and charred wood. Sparks leaped outward, licking at their heels as they stumbled back. The fire pressed in, greedy and unrelenting, turning the exit into a gauntlet of flame.

"This way!" Rhys shouted, pulling Izzie toward what remained of the door.

They ran. Dodging collapsing beams, leaping over smoldering pews, their bodies moving on sheer instinct. Izzie's lungs burned, her vision swam, but she didn't stop—not until the cool late-spring air finally hit her skin, the sunlight beyond the chapel a stark contrast to the inferno behind them.

They stumbled out into the open, choking on smoke, their clothes streaked with soot. Behind them, the chapel blazed like a funeral pyre, the fire's glow stretching high into the sky.

With one on either side, practically lifting her from the ground, Callum and Rhys got her away from the chapel, but they didn't stop there. They sprinted, feet pounding against the earth, adrenaline pushing them forward as the fire began to rage behind them. The structure was coming down, the heat rising higher and higher.

They reached the cliffside, gasping for air, the cold sea breeze cutting through their lungs, their clothes still hot from the blaze. Izzie coughed, trying to clear the smoke from her throat. The chapel was now a wall of fire, burning fiercely, the crackle of the flames mixing with the sounds of the collapsing building.

"We're out." Rhys' voice was ragged but relieved. He glanced over his shoulder at the burning structure. "But the book…"

Izzie's heart sank. She looked back, her chest tightening with the weight of what they'd just lost. The book, the only clue they had to the Harp of Ceòthach Glen, was gone. Somehow she'd dropped it as they fled.

"Damn it." Callum's fists clenched at his sides. His face was hard, his jaw set with frustration and anger. "It's gone."

Izzie's hands shook as she wiped her forehead, her fingers slick with sweat. But then something caught her eye—a flash of paper in the distance. She turned, squinting through the haze of smoke.

Just outside the fallen wall of the chapel, where the stone had cracked and collapsed, the book lay in the gorse. The wind had blown it out of the fire's path, but it was precariously close to the wreckage. Before she could say anything, Callum and Rhys were already moving toward it. Callum's gaze was hard as he stared at the book, but his steps didn't slow.

"That's our only lead." Izzie yelled after them, pulse racing, relieved that they hadn't lost everything. "We can't let it burn."

Rhys reached the book first, bending down to pick it up. The pages were scorched, the cover marred, but it was still salvageable.

"I've got it." His voice was taut but relieved. He carefully cradled the fragile relic.

As they gathered around him, Izzie couldn't shake the feeling that someone — something — had been watching them as they'd fled. But there was no time to dwell on it. The book was their only hope, and it had barely escaped destruction.

Callum took a deep breath, scanning their surroundings. "We need to get out of here. This isn't over."

Izzie nodded, the weight of their situation settling on her shoulders. The fire raged behind them, but the storm ahead was only just beginning.

* * * *

Outside the chapel, Dario Tejedor crouched low in the gorse, suffocating smoke swirling around him. He had tied a faded bandanna across his nose and mouth, the damp fabric heavy with the rank scent of oil and sweat. It offered minimal relief, but the burning in his lungs only fueled his focus. The fire was doing its job — distracting them, disorienting them.

His eyes remained fixed on the chapel's crumbling entrance, watching for any sign of movement.

Izzie and the shifters burst from the building, their dark figures barely visible through the fiery haze. They looked panicked, rushing away from the chaos, but Dario's attention remained on Izzie — on the book cradled in her arms.

Until it fell from Izzie's hands.

For a split second, the world seemed to freeze as it tumbled through the air, but before Dario could react, Rhys lunged. The dragon shifter was faster than Dario anticipated, diving toward the book and scooping it up with a swift motion. He cradled it to his chest, eyes flicking to Izzie with a look of determination.

Dario's heart pounded with frustration. The book was crucial.

But it was already in Rhys' hands.

Dario gritted his teeth, his fingers twitching with the urge to act. Rhys darted back toward Izzie, the book clutched tightly to his chest, its edges glowing in the flickering firelight. He couldn't risk going after him—not yet. He knew better. The dragon shifters were far too powerful, their strength unmatched. Any attempt to face them head-on, unarmed and alone, would mean certain death.

He flexed his hand around the hilt of the handgun at his side—useless for now. The firelight cast long shadows, but it couldn't hide the fact that he was outmatched. His gaze flicked to the edges of the chaos—the team of mercenaries from Albania were on their way, just a few more hours, maybe less. They would be his backup. Once they arrived, he could make his move.

Patience, he told himself. *Patience*.

As Rhys reached Izzie, Dario's thoughts spun. He'd lost the book for now, but that didn't mean the game was over. He would find a way. He always did.

With a sharp breath, he turned away, his boots sinking into the peat as he retreated behind the curtain of smoke. The mercenaries would be able to take the brothers down. With their help, he would take Izzie. He would accomplish his mission.

He slid back into the smoke, slipping deeper into the shadows. The fire would cover his tracks. Dario backed away, melting into the smoke, his gaze locked on Izzie's silhouette, barely visible now in the distance. Somehow he would get her away from the dragon brothers. Then he could force her to take him to the Harp.

Thorne would pay him well for ensuring that the artifact arrived safely in L.A.

Chapter Seventeen

The lounge of the inn was eerily silent, the faint smell of sea salt still hanging in the air from the morning breeze. The fire at the chapel still burned in Izzie's mind, its crackling flames, the heat, the chaos — and now, here, in the quiet of the inn, the tension between them was suffocating. The inn's other guests had scattered to their sightseeing, leaving the lounge empty, save for the three of them.

Callum's jaw was clenched tight, his fists balled at his sides. His eyes flicked between Izzie and Rhys, his frustration barely contained. The flames of the chapel were still fresh, the image of the burning walls seared into his memory. But it wasn't just the fire — it was the feeling of helplessness, the way they'd been pushed into a corner, forced to run.

Dragons were the ones who set the world on fire, not the ones who ran from it.

Rhys, his posture rigid, was trying to hold back, but Izzie could see the tension in his shoulders, the way he looked at her as if he couldn't quite decide whether to reach out or pull away.

Izzie stood in the center of the lounge, her gaze flicking nervously toward the door. The inn was empty — except for the three of them — but the last thing she wanted was for someone to overhear. The maid, the innkeeper — either of them could be lingering nearby, and the smell of smoke clinging to their clothes was a dead giveaway. She needed to get to her room and shower, but first, they needed to finish hashing this out.

Callum's voice sliced through the silence, sharp and filled with frustration. "We should've set a guard," he muttered, eyes blazing with anger. "We lost sight of the danger to Izzie. We should've done more to protect her."

Rhys' jaw tightened, and he turned toward Callum, his shoulders stiff. "I was protecting her, Callum!" His voice wasn't as loud, but it was thick with tension. "We had to get into that room. Who knows what was down there. You should've been covering the perimeter — while you were shoving in, someone was starting that fire. You just didn't want me to be alone with her!"

Izzie's breath caught, a flash of heat creeping into her cheeks. Her gaze darted toward the hallway again, half expecting someone to walk in on them at any moment. They didn't know how bad it would be if anyone overheard them. "Stop," she said, her voice low but firm. "Arguing isn't helping. What's done is done. We'll do better next time."

The brothers fell silent, the weight of her words hanging between them like a thick fog. The tension simmered, but Izzie wasn't about to let it boil over.

She exhaled, trying to steady herself. "We're alive, and that's what matters." She glanced at both of them, the sharp edges of her frustration evident. "But the book is the reason for all this, and whoever set that fire is still after it. And us. We're not safe yet. We have to figure out why this happened."

Her thoughts snapped back to the man in the souvenir shop. She'd never forgotten his face, the coldness in his eyes when their paths crossed. She was sure he was the one behind it all — the one who had been following her from the moment she landed in Scotland. "I'm sure it's him," she said, her voice low but laced with certainty. "The man in the shop. He's been following me. I know it."

The brothers exchanged a look, their previous argument forgotten for the moment. Callum's frown deepened, and Rhys' gaze grew more focused, his tension sharpening into something more strategic.

"Then we go after him," Callum said, his tone final, a decision being made in an instant. "We don't let him get away with this."

Izzie shook her head, her stomach a twisted knot. "No. Not yet. We need to find out more, make sure we're prepared." She met their gazes, determination hardening her voice. "But I'm sure of this — whoever he is, he's dangerous. And he won't stop until he gets what he wants."

The weight of the moment pressed in on her. This wasn't just about the book anymore. It was about survival.

Rhys' anger simmered just below the surface, his eyes blazing with almost feral intensity. He clenched his fists, his nails digging into his palms. "We need to hunt him down," he growled, his voice low and dangerous. "Whoever set that fire, they're not just messing with us — they're attacking our woman. We have to keep her safe."

Callum crossed his arms, his gaze calm but no less determined. "We don't know who he is yet, Rhys," he said, his voice firm. "Charging in headfirst won't help us. Whoever he is, he's playing a long game. We need to be smart about this."

Izzie's feet felt heavy as she moved toward the door, the weight of the day pressing on her like a physical burden. The chaos at the chapel, the flames licking the air, the smell of burning wood mixed with gasoline — it was too much. She needed a shower — needed to wash away the feeling of the fire and the tension between the brothers.

She gripped the doorframe for a moment, steadying herself before she turned back to face Callum and Rhys. They were still in the middle of their heated exchange, voices low but sharp, frustration crackling in the air between them. The book she had retrieved from the gorse was heavy in her arms, its cover warm against her chest. She'd barely had time to think about it since they'd left the chapel, but now it felt like the only solid thing in her grasp.

"I'll take care of this," she said, her voice cutting through their words like a blade. The silence that followed was thick, both brothers halting mid-sentence to look at her. She pushed the book closer to them, then held it out. "But one of you better guard it while I clean up. We can't just leave it lying around."

Rhys stepped toward the book, reaching for it. Callum's gaze locked on the book, his expression hardening as he stepped forward at the same time. Izzie could feel the tension between them, the silent challenge hanging in the air, as if the book were something more than just paper and ink.

Before it could escalate, she stepped forward, pressing the book firmly into Callum's grasp. "You," she said, her voice firm. "You take it."

The brothers froze for a beat, tension simmering between them. Rhys looked as if he wanted to argue, but Izzie didn't give him the chance. She turned quickly, pulling open the door and stepping out into the quiet hall, eager to escape the energy in the room and find some semblance of peace.

The stairs creaked underfoot as she made her way up to her room. Each step felt like a small victory—a moment to breathe. But the weight of the book in Callum's hands lingered in her mind, a constant reminder of the danger they were walking into. Whoever was after them—after the Harp—wasn't going to give up.

But for now, all she could do was get cleaned up and prepare herself for what was coming next.

Her room was small, but it offered a small measure of privacy. The shower, the steam, the sensation of warm water washing away the grit of the day—it was what she needed now. She closed the door behind her and let the world outside fade for a moment, knowing the calm wouldn't last long.

Izzie stepped into the small en suite bathroom, the soft click of the door closing behind her the only sound in the otherwise quiet room. The bathroom was simple—clean, almost sterile—but it was hers, and the space felt like a small sanctuary. She stripped off her smoke-stained clothes and kicked them in the corner, then climbed into the small shower enclosure. She stood for a moment, just inside the shower's glass door, taking a breath, her chest rising with the effort to hold herself together.

The smell of smoke — thick, acrid, lingering — clung to her skin and hair like a permanent mark, and she felt it in every breath, a reminder of the fire that had nearly consumed everything. Her fingers tightened around the shower's chrome handle as she twisted it, the hiss of water filling the air.

The first rush of hot water hit her skin like a balm, and Izzie let out a breath she hadn't realized she was holding. It wasn't enough to wash away the fear, not yet, but the heat of it — a relief, a comfort — was something she could hold onto. Slowly, deliberately, she stepped forward into the stream, letting the water cascade down her face, over her neck, the soothing pressure of it chasing away the tension that had built up in her shoulders.

The water poured over her, a flood of heat against her chilled skin, and Izzie closed her eyes, tilting her head back, savoring the sensation. The steam from the water began to cloud the small space, and she felt her muscles unwinding slowly with each second, each pulse of the spray. The smoke and gasoline that had clung to her skin started to wash away, the gritty layers of the fire sloughing off. She felt lighter with every passing moment.

Her pale blonde hair, streaked in pastel hues of pink, mint green, and violet, fell around her face in damp tendrils as she reached for the shampoo. The delicate strands had been stained by the smoke, but the colors were now surrendering to the water. She worked the shampoo into her hands, the suds catching in the steamy air before gliding across her scalp.

She scrubbed her hair completely, feeling the pink and green strands surrender to the water, the soot and grime lifting from the silken strands. The bright colors of her hair blurred and swirled together in the water as she worked, the relief of being clean sinking deep into her bones. The warmth of the water loosened the tension that had gripped her all day — the tension from the chapel, the fear of the fire, the worry of what might come next.

The fire had been too close. She'd felt the heat of it, the ferocity, felt it curling around her like a living thing. But they'd made it out — unharmed, all of them. Her dragons hadn't been lost to her.

She slid her hands over her arms, her breasts, her torso, her motions automatic as she scrubbed the smoke and ash away. The weight of everything that had happened today, the confusion, the danger, and the narrow escape, was beginning to settle in her chest, but there was something else, too — something softer, a feeling she hadn't expected.

A sense of safety.

Callum and Rhys had been there, protecting her. They had shielded her from the chaos of the fire, from the unknown dangers lurking just outside the chapel. They were strong — more than strong enough to keep her safe, to keep all of them safe. She could feel the lingering warmth of that thought in her chest as she rinsed the suds from her hair, each lock falling clean, free of smoke.

The world outside the shower — the danger, the uncertainty — seemed so far away for a moment, drowned out by the rush of water and the steam that fogged the mirror. She closed her eyes, leaning her forehead against the wall of the shower as the water washed over her. It was a moment of peace, fleeting but needed. It was just her, alone in the quiet, washing away the day's scars. For now, she could forget about the man she'd met in the souvenir shop, the fire, the book, and just breathe.

Then the glass door slid open, and someone stepped into the shower with her. She hadn't heard the bathroom door open and for a moment terror gripped her, her entire body tensing. Izzie's eyes flew open in shock as she turned to the shower opening, but the sight of Rhys' naked body sent a jolt of desire through her. He wasn't supposed to be there, but as he slid around her and cupped her breasts, she couldn't bring herself to object.

A good, hard fuck was exactly what she needed to release the adrenaline coursing through her veins.

Rhys found her lips immediately, kissing her deeply, his tongue delving into her mouth as he roamed her wet body. Izzie moaned into his mouth, her own hands exploring the hard planes of his chest and abs. She could feel his cock pressing against her stomach, already hard and throbbing with desire.

With the water running, no one would hear them. She didn't need to worry about the innkeeper throwing them out for behaving inappropriately.

Breaking the kiss, Rhys bent his head to her breasts, taking one nipple into his mouth and sucking hard. Izzie gasped, her head falling back against the tiles as he lavished attention on her sensitive peaks. He slid his other hand down her stomach, fingers delving between her legs to stroke her soapy, wet pussy. But it was more than water making her wet.

"Fuck, you're so ready," he groaned, slipping a finger inside her tight channel. "I love that you're ready for me, Izzie."

She could only moan in response, her hips bucking against him as he pumped his index finger in and out of her. He added a second finger, stretching her open as he curled them to hit that sweet spot deep inside.

Suddenly, he withdrew his fingers and pushed her back against the shower wall. Izzie yelped in surprise, but the sound was swallowed by his mouth as he kissed her again. He gripped her thighs, lifting her up and wrapping her legs around his waist.

"Hold on tight," he growled, positioning his cock at her entrance. With one swift thrust, he buried himself deep inside her, filling her completely.

Izzie cried out, her nails digging into his shoulders as he began to move. He fucked her hard and fast, the water from the shower cascading over their bodies as they moved together. The sound of their moans and the slap of skin against skin echoed off the tiles, mixing with the hiss of the shower.

Rhys changed his angle, hitting that spot inside her that made her see stars. Izzie's head thrashed from side to side, her breath coming in short gasps as he pounded into her. She could feel her orgasm building, the tension coiling tighter and tighter in her core.

"Rhys, I'm going to come," she panted, her muscles starting to quiver.

Rhys must have felt it too because he redoubled his efforts, fucking her harder and faster than ever before. With one final thrust, he pushed her over the edge, and Izzie came with a scream, her pussy spasming around his cock as wave after wave of pleasure crashed over her.

He followed soon after, his cock twitching inside her as he spilled his seed deep in her womb. They clung to each other, panting and shaking in the aftermath of their intense fucking.

Slowly, Rhys lowered her back to her feet, his softening cock slipping out of her. He turned her around, pressing her front against the cool tiles as he kissed her shoulder.

"Let me take care of you," he murmured, sliding his hands down her body to her hips.

Izzie moaned as he knelt behind her, parting her legs with his hands. She could feel his breath on her sensitive flesh, then his tongue was there, lapping at her slit and delving inside her.

"Oh god," she gasped, her hands scrabbling for purchase on the slick tiles. He licked and sucked, his tongue circling her clit and dipping inside her, tasting their combined essence.

Izzie's second orgasm built quickly, her hips bucking against his face as he pushed her to the edge. When he slid two fingers inside her and curled them just right, she came with a scream, her pussy gushing around his fingers.

He stood, pressing his body against her back and nipping at her shoulder. "You taste so fucking good," he growled, his hard cock pressing against her ass.

Izzie moaned, reaching back to guide him to her entrance. He slid inside her easily, her pussy still slick with their combined juices. He fucked her slow and deep, gripping her hips as he thrust in and out of her.

The shower had long since cooled, but neither of them cared. They were lost in their own world, their bodies moving together in perfect harmony. Izzie's third orgasm built slowly, her muscles tightening around his cock as he hit that sweet spot inside her over and over again.

When she came, it was with a low moan, her body shaking with the force of it. Rhys followed soon after, his cock pulsing inside her as he filled her with his seed.

They stayed like that for a moment, their bodies pressed together as they caught their breath. Then, with a sigh, Rhys withdrew and wrapped his arms around her from behind, pulling her tight against him.

"Let's get you cleaned up," he said, reaching for the soap.

She didn't bother telling him that she'd already washed the smoke off. Izzie leaned back against him, letting him wash her body with gentle hands. The water was cold now, but she didn't mind. She was warm and sated, her body humming with pleasure.

As they stepped out of the shower and dried off, Izzie couldn't help but smile. She had survived a near-death experience, and now she had the best fuck of her life to show for it. Life was good.

The steam from the shower still clung to the air as Izzie stepped out, the coolness of the bathroom rushing over her skin. Rhys followed close behind, his tall frame moving with his usual predatory grace as he wrapped a thick towel around her shoulders, letting his fingers linger against her damp skin.

He didn't speak, just brushed the towel down her back in slow, measured motions, savoring the moment. Izzie didn't know if it was the warmth of the towel or something else, but her skin felt alive, every nerve electric under his touch.

Then he stopped, his breath brushing against her ear, and his voice — low, intense — reached her. "I love you, Izzie."

Izzie's heart skipped. She froze. His words hung in the air between them like a weight, heavy and unexpected. She hadn't been ready for this, hadn't known how to prepare for it. The water still dripped down her skin, but it was nothing compared to the rush of thoughts flooding her mind.

"I love you."

She blinked, her chest tightening as she tried to process. Could it be real? Could it happen this fast? She could feel the heat of his body behind her, his presence so overpowering it was almost suffocating.

He was a dragon shifter — he moved in a world she didn't fully understand. Was love even the same for them as it was for her? Did dragons say things like that lightly? And if they didn't, what did it mean when one of them said it?

Izzie's throat tightened as she met his gaze in the mirror, the glass fogged and misted from the steam of their shared shower. Their reflections were softened by the condensation, as if the heat had blurred the edges of everything around them, making everything feel more intimate, more fleeting. Her pulse quickened, her breath catching as she tried to read the emotions flickering in his eyes through the haze.

Am I that important to him?

Rhys had always been intense, commanding, wrapped in a kind of certainty she'd never quite figured out. But this? This was different. It was vulnerable. Too much, too soon, or was it?

Then there was the thought that terrified her even more than his declaration — *Are we bonded?* The idea flickered in her mind like a fleeting shadow, something primal, deep in the way his eyes locked onto hers, the way he touched her as if he couldn't stop. Something about it felt undeniable.

Is that what this is? She didn't know. Couldn't know.

Did she even want to know?

She swallowed, trying to steady herself, but her voice came out breathless when she finally spoke. "I...I don't know if this is —" She stopped herself, afraid to say the wrong thing, to shut something down she wasn't sure she was ready to understand.

But Rhys didn't seem to be waiting for her to be ready. He moved his hands to her shoulders, turning her slightly toward him, his gaze never leaving hers. He didn't press her, just held her there for a long moment, searching her face as if she held the answers.

"Whatever it is," he said, his voice a low rumble, "I need you to know this. I never say things I don't mean."

Izzie's breath caught in her throat, and for a moment she just let herself feel the weight of his words, let them settle over her, even though her heart was racing with something she couldn't name.

She took a slow, steadying breath, and when she spoke again, her words were quiet but certain. "I don't know what's happening, Rhys. But I know one thing." She stepped closer to him, feeling the pulse of his heartbeat beneath his chest as she looked up into his eyes. "I'm not running from you."

It wasn't love, not yet — but it was something real. Something she hadn't expected. Something she wasn't sure she could control, and maybe, just maybe, she didn't want to.

The silence that followed was heavy with all the unspoken things between them, but it wasn't uncomfortable. Rhys wrapped his arms around her, pulling her into him, and Izzie let herself melt against his warmth, the feeling of his embrace sinking into her as he kissed her again before she pulled away.

She pulled out a fresh set of clothes, leaving her cinder-scorched, smoky ones crumpled in the bathroom. As she did, she landed on the pile of Rhys' clothes, which he'd tossed on top of hers before joining her in the shower.

"Maybe we should just throw them away," she muttered, staring at the charred fabric.

Rhys chuckled, a low, teasing sound that made her stomach flip. "I don't think it'd go over well with the inn management if I walked down the hallway stark naked to my room."

Izzie shot him a sideways glance as she pulled on a pair of jeans over her lace-trimmed panties. "I'm sure they'd be thrilled with that."

"Of course." He grinned. "But maybe not the kind of thrill you're hoping for."

She rolled her eyes, shaking her head as she reached for her phone. Her smile faded as she dialed Callum, tension creeping back into her body. She needed to check on the book they had recovered from the chapel before the fire. But even more than that, how was he going to react, knowing that Rhys had joined her in the shower? Without Callum?

Callum picked up on the third ring, his voice anxious. "What is it?"

"I need you to bring clean clothes for Rhys to my room," she said, her tone steady but firm.

There was a long pause, just silence on the other end as she felt his mood change. Then she heard Callum's low chuckle, his voice laced with a trace of jealousy. "You two finally get clean?"

"Maybe next time I'll shower alone with you," she replied, her voice smooth, masking the flutter in her chest. "Satisfying two brothers is difficult," she mused more to herself than to him, "juggling both of their needs."

The silence on the other end felt heavy, and she knew Callum had heard. Before he could respond, Izzie hung up and dropped the phone on the bed.

She stood for a moment, her thoughts spinning out of control. What had she just said to him? What was she even getting herself into? There were five brothers. Five Sìol Dòmhnaill dragon shifters, all of them waiting for her — or they would be soon, when they reached the brothers' estate — and wanting her in ways she wasn't sure she understood. The thought made her pulse quicken, and she had to steady herself against the bedpost.

She looked back to Rhys, still lounging in his own towel, a slow, predatory smile curling on his lips. There was no going back now.

Chapter Eighteen

The tension in the air was stretching to the breaking point, every moment thick with the unsaid. The fire had barely burned out in Izzie's mind, and now, with another close call, the weight of it all was closing in — nearer than ever before. Her pulse thudded in her ears, matching the rhythm of her racing thoughts.

Callum's voice broke through the storm inside her head, low and sharp. "We can't keep staying here." He threw a bundle of clean clothes and Rhys caught them, dipping his head in thanks.

The air in Izzie's small room was too warm, too charged with things left unsaid. The scent of soap clung to her skin, a reminder of her shower with Rhys. And now, once again, both Callum and Rhys were here — where they weren't supposed to be.

They were supposed to go for dinner. Izzie knew that Callum would be waiting for his chance to fuck her, as his brother had already. But not here in her room, with the rest of the inn's guests and staff coming and going. It was just too dangerous.

If the innkeeper caught them, they'd all be thrown out. She could already imagine his scandalized expression, the old-fashioned morality that would have him pointing to the door, telling her in no uncertain terms that unmarried women didn't entertain two men in their bedrooms.

But they were here anyway, moving with a dragon's ease in the small space, their presence overwhelming. Callum stood near the door, arms crossed, his jaw tight with frustration. Rhys leaned against the dresser, pulling on his jeans, watching her with sharp, unreadable eyes.

Izzie turned away, looking out of the window at the darkening sky, as if the answer to their problems might be written in the shifting clouds. The wind rattled the glass, carrying the scent of damp earth and distant embers. The chapel was gone. Their enemies knew where they were.

"You're right," she admitted, her voice quieter than she'd meant it to be. "But where else can we go? They've already found us at the cabin. And now here."

Callum raked a hand through his hair, the tension in his shoulders evident. "That's exactly why we can't stay. It's too easy. Whoever's after you, they're closing in, and I—" He exhaled sharply, cutting himself off.

Rhys pushed off the dresser, his movement fluid, deliberate. His gaze flicked between her and his brother, the heat in the room shifting to something even heavier. That friction, always simmering just beneath the surface, was impossible to ignore.

"We take her to Skye," he said, his voice steady. "The family estate. It's isolated. Well-protected. Our brothers are there. It's safe."

Izzie turned to face him, frowning. She had only met two of the Sìol Dòmhnaill brothers, and already, they were consuming her — demanding more of her than she knew how to give. But the thought of more of them, waiting for her on some remote stretch of land, sent a shiver down her spine.

Am I ready for that? Could I really handle all of them?

"Skye?" Izzie asked, her voice uncertain. "How much more isolated could it be? I don't know if I can handle any more of this. Every place we go, it's only a matter of time before they find us."

Callum turned sharply toward her, his eyes narrowing. "You think I don't know that? I'm not going to put you at risk like that again. This isn't just about hiding. It's about being smart about it."

Rhys stepped in, his expression unreadable. "We don't have much of a choice, Izzie. If we stay here, we're dead in the water. Your life is at risk, and we can't keep protecting you if we're just sitting ducks."

There was a beat of silence, thick with unspoken things. The weight of their words pressed down on Izzie. She was in the middle of something she didn't fully understand, something that was much bigger than her.

"I don't like this," Callum muttered, but the edge in his voice softened slightly. "But I know we have to. For her."

Looking at him, Izzie could see his frustration. He wanted her. Needed her. Now. But he was thinking ahead. If there were five of them, how much of her would he get?

Izzie swallowed, her throat dry. "I didn't ask for any of this."

"You didn't have to," Rhys said, his tone unexpectedly gentle. "But it's your reality now. Fate."

Callum shot him a hard look. The undercurrent between them was unmistakable. Rhys was right, and they both knew it. But there was something else there too—a simmering tension neither of them had been able to fully shake.

As Rhys turned toward the door, pushing Callum out of his way, his gaze lingered on Izzie for just a fraction of a second too long. It was like he was studying her, weighing something heavy in his mind. The air grew thick again, charged with that unspoken tension between the men.

Callum's jaw clenched, and Izzie felt it, the way his eyes darkened for just a moment as he stepped aside. She couldn't tell if it was because of the situation or because of Rhys' stare, but whatever it was, it was becoming harder to ignore.

Callum sat down stiffly on the edge of the bed, his jaw clenched.

"I'm heading out," Rhys said, breaking the silence. His gaze flicked between them, lingering on Izzie for a beat longer than necessary. "I'll grab us something to eat. Meet me downstairs in the lounge in half an hour."

Izzie nodded, though she wasn't sure she'd be able to eat a single bite. Too much had been revealed in the past few minutes—too much she was still trying to wrap her head around.

Callum didn't respond, just ran a hand through his hair, exhaling sharply.

Rhys smirked as he opened the door. "Try not to tear each other's clothes off while I'm gone."

Then he was gone, the door clicking shut behind him.

Izzie let out a slow breath, finally turning to Callum. The walls of the inn suddenly felt smaller, pressing in around her. They were running out of time, and the weight of what lay ahead was suffocating.

"We leave first thing tomorrow," Callum finally said, his voice rough. "Pack your things. We'll keep moving forward. We'll find that damned Harp. Together."

But Izzie couldn't shake the feeling that the real danger wasn't lurking outside the inn — it was standing right in front of her. And it wasn't just the threat of the unknown, it was the pull between the Sìol Dòmhnaill brothers and the unsettling reality of what awaited her on Skye.

Callum's voice was quiet, almost reluctant. "My brothers…they'll expect their share of you. Are you ready for that?"

Her stomach twisted. She had known that this was coming. The dragon-shifter way, the reason so few human women were ever brought into their world. It was the whole brothers-of-the-egg thing. But knowing and facing it were two different things.

She swallowed hard, searching his face. "All of them? The other three?"

Callum didn't flinch. "Yes."

"When I can hardly keep you and Rhys…satisfied?" A chill rippled through her, as if the ground beneath her feet had suddenly given way. She had stepped into their world willingly, had taken Callum and Rhys into her bed, knowing there was no turning back. But now, the full weight of what that meant pressed down on her. She hesitated, the words thick on her tongue. "Are you telling me I won't have a choice?"

Callum's expression darkened, his jaw tightening. "You always have a choice, Izzie." His voice was firm, but something in his eyes told her it wasn't that simple.

Her pulse pounded. She wasn't naïve—she knew what was expected. Knew what she had already agreed to by taking the first step. But standing here, in this tiny room, with the danger outside and the walls closing in, she suddenly felt trapped.

Callum's eyes softened, but only slightly. He stood up and stepped closer to her, his expression unreadable. "I don't want this for you. I want you for myself. But I'm not in control of everything that happens, either." He ran a hand through his hair, clearly frustrated with the situation, but his gaze didn't waver. "I've told you, I'll protect you. I always will. But my brothers…they have their own ways."

Izzie recoiled from his touch, her pulse spiking. "And Rhys?" Her voice was quiet, shaky, as if she were afraid to hear the answer.

Callum's gaze flicked to the door, his stance taut, almost predatory. There was something dangerous about Rhys, as careful as he was with her—something she couldn't quite place, but it made her skin crawl.

Callum's voice was calm, almost too calm, as if he were waiting for her to make sense of it. "I see something in you, Izzie." His words wrapped around her like a shadow, dark and enticing. "Something more than just the woman we protect." He stepped closer, too close, until there was barely an inch between them. "I think you feel it too."

Izzie's heart skipped a beat, and for a moment she couldn't breathe. There was an intensity in Callum's eyes — an intensity that went beyond the physical. It was something deeper, darker. Something she hadn't been ready to admit, even to herself.

The pull between them was undeniable, an undercurrent she couldn't escape, and the more she tried to ignore it, the stronger it grew. She couldn't deny the attraction — she could feel it, feel him in the way his presence filled the room, in the warmth of his breath, in the subtle tilt of his head as if waiting for her to come to him.

But the idea of being shared, of becoming an object between them — it made her insides twist. She wanted to escape, to run, to make sense of it all, but she was trapped. Trapped by the dragons' magnetism, by the pull of the unknown.

"How could you ask me to do this?" she breathed, her voice shaky. "How can I possibly…"

Callum's lips curled into a smile, a smile that didn't reach his eyes. "You'll have no choice but to choose, Izzie. The bond between us is already stronger than you think."

The walls closed in, the room spinning as Izzie tried to find something solid to hold on to. The weight of his words, the tension thickening the air — it was more than she could bear.

"You'll have to decide, Izzie," Callum said softly, though there was no comfort in his words, "whether you accept your place with us…or fight it."

Chapter Nineteen

The journey to Skye was filled with quiet tension that weighed heavily on Izzie's shoulders. They had driven for hours along narrow, winding roads that twisted their way toward the Isle of Skye, all the while the shadow of what awaited her at the family estate hung like a storm cloud overhead. Her thoughts spiraled, and despite the beauty of the landscape outside the window — rugged cliffs, sweeping fields, and the sea stretching endlessly — she felt a gnawing sense of dread at her chest.

By the time they reached the ancient stone manor, a brooding castle nestled in the mist, Izzie was utterly exhausted. The journey had taken its toll, both physically and emotionally, and she could barely summon the energy to process the enormity of what lay ahead.

The manor itself was a relic, an imposing structure that seemed carved from the very earth it stood upon. The massive stone walls loomed as a silent sentinel against the jagged cliffs that sloped downward toward the wild ocean. The air was thick with fog, the world muffled and still as though holding its breath.

As they approached the estate, Rhys looked over at her, his eyes unreadable. "Welcome to the Sìol Dòmhnaill's home," he said, his tone just shy of playful, but something in his voice gave away his own inner tension.

Izzie barely nodded. Her body was sore from the long hours of travel, and her mind was filled with too many questions, too many conflicting emotions. She wasn't sure what to expect here, but she knew one thing for certain—this was no ordinary place.

As Callum parked the Land Rover near the front steps leading upward to a porticoed door, Izzie stopped short. There, above the door, a familiar symbol was carved into the lintel. A crescent moon with three jagged lines drawn through the center, as though the moon were being struck by some unseen force. She'd seen it before, on that paper someone had left on her bed in the B and B on Arran.

It had been one of the Sìol Dòmhnaill family, she was sure. The symbol was their family crest. Had it been Rhys laying claim to her? Or Callum?

The front door opened before they even reached it, revealing a tall, broad-shouldered man who regarded them with an appraising stare. He had green eyes that seemed to pierce straight through her.

"Izzie, this is Finn," Rhys introduced, his voice smooth but tinged with something dark. "He's the youngest."

Finn was lean and full of restless energy. His eyes, green with flecks of gold, were filled with mischief and the urge for adventure. His dark brown hair, streaked with gold, framed his face like wild foliage in a forgotten glade. His fair skin, dotted with freckles, carried the mark of youth, but his gaze held the weight of untold experiences, ones that only a dragon like him could understand.

Finn was the embodiment of untamed energy, an adventurer at heart, always pushing the limits of what was possible. His gaze lingered on her for a moment, and she felt an odd shiver creep down her spine. She couldn't decide if it was the chill of the mist or something deeper in the way he looked at her. He said nothing, simply turned and motioned for them to follow.

As they stepped into the manor, Izzie was greeted by the scent of aged wood and the soft crackle of a fire. The entryway was vast, adorned with old portraits of people she didn't recognize, each staring down at her with cold, calculating eyes. The atmosphere in the house was heavy—ancient, yet alive with a sense of purpose that made her skin prickle.

Another man emerged from the shadows of a hallway—was this Lorcan or Tavish? He was older in appearance than Finn but equally striking, with wild, untamed hair and a grin that didn't quite reach his eyes. As they were nearing Skye, Callum had told her all about his other brothers. This one studied her with an intensity that made Izzie pause. Lorcan, for sure. He was sleek and enigmatic, his athletic build speaking of strength and agility. His eyes, a piercing shade of jade, were sharp and observant, always calculating. His dark hair, streaked with hints of green at the tips, cascaded around his face like the midnight sky itself. His skin, pale and almost luminous, reflected the faintest light, an aura of mystery that clung to him like the shadows from which he was born. He carried himself with quiet confidence, his gaze so intense that it could expose the deepest secrets hidden in a person's soul.

"Well, well," he said, his voice smooth and teasing. "I'm Lorcan. The fun one." He winked at her as if daring her to challenge him. "You'll fit right in here, I'm sure."

Izzie offered a tight smile, unsure of how to respond. She had no idea what "fitting in" meant in this world, but it was the last thing she felt she was doing.

Before she could say anything more, the sound of footsteps reached her ears — slow, heavy, deliberate. The third brother appeared, his tall frame silhouetted against the flickering light from the fire. It had to be Tavish, from what Callum had told her. His presence was quiet but powerful, like a storm on the horizon. This brother was tall and lean, his presence serene yet commanding. His eyes, soft blue and as clear as a mountain lake, held a quiet understanding of the world and its mysteries. His platinum-blond hair, falling in soft waves around his face, captured the light in a way that made him appear almost ethereal. His skin, fair with a faint glow, seemed untouched by the years, a reminder of the ancient power he carried.

Tavish had a calming aura, one that "could soothe even the most troubled heart," Callum had said, yet his sharp intelligence was always present, quiet and profound. His eyes met hers, intense and deep, and for a moment, the world seemed to still.

He didn't smile, didn't speak. Instead, he simply stared at her, as if trying to read her soul. Izzie felt a wave of unease rise in her, but she couldn't look away. There was a depth to him, a weight that pressed against her chest. Something raw. Something dangerous.

"Welcome to Skye," Tavish said, his voice low and full of an unreadable emotion.

Izzie stood silently for a moment, feeling as if the walls were closing in. The brothers — Finn, Lorcan, Tavish — each of them so different, yet connected to her in ways she couldn't understand. One thing was certain — she was no longer just a visitor here. She was part of something far greater than she could imagine.

As Rhys and Callum walked into the manor's entry, the tension between them remained palpable. Callum's protective instincts flared, especially around Izzie. The moment they crossed the threshold, he made it clear that Izzie was under his protection — his exclusive protection.

"You two know the rules," Callum growled, his voice low but firm as he addressed his brothers. His eyes lingered on Finn and Lorcan, both of whom exchanged knowing looks. "Izzie is mine to protect. You keep your distance."

"For now," Lorcan said.

Finn raised an eyebrow, his usual icy demeanor unshaken. "We're not here to steal her away, Callum," he said, his voice smooth but edged with something that might have been amusement. "But she'll have to make her own choice eventually."

Lorcan chuckled, his eyes gleaming with mischief. "The choice isn't really yours to make, is it, big brother?" he teased, his gaze flickering to Izzie before returning to Callum. "She's free to choose who she wants to be with, and let's face it, there's a lot of…appeal here."

Callum clenched his jaw, his posture rigid as he shot a warning glare at both men. "Stay away from her,

Lorcan. All of you." His voice was steady but filled with authority. "Give her a chance to feel this out."

"I think we can all agree," Rhys said, stepping into the conversation with a smirk tugging at the corner of his lips, "that the choice won't be just Callum's, no matter how much he wishes it would be."

The words hung in the air, thick with tension. Izzie's breath hitched, a knot forming in her stomach. The brothers' power, their presence, filled the room in a way she wasn't prepared for. They were different — dangerous, each in his own way. And though she could feel Callum's possessiveness, his fierce protectiveness of her, something deep inside her stirred in response to the others.

She wasn't sure what it was yet. Perhaps it was the unfamiliarity of the situation, or maybe just the sheer force of their personalities. But she knew she wasn't prepared for the complexity of the choices ahead.

Later that night, after the brothers had retreated to their respective rooms, Izzie lay awake, staring at the ceiling. The house still thrummed with their presence, the air thick with the tension that never truly left.

All evening, they had circled each other like wolves, not in open conflict but in the constant, quiet battle for dominance. A glance, a clipped word, a smirk that lasted a second too long — every interaction carried an edge. Callum, steady and brooding, had claimed his space beside her first, his hand on the small of her back as if to make it clear that he had been there before any of the others. Rhys, quick to challenge, had nudged him aside under the guise of pouring her a drink, his easy charm belying the sharpness in his eyes.

The others were no different. Lorcan leaned against the hearth, his presence unshakable, making pointed remarks that drew smirks from some and scowls from others. Finn had countered him with a casual laugh, but there had been an unmistakable warning in his posture, his fingers drumming absently against his knee. And Tavish — the quietest of them — had simply watched, his expression unreadable, his silence somehow the most unnerving of all.

They didn't fight, not truly. There was no snarling, no open threats. But every word, every touch, every shift in the room was a move in their endless game, a battle that had nothing to do with violence and everything to do with power.

And at the center of it all was her.

Izzie turned onto her side, exhaling slowly. She had stepped into their world willingly, but she hadn't understood this part of it — the way they tangled, the way they pulled at her, as if each one was determined to stake his claim without ever saying it outright. The weight of their attention was intoxicating, suffocating, impossible to ignore.

Sleep was out of the question. With a sigh, she pushed the blankets off and slipped out of bed, her feet silent against the cold stone floor. She needed air, space, to clear her head. She tiptoed through the darkened hallway, the mansion eerily still, save for the occasional creak of wood. As she passed by the grand staircase, the faintest sound caught her attention — a rustle of footsteps, a shift in the air.

Her heart stuttered in her chest.

She paused, her breath caught in her throat, straining to listen. The footsteps weren't clear, almost as though whoever it was trying to move quietly. But the sounds — slow, deliberate — spoke of someone who knew how to move unseen.

Her skin prickled, and without thinking, she ran back to her room and reached for the handle of her door. She pulled it open and glanced behind her at the dark hallway. No one.

But the feeling remained. She couldn't shake it—someone was watching her. She felt it in the pit of her stomach, like eyes were tracing her every movement.

Closing the door behind her, she pressed her back against it, trying to steady her breathing. Her pulse raced. She wasn't alone.

And that knowledge—cold, creeping, unsettling—clung to her as she made her way back to the bed, the oppressive silence of the house suffocating her from all sides.

Chapter Twenty

The morning light filtered through the thick curtains of Izzie's room, casting soft patterns across the stone walls. The weight of the previous night's unnerving silence still pressed heavily on her chest. The brothers, each in their own way, had been impossible to ignore.

Descending the grand staircase for breakfast, she found Lorcan lounging lazily in one of the deep armchairs near the large hearth in the Great Hall. His eyes were a deep green that seemed to gleam with mischief, and his lips curled into that dangerous, teasing smile.

"Well, good morning, beautiful," he purred, stretching out in the chair, his long legs crossed lazily at the ankles. "Did you sleep well? I do hope we didn't disturb you too much last night," he added with a wink, letting the words linger in the air.

Izzie forced a smile, trying to maintain a sense of control, but her pulse quickened at the way his eyes roamed her.

"Not exactly a restful night," she said coolly, keeping her tone even. "Too much on my mind."

Lorcan chuckled, his eyes never leaving hers. "I imagine so," he said with an amused glint. "After all, it must be hard to keep track of all your desires. You've been quite the subject of conversation amongst us, you know."

Izzie's brows furrowed as she approached the fireplace, eyeing him cautiously. "What do you mean?"

He sat up a bit straighter, the glint in his eye sharp now, almost predatory. "Rhys—well, you know how he is—told us a lot about you. About your interest in dragons. How hot you get when they're near you. How your blood races just thinking about them."

Izzie stiffened. Rhys had shared that with them? She didn't know whether to be furious or intrigued. Her gaze flicked to the door, her mind reeling, but Lorcan's voice stopped her.

"Not that I blame you, sweetheart," he continued, his tone low and suggestive. "It's hard not to be drawn to the power, the heat...the temptation. I mean, why wouldn't you want to sleep with all of us? We'd give you more than you could ever imagine. All of us. Each of us different...but just as good as the next."

His words struck a nerve, and for a moment Izzie wasn't sure how to respond. Was he pushing her? Testing her? Or was he simply trying to break down any walls she'd built around herself?

Before she could answer, Finn's low voice interrupted the charged silence. He stepped into the room, his tall form casting a shadow across the threshold. His face was unreadable as always, but there was something in his gaze—sharp, calculating.

"Enough, Lorcan," Finn said, his tone clipped. "Izzie doesn't need to be told what she wants by anyone, least of all you." His piercing green-gold eyes turned to Izzie then, softer but no less intense. "You'll find your own path. And you'll need strength to handle it. This world we live in—it isn't easy. Can you handle the weight of it?"

Izzie's stomach tightened. Finn was going to be the hardest to read, but his words felt like a challenge. She glanced at Lorcan, whose smirk faltered for just a moment.

But before she could respond, Tavish appeared in the doorway, his silent presence enough to still the room. He said nothing, his eyes studying her from across the room, the blue of a deep mountain lake and just as intense. His silence was his own language, and in that moment, Izzie couldn't escape the feeling that Tavish was watching her, assessing her like an enigma he was trying to solve. His gaze lingered, a silent pressure against her skin.

Her heart raced. Is this really the world I'm walking into?

"Go ahead," Lorcan said with a sly grin. "Take your time. We'll be here when you're ready to decide."

* * * *

Izzie's first morning at the brothers' estate started with tension so thick it might as well have been another presence at the table. Breakfast had been quiet—too quiet—each brother keenly aware of the new weight at their table, the woman who, by all rights, was meant to be theirs. Izzie ate cautiously, casting wary glances between them, no doubt feeling the pressure of their presence as acutely as they felt hers.

It was Callum who broke the uneasy stillness. "Come," he said, standing from the table. "I'll show you around."

The manor house was vast, built of stone that had weathered centuries of storms. He guided her through the great hall first, its heavy beams overhead and the scent of burning peat curling in the air. The walls bore the history of the Sìol Dòmhnaill line — ancient banners, weapons mounted in places of honor, portraits of men long dead but never forgotten. Callum spoke little, but his presence beside her was solid, unshakable, a quiet reassurance amidst the unfamiliar.

When he passed her off to Finn, the shift in energy was immediate. Finn was lighter, smoother, more inclined to ease her discomfort with soft jokes and the easy rhythm of conversation. He took her outside, leading her along winding paths that cut through the sprawling grounds. They passed the cliffs that overlooked the sea, waves crashing below in an endless rhythm. The wind tugged at her hair, and for the first time that day, she smiled. Finn appeared to notice, the glint in his eyes sharpening — he had won that moment, claimed it for himself, a small victory in the silent war between brothers.

Lorcan had been waiting when they returned, his stance near the stables casual but unmistakably deliberate. "Come meet our beasts of burden," he said, leading her toward the horses. He introduced each one by name, his voice softer than usual, though the intensity in his gaze never faded. He showed her how to feed them, how to read their moods. When she hesitated, he took her hand in his, guiding it over the sleek, powerful neck of a dark brown stallion. She relaxed, just slightly, under his touch. Another victory.

Tavish had taken her last, bringing her to the old orchard that lay beyond the main house. The trees were gnarled, their branches heavy with the weight of the coming season. Unlike the others, he hadn't spoken much. Instead, he let the quiet settle between them, watching as she traced her fingers along the bark, absorbing the stillness in a way none of the others had allowed her to. By the time they returned, her shoulders were less stiff, the wary lines around her eyes a little softer.

Yet, when evening fell, the house swelled once more with a tension that refused to dissipate.

* * * *

The fire cast long shadows over the hearth as the brothers gathered, the absence of Izzie only amplifying the unspoken conflict between them.

Callum paced, his jaw tight, the restless energy rolling off him in waves. "I don't want her forced into this," he muttered to Rhys, his voice low but fierce. "If she doesn't want it, then we respect that. She's not a prize to be won."

Rhys, leaning against the mantel, exhaled sharply. "And if she does want it?" His tone was unreadable, but his gaze was sharp, assessing. "She's proven quite…adventurous, beneath that girlish exterior."

Callum's steps faltered, his shoulders stiffening. That was the question none of them had dared to voice. If she wanted this—wanted them—how much of that desire was her own, and how much had been shaped by the world they had pulled her into?

Silence settled between them, the fire crackling in the space where an answer should have been. Rhys, however, didn't flinch. He leaned against the intricately carved wooden mantel, the faintest smile curling on his lips. "You think she doesn't want it? You think she hasn't already felt the pull?" He gave Callum a knowing look, his eyes smoldering with the fire of someone who knew far more than he was letting on. "She's tempted, Callum. That's the truth of it. She's been tempted since the moment she laid eyes on us. And whether she admits it or not, she's already made the choice."

"I'm not pushing her," Callum snapped back, his voice rising. "I won't."

"You're not the one in control, are you?" Rhys said, his words soft but cutting. "This isn't about you, Callum. It's about the geas. She will have to choose. Whether it's now or later, she'll feel the pull stronger with every passing day. We can't change that."

Callum's expression darkened. "I don't care about your damn geas. I care about her freedom."

But Rhys only smiled, a hint of victory gleaming in his eyes. He let Callum's frustration hang in the air for a moment before he turned away, his steps silent as he made his way toward the hallway.

* * * *

Later that night, Izzie found herself alone in one of the darkened corners of the manor. The rest of the house seemed distant, as if the walls were pressing in on her. She couldn't escape the sense of being watched, of being surrounded by temptation in every form. In the library, though, she felt a little more comfortable.

Then Lorcan appeared, seemingly from nowhere. His presence was like a storm, powerful and consuming, and Izzie's breath caught in her throat at the intensity of it.

"Izzie," he said softly, almost tenderly, as if the very word had a spell to it. He stepped closer to her as she was reaching for a book on a high shelf. He reached past her, pulling the book down and handing it to her, the warmth of his body almost tangible. The air around them seemed to thicken. His hand, warm and firm, brushed against her neck, his fingertips grazing the sensitive skin there. She shivered in response, unable to resist the intoxicating pull he exuded.

"You think you can resist us forever?" he whispered, his voice low and hypnotic. He touched her arms, his hands sliding up and down her skin with deliberate, unhurried touches. "Sweet girl, you were made for this. You feel it, don't you?"

Izzie's heart raced in her chest, her breath coming in quick, shallow bursts. She pulled back slightly, but he caught her, cupping her jaw, his thumb brushing against her lips. "You're not just any woman," he murmured. "You were born for this kind of magic. You think you can fight it, but you can't. It's already inside you. You want us. All of us."

Her thoughts were a blur as his touch burned into her skin, his words slithering through her mind like silk. She tried to protest, to say no, but everything inside her ached with a want she couldn't deny.

"I know you're tempted," Lorcan continued, his voice low and insistent. "The geas is strong, Izzie. It's what you were meant for. Say yes."

Izzie swallowed hard, her breath unsteady. She couldn't shake the feelings stirring within her—the heat, the pressure, the pull. She didn't want to give in. But everything about this world, about the dragon brothers, made it impossible to ignore the truth.

She closed her eyes, torn between wanting to be free and the magnetic force drawing her in.

Lorcan smiled, a glimmer of victory in his eyes. "No matter what you think, you're already ours. It's just a matter of time."

Her heart hammered in her chest, and her mind raced, but deep down, she knew something had changed. The choice was no longer entirely hers to make.

Chapter Twenty-One

Callum had decided the wild, untamed landscape north of the Fairy Glen was the perfect training ground. The rocky hillsides, jagged cliffs, and thick patches of mist created a sense of isolation — exactly what Callum wanted. Izzie stood with her feet planted in the soft, damp earth, her breath coming in shallow bursts. The crisp morning air stung her skin, and the weight of the mist swirling around them made everything feel ethereal, like they were training in another world altogether.

Callum, towering before her, was a perfect blend of power and grace. His eyes, as sharp as ever, followed every movement she made, and his stance was unwavering as he prepared for the next strike.

"Focus," Callum said in his low, commanding tone, his eyes never leaving hers.

Izzie narrowed her gaze, trying to control the rush of adrenaline coursing through her veins. She had trained in self-defense at Eldritch Curiosities, but that was nothing like this. The way Callum moved — how he anticipated her every move—left her with the nagging feeling that she was fighting against something she couldn't fully comprehend.

She lunged forward, aiming for his chest. But before she could make contact, Callum shot out his arm, catching her wrist with the precision of someone who'd been through far more battles than she could imagine.

"Again," he urged, his voice clipped, but there was a strange undercurrent of something else—concern?

Izzie huffed and stepped back, wiping sweat from her brow. Her muscles ached, and the weight of her frustration was building. She knew she needed to push harder, but it felt like she was fighting an invisible force every time she faced him. She wasn't sure if it was his overwhelming strength or the connection between them that unsettled her. There was so much more to Callum than he was letting on.

She steadied her breath, trying to center herself. "I'm not giving up."

Callum's lips quirked in a small, approving smile. "Good. But you're holding back. What's really stopping you?"

Izzie clenched her jaw, her hands trembling from the exertion. She could feel it—the fire that simmered beneath her skin whenever she let her mind wander. Rhys. Always Rhys. Even now, as she stood in front of Callum, his haunting presence was still there. A dark pull that made it harder for her to stay grounded.

But now, it was more than just Rhys. She couldn't deny it. She was hungry.

For all five of the brothers.

Her movements became jerky, the strike she aimed for Callum's ribs too wild. He caught her arm easily and looked down at her, his face softening just enough that she caught a glimpse of the concern he'd been hiding. "What's going on in that head of yours?"

"I can't focus," Izzie muttered, her frustration evident. "I keep thinking about—" She stopped herself before saying anything more.

"My brothers," Callum finished for her, his voice low. It wasn't a question, but an understanding.

Izzie nodded, her gaze drifting to the mist swirling around them. "They're always there. In my head. In my dreams. You, too," she added, not wanting him to think she didn't want him as well. In less than a week on Skye, she had fended them off, resisting their subtle advances. She wanted to make this choice for the right reasons. There was so much to this, to making such an important decision for her life.

When it came down to it, she just wanted them to fuck her. All of them. But that wasn't a good enough reason to accept a geas, was it?

Was it?

Callum's expression hardened, his grip tightening around her wrist. "You need to put them out of your mind. You have to be in control of yourself, Izzie. Not us."

Izzie breathed deeply, trying to push away the images of the brothers that haunted her. "I need to see more," she said suddenly, surprising herself with the words. "What you can do. What you really are."

Callum's brow furrowed. "What are you talking about?"

"Shift. I want to see what I've been sleeping with. You did it before, at Machrie Moor. You can do it here. No one will see. Change into your dragon." Her voice wavered with curiosity and a touch of something else — something primal.

For a moment, Callum didn't move. His eyes studied her, as if weighing her request. Then, releasing a slow breath, he nodded. "You're sure about this?"

Izzie met his gaze, the intensity of the moment making her heart race. "I'm sure."

Callum stepped back, stripping off his clothes, his body shifting, the change so fluid it seemed almost effortless. His form began to elongate, the mist around him swirling in response, as his muscles rippled and twisted beneath his skin. The air became charged, and the earth seemed to tremble as Callum's body reshaped into something magnificent, something wild.

The dragon that stood before her was an embodiment of power — tall, broad, with scales that shimmered like a midnight storm. His eyes fixed on her with a smoldering intensity.

Callum's dragon let out a low, resonant growl, his wings unfurling, casting a shadow over the ground beneath him. For a moment, it felt like the entire world had shifted. Everything around her felt small in comparison to the power before her.

Izzie swallowed hard, her mind racing. "That's...amazing," she breathed.

Callum, still in his dragon form, tilted his head, his expression unreadable. "Now you see what you're up against." His voice through his dragon's vocal cords was deep, rumbling.

Izzie's heart raced as she took in the full magnitude of what stood before her. Callum in his dragon form was not just powerful — he was otherworldly. His immense size, the way his scales glinted with an inner fire, the way his wings rippled as though the very air responded to his presence — it was all too much. She had been with him. She had been sleeping with this creature, this ancient force that had the capacity to destroy worlds.

She would never get used to seeing him like this.

Her chest tightened, and she felt a rush of conflicting emotions — fear, awe, fascination. She stepped back, her breath shallow, as if her body needed space to process the impossible reality of what she was facing.

In his dragon form, Callum was the embodiment of ancient strength and quiet wisdom. His scales shimmered in deep shades of midnight blue and silver, like moonlight reflected on the surface of a vast ocean. The tips of his wings glistened with an ethereal, almost translucent iridescence, resembling the edges of waves in the starlit dark. His long, sleek tail curled with grace, crowned by spines that echoed the jagged cliffs of Skye. His eyes, glowing like the moon through a storm, revealed the depth of his age and experience, shifting with his mood like the ever-changing tides.

Callum — the dragon — watched her with a steady gaze. His expression, though the same as it had been in his human form, was tinged with something more. There was raw, unspoken understanding between them. His eyes softened, and for a fleeting moment, his dragon form seemed to reflect the vulnerability he rarely showed.

With a soft grunt, Callum shifted again, his body shrinking, retracting, until the dragon that had towered over her moments ago was now Callum once again. His muscular form was naked beneath the mist, his chest rising and falling with every heavy breath.

Izzie swallowed hard. She hadn't expected this — the rawness of this. She hadn't expected her entire world to shift with a single gaze, but it had. It was as though everything she'd felt, all the tension and yearning, had exploded into clarity in that moment.

Her pulse throbbed in her ears. Everything about Callum felt real now — his power, his presence, and the undeniable pull she'd felt toward him, the pull that had confused her. But it was no longer a mystery. This was real. He wasn't just a man. He wasn't just a lover. He was a force of nature.

Without thinking, Izzie stepped forward, her breath caught in her throat. Her fingers trembled as she reached out to him, brushing against the hard muscles of his chest. Callum looked at her, and there was something in his eyes — something deeper, a quiet understanding, as if he knew exactly what she needed before she did.

"Izzie," he whispered, his voice gravelly, heavy with meaning.

Before she could process another thought, she threw herself at him. She pressed her lips to his in a rush of desperate passion, her hands trembling as they roamed over his body. The cool peat beneath them seemed a distant memory, the heavy mist swirling around them only adding to the intoxicating haze of desire that clouded her mind.

Callum responded immediately, his strong arms pulling her close, his mouth hungry, insistent against hers. He didn't hesitate. There was no distance between them now. He had become part of her, just as she had become part of him.

The world blurred as she gave herself over to him completely. Her hands roamed over the hard planes of his chest, her fingers tracing the lines of muscle and heat that had once seemed distant, almost unreachable. But now, they were hers to claim. Every inch of his skin seemed to burn against hers, and the weight of their connection felt overwhelming.

She could feel the thrum of his heartbeat beneath her fingertips, the rush of blood and life in his veins, and it was as though they were both part of the same pulse, the same rhythm. Her body ached to be closer, her lips tracing down the curve of his neck, his scent filling her senses, making her dizzy with longing.

Callum gripped her tightly, lifting her effortlessly and laying her down against the soft, damp earth. The mist surrounded them, cocooning them in a world of their own. She could hear nothing but the sound of their breaths, their hearts pounding in unison.

Her hands ran over his back, feeling the faintest remnants of his dragon form, the shifting power beneath his skin, and it only heightened the tension between them. He was both a man and something so much more, and the realization of that made her shiver with anticipation.

As he moved over her, their bodies a tangled mess of skin and desire, Izzie felt a surge of something new — a sense of surrender. She wasn't just with him. She was lost in him, and she didn't care.

Callum's lips traced the line of her jaw, his breath warm and uneven against her skin. "You're mine, Izzie," he growled, his voice rough with desire. "I've always known you were."

In that moment, she believed him. She couldn't deny the magnetic pull that had led them here, to this wild place, to this wild connection. She let go of all her fears, of everything she had held back, and surrendered herself to him completely.

And in that moment, everything fell away — the mist, the world, the confusion. There was only Callum. Only the two of them, bound by something ancient and primal, something that neither of them could escape.

And she didn't want to.

The fire and force of their union seemed to mix and meld, creating something neither of them could resist.

Izzie gasped as Callum's mouth crashed down on hers, his tongue plundering her depths. He kissed her with a ferocity that stole her breath, his hands tugging at her clothing. She responded eagerly, her own hands exploring the hard planes of his body.

Callum stripped Izzie's clothes off quickly, tearing at her leggings and tank top. His eyes raked over her body as he revealed her naked flesh. He lowered his head, his tongue flicking out to taste her breasts, her stomach, her thighs. He licked and sucked at her most sensitive places, his mouth a dragon's brand against her flesh.

Izzie moaned, her fingers tangling in Callum's hair as he worked his way lower. When his mouth found her core, she cried out, her hips bucking against him. He lapped at her folds, his tongue delving deep, driving her to the brink of madness.

Just as she was about to crest, Callum pulled back, a wicked gleam in his eye. "Not yet, my love. I want to feel you come around my cock."

He positioned himself between her thighs, his thick member pressing against her entrance. With one swift thrust, he buried himself deep inside her, filling her completely. Izzie cried out at the sensation, her nails digging into his back.

Callum began to move, his hips slamming against hers in a relentless rhythm. He kissed her deeply, swallowing her moans as he fucked her with primal intensity. The sounds of their coupling filled the air, the wet slap of flesh against flesh echoing in the misty stillness.

Izzie's climax crashed over her like a tidal wave, her body convulsing beneath Callum's. He continued to thrust into her, riding out her orgasm. But Callum was far from satisfied. He flipped Izzie over, pulling her up onto her hands and knees. He entered her again from behind, his hands gripping her hips as he pounded into her. Izzie's breasts bounced with each thrust, her nipples grazing the soft moss beneath her.

Callum's mouth found her neck, his teeth grazing her skin. He bit down, marking her as his, as another orgasm ripped through her. Her walls tightened around him, milking him for every drop.

Still, Callum wasn't done. Within moments, he hardened again, his dragon magic lending him strength. He rolled them over, settling between her thighs once more. He took her hands in his, pinning them above her head as he entered her again. His thrusts were slower this time, more deliberate, as if he were savoring every inch of her.

Izzie wrapped her legs around his waist, drawing him deeper. She could feel every ridge and vein of his cock as he slid in and out of her, the friction building to a fever pitch. Callum's eyes locked with hers, his gaze intense and unwavering.

"Come for me, Izzie," he commanded, his voice a low growl. "Let me feel you come undone."

His words sent her over the edge, her body shuddering with the force of her climax. Callum followed soon after, his cock pulsing inside her as he found his release.

They stayed there for a long moment, their bodies entwined, their breaths mingling. The air around them was thick with the scent of the wild — earthy and damp, mingling with the sharp, intoxicating musk of their union. Izzie lay beneath Callum, her heart still pounding as she caught her breath. Every nerve in her body hummed with the aftereffects of their passion, and she could feel the faint remnants of dragon's fire pulsing under her skin, an invisible thread that connected them in ways that went far beyond physical.

But the moment of peace didn't last long.

A distant sound echoed over the cliffs — a low, rumbling growl that seemed to vibrate through the earth beneath them. Izzie's head snapped up, her senses on high alert. She felt it before she heard it clearly — four powerful pairs of wings cutting through the sky, casting massive shadows over the fog-shrouded land.

Callum stiffened, his body tensing as his eyes scanned the sky. The sound grew louder, the unmistakable beat of dragon wings pushing the air in every direction. He cursed under his breath, swiftly standing up and shifting in one fluid motion. His body expanded, scales rippling across his flesh as he transformed into his dragon form, the large, dark wings unfurling to shield Izzie from view.

"Stay down," he growled, his voice now a deep, rumbling command.

Izzie scrambled to her feet, pulling her clothes on hastily, her hands shaking as she tried to cover herself. Her heart raced, panic creeping in as she caught a glimpse of the dragons overhead, circling in a pattern that signaled an approach.

The four dragons broke through the mist, their massive forms gliding low over the cliffs. Callum's brothers had arrived.

Izzie's breath caught as she watched them descend, their scales gleaming in the misty air, each one as powerful and formidable as Callum himself. Finn, Lorcan, Tavish, and Rhys — all in their dragon forms, each one with a presence that was impossible to ignore.

Their eyes glinted with fire, scanning the ground below.

How was she going to tell them apart? She barely knew them in their human forms.

Callum's dragon loomed protectively between Izzie and his brothers, his great wings flaring to block their view. The tension in the air was thick, palpable.

"I told you to stay back," Callum said through gritted teeth, his voice a low growl. "This is my territory."

The other dragons landed with powerful thuds, their massive bodies stirring the mist around them. Finn was the first to speak. His voice was smooth and calm, but there was an edge to it.

"You think you can keep her all to yourself, Callum?" Finn's gaze shifted to Izzie, his eyes gleaming with something far more primal than mere curiosity. Finn's dragon form was a force of wild, untamed beauty, with scales of forest green and bronze. His wings, vast and shimmering, were flecked with gold, like sunlight filtering through the dense canopy of a forest. His muscular body, agile and strong, moved with reckless energy, while his claws gleamed like polished copper. His eyes, vivid green with streaks of gold, reflected his untamable spirit and youthful energy. When he moved, he was like a storm, raw and unpredictable, a force of nature that could not be tamed. "We can all smell her, you know. We know what you've been doing."

Izzie's stomach dropped. She could feel the weight of their gaze, and something primal and possessive in the air made her heart race all over again. But there was also something else, a tension, an unspoken understanding between the brothers.

Lorcan grinned, his expression playful but intense even in his dragon form. "You were never going to keep her from us forever, Callum. She's a temptation, and we all know it." Lorcan's dragon form was a creature of shadow and mystery, born from the mist and the forgotten depths of the earth. His scales were velvety black, tinged with a deep emerald green that seemed to glow faintly in the moonlight. His wings, large and elegant, resembled the wings of a bat, with a translucence that shifted as he moved, like a shadow in the dark. His eyes gleamed jade green, filled with intelligence and an almost otherworldly power. When he flew, there was a quiet grace to him, like the fleeting darkness of a storm cloud, moving too quickly to be caught.

Tavish, ever the quiet one, stepped forward. His dragon form was the epitome of grace and elegance, with scales that glowed pale silver and light blue, like the sky at dawn. His wings were broad, almost translucent, shimmering with an opalescent sheen as though touched by the first rays of sunlight. His long, sinuous tail moved with silken smoothness, and his delicate horns swept back in a gentle arc. His eyes, soft ice-blue, exuded calm serenity, yet a sharp intensity lurked beneath the surface. When he flew, it was with the elegance of a bird gliding on a gentle wind, graceful and potent. His dark eyes locked with Izzie's, and though he didn't speak, she felt the heat of his stare, the intensity of his silent question — *Would you choose me, too?*

Izzie's breath caught, but she didn't have time to process the emotions swirling within her before Rhys' voice rang out, sharp and accusing.

"Enough." Rhys' command sliced through the rising tension. Even as a dragon he radiated power, a creature forged from fire and earth. His scales glowed with molten reds and oranges, pulsing like lava in a restless volcano. When his wings spread, they flickered with golden light, burning as bright as a furnace. His claws, black and sharp as obsidian, gleamed with an unrelenting ferocity. His eyes burned amber, fierce and unyielding, carrying the weight of an alpha's rule. When he soared through the sky, he was a whirlwind of flame, a force of nature that commanded awe and terror in equal measure.

He stepped forward, shifting into his human form. "Callum, we all know the truth. She's the one we've all been waiting for. And you can't keep her to yourself forever. The geas was made for all of us."

Callum growled in frustration, his dragon form towering over the others, his wings spread wide in warning. "She is mine," he insisted, his voice harsh and final.

Izzie's pulse thudded in her temples. She couldn't understand what was happening, why everything was spinning so fast. Her heart raced with confusion, with a desire that she couldn't shake, but there was fear in her too.

"You'll have to go through me first, if you want her," Callum said, his tone like a flame threatening to burn out of control.

"I don't think it works that way," Finn countered, stepping closer, his eyes narrowing as he looked at Izzie. "She doesn't belong to you, Callum. She belongs to all of us."

Izzie's chest tightened, her emotions a tangled mess as the dragons exchanged words. They were arguing over her. She felt drawn to them, but she never expected this—to be the center of a battle between them, to feel like she was their possession.

Her hands shook as she tried to steady herself. She had no idea what she was supposed to do in this situation, but as the brothers turned their attention toward her, she knew one thing for sure—she wasn't just facing a choice between them, she was facing the most dangerous temptation of her life.

Chapter Twenty-Two

The room was dark when Izzie awoke, the weight of the night pressing against her senses. The faint smell of mist and peat lingered in the air, but it wasn't the scent of the wild that unsettled her. It was Rhys.

She heard him before she saw him — his movements silent as he slipped into her room. She should have been frightened, but instead, there was something else. A pull. A need. She felt it, deep in her core, as though her body had been waiting for this moment.

It didn't make any sense. She'd just had brilliant sex with Callum a few hours ago, fireworks and lightning and all. How could she be this hungry again, this soon?

Rhys didn't speak, just moved closer, his presence suffocating and undeniable. He brushed his hand against her cheek, a whisper of a touch that sent a shiver down her spine. Her breath hitched, and she couldn't help the heat that rushed through her. He traced his fingers along her jawline, lingering just enough to make her pulse race.

"Izzie," he whispered, his voice low, rough, like something darker was hiding just beneath the surface. "I've been waiting for you to surrender completely. I'm going to show you what you're capable of."

What more was there for her to give him? Her heart pounded in her chest, her thoughts scattering like leaves in the wind. She opened her mouth to protest—to say she wasn't ready, that she couldn't—but the words got caught in her throat. Rhys had a way of making everything feel inevitable, like there was no escape.

He slid his touch down her neck, slow and deliberate, as though he were memorizing every inch of her. His hands explored, teasing, drawing out gasps from her mouth as he gently but firmly guided her toward surrender. He didn't force her—no, he never did—but he pushed her. Each soft caress, each whispered word, each delicate shift taught her something new about herself.

"Every inch of you belongs to me," he murmured, tracing the delicate line of her collarbone. "And I intend to explore every inch."

Izzie gasped as he slid his hands lower, cupping her breasts through the thin fabric of her nightgown. He brushed his thumbs over her nipples, making them harden and strain against the cloth. "Please," she whimpered, unsure whether she was begging him to stop or to continue.

Rhys chuckled, a low, sensual sound that sent shivers down her spine. "Don't fight it, Izzie. You know you want this. You've been craving my touch since we got here. I don't know why you've held back. But knowing what you and Callum were up to today, I know you need to get fucked again. By both of us. Or is it all of us you're ready for?"

He slipped his hands under her nightgown, pushing it up to her waist as he explored the soft curves of her body. Izzie arched into his touch, her breath coming in short, sharp gasps as he danced his fingers over her skin. He leaned down, pressing his lips against her ear as he whispered, "I'm going to make you feel things you've never felt before. I'm going to drive you to the brink of madness with pleasure."

Izzie moaned as he slid his hands between her thighs, his fingers teasing her most sensitive spots. The heat was building inside her, her body responding to his touch in ways she never thought possible. He guided her toward surrender, each soft caress and whispered word teaching her something new about herself.

Rhys' lips trailed down her neck, his teeth grazing her skin as he sucked and nibbled at every inch of her. Izzie's head fell back, her hands gripping the sheets as she surrendered to the pleasure coursing through her body. He teased her mercilessly, sliding his fingers inside her, pumping in and out as his thumb circled her clit.

"Please," Izzie begged, her hips bucking against his hand. "I need you inside me."

Rhys growled, a sound of pure, primal desire. He ripped her nightgown off, leaving her bare and exposed beneath him. He settled between her thighs, his hard cock pressing against her entrance. "You're mine," he snarled, his eyes flashing with a fierce, possessive light. "Every inch of you belongs to me."

With one powerful thrust, he drove himself deep inside her, stretching her walls and filling her completely. Izzie cried out, her nails digging into his back as he began to move. He set a relentless pace, pounding into her with a ferocity that left her breathless. She could feel every inch of him, his thick length stroking her inner walls and igniting sparks of pleasure with every thrust.

Rhys roamed his hands over her body, squeezing her breasts, pinching her nipples, and gripping her hips as he drove into her. He kissed her fiercely, his tongue tangling with hers as he swallowed her moans and whimpers. Izzie lost herself in the sensation, her world narrowing down to the point where their bodies joined.

He flipped her over, positioning her on her hands and knees. Izzie gasped as he entered her from behind, gripping her hips as he pounded into her. The new angle allowed him to go even deeper, hitting a spot inside her that made her see stars. The tension was building inside her, her body coiling tighter and tighter with each thrust.

"Come for me, Izzie," Rhys growled, finding her clit with his fingers and rubbing in tight circles. "Come all over my cock."

With a scream of ecstasy, Izzie did just that, her body convulsing around him as waves of pleasure crashed over her. Rhys followed her over the edge, his cock pulsing inside her as he filled her with his seed.

They collapsed onto the bed, their bodies slick with sweat, tangled together. Rhys pulled Izzie into his arms, pressing his lips against her forehead as he murmured, "You're mine now, Izzie. Body and soul."

She was aching — aching for something she couldn't quite define. A part of her felt exposed, raw, but another part, the part that had been buried for so long, felt…awakened.

Her door creaked open again.

Callum's silhouette filled the doorway, his frame rigid with fury. His eyes locked on her, and for a brief, electric moment, the entire world seemed to pause.

"Rhys," Callum's voice was a growl, low and dangerous. "What the hell is going on?"

Izzie couldn't move. She didn't even know how to react. The air between them was thick, charged with tension, anger, and something else that made her heart race. She could feel Callum's fury, his jealousy, like a weight in the room.

The room was dim, lit only by the dying embers in the hearth and the soft glow of moonlight through the window. Izzie lay tangled in the sheets, Rhys' warmth still wrapped around her. He traced absent patterns along her spine, lazy in the aftermath.

Callum stood in the doorway, his chest rising and falling with barely contained fury. His gaze flicked over the bed—over Rhys sprawled beside her, over Izzie's flushed skin and tousled hair. His jaw clenched so tightly she could almost hear his teeth grind.

Rhys didn't move. He held Callum's stare with that infuriating calm, his arm still draped possessively around Izzie's waist.

"What the fuck are you doing?" Callum's voice was low, but the anger in it burned hotter than any roar.

Izzie pushed up onto her elbows, her heart pounding. "You know what this is."

Callum's hands curled into fists at his sides. "That's not the point."

Rhys finally shifted, sitting up, but his movements were slow, deliberate. Controlled. "Then what is the point, Callum? Because you know the rules."

Callum's nostrils flared. "She was with me today."

Rhys smirked. "And now she's with me."

Callum took a step closer, his presence a storm pressing into the room. "You think I don't understand what's happening here? You think I don't know how this works?" His voice was rough, barely contained.

"But it's different when it's real, isn't it? When it's not just some ancient law, but—" He cut himself off, dragging a hand through his hair. "She's not one of us. She didn't grow up knowing this."

Izzie exhaled slowly, meeting his gaze. "I know now."

Callum's lips parted as if he wanted to argue, but what could he say? That he hated sharing? That he wanted to be the exception? That he wanted her to choose him, even knowing that wasn't how this worked?

His throat worked as he swallowed hard. "I don't like this," he admitted.

Rhys' expression softened just a fraction. "No one said you had to."

A long silence stretched between them, heavy with things unsaid.

Finally, Rhys sighed and peeled himself away from Izzie, pressing a lingering kiss to her shoulder before slipping from the bed. He grabbed his discarded shirt, pulling it over his head as he strode to the door. When he passed Callum, he murmured something too low for Izzie to hear.

Callum didn't react for a second. Then he followed Rhys out, closing the door firmly behind himself.

They were both gone, leaving her alone in the dim, echoing quiet.

* * * *

That night, sleep did not come easily to Izzie. The hours stretched into an endless blur of tangled sheets and restless tossing. But when sleep finally claimed her, it brought with it dreams—wild, vivid dreams that were unlike any she had ever known.

In her dream, the five brothers stood before her. Callum was first, his towering presence dominating the scene, his dragon form flickering in the back of her mind like a fire waiting to be unleashed. His eyes were intense, predatory, but there was something softer beneath that ferocity. Then there was Rhys, dominant even at rest, his smirk teasing her from the corner of her mind. Finn, with his deep, unreadable stare, followed by Tavish, whose quiet strength spoke louder than any words could. Lorcan was last, playful and dangerous, trailing his fingers lightly over her skin.

One by one, they approached her, and she could feel the weight of their desire, their longing. They all wanted her — needed her — and something deep inside her answered that call. She was trapped in the storm of their power, and she wanted it. All of it. The wildness, the danger, the passion.

As they circled her, she realized she wasn't just a passive participant. She was part of them, part of the storm that raged between them all. Their bodies, their power, their hearts — they were all bound to her, and she to them. A deep, unshakable bond formed, stronger than anything she had ever known.

The geas. The ancient magic that tied them together, that tied her to them. It was there in the dream, and she understood. This wasn't something that could be avoided. This was her fate.

When she awoke, the room was still dark, but she wasn't confused anymore. She wasn't lost in the maze of her emotions. No, she knew what she wanted now. She understood the power and the cost, and she was ready. The decision had been made in the depths of her soul, in the shadowy corners of her dreams.

Izzie sat up in the bed, her heart pounding, her body humming with the residual energy of the dream. She wasn't just some pawn in their game. She was in this now. All the tension, all the chaos — it all had to lead somewhere. And she wasn't going to hide from it any longer.

She rose from the bed, the cool morning air biting at her skin as she dressed quickly, smoothing down the fabric of her clothes. With every step, her resolve grew stronger. She wasn't just walking toward the breakfast room. She was walking toward something much bigger, something that would change everything.

The heavy oak door creaked as she pushed it open, stepping into the room where the brothers sat, talking in low tones. They all paused when they saw her. Callum's eyes darkened, his gaze unreadable, while Rhys gave her a knowing look. Finn watched her with his usual detachment, and Tavish's calm presence stayed contained.

Lorcan's eyes were the first to meet hers, and there was something there — something that told her he had known this moment was coming, that he had been waiting for it.

"I'm ready," she said, her voice steady, filled with undeniable strength. She met each of their eyes, one by one. "I'm ready to accept the geas."

The room fell into eerie silence. The weight of her words hung in the air, a promise and a challenge all at once. The brothers looked between each other, their expressions ranging from surprise to approval, but none of them said a word. The tension was palpable, and she knew that this was the point of no return.

Callum's jaw clenched, and for a moment, Izzie thought he might protest. But then his eyes softened just the slightest bit, and he nodded.

Rhys leaned back in his chair, a slow smile spreading across his face. "Good choice," he murmured.

Tavish's gaze didn't waver, but there was a flicker of something — pride, perhaps — before he looked away. Finn simply studied her, as if assessing the decision she had just made. Lorcan was the last to speak.

"You're sure, little one?" he asked, his voice low, almost teasing. But there was something in his tone that made it clear he wasn't asking lightly.

Izzie didn't hesitate. She nodded firmly.

"I'm sure."

And, in that moment, everything shifted.

Chapter Twenty-Three

The water in the clawfoot tub was warm, the steam rising around Izzie as she sank into the depths. The scented oils Margaret had provided swirled in the water, their floral notes calming, but her thoughts were far from peaceful. The world was shifting under her feet, the ground she once stood on crumbling away, and now — now, everything was changing.

This morning she told the Sìol Dòmhnaill brothers that she would accept the geas, the spell that bound her body and soul to each of the brothers-of-the-egg, at least until she became pregnant with one of the brothers' eggs.

And now, as evening fell across the Isle of Skye, she was preparing herself for the ceremony that would change the entire course of her life.

She didn't know Finn, Lorcan, or Tavish well enough to see one of them as her future husband. Rhys made her scream in bed, hitting all the right spots. But for a husband...

She hoped it would be Callum, truthfully.

She let herself submerge briefly, the water closing over her skin, and for a moment, it was as if she could block out the weight of everything. But no matter how deep she sank, the pull of the brothers — their power, their need — was always there. It was inescapable now. She could feel it, even under the cool surface of the water. The geas was alive inside her, thrumming with energy, and soon, it would be activated.

As the water cooled, she reluctantly emerged, her hands slick as she reached for a soft towel to dry herself. The fire crackled nearby, offering warmth against the growing chill of evening as she stood, towel in hand, and let the flickering orange glow dry her skin and hair. The air smelled faintly of orange and nutmeg, but it wasn't enough to calm the anxious tension tightening in her chest.

Her hair, damp and heavy, clung to her back as she reached for one of the sheer silk negligees Margaret had provided for her. The pale fabric whispered against her skin as she slipped it on, the delicate material clinging in all the right places, accentuating her curves. It was the kind of garment she might have worn in another life, in another time, but now — now it felt like a symbol of something much larger than herself. A symbol of surrender.

A symbol of acceptance.

As she stared at herself in the mirror, her reflection felt like a stranger's, the girl who had entered this place so full of questions now replaced by someone on the cusp of discovery. She was ready to step into whatever awaited her. The negligee might as well have been armor — protective, if only in the sense that it shielded her from the truth of what was happening.

With one last glance at herself, Izzie turned and left the room. The hallway stretched before her, its grand architecture echoing her footsteps, the walls lined with centuries-old tapestries that seemed to watch her with knowing eyes. As she approached the sweeping staircase, her heart began to race. Every step down toward the Great Hall was heavy, each footfall sinking deeper into the weight of what was to come.

The moment she entered the vast room, everything seemed to still. The five Sìol Dòmhnaill brothers stood together, their powerful forms silhouetted against the large obsidian plinth that stood at the center of the room. The plinth was etched with glowing runes, pulsing with an ancient energy that seemed to hum in the very air.

Izzie's breath caught as her eyes swept over them. They were half naked, wearing only kilts, but nothing above the waist. Five bare chests, strongly muscled, each with random patches of scales on their torsos. But it wasn't their state of undress, or the signs of their dragonhood. No, it was their undeniable presence. Each of them was powerful in his own right, his body a reflection of the raw energy they wielded.

A mixture of emotions churned in her — discomfort, awe, fear, desire — but she forced herself to push them aside. She had made her choice. There was no turning back now.

Callum was the first to step forward, his eyes intense and watchful. Rhys followed, a slow smirk curving his lips, and the others followed suit. Finn's intense gaze scanned her, while Tavish's silence was as thick as ever, though his eyes never left her. Lorcan's playful gaze lingered just a moment longer than the others, a glint of something dark in his expression.

They led her toward the plinth, their hands gentle but insistent. The fabric of her negligee whispered against her skin as they carefully removed it, their touch making her breath catch. Izzie didn't resist—couldn't resist—though her heart pounded heavily in her chest as she lay back naked on the obsidian surface. It was smooth, cool beneath her skin, yet it somehow felt comforting, as if the ancient stone was welcoming her.

The brothers stood over her, their presence overwhelming. They had always been larger than life, but now—now, they were the embodiment of everything she had feared and craved. She couldn't deny it any longer. The moment had come. And as they looked down at her, their eyes burning with a mix of hunger and something else—something darker—she knew, with absolute certainty, that her life would never be the same again.

The air in the Great Hall thickened with ancient, powerful energy as Izzie lay on the obsidian plinth, her heart pounding in rhythm with the pulsing glow of the runes. The stone beneath her felt alive, breathing with the secrets of centuries, and the brothers circled around her like a quiet storm, their eyes glittering with a hunger that was both tender and fierce.

Callum stood to the side, his face a mask of frustration and concern, his gaze never straying far from Izzie. His hands flexed, like a man caught between the urge to protect and the need to honor the inevitable. He had not wanted this for her, but in his heart, he knew there was no turning back. This was her choice, and there was a deep, undeniable magic in the air—magic that bound them all to this moment, to this ritual.

Rhys stepped forward first, his smile dark and knowing as he knelt beside the plinth. He reached for a small silver vial that hung from his sporran and produced a glowing, translucent liquid. The scent that wafted up from the vial was intoxicating — floral, rich, with a deep, earthy undertone that reminded Izzie of wild nights in the hills, of hidden things deep within the earth. Rhys uncorked it, and the liquid swirled with soft, otherworldly light.

"Drink, little one," Rhys murmured, his voice a velvet rasp that made her pulse quicken. "This will bind you to us, as we are bound to you."

Izzie hesitated for a heartbeat, but the temptation was too great. She had already chosen, hadn't she? She was ready to face whatever came next. With a slow breath, she took the vial from his hand and tilted it to her lips. The liquid slid over her tongue like warm honey, but there was something sharp beneath it — something that felt like fire and ice both. It burned, but not in the way that would harm. It burned in a way that made her feel alive, connected to something ancient and infinite.

As she finished the last of the potion, the magic began to rise within her, swirling in her veins like liquid lightning. It flowed through her body, wrapping around her heart, her soul, and she gasped, arching into the sensation of it. It was as though the very earth was claiming her — claiming her for them.

The brothers moved in close, their eyes glowing brighter with the magic they now shared. Callum stepped forward, his hands trembling ever so slightly as he reached out to touch her skin. His fingertips traced delicate patterns across her body — marking her with the ancient oil of binding. The oil was warm and fragrant, sending waves of heat through her as he moved over her skin, anointing her with a golden substance that shimmered in the firelight. It smelled of jasmine and sandalwood, and something darker, like smoke curling in the night.

"I will claim you," Callum whispered, his breath hot against her ear. "We will all claim you."

The words were more than just an affirmation — they were a promise, an inevitability, and Izzie couldn't stop the shiver that ran through her. The oil seeped into her skin, carrying with it the essence of the geas. She could feel it — deep within, the bond beginning to form. It was as if every touch was carving their names into her soul, a permanent etching, a part of her that could never be undone.

The other brothers, Finn, Lorcan, Tavish, and Rhys, followed suit, their hands tracing her skin, their own magic intermingling with Callum's, each of them marking her as their own. Each of them placed their hands on her, anointing her with more of the sacred oil, their eyes never leaving hers. She felt the shift in the air, the weight of their collective gaze, the way it both soothed and intensified the fire building within her. Their magic, their power, was merging with hers. There was no retreat.

They were carving their very essence into her, claiming her body, her soul, her fate. The connection was fierce, undeniable.

All-consuming.

The runes on the plinth flickered in time with the pulse of her heart, and the air around them crackled, alive with energy. The brothers whispered words in an ancient tongue, their voices blending with the hum of magic that filled the space. The geas was taking root, settling into her bones.

As the last whispers of the spell faded, Izzie was left breathless. Her skin tingled, alive with their touch, their magic, and the weight of the bond they had forged.

Callum's eyes were dark, filled with something both possessive and protective as he watched her. The ceremony was complete.

But something had shifted within Izzie too. She was no longer just a part of this world — she was tied to it. Tied to them.

And as she lay there on the plinth, the scent of jasmine lingering in the air, she knew that her life had changed forever.

Her awakening had begun.

Chapter Twenty-Four

The heavy wooden door to the ceremonial bedchamber closed behind Izzie with a soft thud, and she was alone with the weight of what had just transpired. The echo of the geas ceremony still buzzed in the air around her, a faint hum that reverberated through her chest like the pulse of a dragon's heart. The room before her felt like a dream — a chamber crafted not just for royalty, but for something far older, far more sacred.

Silk and velvet draped the enormous bed that dominated the center of the room, its deep crimson and gold fabrics shimmering in the low light of the hearth. Plush pillows, some as large as boulders, were scattered across the floor in a welcoming mess of softness. The scent of roses and cedar mingled in the air, rich and intoxicating, swirling with the lingering warmth of the fire in the marble hearth.

Izzie stood frozen with her back against the door, her body still humming with the aftershocks of the magic, the weight of the geas pressing down on her like a living thing. The five Sìol Dòmhnaill brothers had given her everything in the geas ceremony — anointed her, marked her, made her a part of them. Her skin still buzzed with the touch of their hands, and every breath she took was laced with their magic, their power. She felt it in the very marrow of her bones.

It was as if the room was alive, waiting for her to take the next step. To claim her place in this ancient family.

Her heart thundered in her chest. There was no going back, was there? Not now. She had made her choice, embraced the sacred bond that tied her to these five dragons — each of them powerful, dangerous, and utterly compelling. She stepped forward, moving to the bed and running a reverent hand over the velvet coverlet.

The air in the chamber shimmered with something unseen, something old and unbreakable. It was as if the very walls were breathing, waiting for her to take the final step — to seal herself to them, to become part of something far older than any one of them. Her heart pounded, a steady drumbeat against the silence. There was no going back now.

She had made her choice.

Accepting the geas meant belonging to them all — not just one man but five. It was like a marriage in the most profound sense, but unlike any marriage she'd ever imagined. She wasn't just promising herself to a husband — she was tying her soul to five dragon shifters, binding her fate to theirs for the rest of her life. The weight of it settled over her, but it wasn't fear that made her hands tremble. It was the knowledge that nothing would ever be the same again.

Her parents should have been here.

A lump formed in her throat. If things had been different — if they had lived — her mother would have helped her prepare for her wedding day, brushing her hair, adjusting her dress, offering whispered advice. Her father would have walked her down the aisle, placing her hand in another's with a proud but bittersweet smile. But there was no dress tonight. No father's hand to guide her. No mother's gentle reassurance.

And, well…considering that she had been naked on a stone plinth for the ceremony, and now was about to consummate her bond with five men in a sacred rite no outsider could ever know about…

That would've been a hell of a conversation to have over Sunday dinner.

A choked, breathless laugh bubbled up, but she swallowed it down. No one could ever know the truth — not about them, not about what she was becoming. This secret was hers to carry now, hers alone. The weight of her decision settled over her like a cloak, heavy yet exhilarating. She had felt the pull of it ever since she had arrived at the manor. The tension, the temptation, the unspoken promise in every glance shared between them. And now, the time had come to face it all. To be fully claimed, body and soul.

The door creaked open again, and the sound sent a flutter of anticipation through her veins. She turned, heart leaping as the five brothers stepped into the room.

Callum was the first to enter, his eyes dark with something unreadable — a mix of protectiveness and possession that sent a shiver down her spine. His tall, broad frame filled the doorway, the quiet command in his gaze making her knees weak. He had always been the one to watch over her, to guide her, but now...now, he was more than that. He was bound to her.

Finn followed closely behind, his movements fluid, measured, his sharp gaze locked onto her. He was a mystery, a dragon whose cool, unreadable exterior hid a depth of emotion she had yet to fully grasp. With him, there was always more beneath the surface, a quiet fire banked beneath layers of control.

Lorcan sauntered in next, his grin wicked, though his golden eyes burned with something softer now. He was the teasing flame to the others' controlled heat, the one who knew how to stoke her desires with a glance, a whisper. Playful, irreverent, but no less intense—he was the spark that could turn a moment into an inferno.

Tavish entered after, his presence quieter but no less commanding. His silence spoke volumes, and Izzie felt the storm in his gaze as he watched her, his lips slightly parted as if struggling to contain the emotions roiling beneath the surface. There was something about him, something both steady and wild, as though he was a force of nature barely restrained.

Then Rhys.

He didn't stalk or saunter—he simply was. The weight of his presence filled the space effortlessly, his amber eyes knowing, his expression unreadable but for the heat simmering beneath it. He was the alpha, dominant, the one who always held a measure of control over the rest, but there was no arrogance in it—only certainty. The others might fight for dominance in subtle ways, but Rhys had never needed to. His power was woven into every breath he took, every glance, every quiet word.

Izzie's breath hitched. Five dragons. Five men. Five bonds, unbreakable.

They encircled her, and she felt it then — the weight of their collective attention, the fire of their desire, the certainty that she was meant to be theirs. This was her new life. This was the moment she had been waiting for, whether she realized it or not.

Her fingers trembled as they brushed the delicate straps of her negligee, the silk whispering against her skin as she slid it from her shoulders. The fabric pooled at her feet in a silent surrender, leaving her bare beneath their hungry, waiting gazes.

A slow, charged silence settled over the room, thick as a storm before the first crack of thunder. Their eyes burned into her — five dragons, five forces of nature, each tethered to her now in a bond that could never be undone.

Heat surged through her, winding tight in her chest, her belly. There was no shame in this, no hesitation left. She had made her choice. And she had never felt more seen.

Callum's voice broke the silence, deep and commanding. "Are you ready, Izzie?"

She nodded, her voice thick with anticipation. "Yes. I am."

And with that, the world seemed to shift. The five brothers stepped forward, and the next step in her journey began.

Izzie's heart raced as she stood before the five towering dragon shifters, their eyes gleaming with primal desire. The ancient manor house creaked around them, shadows dancing on the walls from the flickering candles. This was the night she had been preparing for, the sacred geas that would bind her to these powerful beings for eternity.

Rhys stepped forward, his muscular chest bare and his kilt fluttering with his movements. "Izzie, daughter of the moon, you have been chosen to be our mate, our queen. Are you ready to submit to us, to take our essence into your body and soul?"

Izzie's breath caught in her throat, her nipples hardening. "I am ready," she whispered, her voice trembling with anticipation.

Callum nodded, and the brothers helped her into the massive bed, draped in rich silks and velvets. They caressed every inch of her soft skin as they lay her down against the soft pillows. Izzie gasped as their fingers found her most intimate places, teasing and stroking until she was writhing with need.

One by one, the brothers shed their kilts, the heavy fabric dropping to the floor in soft, weighted folds. Callum was the first, his movements deliberate, eyes locked on Izzie with a quiet intensity that sent shivers racing down her spine. Finn followed, his expression unreadable, but the hunger in his gaze betrayed the cool control he always wielded so effortlessly. Lorcan smirked as he loosened his kilt belt, dragging out the moment just to watch her squirm beneath his wicked amusement. Tavish was slower, more measured, tracing the edge of his kilt with his fingers before letting it fall, his body tense with barely contained restraint. Then Rhys—always last, always the one to hold back just long enough to remind them all of his place— removed his kilt pin, loosening the fabric with the confidence of a man who had already claimed what was his. The air between them crackled, thick with heat and anticipation, before they moved, climbing up onto the bed where Izzie waited, breathless.

The first brother, Finn, positioned himself between her thighs, his thick cock throbbing with desire. "We will take you one by one, my love, until we have all claimed you as our own."

Izzie nodded, spreading her legs wider in invitation. Finn entered her slowly, filling her completely. She cried out at the delicious stretch, her walls squeezing him tight. He began to move, thrusting deep and hard, his balls slapping against her ass.

As Finn fucked her, the other brothers caressed her body, their hands and mouths exploring every curve. They pinched her nipples, sucked on her neck, and teased her clit until she was a writhing mess of pleasure. Izzie felt her orgasm building, her body tensing as Finn drove into her harder and faster.

With a roar, Finn came, his hot seed spurting deep inside her. He pulled out, and the next brother, Tavish, took his place. Tavish was even larger than Finn, his cock stretching her to her limits. He fucked her with wild abandon, his hips slamming against hers as he pounded into her.

The other brothers continued their sensual assault, their hands and mouths never leaving her body. Izzie lost herself in the sensations, her mind hazing with pleasure. She came again and again, her body shaking with the force of her orgasms.

As Tavish finished, spilling his load inside her, Lorcan took his turn. Lorcan was gentle but no less passionate, his cock sliding in and out of her slick pussy with a slow, steady rhythm. He brought her to the brink of ecstasy and held her there, teasing her with his movements until she was begging for release.

When Lorcan finally let her come, Izzie screamed with pleasure, her body convulsing around his cock.

He filled her with his seed, his laugh of satisfaction mixing with her own cries of bliss.

Finally, Callum took his place. He flipped her over, positioning her on her hands and knees. He entered her from behind, his cock plunging deep into her soaked cunt. Izzie pushed back against him, meeting his thrusts with her own, the bed creaking beneath them. They'd fucked before, several times, but tonight Callum was…more than he'd ever been.

Did he have something to prove to his brothers? If so, Izzie was willing to accept it.

The other brothers gathered around her, their cocks hard and ready for another round. They fed her their dicks, one at a time, as Callum fucked her from behind. Izzie sucked and licked, her mouth filled with their musky taste.

At last Callum came with a growl, his cock pulsing inside her as he filled her with his hot cum. He pulled out, and finally Rhys took his place. Rhys was the largest of them all, his cock stretching her to her limits.

Kneeling on the bed, he lifted her into his arms, facing him, impaling her on his massive shaft. He bounced her on his cock, gripping her ass with his hands as he drove into her. Izzie clung to him, her nails digging into his shoulders as he fucked her with wild, animalistic passion.

The other brothers joined in, their hands and mouths on her body once more. Izzie was lost in a sea of sensation, her body overwhelmed with pleasure. She came again and again, her orgasms blending into one endless wave of ecstasy.

Finally, Rhys came, his cock erupting inside her with a force that sent her over the edge once more. They collapsed onto the bed, their bodies tangled together, slick with sweat and cum.

As the sun rose over the ancient manor, Izzie snuggled into the arms of her new mates, ready to face whatever the future held. She was theirs, and they were hers, bound together by the sacred geas, an unbreakable bond.

Chapter Twenty-Five

The dim glow of her own bedroom cast everything in soft shadows as Izzie stood there, her body still humming with the echoes of the night's passion. The ceremonial bedchamber, heavy with the scent of sex and magic, felt like a dream slipping through her fingers, but the reality of what she had done — what she had become — settled deep in her bones. She pressed a hand to her chest, her heartbeat unsteady, as if the geas itself pulsed beneath her skin. The weight of her choice, of the five brothers bound to her as surely as she was bound to them, was already pressing down, but something else coiled in the air around her. A darker presence. A whisper at the edge of her thoughts. The night had reshaped her, but the world outside the chamber had not stopped turning — and something unseen was waiting. Watching.

The knock at the door was soft, but it pierced the heavy silence of the room like a knife. Izzie froze, every instinct screaming that something was wrong.

Callum's voice rumbled from just outside the door. "Izzie, open up. We need to talk."

Her heart skipped a beat. She threw a robe over herself, then moved to the door, opening it to reveal Callum's brooding form. His face was tight with tension, his eyes sharp and piercing. Behind him stood Rhys, his casual stance a stark contrast to the storm brewing in Callum's expression.

"What's going on?" Izzie asked, her voice laced with concern.

They stepped into the room, the door shutting softly behind them. Callum didn't answer right away, instead pulling a folded piece of paper from his jacket and tossing it onto the bed in front of her. The wax seal had already been broken, the words hastily scrawled in a hand that was all too familiar.

Izzie's breath caught as she read the note.

Tell me what you know about the Harp. If you don't, Thorne will make sure you regret it.

Her pulse pounded as she stared at the crumpled letter in her hand. The mention of Thorne — the collector — sent a chill down her spine. She hadn't heard from his fixer in nearly two weeks, but that didn't mean he had stopped watching. Now, after everything, he was back. He wanted the Harp. He was going to use her to get to it.

"Dammit," she muttered, her fingers tightening around the paper. "This isn't over."

Rhys leaned against the wall, arms crossed, his golden gaze sharp. "This Thorne's threats don't scare me," he said, voice edged with challenge. "We've fought off worse. You know how this works, Izzie. Give him just enough to make him think he's winning, keep him off our backs while we find the Harp and get it to the Draconic Council's vault."

Callum's expression was darker, his stance rigid with tension. "We can't play his game," he said, his voice low but firm. "This isn't just about us — it's about the Harp. If he gets his hands on it, we have no idea what he'll do. And I won't risk you, either, Izzie."

The weight of their gazes pressed on her. Rhys' approach — bold and head-on — was tempting, but Callum's caution carried a different weight, one laced with something more than just strategy. Protection.

"So what's the plan?" she asked, her voice tight, the weight of the night still lingering in her bones. The magic of the geas still pulsed beneath her skin, but the reality of the danger closing in was impossible to ignore.

Callum exhaled, jaw clenched. "We can't stay here. The longer we wait, the closer Thorne gets."

Rhys pushed off the wall, stepping toward her. "Then we stop waiting. We take the fight to him."

Her breath caught as their words settled between them. The Harp, the geas, the danger — it was all tangled together now. There was no turning back.

A sharp exhale escaped her lips. She felt like she was standing on a precipice, the ground slipping beneath her feet as the choice between danger and desire pressed on her shoulders. There was no easy answer. And the choice — her choice — would define everything from this point onward.

* * * *

Izzie stood at the edge of the cliffs, wind sweeping through her hair, the scent of salt filling her lungs.

Below her, the sea churned, its rhythmic crash against the rocks hypnotic. Sunlight bathed everything in a pale, almost ethereal glow, casting shadows across the landscape as if the world itself was holding its breath.

Something stirred within her, a pull deeper than any physical attraction she had ever known. The world she'd been thrust into — the dragons, the geas, the brothers — was no longer something she simply had to navigate. It was a call, and in the depths of her being, she could feel herself answering it. The lines between desire, fear, and destiny blurred in that moment, and it wasn't just a matter of choice anymore.

She wasn't just here because the brothers had claimed her. She was here because she belonged.

A soft, steady step behind her interrupted her thoughts. She didn't need to turn around to know who it was. Tavish had a way of moving, an almost silent presence that spoke of quiet strength and unspoken power. He had been watching her since the ceremony, his dark gaze never far from her, assessing, waiting.

"You should be back in the manor," he murmured, his voice a low rasp that slid across her skin like velvet. "It's not safe for you to be away from at least one of us." His breath brushed against the back of her neck, warm and intimate, sending a shiver down her spine.

Izzie took a slow breath, steadying herself before turning to face him. He was just as she remembered — dark, brooding, with eyes that seemed to hold the storm of a thousand unspoken thoughts. Tavish wasn't like the others. Where Callum was protective and Rhys was a challenge, Tavish was an enigma, his presence magnetic in a way that unsettled her and drew her in all at once.

She gazed at him, something flickering in her chest, a pull she couldn't explain. The moment felt heavy with anticipation, as if the world was holding its breath, waiting for her to make a decision.

"I've been thinking," she said, her voice barely above a whisper, but carrying the weight of everything that had been building since the moment the geas had bound her to them. She swallowed, her throat tight. "I'm not just here by accident. I'm not just here because of the geas or because of...whatever this is." She stepped closer to him, her eyes never leaving his. "I'm here because I want to be."

Tavish's gaze softened, the storm in his eyes giving way to something gentler — though it was no less intense. He smiled, something that could have been a smile, but it was elusive, like a secret he wasn't ready to share.

"And what is it you want, little one?" he asked, his tone almost teasing, but the underlying tension in his voice made it clear he was just as ready as she was to step further into whatever this was.

Izzie's heart thundered in her chest. Every moment, every choice she had made had led to this. She could feel it in her bones, in the very air around her — the draw to this world, to these men. And right now, to Tavish, whose quiet intensity both comforted and unnerved her.

She reached out, her hand brushing against his chest, feeling the steady beat of his heart under her fingertips. She closed the distance between them, her voice low but filled with certainty.

"I want you. All of you."

Tavish's eyes darkened, slipping his hand around her waist, pulling her into him. The air between them sizzled, crackling with electricity as he leaned down, his lips barely brushing against hers.

"I thought you might say that," he murmured, and in that moment, all of Izzie's doubts, all of her fears, melted away. She knew, without question, that she was ready to claim her place in their world.

And Tavish would be the one to help her take that first step.

"You know," she said, her voice trembling slightly, "I'm glad you followed me out here. I feel like we barely know each other, and yet...here we are, bonded."

Tavish turned to face her, his gaze thoughtful, his touch featherlight as he brushed a stray lock of hair from her face. "Dragons have long lives, Izzie," he murmured. "Time moves differently for us. Even if we're not together forever, that doesn't change what you mean to me now." He smiled the smallest of smiles. "We have time to figure this out — to truly know each other. And I want that."

Warmth spread through Izzie's chest, a sense of hope and possibility that she hadn't felt in a long time. She reached out, her hand finding his, their fingers intertwining as if they had been meant to do so.

"I'd like that," she whispered, her eyes searching his. But all she saw was a deep sincerity, a genuine desire to understand her, to know her.

Tavish smiled, a slow, sensual curve that sent a shiver down Izzie's spine. "Good," he murmured, tracing circles on the back of her hand with his thumb. "Because I want to know everything about you, Izzie. I want to learn your secrets, your desires, your fears."

Izzie's breath caught in her throat, her pulse quickening at his words. She knew that she should be cautious, that she should take things slow, but there was something about Tavish that made her want to throw caution to the wind.

She stepped closer, her body pressing against his as she looked up at him through her lashes. "And what about you?" she breathed, her lips just inches from his. "What are your secrets, your desires?"

Tavish's eyes darkened, his gaze dropping to her mouth. "I have many desires, Izzie," he said, his voice a low growl. "But right now, the only thing I desire is you."

Izzie's heart raced as he leaned down, pressing his lips against hers in a feather-light kiss. She gasped, fisting her hands in the fabric of his shirt as she pulled him closer, deepening the kiss.

Tavish groaned, wrapping his arms around her waist as he lifted her off her feet, carrying her away from the edge of the cliff. He laid her down on the soft peat, his body covering hers as he continued to kiss her, moving his lips from her mouth to her neck, his teeth grazing her sensitive skin.

Izzie arched beneath him, roaming her hands over his back, feeling the hard muscles beneath his shirt. She wanted him, needed him in a way special to him.

Tavish moved his hands to the buttons of her shirt, deftly undoing them one by one until her shirt fell open, revealing her lacy bra. He paused, his eyes drinking in the sight of her, his breath coming in short, sharp gasps.

"You're so beautiful," he murmured, cupping her breast through the thin fabric of her bra. "So fucking beautiful."

Izzie whimpered, her hips bucking against his as he rolled her nipple between his fingers, sending sparks of pleasure shooting through her body. She reached for his shirt, tugging at it impatiently until he sat up, allowing her to pull it over his head and toss it aside.

His chest was broad and muscular, his skin tan and smooth. Izzie ran her hands over his chest, marveling at the way his muscles rippled beneath her touch. She leaned forward, trailing her lips over his skin, her tongue darting out to taste him.

Tavish groaned, tangling his hands in her hair as he guided her lower, his erection pressing against her through his pants. Izzie fumbled with his belt, her fingers trembling with anticipation as she finally freed him from his confines.

He was hard and thick, his cock pulsing with need. Izzie wrapped her hand around him, stroking him slowly, feeling him twitch in her grasp. Tavish's head fell back, his hips rocking into her touch as he moaned her name.

But Izzie wanted more. She wanted to taste him, to feel him in her mouth. She shifted, positioning herself between his legs as she leaned down, flicking her tongue out to lick the bead of moisture from the tip of his cock.

Tavish hissed, gripping her hair as she took him into her mouth, her lips stretching around his girth. She bobbed her head, taking him deeper with each stroke, her tongue swirling around his shaft.

"Fuck, Izzie," Tavish groaned, his hips thrusting up to meet her mouth. "Your mouth feels so fucking good."

Izzie moaned around him, the vibrations sending him closer to the edge. She could feel him throbbing, could taste the salty tang of his pre-cum on her tongue.

She wanted him to come, wanted to feel him lose control.

But Tavish had other plans. He pulled her off him, gripping her shoulders as he pushed her onto her back. He quickly divested her of her shirt and jeans, bra and panties, his eyes dark with lust as he took in the sight of her naked body.

"God, you're perfect," he breathed, roaming his hands over her skin, dipping his fingers between her legs to find her wet and ready. "I want to taste you, Izzie. I want to feel you come on my tongue."

Izzie whimpered, her hips arching into his touch as he stroked her, sliding his fingers through her folds, teasing her clit. She was so close, so desperate for release.

Tavish lowered his head, his tongue replacing his fingers as he licked her, closing his lips around her clit and sucking gently. Izzie cried out, fisting her hands in his hair as he worked her, his tongue delving deep inside her, tongue-fucking her with a rhythm that had her thighs quivering.

She came with a sharp cry, her body convulsing as waves of pleasure crashed over her. Tavish didn't stop, lapping at her with his tongue, drawing out her orgasm until she was boneless and spent.

He kissed his way back up her body, trailing his lips over her stomach, her breasts, her neck until he reached her mouth. He kissed her deeply, his tongue tangling with hers, letting her taste herself on his lips.

His erection pressed against Izzie's thigh, hot and hard. She reached between them, guiding him to her entrance, moaning as he slid inside her, stretching her, filling her completely.

Tavish groaned, his hips rocking against hers as he began to move, his thrusts slow and deep. Izzie wrapped her legs around his waist, her heels digging into his ass as she urged him on, wanting him deeper, harder.

They moved together, their bodies slick with sweat, the sound of their moans and the crash of the waves below filling the air. Tavish's thrusts became more urgent, more desperate, his hips snapping forward as he chased his release.

Izzie's own orgasm was building again, her walls tightening around him as he hit that spot inside her that made her see stars. She clung to him, her nails raking down his back as she teetered on the edge, her body tense and ready.

"Come with me, Izzie," Tavish growled, his voice rough with need. "I want to feel you come around my cock."

Those words were all it took. Izzie shattered, her body convulsing as she came with a scream, her inner walls squeezing him tight. Tavish followed her over the edge, his cock pulsing inside her as he filled her with his seed.

They collapsed together, their bodies still joined as they panted and trembled in the aftermath of their lovemaking. Tavish rolled to the side, pulling Izzie into his arms, pressing his lips to her forehead, her cheeks, her lips in soft kisses.

"That was incredible," he murmured, tracing his fingers in patterns on her skin. "You're incredible, Izzie. I'm so glad Rhys and Callum found you. I'm so glad they brought you to us."

Izzie smiled, her heart full and her body sated. Their relationship was still new, and they had a lot to learn about each other. But in that moment, as she lay in his arms, feeling the warmth of the setting sun on her skin, she knew that she had made the right choice.

Chapter Twenty-Six

Margaret Alden arrived on the Isle of Skye as the evening fog rolled in from the sea, cloaking the island in ethereal mist. Her boat cut through the waters toward the manor house, its high stone walls barely visible through the twilight haze. The air was thick with anticipation, both for her reunion with Izzie and the purpose of her visit.

The brothers were already waiting at the estate's dock, greeting her warmly. Finn regarded her with a steady, unreadable gaze. Lorcan's mischievous smile remained intact, and Tavish offered a quiet nod of acknowledgment. Rhys was conspicuously absent, disappearing into the estate's shadows as he often did, his mood dark and brooding. And Callum was back at the house with Izzie, unwilling to leave her alone even behind the safety of their gates.

Margaret gave them a knowing look as she disembarked. She had heard the stories of Izzie's time with the five brothers. She'd felt the pull of the situation from afar. This was something she'd been expecting, though she didn't yet know how it would unfold. Izzie had made her choice, but the reality of it was still unclear — both for Izzie and those who cared for her.

As the brothers ushered Margaret into the study, gravity filled the room. Margaret could already sense the tension building in the manor — she had always been attuned to such things. There was a weight to this visit, something not entirely known, even to her. The air seemed heavy with secrets, and as they moved to sit, the silence stretched, almost unbearably so.

Once the social niceties were handled, the brothers settled down to business.

"I trust you've come to check in on our bondmate," Finn said, his voice as cool and distant as the wind from the sea. He was trying to mask his unease, but Margaret could see through it.

Margaret's eyes narrowed, taking in his words, the subtle wariness in his posture. "In a way," she replied. "I've come to see how she is…how all of you are. This arrangement — well, I'm curious about its consequences."

Tavish, ever observant, remained silent. His gaze shifted between Margaret and the others, though he said nothing. He didn't need to. His presence alone was enough to stir the atmosphere.

Callum came through the door to the study just then, having left Izzie in her bedroom changing. She hadn't known her employer was coming. It was a surprise to her, and she wanted to present a mature image. As the oldest, Callum stepped forward, his expression serious. "I trust this is more than just a check-up, Ms. Alden," he said, voice low. There was something in his tone — an edge — that hinted at the deeper emotions he was grappling with. "Is this something you think we can sustain? This choice she's made?"

Margaret's gaze softened, though her answer was weighted with experience. "The path she's chosen has consequences, Callum. That much is clear. But I know Izzie well enough to understand she'll come to terms with it. Just as you all will."

The silence that followed was thick with understanding, each person in the room feeling the gravity of the situation. Just as the tension reached its peak, the door creaked open. Izzie stood at the threshold, her presence commanding the room. She was different now—changed by the choices she had made and the path she was now walking.

Izzie stepped into the room, her posture rigid with both anticipation and uncertainty. Margaret's eyes softened as she took in Izzie's appearance. There was a new aura around her—something that hadn't been there before. The energy in the room shifted as Izzie crossed the threshold, a quiet, magnetic pull to her presence that spoke of both vulnerability and power.

Margaret's smile widened at the sight of her. "So you've done it. You've accepted the geas. I knew you could do it." Her tone was warm yet perceptive. "I knew it, Izzie. I could feel it in the air when we spoke before." She motioned for Izzie to sit, and the two women locked eyes for a brief moment, both understanding the weight of the conversation that was about to unfold.

Izzie sank into a chair across from Margaret, her fingers brushing against the soft fabric of her wool skirt. Her gaze was distant, lost in her thoughts, as she tried to process the storm of emotions that had been flooding her since the ceremony a few days earlier. "I thought I understood what it meant," she began quietly, her voice soft but steady. "But I was wrong."

The study was quiet, the fire in the hearth crackling softly, casting flickering light over the dark wood paneling and the collection of books lining the shelves. Callum stood near the fireplace, arms crossed over his broad chest, his expression unreadable. Finn leaned against the far wall, his fingers rolling a coin across his knuckles, his face neutral. Lorcan, perched on the edge of the desk, stilled where he had been flipping through a book, his easygoing demeanor sharpened with focus. Tavish sat in the high-backed chair closest to Izzie, his eyes shadowed as he listened.

Margaret raised an eyebrow, waiting for Izzie to continue.

Izzie swallowed, aware of how still the room had become, how each of the men—her men—was watching her. She took a steadying breath, pressing her lips together before speaking.

"The night of the meet and greet at Eldritch Curiosities," she said, voice quieter than she intended, "when I slept with the three shifters, I thought it was just that. Sex. Hot, intense, mind-blowing sex." She forced herself to meet Margaret's gaze, but she could feel the weight of the others' attention. "But that was just physical. Just a release. I expected it to be like that."

She glanced around then, gauging their reactions. Callum's jaw was tight, his arms still crossed, but his fingers curled, as if gripping something unseen. Finn's coin had stopped moving, his knuckles white. Lorcan's lips had curved, but the usual mischief in his expression was absent, replaced by something sharp and assessing. Tavish, quiet as ever, stared at the floor, his throat working as if swallowing words before they could escape.

Izzie pressed on. "Even here, when I had sex with Callum and Rhys, before…it was different. But when I went through the geas ceremony," she said, her voice thickening with emotion, "it wasn't just sex. It was like…I became part of them. Like I wasn't just bound to them by physical desire but by something deeper, something I can't quite explain. It's like my soul is tangled with theirs. It's not just my body, Margaret. It's every part of me."

The silence stretched, heavy and charged. The tension in the room was palpable, unspoken thoughts simmering just beneath the surface.

Chapter Twenty-Seven

Izzie's thoughts whirled with emotions as she wandered through the estate's lush gardens, the cool breeze of Skye carrying the scent of the sea and earth. The sound of waves crashing against the cliffs echoed in the distance, but all Izzie could hear was the hum in her chest — the constant, vibrating pulse that tied her to the brothers.

Margaret Alden had left that morning, but her visit left a lingering mark on Izzie's soul, one she couldn't quite shake. The reality of what she'd agreed to, what was expected of her, was sinking in, and it terrified her. The thought of losing any part of what she'd built with the five brothers — of becoming separated from them — was like a raw wound that refused to heal. She wasn't ready. She wasn't ready for the changes that would come, the inevitable pulling away from some of them once she conceived.

From four of them, leaving her bonded for life to only one.

But even now, her connection to them had deepened, and as much as the fear gnawed at her, there was an undeniable pull, an ache that had become a part of her.

When Rhys found her in the garden, the emotions she was struggling to contain came surging to the surface. He appeared at her side, his presence a shadow in the shifting light of the day. The heat from his body radiated, and she felt it immediately, the way his energy wrapped around hers. A possessive pulse. A heavy breath in the air.

"You're thinking about it," Rhys murmured, his voice soft but threaded with intent. "The change that's coming. The change you'll have to accept."

Izzie stiffened, but before she could turn to face him, he was there, his hand on her waist, tugging her against him. His thumb stroked the skin of her side beneath her sweater, his gaze intense as he stared down at her.

"I can feel it," he said, his breath warm against her ear. "You're afraid. But you're not afraid of me, are you?"

Izzie couldn't breathe, couldn't think. She opened her mouth to respond, but Rhys cut her off, his voice dropping lower, his tone thick with dominance. "You know you belong to me just as much as you belong to the others. I can feel it in you, feel it deep inside."

Her breath hitched in her throat, and a shiver ran down her spine. Rhys was playing with her, teasing her—and she hated how much she liked it. His words wrapped around her like chains, and for a moment, she could do nothing but submit to him. Give in completely.

"Tell me you can feel it too, Izzie," Rhys murmured, his lips brushing her ear. "Tell me you can feel me inside you, in your blood."

She gasped at the intensity of the reaction that surged through her—hot, overwhelming desire, pooling low in her belly. The pleasure was undeniable, but so was the power. Rhys was exerting his control over her again, pushing and pulling at her emotions, drawing out her responses with frightening ease.

"I can feel it," she whispered, her voice barely audible.

Rhys smiled, a slow, predatory curve of his lips. "Good girl."

Izzie could barely contain the storm that raged inside her. The bond wasn't just about pleasure—it was a power that left her breathless, a pull so strong it made her dizzy. Rhys wasn't just enjoying her reactions—he was controlling them. Her body, her mind, were all at his mercy.

What if he turned out to be the one? The one she spent the rest of her life bonded to?

Was she strong enough to find her place in a relationship like that? The thought left her shaken, but the feeling that lingered—the mix of desire and something darker, something more dangerous—was enough to make her heart race.

But as much as she longed to ignore it, the truth was undeniable. Rhys, and all of the brothers, held more power over her than she had ever imagined. And the consequences of this bond, of this life she had chosen, were only just beginning to make themselves known.

Callum stood at the edge of the garden, hidden in the shadows where the stone walls of the manor met the overgrown vines and moss. His piercing gaze tracked Izzie and Rhys from a distance, the pull of their connection too strong for him to ignore. His jaw tightened, a low growl rising in his chest as he watched Rhys, the alpha of the brothers, exerting his dominance over her with ease. It wasn't the first time Rhys had tested Izzie—no, he'd been doing it since the very first day she arrived in Scotland. But today, something in Callum stirred that made the possessiveness he felt for her surge, unbidden and raw.

Izzie's response was clear to him, even from across the garden. Her pulse quickened, her body reacting to Rhys' words. Callum could see the conflict in her—a part of her was undeniably drawn to it, to him. And yet, Izzie was not like any other. She was not made to be bent by force alone.

That's what I have to remind her of.

He took a step forward, his large form moving with quiet grace, and approached them, brushing his hand against the stone wall as he made his way toward her. Rhys' predatory smile faltered as he noticed Callum's approach. But he said nothing—Rhys knew better than to challenge the firstborn dragon in the presence of their mate.

"Izzie," Callum said softly, his voice carrying the weight of affection and concern. His hand reached out, cupping her face as he guided her gaze to meet his. "You don't have to let him pull you like that. You don't have to be at his mercy."

Rhys' sharp eyes flicked between them, the tension thickening. The air between Callum and Izzie seemed to hum, but it wasn't the electric charge of desire—it was something more protective. Callum was not playing games with her like Rhys. He wasn't going to make her feel small and uncertain.

"I feel it, too," Izzie whispered, her eyes flicking between Rhys and Callum. "But it's not just him — it's all of you. You all have this...power over me, and I'm not sure what to do with it."

The vulnerability in her voice made something tighten in Callum's chest. His thumb stroked her cheek, brushing away a tear that had fallen unbeknownst to her.

"You don't have to do anything, love," he said, his voice low and firm. "You just need to be with me. With us. But not like this." He glanced at Rhys, who was now watching them with an unreadable expression. "You deserve more than this."

Izzie looked down, the weight of the situation sinking in deeper than ever before. She felt as though she were being pulled in so many directions, each brother offering something different, something intense and unfamiliar. But she knew one thing for certain.

This was only the beginning.

Chapter Twenty-Eight

Dario sat in his cramped bedroom in the Skye B and B, the faint scent of pinewood from the furniture mixing with the cool, salty air drifting in from the sea. The room was sparse, almost Spartan, with whitewashed walls that closed in on him, reflecting the somber nature of his task. The desk in front of him was made of golden, polished oak, its surface gleaming under the overhead light. A window across the room was ajar, distant waves crashing in the background, but the noise felt muffled, distant, like everything around him was pressing in.

Dario adjusted his chair, leaning forward, his body angled just so, as though the precise alignment of his form could somehow influence the outcome of the moment. His gaze was fixed on the tablet before him, the flickering glow from its screen casting a pale light across his sharp features. His fingers hovered above it, poised yet twitching with the tension that hummed through the air. His hands were clammy, betraying the calm he tried to project. Every instinct in his body screamed at him to move, but he remained still, like a man about to pull a thread that would unravel everything.

He took in a slow, steadying breath, but even that felt forced, as if his lungs were reluctant to fill. His mind raced, calculating every possible angle, every potential consequence. This wasn't going to go well.

The stillness in the room was oppressive, but it was the kind of silence that demanded action. And he wasn't sure he was ready for what would come next. The flicker of unease that passed over him wasn't something he could easily dismiss. But there was no turning back now.

"Here goes nothing," he muttered under his breath before the screen lit up, his voice carrying a note of resolve but also hesitation, a subtle crack in his armor.

"Mr. Thorne, I have the information you requested." Dario's voice broke the silence, clipped and efficient, but with a trace of something deeper that lingered beneath his words. The kind of hesitation that could never be fully hidden.

Across the screen, Maximilian Thorne's eyes gleamed with cold intensity, a dangerous focus that sent a chill down Dario's spine. Thorne's broad shoulders were hunched forward as he leaned toward the screen, his entire being coiled tight with anticipation. In the shadows of his opulent office, soft light glinted off the wall of windows behind him, a reflection of the hardness in his expression.

"Go on," Thorne growled, his voice low and gravelly, thick with the weight of a man who had waited far too long, thirsting for the information that

Dario now held. His presence, even through the call, demanded respect.

Dario's throat tightened, the weight of the revelation pressing heavily on his chest. "I bribed one of the servants who works for the dragon brothers," he began, his tone steady, though the faint tremor of discomfort lingered in the air. He kept his eyes on the tablet in front of him, unwilling to meet Thorne's gaze directly. "He's been with them for quite some time and knows their comings and goings. He confirmed…rumors about a ceremony. And about Miss Rhodes."

At the mention of Izzie, Thorne's face hardened, his brows knitting together in a deep frown. The sharp lines of his jaw flexed as his expression turned calculating.

"What ceremony?" Thorne demanded, his voice rising with a simmering anger, now unable to hold back. His fingers dug into the arms of his chair, the need for answers clear in every taut muscle of his body.

Dario exhaled, attempting to steady himself. He brushed his fingers across the screen of the tablet as he began recounting the details, his words now hesitant, as though reluctant to voice the unspeakable. "The servant mentioned…a ritual. A ceremony where the five brothers — those wicked men — had their way with Miss Rhodes. She was, as he described it, led by them, dressed only in her skin. And there, in front of them, she was laid bare on a stone table."

Thorne's eyes flashed with dangerous, volatile fury. His teeth clenched so tightly that his jaw muscle twitched, and his breathing became heavier. His pulse quickened with the rage building inside him. The darkness of the words hit him harder than he expected. The blood drained from his face, leaving a cold, grim pallor. His chest tightened, as if the very air around him had thickened with the weight of his mounting disgust.

Dario's hands trembled as he clicked a button on the tablet, bringing up the video the servant had taken from the hidden camera in the room during the ritual. The grainy footage flickered to life, and Dario didn't dare look up. Instead, his gaze remained focused on the screen before him, the sharp edge of dread making his heartbeat erratic.

On the screen, Izzie appeared, fragile and exposed. Surrounded by the five men, each wearing a kilt, they towered over her with a hunger in their eyes that chilled Thorne to his core. As the video zoomed in, Thorne saw Izzie, hesitating but not fighting back, as the men removed her negligee, their hands brushing over her delicate form. She looked small, almost childlike in that moment, overwhelmed by the presence of these men, though she did not resist.

Had she been drugged? Was this what his daughter Mia had endured?

The next moments were far worse. The camera captured Izzie being led toward the obsidian plinth, a massive slab of smooth, black stone, its sharp angles casting eerie reflections in the dim candlelight. The men moved with slow, deliberate steps, their power dominating the scene, as they laid her bare—completely vulnerable—atop the stone. Golden runes flickered on the video, and the girl was forced to drink something. Drugged, for sure.

Thorne's fist shot out, slamming against the edge of his desk with a sharp crack, the sound echoing throughout the room. His chest heaved with the rush of emotion that swept through him. Rage. Sorrow.

Desperation. A mixture of fury and heartbreak that left him gasping.

"No…" Thorne whispered, his voice barely audible, thick with pain and disbelief. His fingers, white-knuckled, dug into the edge of the desk as the image of his daughter, Mia, flashed into his mind. His heart shattered with the sickening realization — this had been done to Mia. He could feel it in his bones.

Dario let the silence linger for a moment, before speaking softly, almost apologetically. "I'm sorry, Mr. Thorne. But this is what happened. I thought you should know."

Thorne ran a shaking hand through his hair, his mind spinning as his heart sank deeper into the abyss. His daughter had been through this. The same evil. The same darkness.

"Damn them," he muttered under his breath, his voice filled with venom and pain. His eyes were burning with a single, unrelenting desire.

Fucking dragons. He would make them all pay.

Dario's gaze softened for just a moment, his expression faltering as he glanced at Thorne, the man whose orders he had followed without question for so long. The cold, steely resolve that usually dominated Thorne's features was still present, but beneath it, Dario could sense a deep, simmering fury that threatened to consume everything in its path.

"Mr. Thorne, I know you feel this deeply," Dario began, his voice quieter now, almost reluctant, as if the words weighed on him. "But I'm afraid it doesn't end there. Miss Rhodes…she's changed." His eyes lingered on the tablet in front of him for a moment before he met Thorne's gaze again, his face softening with genuine concern. "She's showing signs of heightened senses.

She can feel things—things she didn't before. Magic is flowing through her."

Thorne's posture immediately shifted, his broad shoulders tensing as his eyes snapped to Dario. His once casual demeanor evaporated, replaced by a hard, calculating edge. "What do you mean?" he demanded, his voice low but sharp, like a knife being unsheathed. "What kind of power?"

Dario hesitated, unsure how much to reveal, the weight of it all pressing down on him. He wasn't sure he could stomach keeping any more secrets. "She can sense the magic around her," Dario explained, his fingers fidgeting with the edge of his tablet. "She reacts differently to it. It's…not just a change in perception. She's—" He stopped himself, unwilling to voice what he feared most.

After a long pause, he continued, his voice quieter, filled with a mix of awe and dread. "She's something more now. I think the ceremony did something to her, something that's awakened her magic. And I'm worried that with each passing day, she'll grow stronger. She could become a serious threat."

The words lingered in the air between them, heavy and foreboding. Thorne was silent for a moment, his face hardening as his mind began to race. He sat back in his chair, eyes narrowing in thought. "No," he growled, his voice colder now, sharper than ever. "That's not what I want." His eyes gleamed with an almost predatory hunger. "I want her for myself. I want to control that power." His lips curled into a cruel smile. "And to do that, I need her. She is the key."

A cold shiver ran down Dario's spine at the way Thorne's gaze darkened, becoming almost predatory. He had known Thorne was ruthless, but hearing him speak so openly about his intentions for Izzie sent a wave of unease through him. Thorne's eyes locked on Dario with a weight that pinned him to the spot.

"What do you plan to do with her once you have her, sir?" Dario asked carefully, his voice betraying a subtle undercurrent of fear. He had always followed Thorne's orders without question, but something about this felt different. The coldness in Thorne's words, the way he spoke of using Izzie as a pawn in his own twisted game—it unsettled him.

Thorne leaned forward, his fingers drumming a steady, menacing rhythm on the edge of his desk as his voice dropped to a dangerous murmur. "I'll make her mine," he growled, each word edged with an unmistakable malice. "I'll use her magic, twist it to my will. She'll help me find Mia. And when I do...the dragons will regret ever crossing me."

Dario nodded, the familiar weight of agreement settling over him, but a darker thought slithered through his mind. Thorne's hunger wasn't just for power. The way he spoke, the gleam in his eyes... Dario's stomach tightened as he imagined what else Thorne might claim. A sudden shudder ran through him, an unsettling realization creeping in. *Maybe it's not just her power he desires...*

He forced the thought aside, but the flicker of pity for Izzie lingered. She was nothing more than a pawn in a game far darker than she could imagine, and Dario wasn't sure she even realized what was coming for her.

"I understand," he said, his voice more distant than he intended.

Thorne's gaze grew colder, harder. His eyes locked onto Dario's with an intensity that felt like a weight pressing down on him. The air in the room seemed to thicken, suffocating. "Make no mistake, Dario," Thorne said, his voice colder than the deepest winter. "Bring her to me. If you fail, I'll make you regret it."

Dario swallowed hard, the lump in his throat a heavy, uncomfortable weight. His chest tightened, and for a moment, he wasn't sure if he could carry out the orders Thorne had given him. But he had no choice. He couldn't back out now, not when the stakes were this high.

"I'll do what needs to be done, sir," Dario replied, his voice barely above a whisper as he turned off the video feed.

The screen went dark, and for a long moment, the silence in the room felt suffocating. Izzie would soon be Thorne's, and the dragons would pay.

Chapter Twenty-Nine

The night was heavy with silence, the kind that only settled over the ancient stone walls of the Skye manor, where shadows lingered long after the sun had disappeared. The fire crackled softly in Izzie's bedroom hearth, its warmth a gentle pulse against the chill that had begun creeping through the cracks in the window frame.

Izzie lay between Lorcan and Finn, the heat of their bodies on either side, their steady breathing a slow rhythm that seemed to echo in the dim room. Her skin thrummed with the aftershock of their touch — electric, demanding, hunger fulfilled. There was a deep ache in her bones, but it wasn't pain... It was the strange and satisfying weight of satisfaction, of something carved into the marrow of her being. The air around her was heavy with the scent of them — wild, primal, with a thread of smoke and earth, a heady mixture that clung to her skin like a spell.

For a moment, she let herself drift, the edges of her thoughts fading into a fog of sleep, her heart still racing from the fire that had burned through them only a short time ago. The warmth of their bodies enveloped her, pulling her deeper into the quiet, safe cocoon they had built around her.

The world split open.

Izzie's ribs seized, her breath strangled in her throat as something razor-sharp tore through the night. Glass exploded somewhere below — a thousand crystalline fragments screaming against stone. The vibration slammed into her chest like a fist, her heart lurching sideways before hammering against her sternum.

The peaceful warmth between the brothers shattered. Every muscle in her body coiled tight, her skin suddenly electric with the wrongness flooding the manor. Sleep fled as if burned away, leaving her raw and exposed to whatever had just violated their sanctuary.

Lorcan and Finn were awake before the last echo of breaking glass had finished trembling through the manor. She could feel the change in them — the sharpness, the predatory focus that slid like ice into their bones. She felt it as if it was her own skin that suddenly became too tight, as though the air had turned thick with their growing tension. She was caught in their wake, a bystander to the sudden shift in the atmosphere.

Lorcan's voice, low and guttural, broke the stillness, carrying with it the weight of command. "Dress. Now."

There was no time for questions. No time for hesitation. His tone was cutting, and something deep inside her responded. She scrambled from between them, the bedclothes tangled around her as she fumbled to the edge of the bed, her bare skin cold as the night air cut through the room. But even as she moved, she could feel them. The brothers were already rising, their bodies shifting in sync, a fluid movement of muscle and bone as they pulled on their clothes and slipped into their shoes.

Their movements were a blur, fast, like shadows cast by moonlight, their power vibrating through the house in waves that made the very floor beneath her seem to hum. The weight of their presence filled the room like a storm gathering strength.

Izzie didn't question. She grabbed for the clothes tossed across the room, her fingers shaking with energy. Her pulse was frantic, dancing in her throat, an ache that wasn't just physical anymore—it was a visceral, raw connection to whatever danger was now creeping through the manor like an unwelcome specter.

She dressed quickly, her mind spinning, the heat of the brothers' presence lingering on her skin, the scent of them tangled in her hair. Her body was heavy with the aftermath of their union, but her heart raced in a different way now. She grabbed her running shoes, then followed Finn and Lorcan. Her feet were bare against the cold floor of the hallway, the chill sharp against her skin, but it was nothing compared to the urgency that hummed beneath her ribs.

Izzie's breath came in ragged gasps as she met the brothers in the hallway, their powerful frames blocking the wide passage, their eyes blazing with an intensity that mirrored her own panic. Rhys stood at the forefront, his gaze fierce, a stark contrast to the sharpness in his movements as he scanned the area. Finn, Lorcan, and Tavish flanked him, their expressions taut. Each of them was ready for whatever came next, but none of them hesitated when their eyes found Izzie. Callum moved closer, taking her hand in his.

Her heart pounded against her ribs, but there was no room for questions. There was only the undeniable urgency that filled the air like smoke, thick and choking. Rhys' voice broke through the chaos, low and demanding.

"Izzie's safety comes first," he commanded, his tone firm and unwavering. "Callum, take her to the roof. Get her out of here. Shift and carry her into the wild. We'll handle this."

Izzie's pulse surged as Callum pulled her against him. His eyes flickered with concern, making her breath catch. Without a word, he wrapped an arm around her shoulders, his grip gentle but sure, pulling her toward the narrow staircase that led to the attic.

As they moved swiftly up the stairs, Izzie could hear the sharp, echoing crack of gunfire from below, sharp and staccato, followed by the thudding of boots on stone. A cold knot formed in her stomach. Her mind screamed for her to turn around, to run back to the brothers, to demand that she stay and fight with them.

This was her home now, too.

But Callum didn't pause. His pace quickened, his hand tight around hers as he guided her up to the top of the house, where the rafters creaked with the weight of centuries. The attic smelled of dust and old wood, the walls seeming to close in as they reached the farthest end.

Callum yanked open a pair of wide doors, the hinges screeching as they swung open to reveal a sky full of stars.

"Get ready," he said, his voice low, the urgency in his words a knife to her gut.

Before she could respond, his form shifted, and in a whirl of midnight blue and silver scales, Callum transformed before her eyes. His body elongated, wings unfurling with a snap that sent a gust of air swirling through the attic. The air smelled of musk and heat, an intoxicating mix of his dragon's essence. Izzie blinked, her mind struggling to adjust to the breathtaking sight.

She'd seen his dragon before, but never like this. Never this powerful. He loomed over her in the dim light from a single overhead bulb, sniffing at her torso. With a soft growl that vibrated the air around her, Callum lowered his head, his glowing amber eyes locking onto hers.

The urgency in his gaze was palpable. "Climb on," he urged.

Her pulse thudded in her throat, but there was no time to hesitate. Trembling, she swung herself onto his back, clutching to the ridged scales that spanned across his shoulders. His dragon's body was hot, thrumming with raw, ancient energy that sent a shiver through her as she pressed herself against him.

Below, the sounds of gunfire continued, sharp and frantic, a battle unfolding in the shadows of the manor.

Callum turned to face the moon. He opened his wings to their full length, and in an instant, they were airborne. The cold night wind whipped past them, pulling at Izzie's hair and stinging her cheeks. Her body pressed against Callum's back as the ground fell away, the manor shrinking beneath them as they soared into the wild unknown. Together they ascended into the inky darkness above the hills.

Izzie clung to him, every instinct screaming at her to look back, to check on the safety of the others. But Callum's form was a solid anchor beneath her, and she trusted him — trusted him to keep her safe, even as the world below her seemed to spiral into chaos.

The wind howled in her ears as they flew higher, the dark silhouette of the manor outlined beneath them. It wasn't until they reached a high hill that Callum's wings slowed, the rush of the air dying down as they landed with a heavy thud.

Izzie slid off his back, her legs weak beneath her, looking back, hoping to see the other brothers following. Her eyes were drawn immediately to the flames licking at the windows of the lower floor of the manor. The fire burned bright against the dark night sky, a stark and terrible contrast to the stillness that had once reigned there.

She turned to Callum, her heart hammering in her chest. "Are they — "

But he held up a hand, his expression hard. "We'll know soon enough. They're not dead, not yet." He placed a hand on her chest. "Breathe. Feel. You can feel them." His voice was calm, but there was a storm building beneath it, a primal edge that made the air between them crackle with tension.

But he was right. Izzie could feel them, inside her. They were fighting, their pulses rapid. They didn't have guns, but they'd all shifted into their dragon forms.

"Are they bullet-proof?" she wondered, her voice low.

Callum shifted beside her, putting his arms around her and pulling her close against the chill of the night.

"Near enough, little one," he said. "Dragon scales are like armor."

It wasn't enough, but it would do. As long as they all made it through unharmed. Together, they looked back at the manor, the smoke rising from its heart like a foul omen.

Above them, the night sky rippled with the movement of vast wings. A gust of wind swept through the glen as four enormous shapes descended in the moonlight, their dark forms cutting through the sky. The ground trembled as they landed atop the ridge, talons sinking into the damp earth before scales shimmered, twisting and contracting. In a heartbeat, the dragons were gone, replaced by the four other brothers — Rhys, Lorcan, Finn, and Tavish — each of them fierce, battle-worn, and breathing hard.

Izzie turned, scanning their faces, searching for any sign of injury. "Are you all okay?"

Rhys, ever the leader, nodded sharply. "We're in one piece." His gaze flicked toward the manor below, where smoke still curled into the night. "Can't say the same for the house, though. We'll need some serious remodeling after that fire on the ground floor."

Finn, brushing soot from his sleeve, let out a low chuckle. "It's built to withstand dragon fire, Izzie. A little pitched battle with mercenaries isn't going to bring it down."

Mercenaries. The word sent a fresh chill down her spine. Izzie swallowed hard. "Is that what this was?"

Lorcan's jaw tensed. "Whoever's after the Harp isn't messing around."

Her heart clenched. It wasn't just the attack, the destruction, or the lingering scent of charred wood that unsettled her — it was the loss of the book they had risked everything to recover from the chapel. "The book," she whispered, devastation creeping into her voice. "We lost it."

For a moment, no one spoke. Then Tavish — silent, steady Tavish — stepped forward. "I read it." His voice was quiet but certain. "Cover to cover."

Callum smiled. "Tavish has the memory of a...well, of a dragon."

Izzie exhaled shakily, torn between relief and disbelief. She met Tavish's gaze, searching. "You remember all of it?"

He inclined his head. "Every word."

Rhys stepped closer, placing a hand on her shoulder. "Right now, we need to get to a safe place and regroup. We'll figure out the search for the Harp once we know you're secure."

Izzie hesitated, casting one last glance toward the burning manor. Then, she let out a breath, nodded, and turned toward the darkened hills beyond.

Izzie's pulse thrummed in her ears as they set off on foot through the thick heather and moss-covered stones, the distant chaos at the manor fading with each step. The weight of the moment pressed heavily on her chest, but she could feel the brothers around her — each one providing a protective force, a shield against the unknown.

Callum's hand was firm on her back, guiding her forward. His body was tense, his shoulders tight with the strain of the situation, but his voice, when he spoke, was calm, as if to assure both of them that no matter what came next, they would be safe.

"We'll protect you. Always," Callum murmured, his breath warm against her ear.

His words should have been comforting, and for a moment, they were. But as they made their way deeper into the wilderness of Skye, Izzie's mind swirled with thoughts she couldn't shake. Her body thrummed with the power of the geas, the connection she shared with the brothers more intense now than ever before. But it wasn't just the bond. It was the growing realization that she didn't need to be protected. Not in the way they thought.

Behind them, Rhys kept pace with the others, his strides long and smooth, the fire of his presence ever palpable. Every so often, Izzie felt the weight of his gaze on her, a searing intensity that made her heart race. There was something in the way he watched her — something that made her question her place in this world.

As they moved further into the wilds of the island, the land untamed and rugged, she caught Rhys' gaze, locked in a silent challenge. His deep, molten eyes seemed to see straight through her, and she found herself holding her breath.

"Are you afraid, Izzie?" Rhys asked, his voice low and almost teasing.

Izzie paused, standing still for a heartbeat as the others moved past, her thoughts spinning faster than she could organize them. The fire inside her was no longer just the heat of attraction — it was something darker, something fiercer, that mirrored the power rising in her veins.

"No," she whispered, her voice carrying an edge of certainty she hadn't realized she possessed. "I'm not afraid."

There was a fleeting moment where Rhys' lips twitched into a faint, knowing smile, and something dangerous flickered in the air between them. It wasn't just sex, it wasn't just the geas — it was something more.

But before she could fully comprehend what was happening between them, Callum was there again, his hand squeezing her shoulder.

"Izzie," he said, his tone firm, but his gaze softening when it met hers. "We'll be safe at the bothy. We'll keep you safe. You've been through enough."

Izzie looked at him, really looked at him, and something twisted in her chest. The weight of her feelings for Callum was undeniable, but she couldn't ignore the simmering tension that bubbled between her and the others. It was more than just attraction. It was a deeper connection — one that made her question the limits of what she thought she knew about herself.

She stepped closer to Callum, her breath catching in her throat as she placed her hand on his chest. "I know you will," she said softly. "But I'm not the same woman I was when I came here."

Callum's eyes softened as he placed his hand over hers. "I know. And that's why we'll help you with whatever comes next."

Izzie's gaze flicked back to Rhys. The spark between them was undeniable, but she was no longer sure of the role she should play in this. She had crossed a line, one that she didn't fully understand yet. She wasn't sure she needed to be sheltered anymore, and part of her wasn't sure if she ever wanted to be.

The wilds of Skye stretched endlessly before them, and the future felt like it was still open for her to choose.

Chapter Thirty

The village was a welcome change from the bothy, the cramped old cottage on the farthest moors. Cobblestone streets wound between whitewashed, slate-roofed cottages, their chimneys trailing thin curls of smoke into the crisp afternoon air. Window boxes spilled over with trailing ivy and climbing roses, bright against the gray stone walls. It was the kind of place that smelled of peat smoke, fresh bread and damp earth — a place where life felt ordinary.

Izzie breathed it all in as she walked beside Lorcan, her fingers brushing the wool of her borrowed coat. For the first time in days, she felt almost normal. No magic thrumming through her veins, no ancient geas pressing against her soul. Just a girl on an outing with a man who, despite his dragon blood, had an easy, human charm about him.

"This was a good idea," she admitted, smiling up at Lorcan. "I needed this."

He grinned. "Aye, I thought you might. You looked ready to claw the walls back at the bothy."

"Did not."

Lorcan gave her a sideways glance. "Did too. Thought Rhys was about to chain you to the floor just to keep you from pacing."

Izzie snorted. "Don't even joke about that."

They passed a butcher shop with strings of sausages hanging in the window, and a baker's stall where a stout woman with ruddy cheeks was stacking fresh scones onto a tray. A few villagers nodded to them as they passed, and for once, no one looked at her like she was something other. Just another visitor, out for a stroll.

Lorcan led Izzie down the narrow lane, heading toward a tiny clothing shop tucked between a post office and a grocer's. The bell above the door jingled as they stepped inside, and the scent of wool and cedar greeted them.

The shop was small, the shelves lined with neatly folded sweaters, sturdy denim and practical outdoor gear suited for the moors. No silks, no delicate lace, nothing like the beautiful things Margaret had curated at Eldritch Curiosities. The fanciest thing there were the floral print cotton dresses, looking like something Princess Diana might have worn on an outing to the country. Izzie swallowed her sigh. She hadn't expected luxury, not after the night they'd had, but the reality of her situation settled a little deeper in her bones.

A stout woman with steel-gray hair peered at them over the counter, adjusting the spectacles perched on the bridge of her nose. "Help ye find somethin'?"

Lorcan, hands shoved in his pockets, tilted his head toward Izzie. "She needs a full kit."

The woman gave her a quick once-over and nodded. "Aye, we'll sort ye out."

Izzie browsed through the offerings, fingers trailing over thick woolen jumpers and flannel-lined coats. Everything was practical, made for bracing winds and long walks over rough terrain. She selected some plain blouses, several Shetland and Fair Isle sweaters, three more pairs of jeans, and a puffy rose-pink jacket that smelled faintly of rain and pine.

Then came the underthings.

The selection was...bleak. No silk chemises, no delicate lace-trimmed bralettes. Just sturdy cotton in white, beige, or a single uninspiring shade of blue. Functional, sensible, and entirely unremarkable. She sighed and grabbed what she needed, ignoring Lorcan's smirk as she tossed them onto the counter.

"Don't say a word," she muttered.

"Wasn't gonna." But the amusement in his eyes betrayed him. He moved closer to whisper in her ear. "We'll have 'em off ye in seconds, ye know it. Doesna matter how girly they are...or aren't."

Izzie couldn't help blushing at the thought.

The woman rang up their purchases, wrapping them neatly in brown paper before sliding them into a large cloth duffel bag. "Ye'll be wantin' boots, too, if ye mean to be trampin' about."

Izzie glanced down at her battered running shoes, remnants of their mad dash from the estate, and nodded. "Aye, I will."

A pair of well-worn leather boots, a bit scuffed but sturdy — and most importantly, already broken in so she wouldn't get blisters — completed the haul. When they stepped back onto the lane, the wind had picked up, carrying the scent of rain.

Izzie hugged the duffel to her chest, the wide strap digging into her shoulder. "Not exactly a fashion statement."

Lorcan chuckled. "Aye, but at least ye won't freeze."

She rolled her eyes but couldn't suppress a small smile. Practical wasn't the worst thing in the world. And for now, warmth and anonymity were more valuable than silk and lace.

Eventually, weary from their long walk and the morning spent shopping, they slipped into a small, dimly lit pub, eager for a moment's rest. The warm, yeasty scent of ale and meat pies filled the air, mingling with the low hum of conversation. A fire crackled in the hearth, and a fiddler played a slow, mournful tune in the corner.

They found a table near the back, and Lorcan ordered them a round of thick, foamy ale along with two plates of shepherd's pie. Izzie cupped her hands around her mug, savoring the solid weight of it as she let the rich scent of malt and hops fill her senses.

"Feels good, doesn't it?" Lorcan said, leaning back in his chair. "Being around people. No dragons, no magic. No mercs wi' machine guns. Just folk going about their day."

Izzie nodded, taking a sip of her drink. "Yeah. I almost forgot what that felt like."

They ate in comfortable silence, savoring the simple, hearty food. When they were nearly finished, Izzie wiped her hands on her napkin and stood.

"I'm going to use the restroom," she said, pushing back her chair.

Lorcan smirked, his green eyes gleaming with mischief. "Want me to come with you? Quickie in the Ladies' room?"

Izzie rolled her eyes. "Absolutely not."

He laughed, lifting his hands in mock surrender. "Your loss, lass."

Shaking her head, she made her way through the pub, weaving past occupied tables until she reached the narrow hallway leading to the restrooms. The wooden door creaked as she pushed it open, stepping inside. The air inside the narrow bathroom was damp, heavy with the scent of lavender soap.

Then she stopped short.

She wasn't alone.

Izzie barely had time to register the presence behind her before a strong arm wrapped around her waist, yanking her backward. A cloth pressed over her mouth and nose, carrying a sickly sweet scent.

She fought, jerking her body, but whoever held her was stronger. Her magic flared, a wild pulse beneath her skin, but it was sluggish, tangled with the sedative working its way into her system.

Lorcan. He's right outside. If she could just—

Darkness swept in, swift and merciless.

* * * *

Izzie woke to the scent of cold stone and damp earth. Her head throbbed, the edges of her awareness fuzzy. She shifted, but her wrists wouldn't move—bound. A sharp chill crept into her bones, and she shivered as she blinked away the haze clouding her vision.

She was in a vast chamber, the walls built from ancient stone. The floor was uneven, worn by time and weather. Faint moonlight slanted through the tall, narrow windows, casting eerie shadows across the ruined space. Somewhere in the distance, wind howled through the broken remains of an upper level, its voice hollow and mournful.

An abandoned castle.

A presence stirred nearby. A figure moved out of the darkness, slow and deliberate.

Dario.

His sharp features were cast in shadow, his dark eyes unreadable. He leaned against a crumbling archway, arms crossed, watching her wake with the patience of a man who had done this many times before.

"You're tougher than I expected," he murmured. "Most would still be unconscious."

Izzie swallowed against the dryness in her throat. "Lucky me," she rasped.

Dario tilted his head. "Not luck. You've got magic in your blood. It's fighting off the drugs faster than it should. Impressive."

She pulled against her bindings—leather straps looped tight around her wrists, anchored to an iron ring in the floor. Not rope, not chain. They were trying to control her without triggering her magic's defenses.

She forced herself to breathe, to think. Lorcan would realize she was missing. He'd come for her. They all would. She just had to hold on.

A slow, deliberate clap echoed through the chamber.

Izzie stiffened.

A second figure emerged from the shadows, his presence sharp as a blade. Tall, dressed in black, his coat sweeping behind him like the shadow of a bird of prey. He stopped a few feet away, his pale blue eyes cold and calculating as they raked over her.

She didn't know him.

Dario had never given a name—only vague warnings about the powerful man he served. But now, staring into the eyes of this stranger, she knew without a doubt that he was the one.

"Who the hell are you?" she demanded, her voice edged with fury.

The man tilted his head, amusement flickering over his sharp features. "You mean Dario never told you?" His lips curled. "I'm almost offended."

She fought against the cuffs biting into her wrists. "I don't care who you are. Let me go."

He chuckled, a rich, indulgent sound. "Oh, Izzie. I think you'll find that's not how this works." He stepped closer, his presence suffocating. "You may not know me, but I know you. I've been watching. Waiting." His gaze darkened. "And now you are mine."

Izzie's pulse hammered. Cold fury surged through her veins, cutting through the fear. "Like hell I am."

His smirk widened. "I do love a challenge."

Chapter Thirty-One

Two days had passed since the kidnapping. The air inside the ruined castle was thick with the scent of damp stone and old magic. Izzie sat where they had left her, bound at the wrists, her butt pressed against the cold floor. Her muscles ached, her magic simmering beneath her skin, restless, hungry for release. But she held still. She listened.

Footsteps echoed against the stone, deliberate and unhurried.

Thorne.

He emerged from the shadows like something conjured from a nightmare — tall, sharp-featured, draped in a black wool coat against the chill. He carried himself with the confidence of a man who owned the world and expected everyone in it to bow to him.

Izzie sat taller.

She met his gaze and forced steel into her voice. "What do you want from me?"

Thorne studied her, the corners of his mouth tilting slightly. "What I want, Izzie, is for you to make this easy on yourself." He crouched in front of her, close enough that she could see the faint scar along his jaw, the flicker of something unreadable in his pale blue eyes. "Join me willingly, and you might even enjoy yourself."

She snorted. "Not likely."

His expression didn't change. "I thought you'd say that." He reached into his coat and withdrew a small, wickedly sharp dagger, letting it catch the dim light as he turned it between his fingers. "I had hoped to avoid the unpleasant route. But make no mistake, I *will* get what I want."

Izzie kept her breathing steady. "And what exactly is that?"

Thorne twirled the dagger once before slipping it back into his coat. "That depends on you." He leaned in, his voice low, almost conspiratorial. "For now, I want to know what you know about the Harp."

The blood in her veins turned to ice.

The Harp of Ceòthach Glen.

Ancient. Powerful. Dangerous.

She had only begun to scratch the surface of its history, but she knew enough. She knew that in the wrong hands it could bring dragons to their knees, stripping them of their strength, bending them to the will of its master.

She also knew that Thorne wasn't telling her the whole truth.

"You collect artifacts," she said carefully.

Thorne's smile was slow, deliberate. "I do."

"Draconic artifacts."

He inclined his head. "You've been paying attention."

Izzie swallowed the bitter laugh that threatened to escape. He wanted her to believe this was about history, about acquiring rare objects. But she had spent enough time around dragons to understand what this really was.

Power. Control.

She met his gaze, searching for any flicker of hesitation, any weakness. "The Harp isn't another artifact, is it?"

Thorne's smile widened. "Very good." He tapped a finger against his temple. "I knew you were clever."

She forced herself not to react. She couldn't let him see that she knew exactly what he was after.

Because if he found the Harp before she did, the dragons — her dragons — would never be safe again.

A low rumble shuddered through the stone floor beneath Izzie's legs. At first, she thought it was the wind howling through the ruined castle's crumbling walls. But then the vibrations deepened, a steady, ominous rhythm that sent dust cascading from the ceiling.

Thorne stiffened.

Izzie swallowed a smile. *They're here.*

A deafening roar split the night, the kind that didn't belong to anything human. It echoed off the ancient stone, reverberating through her chest, drumbeat of fury. Thorne's gaze snapped toward the castle's arched entrance as the heavy doors exploded inward, ripped from their rusted hinges by a force too great to be mortal.

Smoke and fire filled the threshold.

Then they came.

Callum was first, stepping through the haze with the calm, relentless purpose of a storm rolling toward shore. He'd shifted back into his human form, but even so, he was a force to be reckoned with. His eyes burned, his power leashed beneath his skin. Behind him, Lorcan and Finn flanked his sides, their faces grim, their bodies thrumming with contained fury. Tavish followed, his intense gaze scanning the chamber with silent calculation, every muscle coiled for violence.

Then there was Rhys.

He emerged last, his golden eyes alight with something dark and unrelenting. His fingers curled at his sides, tension coiled tight in his frame. The air around him crackled, the temperature in the room dropping as he exhaled a slow breath.

For the first time since she'd met him, Rhys wasn't a dominant force of will—he was something ancient, something terrifying.

Something draconic.

Thorne exhaled, long and slow. "Ah," he murmured. "So the princes of the sky finally grace us with their presence." He turned his sharp gaze on Callum. "You always did have terrible timing."

Callum didn't answer. His gaze flicked to Izzie, his jaw tightening when he took in the leather straps binding her wrists. He took one deliberate step forward, his power rolling outward in a suffocating wave.

"Let her go." His voice was low, edged in steel.

Thorne moved his dagger closer to Izzie's neck. "And if I don't?"

Rhys answered before Callum could. He didn't speak. He didn't need to.

He moved.

Faster than Izzie could blink, Rhys was across the room, a blur of violence and rage. Thorne had time to throw up a defensive arm before Rhys was on him, slamming him back against the stone wall with enough force to crack the surface. The sound of the impact echoed through the room, a sharp, sickening thud that reverberated in her chest.

Thorne gasped, choking out a laugh, even as blood trickled from the corner of his mouth. "Now this is more like it," he sneered, his eyes glinting.

Lorcan and Finn were already at her side, Finn's blade flicking through the leather straps around her wrists with ease. She noticed, her eyes locked on Rhys, watching as he pressed his shoulder into Thorne's chest, pinning him to the wall. The fury on his face was cold, unrelenting—he wasn't holding back anymore. Neither were the others.

The sound of heavy footsteps echoed in the corridor, too many to be ignored. A door burst open, and mercenaries poured into the room, guns raised, faces hard with intent.

"Step away from him," one of them barked, his voice low but thick with menace, the barrel of his gun aimed directly at Rhys' head.

Izzie's heart skipped a beat as the men fanned out, surrounding them. Each one was a threat, their fingers twitching on the triggers, the metallic scent of danger hanging heavy in the air. She knew these men—had seen them on the estate, part of the group who'd attacked the manor. They had survived the assault. And now, they were here.

"Is this how it ends?" Izzie asked, her voice shaking with the weight of it all. She didn't want to see them hurt, but the fear was gnawing at her insides.

Rhys didn't flinch. He didn't even look at the guns. He pressed harder against Thorne, pinning him with his strength. "You think these will stop us?" he snarled.

The mercenary leader sneered. "You're outnumbered." He motioned for the others to aim their guns. "Drop him. Now."

For a moment, time hung suspended in the heavy air, the tension thick and tight. The mercenaries closed in, ready to fire.

Then, without warning, a low growl rumbled from the back of the room. It wasn't human — it was something far more dangerous. The men faltered for a split second, their eyes darting toward the source of the sound.

But it was already too late.

Rhys' gaze flicked to the side, to Lorcan, who grinned darkly, his hands already raised. A flash of light and a rush of energy exploded in the room, filling the space with a deafening roar. Magic crackled around them, searing the air. The mercenaries scrambled, confusion filling their faces, but they didn't have time to react.

A wall of fire ignited, forcing them back.

Izzie's breath caught in her throat. She had never seen them this ruthless, this untamed. They weren't fighting for her anymore. This was war.

Chapter Thirty-Two

The world fractured into chaos—gunfire crackling through stone corridors, magic thrumming beneath Izzie's skin like a second heartbeat, the acrid scent of scorched stone and iron burning her lungs.

The mercenaries had come prepared. Too prepared. Izzie recognized the reinforced armor from the brothers' descriptions of the estate attack, each piece shimmering with sigils designed to withstand draconic fire. Their bullets couldn't penetrate dragon hide, but their traps—runes carved deep into ancient stone, nets pulsing with dampening magic—were working with brutal efficiency.

Callum and Finn struggled against enchanted chains that tangled around their wings, the metal glowing with each futile beat. Lorcan and Tavish fought with desperate fury, but the sheer number of mercenaries pressed them back toward the crumbling walls. Rhys stood at the center of it all, silver eyes blazing, power rolling off him in waves that made the air itself tremble — but even he was faltering under the coordinated assault.

Izzie felt it through the geas.

She felt them.

The bond that tethered her to the five brothers pulsed with their pain, their struggle threading through her ribs like molten wire. Their anguish lanced through her chest, their exhaustion dragging at her limbs as if she fought beside them.

She pressed her back against the cold stone wall, watching her dragons — her bondmates — being overwhelmed by enemies who understood exactly how to neutralize their greatest strengths.

She couldn't just stand there.

She wouldn't.

Izzie closed her eyes and reached deep into the bond, past the pain, past the fear, to the source of what connected them. The sensation was like plunging into an ocean of liquid fire — dragon essence thundering beneath her skin, ancient and wild and utterly alien to her human nature. Power rushed through her veins, igniting something that had slumbered until she'd accepted the geas, something that had only stirred when the brothers' lives hung in the balance.

Magic unlike anything she'd ever known.

She exhaled slowly and flung that power outward, weaving her energy into theirs, letting the bond carry her strength to each of them.

Callum gasped, his head snapping toward her.

Rhys went completely still.

Their magic answered her call.

Golden fire erupted around Callum, incinerating the chains that bound his wings in a cascade of sparks. Tavish and Lorcan broke free of their attackers, renewed strength flooding through them as Izzie's power fed into their own. Finn let out a victorious snarl, his flames burning blue now—colder, sharper, more dangerous than before.

Rhys turned to find her against the wall, something wild and wondering in his silver gaze.

"You're doing this." Not a question. Recognition.

Izzie didn't waste breath on answers. She reached for him—physically, magically—and pushed everything she had into the bond, into all of them.

A shockwave rippled through the ruined castle. The mercenaries staggered backward, their enchanted armor flickering as Izzie's magic tore through their protective wards like paper.

"Now!" Callum's roar echoed off broken stone.

Wings unfurled, the brothers surged upward in perfect synchronization. Callum swept Izzie into his arms as he launched through a shattered window, her fingers clutching at his scales while wind roared around them.

The wild moors of Skye stretched endlessly below, dark and ancient under the star-scattered sky.

Izzie pressed her cheek against Callum's warm scales and let herself breathe for the first time since the attack began.

They were free.

For now.

* * * *

The night sky stretched above them like black velvet studded with silver, the wind howling past Izzie's ears as Callum carried her through the air. His massive wings cut through the currents with ease, each beat steady and reassuring. Behind them, his brothers flew in tight formation, their scales gleaming under starlight as they left the Isle of Skye far behind.

They crossed the Little Minch in minutes, the body of water that separated the island from the mainland nothing more than a dark ribbon below. The mainland village of Kyle of Lochalsh passed beneath them, its scattered lights like fallen stars, before they turned inland toward the heart of the Highlands.

Izzie's heart still pounded—not from the flight, but from the power that continued to hum beneath her skin. It hadn't faded when the battle ended. It was there now, simmering just beneath the surface, waiting for her to call on it again.

Eventually, Callum angled downward, leading the group toward a hidden glen nestled deep in the mountains. A waterfall cascaded over jagged rocks, feeding a small loch that reflected the stars like scattered coins. A crumbling stone outpost stood at the water's edge, half-consumed by ivy and centuries of Highland weather.

The moment Callum's feet touched earth, Izzie scrambled from his arms, her legs unsteady beneath her. The second she stood, dizziness swept through her like a wave. Lorcan shifted back to human form and caught her, his hands firm and steady.

"Easy." His voice was rough with exhaustion. "You just poured a lot of power into us back there."

Izzie swallowed hard, her throat tight. She looked at the brothers—her dragons, her bonded ones—as they shifted back to human form one by one. Each of them looked worn, as if the battle had taken more than they cared to admit. Their eyes were heavy with exhaustion, but there was something else there too.

They were watching her as if she were something new, something they didn't quite recognize.

Her chest tightened. They had always been her protectors, the ones who held her when fear overwhelmed her, who guided her when she didn't know which direction to turn. Now their eyes searched her face with a mixture of awe and uncertainty, as if they weren't sure what she had become.

She could feel their emotions through the bond — exhaustion, relief, and a deep undercurrent of confusion mixed with gratitude. They didn't know what to make of her newfound power, the magic that had surged through her when she reached into their bond and pulled them back from defeat.

"I didn't even know I could do that." Her voice barely rose above a whisper, but it seemed to echo in the glen's tense silence. She ran trembling fingers through her disheveled hair. "I just — felt it. All of you. I felt your magic, your pain, your struggle. And I knew I could help."

The words felt inadequate compared to what had happened. The raw, unrestrained power that had coursed through her, the way her consciousness had expanded to encompass all five of them — it was beyond her comprehension, yet it had felt as natural as breathing.

Finn was the first to speak, his voice hoarse. "Izzie..." He swallowed, shaking his head as if grappling with forces too large to process. "You saved us."

His words carried weight — not just gratitude but recognition of something profound.

Rhys stepped closer, his silver gaze never leaving hers. "We've always fought together, but this..." His voice remained steady despite the tremor of exhaustion that lined his features. "This is different. You're different. You're ours, our bondmate, but now you're something more."

There was reverence in his eyes, a kind of wonder that made her pulse quicken.

"I couldn't just stand by." The rush of emotion still coursed through her veins, making her voice shake. "I couldn't watch you all—" Her voice cracked. She steadied herself before continuing. "I couldn't let you fall."

Lorcan's hold on her shifted slightly, his eyes soft with understanding and pride. "You didn't just save us, Izzie. You saved yourself, too."

Izzie felt tears prick at the corners of her eyes, but she pushed them back. She wasn't broken—not anymore. She wasn't just the girl they had protected, the one who had leaned on their strength. She was more now—something forged in the fires of their shared struggles.

Part of them, and they were part of her.

Rhys folded his arms, his sharp gaze assessing her with new intensity. "That kind of magic doesn't just happen, Izzie. The geas gave you a link to us, but this?" He shook his head slowly, disbelief warring with awe. "This is something more."

Finn knelt at the water's edge, his fingers trailing absently through the still surface. His expression was distant, contemplative. "A human shouldn't be able to wield dragon magic, but she did."

Izzie's hands tightened into fists, urgency threading through her voice. "We don't have time to figure out why I can do this. Right now, we have a bigger problem."

Callum gave her a measured look, his storm-gray eyes unreadable. "Tell us."

She took a deep breath, forcing herself to focus past the lingering adrenaline. "The man who held the knife to my throat back there—he's the one behind all of this. His name is Maximilian Thorne. Dario works for him."

The mention of Dario's name made the brothers tense. Lorcan's brow furrowed. "The man who took you from Mull? We thought he was just hired muscle."

Izzie shook her head. "He is just muscle. The one who kidnapped me from the pub, yes. But Thorne's the mastermind." She paused, her mind racing as the full scope of the situation hit her again. "He's a collector—a billionaire who hunts down rare and powerful dragon artifacts." Her voice dropped. "And he's after something very specific. The Harp."

Tavish cursed under his breath. "The Harp of Ceòthach Glen?"

Izzie nodded grimly. "That's the one. But it's not just the Harp he wants." She hesitated, her heart pounding with the weight of what she had to tell them. "He wants me, too. Because of my magic. He plans to use me as a weapon against you."

The brothers went completely still, the weight of her words settling over them like a shroud. Callum's face darkened, his jaw tightening with barely controlled fury.

"Why the Harp? Why you?"

Izzie's voice carried the bitter truth she'd learned in those terrifying moments of captivity. "Thorne doesn't just collect artifacts—he wants to control dragon magic. He sees me as a way to weaponize it. To use me against you, to bend you to his will."

The silence that followed was thick with tension and growing rage. Rhys' silver eyes flashed with deadly fury as he spoke in a low growl that promised violence.

"Then he'll have to be taught a lesson."

The resolve in his voice was unmistakable. From the way his brothers nodded, their faces set with grim determination, it was clear—Maximilian Thorne had just made some very dangerous enemies.

Chapter Thirty-Three

The air in the ruined outpost crackled with tension, thick and unrelenting. Izzie stood between Callum and Rhys as they glared at each other, their bodies rigid, their breathing shallow and sharp.

"She's not leaving our sight." Callum's fists clenched at his sides. "Not for a second."

Rhys sneered. "And what, you're going to keep her on a leash? That's not protection—that's imprisonment."

"She was taken from us. I won't risk her being taken again." Callum's voice turned sharp. "This man Thorne is too dangerous."

Rhys stepped closer, his jaw tight. "And you think suffocating her is the answer?"

The energy between them was volatile, barely leashed, like the snap of a storm just before lightning struck. The others stood at a distance, watching— waiting. Lorcan sighed, rubbing the bridge of his nose, while Finn muttered something under his breath.

Tavish leaned against the moss-covered stones, looking entirely unbothered by the brewing fight.

Izzie exhaled sharply. "Enough."

Neither man moved. Neither looked at her.

She stepped between them, placing a hand on Callum's chest, then one on Rhys'. The heat of their magic pulsed beneath her palms. Oh. That was it.

This wasn't just about her safety. Not really.

She closed her eyes, focusing, stretching that new sense the geas had awakened. The same power she had called on to strengthen their magic during the fight now whispered another truth. It wasn't just tension — wasn't just fury.

It was desire.

A sharp, aching need neither of them had indulged in since the day before the attack.

"You're both wound so damn tight you're about to explode." She opened her eyes. "And it has nothing to do with strategy or keeping me safe."

Callum's nostrils flared. "Izzie —"

"No." She turned to Rhys. Her gaze swept over him. Dominant. Dangerous. Always pushing. She lowered her voice. "This is about me, isn't it?"

Rhys tilted his head, considering her. Then — slowly — he smirked.

"Figured that out, did you?"

Callum growled, his hands balling into fists again. "Izzie —"

She turned on him. "You too. Don't act like you don't feel it."

The muscles in his jaw twitched. His golden eyes burned into hers.

Izzie swallowed, her own pulse quickening. She had spent so long trying to make sense of what was happening between them — between all of them. Lorcan, Finn, and Tavish had their own ways of showing care, of anchoring her in this strange, powerful bond.

But Callum and Rhys? They demanded.

Two forces pulling at her, opposite and yet alike.

Her fingers curled against Callum's chest, then slid away. "You need an outlet." Her voice barely rose above a whisper. "We need an outlet."

Silence.

Then, slowly, Rhys chuckled.

"Well now." His silver eyes flashed. "This just got interesting."

Izzie's breath came shallow as she lifted her chin, her gaze sweeping over the five men surrounding her. A decision thrummed in her blood — not one born of fear or confusion, but of something deeper. Need. Power. Fate.

Her fingers tingled as she reached for Callum first, tracing the line of tension in his jaw. He was always so in control, the steady foundation beneath her shifting world. But now? That control was slipping, barely restrained, his dragon close to the surface.

"You don't have to hold back."

His breath hitched.

Then she turned, stepping toward Rhys, watching the way his amber eyes darkened, his smirk faltering just for a moment. He pushed her, challenged her, but right now, he was the one waiting. Watching.

She smiled, slow and knowing. "Neither do you."

A sharp breath behind her — Finn. Always the watchful one, his protective warmth a steady presence. She reached for him next, trailing her fingers down his arm, feeling the shudder in his body. "You're always taking care of me. Let me take care of you."

Lorcan and Tavish stood just beyond him, their postures tense, their gazes locked on her like she was the center of their world. Maybe she was. The geas had bound them all, but this? This was her choice.

No more uncertainty. No more holding back.

She moved to Tavish, letting her fingers drift across his chest. His heart raced beneath her touch. He had always been the quiet one, the thoughtful one. But there was fire in him too, barely banked beneath the surface.

She wanted to see it burn.

Then—Lorcan. The one who always laughed, always deflected, but now his smirk was gone, his throat working as she stepped closer. She reached for him last, tilting her head, her voice softer now.

"You hide behind jokes, but I see you."

His breath escaped in a harsh exhale, and she knew she was right.

The power of the geas pulsed between them, a force greater than any of them could fight. It wasn't just magic—it was connection. Desire.

Her choice.

Izzie inhaled deeply, feeling the weight of their gazes, the energy crackling between them. She wasn't just the woman they'd sworn to protect—she was their match.

And tonight, she would prove it.

She stood at the edge of the still loch, the moonlight shimmering on its surface. The forest was quiet, but for the gentle rustling of leaves and the distant hoot of an owl. She could feel the magic that bound her to the five dragon shifter brothers pulsing within her, a constant reminder of her choice.

Izzie's breath caught in her throat as they approached her, their gazes fixed on her with a hunger that made her shiver.

"Our mate." Finn's voice was deep and rough. "We've earned this tonight."

Izzie nodded, unable to speak. She had accepted the geas willingly, knowing that it would bind her to these powerful creatures for the rest of her life. Now, she could feel the magic pulling at her, urging her to submit to them.

The brothers surrounded her, their large hands caressing her body through her clothes. Izzie gasped as she felt their hot breath on her skin, their mouths and tongues trailing kisses and licks over her neck, her shoulders, her breasts.

With deft movements, they undressed her. Izzie stood naked before them, her body trembling with anticipation. The cool night air caressed her bare skin, making her nipples harden.

Finn knelt before her, his face inches from her wet pussy. "You smell divine." He buried his face between her thighs. Izzie cried out as his tongue delved into her folds, licking and sucking at her sensitive flesh.

The other brothers continued to touch and kiss her, their hands roaming over her breasts, her ass, her thighs. Izzie's head fell back as she lost herself in the sensations, the magic within her growing stronger with each touch.

After Finn had brought her to the brink of orgasm with his talented mouth, he moved away, allowing Callum to take his place. Callum's tongue was long and he used it to great effect, thrusting it deep into Izzie's pussy while his hands gripped her ass.

Izzie's moans grew louder as Callum pleasured her, her body writhing with pleasure. The other brothers continued to stimulate her, their fingers and mouths bringing her to new heights of ecstasy.

When Callum finally brought her to a shattering climax, her legs shaking as the others held her upright, he stepped back, his face slick with her juices. Tavish took his place, his tongue swirling around her clit as two of his fingers slid into her tight channel.

Izzie's hands fisted in Tavish's hair as he brought her to another orgasm, her body shuddering with the force of it. Then Rhys took his turn, moving in front of her and gripping her hips. As he kissed her deeply, his long tongue snaking into her mouth, he slid his fingers along her folds. After the attentions of his brothers, she was soaking wet. Ready. Pushing her legs further apart, he held his long, thick cock at her entrance, then thrust deep inside her pussy as he kissed her.

Rhys fucked her hard and fast, his hips slapping against hers as he drove into her. Izzie wrapped her legs around his waist, urging him deeper, her nails digging into his back.

As Rhys brought her to yet another climax and stepped aside, Lorcan positioned himself beneath her, his cock hard and ready. Izzie straddled him, sinking down onto his length with a moan of pleasure.

Lorcan's hands gripped her hips as she rode him, his mouth latching onto her breast and sucking hard. Izzie's head fell back as she lost herself in the sensations, the magic within her pulsing in time with her heartbeat.

The brothers continued to fondle and kiss her as she fucked Lorcan, their hands and mouths bringing her to new heights of pleasure. When Lorcan finally brought her to a shattering climax, he took her to the ground, pounding into her with renewed vigor as she wrapped her legs around his back.

When Lorcan came with a deep moan, spurting his cum inside her, Callum stepped forward and nuzzled Izzie's neck. She could feel the heat of his breath on her skin, shivering with anticipation. Callum lowered his head and gently pushed her onto her hands and knees, his strong body looming over her.

Izzie felt a rush of excitement as Callum positioned himself behind her, his long, thick cock pressing against her dripping slit. She arched her back, presenting herself to him, and he wasted no time in thrusting into her with a low growl.

Izzie cried out in pleasure as Callum filled her, his girth stretching her tight walls. He began to move, his hips slapping against her ass as he pounded into her from behind. He reached around to swirl his fingers around her sensitive clit, sending jolts of electricity through her body.

As Callum fucked her, the other dragon brothers gathered close around her, their eyes gleaming with lust. Izzie could feel their gazes on her, watching her body writhe and bounce with each powerful thrust. She felt like a goddess, worshipped and adored by these magnificent creatures.

Just as Izzie was on the verge of climax, Callum pulled out of her with a snarl. Before she could protest, Finn scooped her up in his arms and carried her to the nearby loch.

Izzie gasped as cool water enveloped her, the contrast to her overheated skin sending a shock through her system. Finn held her aloft, his strong arms supporting her as he spread her legs on either side of his hips, positioning himself at her entrance.

With a swift thrust, he buried himself inside her, his length sliding deep into her core. Izzie moaned, her head falling back as Finn began to move, his hips rolling against hers in a sensual rhythm as the water lapped around her.

The other dragons gathered around them, their massive forms creating waves in the water as they shifted to surround Izzie. She felt a sense of overwhelming pleasure as they touched her, their hands caressing her skin and their tongues laving her nipples.

One by one, each brother took his turn again with Izzie, lifting her from the water and impaling her on their thick cocks. She lost herself in the sensations, her body trembling with the force of her orgasms as they filled her again and again.

As the sun began to rise, the dragons carried Izzie back to the forest floor. They lay her down gently, their bodies surrounding her in a protective circle. A sense of peace washed over Izzie, her body sated and her heart full.

As the sun began to rise, painting the sky in hues of orange and pink, the brothers finally brought Izzie to her last orgasm. They collapsed onto the grass beside her, their bodies slick with sweat and other fluids. Izzie lay there, her body trembling with the aftershocks of her pleasure. The magic that bound her to the brothers was now a part of her, a constant presence within her soul. As she drifted off to sleep, she knew that this was only the beginning. The geas that bound her to these dragons was eternal, and she would spend the rest of her days in their embrace, lost in a world of unending pleasure.

As she looked at the brothers, their faces still flushed with passion, Izzie knew that she had made the right choice in accepting the geas. She was theirs now, forever bound to them by the magic and the love they shared. She knew she would never want to be anywhere else. She was home, and she was complete.

Chapter Thirty-Four

A morning breeze wafted through the glen, carrying the scent of damp earth and wild heather. Izzie pulled her sweater tighter around her shoulders, her breath misting in the crisp morning air. Beside her, Lorcan stood with his arms crossed, his keen eyes scanning the horizon. Unlike the others, who wore their emotions openly—Callum with his steady intensity, Rhys with his biting dominance—Lorcan typically hid behind humor and deflection, though his usual lightness seemed subdued this morning.

"Again." He nodded toward the cluster of stones ahead.

Izzie exhaled sharply. The magic inside her had awakened like a beast roused from slumber, but wielding it was another matter entirely. It didn't obey her—not yet. She stretched out a hand, willing the energy within to bend to her will. The air hummed, her fingers tingling as a faint golden light flickered between them.

Nothing.

Lorcan sighed. "You're still hesitating."

"I'm trying."

He stepped closer, lowering his voice. "You're afraid of it."

She opened her mouth to argue but closed it again. He was right. This power—her power—felt vast and unpredictable, and after everything that had happened, she couldn't shake the fear of what she might become.

Lorcan studied her, his golden eyes unreadable. "You are not a weapon, Izzie. But you must learn to control this, or others will control it for you."

The truth of it settled heavily on her chest. Thorne wanted her, not just for the Harp but for what she could do. What she was.

She gritted her teeth, planting her feet more firmly in the grass. "Again."

Lorcan gave a satisfied nod. "Good."

This time, she didn't overthink it. She let the magic rise, let it pulse beneath her skin, let it move. Heat flooded her veins, and when she thrust her palm forward, the energy answered. A force rippled from her, sending the stones skidding back across the clearing in a neat, controlled arc.

Izzie gasped.

Lorcan smirked. "Better."

Her heart pounded, exhilaration rushing through her. It wasn't just about power. It was her power.

They trained for hours, the sky shifting from morning gray to the deep blue of late afternoon. With every attempt, her confidence grew. The hesitation faded. She was stronger than she'd ever imagined.

But as they stood on the rocky outcrop, the last of the sun sinking behind the mountains, Lorcan's expression turned somber.

"There's something you need to know."

Izzie frowned. "What is it?"

He hesitated. And Lorcan never hesitated.

"Your power isn't just rare. It's the mark of something much older."

Dread curled in her stomach. "Older?"

He met her gaze. "There's a prophecy, Izzie. One that speaks of a woman who will rise alongside dragons. One who will change the balance of power forever."

The wind picked up, howling around them.

Izzie swallowed hard. "What does it say? This prophecy?"

Lorcan's gaze was distant, his expression unreadable as the wind whipped through the heather. The silence between them stretched for a moment too long, and Izzie's heart began to thud louder in her chest. She could sense the weight of what he was about to say, the gravity of the truth that hung in the air like a storm cloud.

"You're not just any woman with a geas." Lorcan's voice was quieter than she'd ever heard it. "You are the one the prophecy speaks of. The one who is tied to the future of all dragonkind."

Izzie blinked, trying to process the words, the weight of them. A prophecy? She wasn't the sort of person who believed in destiny or fate. Her life had always been more about surviving, more about making her own way than being caught in some ancient story. But the power that surged through her veins told a different story.

Lorcan stepped closer, the shadows of the mountains stretching long behind him. His green eyes were intense, locking with hers as if trying to force her to understand.

"The prophecy speaks of a woman who will come from beyond our kind, a woman who will wield power greater than anything the dragons have known before. And it says that this power will either save us or doom us all. But more than that, it's tied to the dragon clans. To the bloodlines."

Izzie's stomach twisted. She didn't want to believe it, didn't want to accept that she might have been brought here for some grand cosmic purpose. She had just started to feel like she might fit in with this family, just started to feel like she could control what was happening to her. But this? This was too much.

"I don't even know what this power is." Her voice trembled despite her best efforts to steady it. "I don't know what I'm supposed to do with it."

Lorcan looked at her for a long moment before speaking, his voice softer, more vulnerable than she'd ever heard it. "You're not alone in this. You have the brothers. You have us. And as long as you're with us, we'll help you figure it out. But we need to trust you — and you need to trust yourself."

Izzie took a deep breath, trying to steady her racing heart. She wanted to believe him. She wanted to believe that she could handle whatever this prophecy was throwing her way. But the doubt was still there, gnawing at the edges of her resolve. She didn't want to be a pawn in some ancient dragon game. She didn't want to be used or, worse, controlled.

"I'm not sure I can do this." Her eyes remained downcast, unable to look him in the eye. "I'm not sure I even know who I am anymore."

Lorcan's hand brushed her shoulder, his touch gentle. "Izzie, you are exactly who you're supposed to be. Trust me. And trust us."

She nodded slowly, but a dark thought flashed through her mind, one she couldn't quite shake. What if the prophecy is right? What if I really am the key to something I don't understand? Something dangerous?

"Thank you." Her voice barely rose above a whisper.

For a moment, they stood there together, in the quiet of the Highlands, as the last of the daylight faded. And as the stars began to appear in the sky above, Izzie's heart felt heavier than it had ever felt before. There was something ancient and dangerous awakening inside her, and she wasn't sure she was ready to face it.

* * * *

A fire crackled in the clearing beside the loch, the scent of roasting meat mingling with the crisp evening air. When Izzie and Lorcan stepped into the warm glow of the flames, the four other brothers glanced up from their tasks. Rhys crouched by the fire, turning a skewer of rabbit, while Callum sharpened a blade with slow, deliberate strokes. Finn and Tavish sat cross-legged nearby, murmuring over a map spread between them. The quiet, watchful way they took in her and Lorcan's arrival sent a shiver down Izzie's spine.

She sat on an empty log near the fire, rubbing her hands together to chase away the chill. For a moment, she hesitated, unsure of how to begin. The weight of

Lorcan's revelation still pressed on her chest. Finally, she exhaled and looked up at the others.

"Lorcan told me about the prophecy." Her voice remained steady despite the unease twisting in her gut. "About what I might be. What I might become."

A beat of silence followed. Tavish's fingers stilled over the map. Finn's easy smirk faded. Callum's sharpening stone scraped against steel before he set it aside. Rhys merely sighed, as if he had expected this moment.

"And what do you make of it?" Callum's gaze pierced as he met her eyes.

Izzie let out a short, dry laugh. "I don't know what to think. I didn't wake up this morning expecting to be some kind of prophesied force of change for dragonkind."

"Prophecies are tricky things." Tavish rested his elbows on his knees. "They can be vague, twisted. Sometimes they don't mean what they seem to."

"Or sometimes they mean exactly what they say." Rhys' amber eyes reflected the firelight. "And that means we need to figure out what this one is really saying."

Finn leaned forward, arms resting on his thighs. "This prophecy—what does it say about her? About us?"

But it was Izzie who answered. She swallowed, glancing at Lorcan for support before turning back to the others. "It says I'm tied to the dragons. To your bloodlines. That my power will either save you...or doom you."

The weight of those words settled over them like a suffocating mist. The brothers exchanged glances, each of them processing the implications.

"And what does that mean for you?" Callum's voice was quiet. "For your future with us?"

Izzie shook her head. "That's what I don't know. And that's what scares me. What if I lose control of this magic? What if I become something dangerous? What if I hurt you?"

"You won't." Finn's voice was firm and immediate. "Because you won't be facing this alone."

She looked at each of them, seeing the unspoken vow in their eyes. They weren't afraid of her. They weren't turning away.

"You are our bondmate, Izzie." Lorcan's usual lightness gave way to sincerity. "Whatever this prophecy says, it doesn't change that. It doesn't change us."

Rhys nodded. "You're one of us now. And no prophecy — no fate — will change that."

The fire crackled between them, but the warmth of their words reached her first. For the first time since Lorcan's revelation, Izzie felt something close to hope.

Chapter Thirty-Five

The fire crackled low, casting flickering gold across the surface of the loch. Beyond the water, the Highlands stretched dark and endless, their jagged peaks swallowed by the night. Izzie pulled her sweater tighter around her shoulders, pressing closer to the warmth of the flames. Across from her, Tavish crouched over the map he and Finn had studied earlier, smoothing its worn edges against the rough-hewn log they used as a table.

"There." He tapped a point near the western coast. "That's where we start."

Izzie leaned in, her breath misting in the cool air as she traced the faded ink lines with her eyes. "You're certain?"

Tavish's mouth quirked in a half-smile. "Aye. As certain as I can be."

A sharp pang shot through Izzie's chest. The book—the one they had risked everything to recover from the abandoned chapel on Mull—was gone, lost when mercenaries stormed the brothers' estate on Skye. She had barely let herself think about it, the grief too sharp. It had been her only real lead, the only true clue to finding the Harp.

She swallowed hard. "I thought we'd never piece it together without it."

Tavish exhaled, rubbing the back of his neck. "Finn says I've a mind like a trap." He tapped his temple. "Read every page. Remember every word."

Izzie stared at him. "You're sure you memorized it?"

He shrugged. "Didn't have much choice, did I?"

Hope flared in her chest, tentative and uncertain. "Then tell me."

Tavish nodded, shifting so they could both see the map more clearly. "The book spoke in riddles. Half the time, I wasn't sure if it was meant to guide or confuse, but one thing was clear—it kept returning to a name." He ran a finger along the parchment. "An Gearasdan. Now known as Fort William."

Izzie frowned. "Fort William?"

"Aye. But not the town itself. There's something older beneath it, something buried in the bones of the land." His brow furrowed. "The book called it 'The Hollow of Echoes.' I think it's a cave system, hidden somewhere near the loch."

Izzie let the words settle, the weight of them pressing against her ribs. "And you think that's where the Harp is?"

Tavish tilted his head. "I think it's where we'll find the next piece of the puzzle." He moved his hand, pointing further north. "The book spoke of a guardian—no name, only a title. The Silent Watcher." His expression darkened. "Whatever it is, whatever it guards, the book made one thing clear. No one who seeks the Harp reaches it unchallenged."

A shiver ran through Izzie. "Then we'll be ready."

Tavish met her gaze, his own filled with something unreadable. "Aye. We'd best be."

The fire popped, sending a spray of embers into the night, and the loch stretched silent and still before them. The hunt had only just begun.

* * * *

Izzie studied the map, the glow of the fire casting shifting shadows over the parchment. The Hollow of Echoes. The Silent Watcher. Names pulled from the book now lost in the ruins of the brothers' estate. If not for Tavish's near-perfect memory, their search might have ended there. But he had read every word, absorbed it, and now it was their key to finding the Harp.

She exhaled slowly. "So, we start in Fort William."

Tavish nodded, tapping a point on the map. "Aye. Finn has an old friend there — well, more than a friend." His lips curled in something between amusement and resignation. "Rhona MacKinnon. She runs a smithy, but she's got her hands in a few other trades. She knows people, hears things, and if there's any truth to this Silent Watcher, she'll have caught wind of it."

Izzie arched a brow. "A lover, then?"

Tavish shrugged. "At one time. But Finn doesn't stay in one place long enough for things like that to last." His eyes were piercing as he stared at her across the low flames. "He was never serious about her, or any lass. None of us have been. Until you."

That left Izzie with a very warm feeling. "And you think she'll help us? This ex-lover?"

"She's got no love for men like Thorne." Tavish's expression hardened as he spoke the billionaire's name. "She's dealt in relics before, but not in the way he does. She doesn't take them for greed or glory."

Izzie nodded. That was all she needed to hear. If this Rhona knew anything, they'd get it out of her.

Tavish reached for a piece of charcoal and marked the map. "We'll need supplies — ropes, torches, climbing gear. If the entrance to this cave is anything like the book described, it won't be easy to reach."

Izzie leaned forward, studying the topography. "And what happens if we do find the Silent Watcher?"

His gaze flickered to hers. "Then we pray we're not still being watched."

She shivered. Not because of any ancient guardian, but because she knew exactly who might be watching.

Thorne's men were still out there. The billionaire himself. His fixer, Dario. And a team of mercenaries.

She rubbed at the bruises on her wrist, a phantom ache reminding her of the rough leather straps Dario had bound her with in the ruins of that castle on Skye. They'd held her captive in that cold, lifeless building for two days, waiting for Thorne to decide what to do with her. If the brothers hadn't found her in time…

Tavish's jaw tightened as he caught her movement. "He won't get another chance at you, Izzie."

She swallowed. "We don't know that."

"Aye, we do." He folded the map with deliberate care. "We leave at first light. We'll be on foot. Keeping a low profile. The fewer people who know what we're about, the better."

She nodded, though a knot of unease still coiled in her stomach. They weren't just searching for a lost artifact. They were racing against a man who wouldn't hesitate to kill to keep it for himself.

The fire crackled between them, casting fleeting warmth against the chill Highland air. She glanced at Tavish, his face half-lit in the golden glow.

"You're sure about this?"

His gaze held hers, steady and unwavering. "Aye, Izzie. I am."

And, despite the dangers ahead, she believed him.

* * * *

The fire burned low, the embers pulsing red and gold in the darkness. A soft wind rippled over the loch, carrying the crisp scent of peat and pine. Izzie pulled her knees to her chest, resting her chin on them as she studied Tavish.

He was always like this—watchful, unreadable. Where Lorcan spoke his mind with reckless certainty, Tavish measured his words as if each one carried weight. He had been quiet when she first arrived on Skye, quieter still when she had learned of the prophecy tying her fate to dragonkind. He never argued, never scoffed. But he never offered his own thoughts, either.

Now, with the firelight flickering over his sharp features, she decided to press him.

"You never said what you thought about all this."

Tavish didn't look at her, his gaze fixed on the glowing embers. "All what?"

"You know what." Her breath curled in the chill night air. "The Harp. The prophecy. Me." She exhaled, watching the mist dissipate. "Lorcan has all these theories. That I'm meant to change the world or whatever. But you—you never say anything. I don't even know if you believe it."

Tavish remained still for a long moment, his fingers idly rolling a smooth stone between them. Then, he spoke quietly. "Belief doesn't change truth."

Izzie frowned. "What's that supposed to mean?"

He finally met her gaze, his dark eyes steady. "I don't have to believe in a thing for it to be real."

She waited, knowing that was only part of the answer.

Tavish turned the stone in his palm before tossing it into the fire. The coals flared, sparks snapping upward into the night. "You want to know what I think?"

She nodded.

He sighed, rubbing a hand along his jaw. "I think you didn't ask for any of this. I think you had a life before all this madness found you, and now you're in the middle of something you can't walk away from." He paused. "And I think you're handling it better than most would."

That wasn't quite what she had been expecting.

She swallowed. "But the prophecy—"

"The prophecy." His voice turned wry, though not unkind. "You think we don't have enough old legends hanging over our heads? Another tale written by men who don't have to live it?"

She stared at him. "But if it's true…"

He leaned forward slightly, resting his forearms on his knees. "Then what? What does it change for you, Izzie?"

She hesitated. "I don't know."

Tavish nodded, as if that was the answer he expected. "Neither do I. That's the thing about fate. It doesn't tell you what to do with it."

A silence settled between them, heavy with unspoken things.

Then he stood, stretching. "Get some rest. We've got a long day ahead."

And just like that, the conversation was over.

But his words lingered.

And she knew—despite his quiet, despite his reluctance—Tavish believed in her. Even if he would never say it outright.

Chapter Thirty-Six

Izzie stood at the edge of the cliff Finn had brought her to, the wind biting at her skin as it whipped across the vast expanse of the Scottish Highlands. Beneath her, the mountains stretched endlessly, their jagged peaks rising into the twilight sky. The stars had started to twinkle above, but it was the presence of Finn beside her that held her attention.

He stood just a few steps away, his silhouette a sharp contrast against the fading light, his aura quiet but undeniably potent. He hadn't said much since they'd arrived, but had only watched her with that intensity of his that seemed to see through her, into her deepest, most vulnerable places. And that was the problem. She felt as if she were standing on the edge of something she couldn't control, and Finn — so calm, so confident — was the one drawing her further in.

"You're thinking too much." Finn's voice was low and smooth, like velvet sliding over her skin.

Izzie glanced at him, unable to hide the wariness in her eyes. "I have to think. If I don't, I'm afraid I'll lose myself."

His smile was small but knowing, his gaze unwavering. "You're not going to lose yourself. You're going to find a part of you that's always been there."

His words stirred something deep inside her—something that, in the light of day, she tried to suppress. The connection between them, the bond she felt with him and his brothers, was undeniable. It wasn't just the geas that tied her to them anymore. No, it was more than that. Her magic—wild, untamed, and growing stronger by the day—was pulling her toward them, urging her to trust in the connection they shared.

She swallowed hard, taking a slow, shaky breath. "I'm scared." Her voice was barely audible. "I don't know what's happening to me."

Finn's eyes softened with something like understanding, and in a few strides he was beside her, his presence comforting yet overwhelming. He reached out, his fingers brushing her arm lightly, sending a spark of electricity coursing through her veins. The contact was brief, but it was enough to make her pulse quicken.

"You don't have to be scared of us, Izzie." Finn's voice was full of that calm assurance that always seemed to wrap itself around her like a blanket. "You don't have to be scared of your power either. You were always meant for this. Meant for us."

She met his gaze, her heart pounding in her chest. "But...what if I lose control? What if I—"

"You won't." Finn's hand now rested on her shoulder, his touch warm against the cold wind. "Not with us. Not when we're here. We're not just your family. We're your anchors."

Izzie felt the heat of his touch sink deep into her, the magnetic pull between them growing stronger, harder to resist. Her body responded before her mind could catch up, her skin flushing with heat. Her magic thrummed under the surface, the familiar sensation of power building inside her, wild and insistent.

"I can feel it." Her voice was thick with the intensity of the moment. "The magic, it wants…more."

Finn smiled then, a slow, deliberate curve of his lips, and he leaned in closer, his breath hot against her ear. "Then let it, Izzie. Let us show you what it means to truly feel alive."

Her heart pounded, the tension mounting inside her as desire and fear tangled together, knotting deep within. But more than anything, she felt alive.

Finn's hand slipped to the small of Izzie's back, his touch searing through the fabric of her sweater as though it was nothing. The wind around them stilled, the world quieting for the briefest of moments, and all Izzie could feel was the heat of his presence, the way his body seemed to press against hers, pulling her in, anchoring her to the moment. Her heart fluttered in her chest, her pulse quickening under his touch.

"Feel that?" Finn's voice was a deep, soothing murmur against her ear. His breath was warm, his lips so close to her skin that she shivered. "The magic…it's waking up inside you. And it's yours, Izzie. It's a part of you, always was."

Her body hummed with energy, like a string pulled taut, and yet she felt anchored by his touch. His fingers traced circles along her spine, sending ripples of warmth and electricity through her. The heat deepened with every movement, with every word. Her breath came in short gasps, her body straining toward him, but she held herself back.

"I don't know how to control it." Her voice was barely more than a whisper. Her hands were trembling now, but she could feel the pull of his energy, a steady beat beneath her skin that matched the erratic rhythm of her heart.

"You don't need to control it." Finn's hand slid upward to her neck, his thumb gently brushing against her pulse point. "Let it flow through you. Let us help you." His voice was deep, darkened with something that felt like desire but was layered with a magnetic authority she couldn't resist. "We're here for you, Izzie. We always will be."

His words wrapped around her, the promise in them settling deep in her chest. The way he said we made her feel like it was all of them — his brothers, him, the power they shared — that were waiting for her to give in. To feel the same thing that they did.

And as his thumb brushed her skin again, a spark of light flared in her chest, a flare of magic igniting within her. It was like fire inside her veins, a fire she wanted to feed. It wasn't just a need — it was an urge, something primal that pushed against the surface of her soul, begging to be let loose. She gasped, a shock of energy shooting through her, and her hands shot forward, grabbing the front of his shirt in reflex, needing something to ground her.

Finn's body stiffened for just a moment before he let out a low, approving growl, his hands moving to her waist, pulling her closer. The scent of him, all musk and something sharper — something magical — wrapped around her, and she could feel the heat of him through the layers of her clothes.

"You're so much more than you realize, Izzie." Finn's words were a whisper. "You're part of something bigger now, a part of us. And I can feel it...this connection between us. It's real."

Her magic surged at his words, the geas, the bond, everything wrapping around her, pressing against her heart. She didn't know how to handle it, didn't know how to navigate the intensity of the pull she felt toward him. But everything in her, every instinct, told her to lean into it.

The air around them seemed to shimmer with the force of it—an electric pulse building with each touch, each shared breath. Finn's lips brushed against her jaw, his voice now hushed as he whispered, "Don't be afraid. We're here. And I'm here with you, Izzie. Let go."

His words were like a command, and something deep within her shifted, the uncertainty melting away as her body responded to him. The fire inside her wasn't just her magic—it was desire, pure and consuming. And as Finn leaned in, his lips capturing hers in a kiss so heated, so urgent, Izzie knew, without a doubt, she wasn't alone. She would never be alone again.

As their kiss deepened, the magic coursed through her, pulling her into him, into them, and she let herself surrender to it. To them. To the wild, passionate connection they shared, knowing she was a part of something far greater than she could understand. She could feel her magic pulsing within her, responding to his touch, urging her closer.

Kiera McKenna

"Finn." Her voice was thick with desire. "I…I don't know what's happening to me. This prophecy, it's so intense."

Finn reached out, his large, calloused hand cupping her cheek. His touch was electric, sending sparks of magic dancing across her skin. "Shh, my love." The endearment rolled off his tongue like honey. "Don't fight it. Let it flow through you. Let it guide you."

Izzie leaned into his touch, her eyes fluttering closed as the magic swirled around them, caressing their bodies with phantom fingers. She could feel it building, the tension coiling tighter and tighter in her core. When she opened her eyes, she found Finn was staring at her with an intensity that stole her breath.

In a sudden burst of movement, Finn pulled her flush against him, his lips crushing against hers in a searing kiss. Izzie moaned into his mouth, her hands fisting in his shirt as the magic surged through her, igniting every nerve ending. Finn's hands roamed her body, leaving trails of fire in their wake as he explored every curve and dip.

Their clothes were shed with frantic urgency, the fabric tearing in their haste to feel skin against skin. The forest seemed to come alive around them, the trees swaying in a nonexistent breeze, the leaves whispering secrets in a language only they could understand. The magic wrapped around them, a third party in their passionate dance, its tendrils stroking and teasing, driving them higher and higher.

Finn laid Izzie down on a bed of soft moss, his body covering hers as he gazed down at her with reverence. "You are a goddess." His voice was rough with emotion. "And I am but a humble servant, here to worship at your altar."

Izzie's heart swelled with love and desire, the magic within her responding to his words, surging through her veins like liquid fire. "Then worship me." She arched up into him, craving his touch, his kiss, his everything. "Serve me."

Finn obliged, his mouth trailing hot, open-mouthed kisses down her neck, her collarbone, her breasts. He lavished attention on her nipples, his tongue swirling and flicking, drawing gasps and moans from her lips. The magic danced along with his movements, its touch adding to the pleasure, intensifying every sensation until Izzie thought she might combust from the sheer intensity of it all.

When Finn finally entered her, it was with a slow, deliberate thrust that had them both crying out in ecstasy. The magic wrapped around them, binding them together, its presence a constant, pulsing reminder of their connection. They moved as one, their bodies perfectly in sync, the magic guiding their movements, urging them to new heights of pleasure.

Izzie's world narrowed down to the feel of Finn's body against hers, the sound of his ragged breaths, the taste of his skin. The magic was a living, breathing thing, a part of them, a part of this moment. It whispered to her, urging her to let go, to surrender to the pleasure, to the love, to the bond that tied her to Finn and his brothers.

And so she did, her body tensing, her back arching as her orgasm crashed over her, wave after wave of pure, unadulterated bliss. Finn followed soon after, his body shuddering with the force of his release, his name a reverent prayer on her lips.

As they lay there, entwined in each other's arms, the magic slowly receded, its presence a gentle caress rather than a driving force. Izzie could feel it within her, a part of her now, a part of her very essence. She knew that this was just the beginning — that there would be more to explore, more to discover as she navigated this new world of magic and passion with her dragon shifter mates.

Finn kissed her forehead, his lips curving into a soft smile. "Welcome to your new life, my love." His words were a gentle murmur. "Welcome to the magic, the passion, the love that will be yours for all eternity."

Chapter Thirty-Seven

Fort William had changed in the years since Finn had last set foot there, but the air still smelled of peat smoke and the sea, and the mountains still loomed, silent sentinels over the town. He led them through winding streets without hesitation, his steps sure.

Izzie barely had time to take in their surroundings before they stopped in front of a modest cottage tucked between taller stone buildings. A tangle of wild roses climbed the front gate, their blooms faded with the season. Finn led them up the flagstone walkway and rapped on the door—three sharp knocks—then stepped back.

There was a long pause before the door creaked open, revealing a woman framed in firelight. She had once been striking—Izzie could see it in the high bones of her face, the blue of her eyes—but time had drawn faint lines at the corners of her mouth and eyes, silver threaded through her auburn hair. She looked good for a woman in her sixties.

Izzie stared at Finn's former lover, Rhona, and for the first time, a thought struck her with unexpected force — dragons lived so much longer than humans. It was something she'd never really considered before, not until now, when she saw the lines of age etched on Rhona's face. No doubt, she had been young when she was with Finn. Someday, though, Izzie would be in Rhona's place — aging, hopefully as gracefully, while Finn and the other dragon shifters would continue to maintain their eternal youth. The thought was both comforting and unsettling, a reminder of the delicate balance between love and time.

Rhona's gaze landed on Finn, ignoring the rest of them. She went still.

"Saints preserve me."

Finn smiled, all easy charm, but Izzie saw the tension in his shoulders. "Hello, Rhona."

Rhona's fingers tightened around the doorframe. "I thought you were dead."

"I've been...otherwise occupied."

She scoffed. "Aye? That why you look exactly the same as the morning you slipped from my bed, never to be seen again?"

Izzie tensed, but Finn only tilted his head, offering a lopsided grin. "Good genes."

Rhona's gaze flicked to the rest of the brothers, then to Izzie, and back to Finn. "What do you want?"

"Just to talk."

She hesitated. Then, with a huff, she stepped aside. "Well, no sense standing in the air. Get in, then."

Inside, the cottage felt smaller than it was, the air thick with the scent of burning peat and dried lavender. The fire's glow flickered over crowded shelves crammed with books, trinkets, and jars of unknown substances. The six of them barely fit, the brothers looming in the cramped space, their broad shoulders brushing against hanging bundles of herbs and low wooden beams. Rhona shot them a wary glance as she moved to the sideboard, pulling down mismatched cups and pouring whiskey with steady hands. She set them down on a battered table, the only surface not cluttered with old maps and forgotten relics.

She took her seat and fixed Finn with a sharp look. "You disappeared for over forty years. Not a word, not a letter. And now you show up, looking like you just walked out of the past. You best start talking, Finn, because I don't have the patience I once did."

Finn exhaled, taking a cup of the single malt. "We're looking for something. A way into the caves beneath Fort William."

Rhona's brow furrowed. "The caves? What in the world for?" She motioned to the cups sitting on the table and the rest of the brothers moved in, taking them up to sip at the precious golden liquid.

Izzie just held hers, too absorbed in the connection playing out between Finn and the older woman to drink.

Finn gave Rhona his most disarming smile, his voice lowering into that rich, smooth cadence that made the air seem to hum. "You always had a way of knowing things, Rhona. I was hoping you'd help us find what we're looking for."

She scoffed again, shaking her head, but her expression had softened just slightly. "Flattery won't get you very far."

"Are you sure?" Finn's gaze held hers, and Izzie felt it—magic curling in the air like smoke. Not enough to take away Rhona's will, but enough to warm her, to remind her of what it had once felt like to be wrapped in his presence.

Rhona's fingers twitched against the tabletop. She exhaled, shaking her head as though clearing a fog. "Damn you, Finn."

Finn only waited.

Finally, she sighed. "There's an old stone circle, out in a farmer's fallow field. You'll find the entrance there."

Izzie watched the exchange between Finn and Rhona with a mix of awe and unease, her fingers tightening around the cup she still hadn't touched. There was a certain magic to the way Finn could sway Rhona, bending her resolve with nothing more than his presence. Izzie wondered, a cold shiver creeping over her, if someday she'd be just as easy to manipulate — if Finn's charm, his voice, his power would eventually chip away at her own will. Would she, too, find herself helplessly bending to him, as Rhona had?

Rhona stood abruptly, reaching for her coat. "Come on, then. I'll take you there."

Shaking off the disturbing thought, Izzie pushed it aside, downing her whiskey in one burning gulp before following the brothers out of the door. As Rhona led them to the van, Izzie swallowed the nagging sense of vulnerability, focusing instead on the task ahead.

* * * *

The standing stones rose around Izzie like ancient sentinels, their jagged edges scraping against the lowering sky, weathered and worn by time. Lichen clung to their surfaces like faded scars, marking the centuries they had stood watch over this land. A hush had fallen over the landscape, the usual sounds of the countryside—birdsong, the rustle of leaves—muffled as though the stones drank in the noise, leaving only the whisper of the wind. It wove between the monoliths with an eerie, sacred hum, shifting in pitch as if whispering secrets meant only for those who dared to listen.

The air thickened with magic, the taste of it metallic on Izzie's tongue. The very earth beneath her feet thrummed with ancient power, something deeper than words, deeper than thought—something elemental. This was a place of ritual, a place where the veil between worlds thinned. Izzie could feel the weight of it pressing down on her shoulders, settling in her bones.

Finn stood just outside the circle, his expression unreadable, but she sensed his unease. He was older than these stones, older than the magic that clung to them, yet he treated the place with reverence. Even dragons, it seemed, recognized power when they stood in its presence.

Rhona had left them moments before, her old van rumbling away down the dirt road, kicking up dust that hung in the still air. She had not lingered, had not even wished them luck. Just a curt nod and a glance that held something unreadable—concern? Regret? Perhaps she knew more than she had let on.

Izzie inhaled deeply, steadying herself. The circle called to her, beckoning her forward. A shiver raced up her spine as she stepped into the very center. The moment her boot touched the mossy ground, a pulse of energy surged through her, sharp and electric, like the moment before a lightning strike. The wind shifted, swirling around her, carrying the scent of damp earth and something else — something old and forgotten.

She turned to Finn, but before she could speak, the first whisper reached her ears, curling through the air like smoke. A voice, distant yet close, rising from the stones themselves.

A warning. A summons. Or an invitation.

She wasn't sure which.

She wasn't alone — at least, that's what she told herself as she stood at the center of the stone circle, her hands trembling but determined. There was something stirring within her, something far more powerful than the magic she had been learning to harness. The geas, the bond, had awakened a hunger in her, a need she didn't understand but couldn't ignore. It was as if the stones themselves were calling to her, beckoning her to do something she wasn't sure she could control.

But Izzie had never been one to shy away from the unknown.

She let her hands roam over her body, each touch sparking a thrill that shivered through her like lightning. Her pulse quickened as her fingers traced the edges of her clothing, peeling away layers, revealing her skin to the cool air of twilight. Her breath came in shallow gasps, the energy within her building, thrumming beneath her skin like the pulse of a dragon's heart.

She didn't know what she was doing — not really — but she felt it. A deep, primal connection to the stones, to the land, to the brothers. Her magic, her desires — everything had become tangled together in a way she couldn't untangle.

Izzie closed her eyes, drawing a deep breath and exhaling slowly. When she opened them again, the world seemed to shimmer, the stones before her glowing faintly in the twilight. She could feel them there, watching. She didn't know if it was the geas, the magic, or something more intimate, but she could sense their presence, their thoughts brushing against her own.

It is here.

She reached out, not with her hands but with her mind, her soul. The connection was a thread woven so tightly that she couldn't escape it if she tried. And she didn't want to. With a soft, almost imperceptible moan, she let the desire coursing through her run free, unraveling the tension that had been building inside her since the moment she had first felt it—the connection that had always been there but was now sharper, clearer, overwhelming.

"I need you." Her words were almost a prayer, though she didn't know who she was praying to. The stones? The Silent Watcher? The brothers? Herself?

But the moment the words left her lips, she felt it—their presence, moving into the circle, surrounding her. She felt their energy drawing closer, as if they were reaching for her, responding to her call.

The magic surged again, and she wasn't sure if it was hers, theirs, or something else, but it didn't matter. All that mattered was the pull, the hunger, the need.

Then she called again, this time without hesitation, without doubt. A pull from deep within her, strong and primal, reaching out to them all.

"I'm yours." The words were more of a surrender than a declaration, but she felt the heat of her magic flare in response.

The wind around the standing stones howled, its mournful cries carrying the weight of centuries.

Shadows stretched long across the ancient stones, their surfaces etched with forgotten symbols and worn by the passage of time. The twilight dimmed, the sun dipping lower as the evening swallowed the last remnants of daylight. Yet, in the center of the circle, Izzie stood illuminated, her skin glowing faintly in the ethereal light, the very air around her pulsing with magic.

Her body trembled, not from cold but from the power coursing through her veins. It was wild, untamed, just like the storm that had been building inside her since the moment she first joined with the brothers. Each breath she drew seemed to feed the flame inside her, making her heart race faster, her senses more acute. She could feel them — they were here, close, their presence thrumming through the stones, surrounding her, like a gravitational pull she couldn't resist.

Then, as if summoned by her unspoken need, they began to emerge from the shadows between the stones.

Tavish was the first, stepping through with silent grace, his long strides barely making a sound. His eyes glowed with a fierce light, his aura heavy with power. He was the rock, the foundation — always the steady one. His gaze never left Izzie as he moved closer, the earth beneath him seeming to tremble at his approach.

Next came Lorcan, his presence like a flare in the dark, sudden and burning bright. His fiery energy ignited the space around him, adding to the intensity of the moment. He was a spark, a flame that could not be contained, and he was drawn to Izzie as if she were the match, waiting to set everything ablaze.

Finn followed, his movements measured but full of purpose. There was an air of calm in him, but Izzie could feel the storm that simmered beneath. His magic was quieter, but no less intense — a soft hum that resonated deep within her. His eyes locked onto hers with an unspoken promise, a connection neither could deny.

Then, with a presence that seemed to fill the very air, Rhys entered the circle. He was a towering figure, his alpha aura undeniable, heavy, and commanding. The air seemed to thicken with his arrival, as if the earth itself bowed to his strength. His gaze was sharp, unyielding, and when it swept over the group, it was as if he were weighing each of them in a single, decisive glance. He moved with an assured, almost domineering stride, his power radiating in a way that left no room for doubt — he was the one who led, the one who commanded. Izzie could feel it, the pulse of his dominance, and it stirred something deep within her.

Callum was last, stepping into the circle with a quiet intensity, his presence commanding. He didn't need to speak — his aura was enough. The eldest, the leader. He held himself differently from the others, a calm authority that wrapped around him like an invisible cloak.

They moved as one, drawing closer to her, and Izzie's breath caught in her throat. The energy between them was undeniable, electric, and every step they took brought them closer to her. She reached out, her hand trembling as it extended toward them, and immediately they responded. Lorcan was the first to touch her, his hand grazing her face, his touch a steadying force as he cupped her cheek, his thumb tracing the curve of her jaw.

Tavish was next, his fingers trailing down her neck, leaving a trail of heat in their wake, the sensation both comforting and incendiary. His touch burned through her skin, sparking something deep inside her. Finn's hands roamed her arms, gently caressing her, as if memorizing the feel of her body beneath his hands. His fingers curled around her, pulling her closer, grounding her in a way only he could.

Rhys moved forward, taking his place as if it were his by right, pulling Izzie to him and devouring her mouth with his. And finally Callum, the last to reach her, his eyes dark with desire. He cupped her face in his large hands as Rhys released her, his gaze burning into hers. There was something tender in his touch, but also a raw edge, a promise of something more.

Izzie closed her eyes, the intensity of their touch overwhelming her, each caress igniting the magic within her. The heat, the power, the yearning—it all coiled together inside her, a cyclone of emotions, magic, and desire. She leaned into them, unable to resist. This was the moment—the moment she had been drawn to from the very beginning.

As the brothers surrounded her, their combined power and magic seemed to merge with hers, their bond strengthening, growing. The air crackled with anticipation. She had called to them, and now they had answered. They were one, their energies entwined, as the magic of the stones, the land, and their ancient connection to her surged, carrying them all to the edge of something new. Something inevitable.

Chapter Thirty-Eight

The magic flared, and the ground beneath their feet shifted, trembling as if it were alive. Izzie gasped, the sensation so strong it almost felt like a physical force pushing against her. A vortex of energy spiraled around them, swirling with colors that didn't exist in the natural world, pulling them into the earth itself. It was as if the very ground was parting, splitting open to welcome them into its depths. Izzie's pulse raced, her breath shallow, but there was no fear—only the exhilaration of knowing they were all connected, bound together in this moment.

The earth trembled again, the force of the vortex growing, and before she could take another breath the world dropped away. Izzie felt herself sinking, her body weightless in the thickening magic. The stone circle above her faded into nothingness as the ground swallowed them whole, pulling them downward into darkness. The light from the circle disappeared, replaced by the overwhelming, suffocating blackness of the tunnels beneath.

Izzie shivered as they descended into the abyss. On impulse, she had shed her clothes before entering the circle, and now the coldness of the underground world seemed to bite at her skin. She shivered, her body reacting to the loss of warmth, but she refused to let it shake her resolve. Instead, she reached out, fingers brushing against the shifting air, searching for any trace of the brothers.

Her senses strained, and she felt the reassuring pull of their presence — their warmth, their power — closing in around her. She wasn't alone. She wasn't afraid.

The brothers had followed her lead, their bodies just as bare as hers, their skin flushed with the heat of their combined magic. She could feel them moving around her in the darkness, their powerful auras a beacon of strength, pulling her back from the edge of uncertainty.

"Here." Lorcan's voice was a low rumble, his hand finding hers in the dark. "We follow you."

Tavish's steady presence brushed against her on the other side, a silent reassurance. Finn's hum of magic vibrated in the air, a deep, soothing resonance that calmed the edges of her mind, even as it urged her forward. Rhys stood close behind her, his dominant aura pressing down on her, making her feel protected.

Then there was Callum, his calm authority reaching out, anchoring them all in the midst of the chaos that swirled around them. His hand brushed over her shoulder, a soft touch that felt like an unspoken command, grounding her in the vortex of their combined power.

The darkness seemed to lift, if only slightly, as a faint glow appeared down one of the tunnels ahead. A light that beckoned them, like a distant star shining through the suffocating blackness. It wasn't much, but it was enough. Izzie turned toward the glow, her heart pounding with anticipation.

The brothers moved as one, the air around them thick with magic as they followed her lead. She stepped forward, the weight of their presence at her back, and they all turned toward the glowing path. The tunnel stretched before them, an unknown road that promised answers — or perhaps more questions. But they were united, their bond unbreakable, and together they would face whatever came next.

In the silence of the dark, with only the faint glow to guide them, Izzie moved down the tunnel. The brothers followed, their power flowing in a unified pulse, a promise that they would never let her face this journey alone.

* * * *

The glow at the end of the tunnel grew brighter as they moved, the air pulsing with ancient energy. It wasn't just light — it was life, the pulse of something timeless. The stone walls seemed to hum with it, as if the very tunnel was alive, watching them.

Then they saw her. Glowing.

The Silent Watcher was a creature out of legend, a dragon whose presence filled every inch of the cave they entered, her immense form coiled gracefully between masses of stone. Her scales were as white as moonlight, gleaming with ethereal radiance that illuminated the space around her. Her eyes were deep, unfathomable blue, ancient and full of wisdom, holding centuries of knowledge in their depths. The air around her thickened as they came closer, heavy with the weight of her age, her power, and the stories of countless years.

Izzie and the brothers had stopped just beyond the tunnel, where a wide cavern opened around them. The air shifted, the silence pressing in on them. They had faced many dangers, but none like this. Even Rhys, usually so confident in his own strength, stood a little taller, his posture wary, respectful. The Silent Watcher wasn't just a creature of legend—she was power incarnate.

The Silent Watcher's gaze swept over them, lingering on each of the brothers, her eyes sharp and calculating. Then she turned her attention to Izzie, steady and searching. A pause stretched between them, thick with silent expectation, as if the very air held its breath.

Izzie lowered her gaze respectfully, placing a hand over her heart before bowing her head. "Silent Watcher. We honor your wisdom and your years. We do not seek to disturb your vigil but to ask for your guidance."

She lifted her head, meeting the dragon's glowing eyes with quiet determination. "The Harp of Ceòthach Glen is no mere artifact. It is a weapon, a danger to all dragonkind. In the wrong hands, it could subdue even the strongest of your kind, forcing them into sleep or bending them to another's will. We must find it before it can be misused."

The stillness stretched, heavy with unseen currents of thought. Then, at last, the dragon stirred.

"You come seeking my guidance." The Silent Watcher's voice was like distant thunder. "But I do not know who you are." Her gaze sharpened, sweeping over the brothers once more. "You stand before me as men. Shift. Show me your true forms, and then I shall decide whether you are worthy of my aid."

The brothers hesitated only a moment before yielding to the demand. One by one, they let their human shapes dissolve, their bodies expanding, stretching, shifting. The cavern filled with the sound of bones reshaping, muscles stretching, and the whisper of scales sliding into place. One by one, the five brothers completed their transformations, their dragon forms towering in the dim, shifting glow of the Silent Watcher's light.

Finn stood at the forefront, his wings half-spread, the edges of his dark green scales catching the faint illumination. To his left, Lorcan's black hide shimmered, his long tail curling behind him. Beside him, Tavish's silver-blue form radiated a quiet, smoldering heat, his keen eyes locked onto the Silent Watcher. To the right, Rhys, the largest of them, let his red-orange wings flex as if testing the weight of the air, while behind him, Callum's smaller but no less formidable form crouched, his storm-touched hide flashing with sparks of silver across the midnight blue scales.

The Silent Watcher observed them in silence, her great, luminous eyes traveling over each of them, measuring, weighing. Then she gave a slow, rumbling exhale, like the settling of ancient stone.

"Sìol Dòmhnaill." She repeated the name with something almost like amusement. "I knew your parents. Aodh was a firebrand, always seeking, always pushing against the edges of what was known. And Eilidh..." Her voice softened. "Eilidh had a heart of iron and gold. It does not surprise me that their sons now stand before me, seeking to correct the mistakes of the past." She let the words settle before adding, "Your parents were worthy. Let us see if their sons are as well."

The brothers did not speak, but their massive heads dipped slightly in acknowledgment.

The Silent Watcher turned her gaze to Izzie, still in her human form amidst the dragons. "And you, little one." Her great head tilted. "You are not of their blood, but you do not flinch before them. Nor before me. Why is that?"

Izzie straightened her spine, feeling the weight of the dragon's scrutiny pressing down on her. "Because I believe in what we are doing. Because I know the danger of the Harp. And because I will not stand aside while a weapon that could enslave dragonkind is left for anyone to claim."

Deep silence followed. Then the Silent Watcher nodded, her great white mane shifting like mist.

"Very well. I will tell you what you wish to know. But hear this — finding the Harp is one thing. Keeping it from those who seek it will be another."

Izzie exchanged a glance with the brothers. They all knew the dangers, but this was something darker than they had imagined.

"The Harp must not fall into the wrong hands." The Silent Watcher's voice carried a low warning. "If it does, it will spell disaster for dragonkind. We have fought for centuries to remain free, to keep our will our own. But the Harp, in the wrong hands, could change all of that."

Rhys shifted back, his jaw tight, and the other brothers followed, the air shimmering with the remnants of their transformation. Izzie pulled in a deep breath, her heart still thrumming from the Silent Watcher's gaze.

"We know. That's why we must take it to the Draconic Council's vaults, where it cannot be misused."

The Silent Watcher studied them, her luminous eyes unwavering. Then, her gaze settled once more on Izzie, piercing and ancient.

"But you are human, despite your geas." Her voice carried a weight that sent a shiver down Izzie's spine. "You walk among dragons, you are bonded to them, yet you are not one of them. Do not think that makes you immune to the Harp's influence."

Izzie swallowed, but she did not look away. "I won't be corrupted. I know what's at stake."

A slow, rumbling chuckle escaped the Silent Watcher, though there was no humor in it. "They all believe that. Until the Harp sings to them."

She swept her wings wide, the shifting light around her flickering like a living thing. "The path to the Harp will not be easy. The guardians of Ceòthach Glen will test you. They will challenge you in ways you cannot yet foresee. And if your will falters, if your heart wavers even once, the Harp will know."

Her gaze hardened. "And it will take."

The cavern seemed to darken for a moment, a chill settling into the air. Izzie felt the weight of the warning settle into her bones, but she lifted her chin.

"We'll stop it. No matter what."

The Silent Watcher exhaled, a sound like distant thunder. "You will find the Harp where the mist never lifts. Beyond the Vale of Ceòthach, where the land swallows the unwary and time bends upon itself. There lies the Glen of Echoing Songs, hidden in the heart of the oldest forest, where no man nor dragon walks unchallenged."

Finn frowned. "And how do we find this place?"

"The path is not marked. But listen, and the land itself will guide you. Follow the river as it winds eastward until the waters turn silent—where no bird sings and no beast stirs. When you reach the hollowed yew, step between its roots at twilight. Only then will the glen reveal itself to you."

Izzie felt a prickling along her skin, as though the very air carried the weight of the Silent Watcher's words. "And once we reach the glen?"

The dragon's gaze sharpened. "You must be prepared. The Harp is not unguarded. Its keeper has stood watch for centuries, bound to its song. He will not yield it easily."

Rhys crossed his arms. "And if he refuses to let us take it?"

The Silent Watcher's light flared for a moment, casting deep shadows along the cavern walls. "Then you will have to make a choice. One that may cost you dearly."

A heavy silence followed. Izzie's pulse thudded in her ears, but she squared her shoulders. "Then we have our path. And we won't fail."

The Silent Watcher studied them a moment longer, then dipped her great head. "Go, then. And may you be stronger than those who came before."

With those final words, the Silent Watcher unfurled her massive wings, the sound of them stirring the air around them, and slowly began to retreat into the shadows of the cavern. Her light dimmed, but her presence remained, heavy in the air, as if she were still watching, still guiding them.

Izzie stood still for a moment, the weight of the dragon's warning pressing on her. The brothers were silent, each lost in their own thoughts, but she could feel their resolve hardening. They had come this far. They couldn't turn back now.

"Let's go." Finn's voice was quiet, filled with determination. "We have to stop it. For dragonkind."

Without another word, they turned back, the weight of their mission heavy in their hearts. The Silent Watcher had given them the directions they needed, but the true test was yet to come. They could only hope they were ready for what awaited them in Ceòthach Glen.

* * * *

As the last remnants of the magical glow faded from around them, Izzie and the five brothers suddenly found themselves back in the very place they had begun — at the center of the stone circle. The chill night air wrapped around them, and the ground beneath their feet felt solid, familiar. But as the strange haze of their journey lifted, reality slammed back into focus with unsettling clarity.

Izzie blinked, her body tingling with the aftershocks of their magical return. The brothers, equally disoriented, stood in stunned silence for a beat, before the distinct sound of a voice, sharp and agitated, sliced through the air.

"What in blazes is this?!"

The group whipped around, eyes wide, and there, standing just beyond the circle of stones, was a farmer pointing a flashlight at them. His face was mottled with fury, his hands on his hips, and he was glaring at them as if they were the most offensive sight he'd ever seen. Izzie's stomach dropped. He was holding a pitchfork, and it was pointed in their direction as if he might use it to skewer them.

"Oi! What do you think you're doing on my land?" The farmer's accent was thick with anger. "And why are you lot stark naked? What kind of nefarious activities have you been up to, eh? In my stone circle!"

The words hit them like a slap in the face. Izzie's heart raced, her cheeks flushed with embarrassment as the brothers scrambled to cover themselves, fumbling for their clothes in the darkness. The farmer's accusatory gaze swept over them, and Izzie felt herself shrink under the weight of his scrutiny.

She couldn't stop herself from glancing at the brothers. Rhys and Finn were already trying to pull on their pants, a tangle of limbs, and Lorcan was slipping on his shirt, looking far too amused for the situation at hand. Yet, all of them shared the same frantic energy, trying to shield themselves from the farmer's unforgiving gaze.

"You think I won't see through your little games?" The farmer's voice rose in pitch as he shook the pitchfork at them. "Get out of here! This is no place for your fewking!"

"Sorry, sorry!" Finn's voice was strained as he finally tugged on his trousers. "We—ah—we didn't mean to…trespass."

"Didn't mean to?!" The farmer was now nearly frothing with rage. "You don't just accidentally end up naked in my circle at midnight! And five of you bastards, fewking one wee lass!"

The brothers, now fully dressed, exchanged glances, trying to contain their laughter at the absurdity of it all.

Izzie was no better, struggling to stifle a giggle as she quickly pulled on her jeans. The tension in the air, mixed with their sheer disbelief, made it impossible to remain serious.

The farmer's ranting continued as they hurried toward the road, not daring to look back. Muttered curses followed, along with "Bastards!" and "Slut!" thrown after them. They began walking down the dirt lane, the evening air now crisp and cool against their skin.

Just out of earshot, they let their laughter bubble up, finally finding a moment of release after the intensity of the night.

For the first time since they had started, the weight of their quest felt a little less heavy, and the promise of what lay ahead — of stopping the Harp from falling into Thorne's hands — burned a little brighter in Izzie's chest. With the brothers laughing beside her, their footsteps echoing down the lane, Izzie couldn't help but feel that, no matter the obstacles ahead, they were one step closer to saving dragonkind. And that was all that mattered.

Chapter Thirty-Nine

The morning air was crisp, the scent of damp earth and pine thick around the hidden refuge on the loch's edge. The others had gone, their massive dragon forms vanishing into the mist-draped peaks to hunt, leaving only Rhys behind to guard her.

Izzie stood near the water, arms wrapped around herself, though the chill in the air wasn't what made her shiver. Last night still lingered in her mind — the blinding light in her eyes, the farmer's accusations, the frantic scramble for clothes. And before that, the Silent Watcher's warning, heavy with unspoken consequences. But now, in the quiet of morning, another kind of tension settled over her, more immediate, more demanding.

She turned, finding Rhys watching her. He leaned against a broad stone, arms crossed over his chest, the faintest smirk curving his lips. That look — steady, knowing — sent a shiver down her spine.

Since the beginning, there had been a pull between them, something elemental, undeniable. She had fought it, ignored it, pushed it aside to spread her attention around. But now, alone with him, with the memory of last night's magic still humming in her veins, resistance felt like a lost cause.

"You're thinking too hard." Rhys' voice was rough, edged with amusement.

Izzie huffed a breath, shaking her head. "I doubt thinking has ever been my problem."

He pushed off the stone and closed the distance between them in a slow, deliberate stride. "No." His fingers brushed her wrist, sending sparks skittering across her skin. "But fighting what you want? That might be."

Her breath hitched. The space between them felt charged, electric. This had always been inevitable.

And this time, she wasn't going to run.

She knew Rhys. She understood him in ways she didn't want to, and now, she couldn't help but feel that he was about to push her boundaries in a way that would change everything. The air shifted, and the sudden presence of him was like a storm bearing down on her.

"Rhys." Her voice shook as she turned to face him.

His eyes glowed with something darker than before, like a predator waiting to pounce. He closed the distance between them in a single stride, the intensity of his presence overwhelming her senses. His gaze never wavered from her face, reading her in ways that made her feel exposed — raw, vulnerable.

Without a word, Rhys lifted his hand to her cheek, his fingers grazing her skin possessively. He tilted her head back, forcing her to meet his gaze, and his lips curled into a knowing smirk.

"You're craving it, Izzie." His breath was hot against her ear. "You want me."

The words sent a shiver down her spine. She hated how much truth they held. She did want more — she had wanted him, from the very first moment, before any of the others. His hand slid to the back of her neck, gripping her tightly as his lips found her jaw, his teeth grazing her skin in a way that made her breath hitch. A soft gasp escaped her lips before she could stop it, and she felt herself melt against him. He knew exactly what he was doing, exactly how to make her respond. His touch, the sheer dominance in his movements — it was as intoxicating as it was terrifying.

"Don't fight it." His voice was rough, his breath heavy with desire. "You've always wanted me to take control."

Izzie's heart hammered in her chest. She could feel his pulse against hers, the raw heat that radiated from him, and the force of his magic clinging to her like a second skin.

"No." The word felt hollow, even to her own ears. She wanted to push him away, to make him stop, but every inch of her body betrayed her. Being alone with him — without the others to rein him in — terrified her. But at the same time, she couldn't deny the thrill of the chaos he stirred within her.

Without warning, he pushed her back against the stone wall of the ruined hut, his lips crashing into hers, bruising with intensity. It wasn't tender, wasn't gentle — it was raw, demanding, a clash of wills. Within seconds he'd stripped her naked, leaving her shivering in the chill of early morning. Izzie's body screamed at her to pull away, to break free, but she couldn't. The pull of him, of what he was offering, was undeniable.

Rhys didn't give her the time to think, not a second of space to breathe. "On your knees, Izzie." He left no room for argument. Every inch of her, every nerve, was on fire, and she hated herself for how much she wanted it. How much she needed it.

She knelt on the ground at his feet, her naked body shivering. Rhys stood before her, his muscular form silhouetted by the sunlight filtering through the canopy above. His golden eyes glowed with primal hunger as he gazed down at his bondmate.

"From this moment on, you belong to me." His deep voice resonated through Izzie's very core. "Your body, your mind, your soul — all of it is mine to command. I am first among my brothers-of-the-egg."

Izzie trembled, a heady cocktail of fear and anticipation coursing through her veins. She had known what she was getting into when she agreed to become the dragon brothers' mate, but now, alone, face to face with Rhys' raw power, his dominance, she couldn't help but feel a twinge of doubt.

"Y-yes, Rhys." Her voice was barely above a whisper. "I am yours to command."

Rhys' lips curled back, revealing a set of razor-sharp teeth. "Good girl." His tone was laced with dark promise. "Now, show me your submission. Worship me with your mouth."

Izzie's heart raced as she leaned forward, her lips parting to take in his thick, throbbing cock. She started slowly, her tongue flicking out to taste the salty musk of his flesh. The alpha dragon groaned above her, his fingers tangling in her hair as he guided her deeper onto his shaft. Izzie gagged slightly as he hit the back of her throat, but she forced herself to relax, to take him deeper still.

"Fuck, yes." Rhys' hips rocked forward to meet her mouth. "That's it, my little mate. Take it all like a good girl."

Izzie's eyes watered as she struggled to breathe, but she didn't pull away. She wanted to please him, to prove her worth as his mate. She sucked harder, her tongue swirling around his shaft as she bobbed her head in time with his thrusts.

Rhys growled in approval, his grip on her hair tightening. "Such an obedient little pet." His voice was thick with lust. "I'm going to enjoy breaking you in."

Izzie's stomach fluttered at his words, a heady mix of fear and anticipation coursing through her. Rhys had never been so blatant in his dominance over her before. He'd always kept it in check, reined in by the presence of one or more of his brothers. Now he was unchained in his demands. She knew this was only the beginning, that the alpha had plans for her that would push her to her very limits.

As if reading her thoughts, Rhys suddenly pulled her off his cock, his eyes gleaming with dark promise. "On your back." His voice brooked no argument. "I want to taste your cunt."

Izzie scrambled to obey, lying back on the cool forest floor and spreading her legs wide. The dragon shifter loomed over her, his massive form casting her in shadow. He knelt between her thighs, his hot breath ghosting over her most intimate flesh.

"Mmm, you smell delicious." His tongue flicked out to taste her. "I can't wait to devour you whole."

Izzie cried out as he sealed his lips around her clit, his tongue swirling and flicking in a maddening rhythm. She bucked her hips against his face, tangling her fingers in his hair as she lost herself in the sensations he was awakening between her legs.

Rhys feasted on her like a man starved, his mouth and tongue working in tandem to drive her to the brink of madness. Izzie's moans echoed across the still waters of the loch, her body trembling with the force of her impending orgasm.

Just as she was about to tumble over the edge, he pulled back, a cruel smile on his lips. "Not yet, my pet." His voice was dark with promise. "I want to hear you beg for it."

Izzie whimpered, her body aching with need. "Please, Rhys." Her voice was ragged with desire. "Please let me come. I need it so badly."

He chuckled, a low, rumbling sound that vibrated through Izzie's very core. "Since you asked so nicely." He dove back between her thighs.

His mouth was relentless, his tongue delving deep into her core as he sucked hard on her clit. Izzie screamed as her orgasm crashed over her, her body convulsing with the force of it. The dragon didn't let up, continuing to lick and suck until she was reduced to a quivering, whimpering mess.

As she lay there, gasping for breath, he stood, his cock throbbing with need. "On your hands and knees." His voice was rough with lust. "I'm going to fuck you now, my little mate."

Izzie scrambled to obey, presenting herself to him like the obedient pet she was. Rhys knelt behind her, his fingers digging into her hips as he positioned himself at her entrance.

"Remember, you belong to me now." His voice was a dark promise. "Every inch of you is mine to use as I see fit. My brothers come after me."

With that, he slammed into her, his thick cock stretching her impossibly wide. Izzie cried out at the sudden invasion, her body struggling to accommodate his size. The dragon shifter didn't give her time to adjust, setting a brutal pace that had her breasts bouncing with each thrust.

He fucked her like a man possessed, his hips snapping forward with a force that left her breathless. Izzie could only hang on for dear life, her fingers digging into the soft earth as he pounded into her.

His predatory growls filled the air, his teeth grazing her shoulder as he marked her as his own. Izzie shuddered at the feeling, a primal part of her reveling in the knowledge that she belonged to this powerful creature.

As he fucked her, Rhys reached around to circle her clit with his fingers, his touch expert and relentless. Izzie's body responded instantly, her inner walls tightening around his cock as she hurtled toward another orgasm.

"Come for me, my little mate." His voice was a dark command. "Let me feel you come on my cock."

Izzie screamed as she obeyed, her body convulsing with the force of her release. Rhys followed soon after, his cock pulsing as he filled her with his seed.

They collapsed together onto the forest floor, the dragon shifter's body blanketing Izzie's as they caught their breath. As the aftershocks of their shared climax faded, a sense of contentment washed over Izzie.

She knew this was only the beginning, that the alpha dragon had plans for her that would push her to her very limits. But for now she was content to bask in the glow of his possession, knowing that she had found her place in the world. Though how his brothers would react to his possession, his dominant control of her, she couldn't imagine.

The alpha rolled off of her, his golden eyes gleaming in the sunlight through the trees. "You did well, my pet." His voice was laced with dark promise. "But we're far from done. I have so much more in store for you."

Izzie shivered at his words, a heady cocktail of fear and anticipation coursing through her veins. She knew that she was in for a wild ride, that Rhys would take her to the very edges of her limits. There would be conflicts to come, especially with Callum. He and Rhys were always pushing at each other, even though Callum had admitted to her that Rhys was the clutch's alpha. But Callum had always been gentle with her, kind and considerate. Seeing Rhys treat her roughly would push him over the edge — she was sure of it.

But she also knew that she was exactly where she was meant to be, the alpha's obedient mate, ready to submit to his every whim and desire.

* * * *

The tension in the air was thick, like a storm ready to break. Rhys stood in the center of the clearing, his chest heaving with deep breaths, his eyes glowing with that same primal intensity that had ignited the chaos between him and Izzie. But now, as the dust settled and the realization of what had just happened hung in the air like a heavy fog, the fury that radiated from Callum was palpable.

The scent of intense, dominant sex hung in the air like a fog.

"I warned you, Rhys." Callum's voice was low, dangerous, a sharp edge to it that sliced through the charged atmosphere. He stepped forward, his posture rigid, his fists clenched at his sides. "You pushed her too far. You've crossed a line, and I can't—won't—let this go."

Izzie stood, trembling, her body still thrumming with the aftermath of Rhys' overwhelming fucking, her mind a whirlwind of confusion, fury, and...desire. She hated how much of her wanted to succumb to him, but she couldn't deny the ache deep inside her.

But it was Callum's disappointment that stung the most. His eyes, usually warm and steady, were now cold, narrowing with anger.

"You think this is acceptable?" Callum's voice cracked like thunder. "What the hell is wrong with you? Izzie is part of this family now. You don't do that to someone you're supposed to protect."

Rhys stood unfazed, his eyes still locked on Izzie, as if searching for a sign, any sign, that she didn't hate him. But Izzie couldn't even meet his gaze. A part of her wanted to scream at him, to tear into him with the fury she felt, but another part—one she didn't want to acknowledge—was still too tangled in the fire he'd lit inside her. She loathed herself for it, for needing him in ways she couldn't control.

"You think I don't know what I did?" Rhys' voice was low, his gaze finally leaving Izzie to focus on Callum. "I'm not some damn monster, Callum. I did what needed to be done. I am the alpha!"

"Not like this." Callum's hands tightened into fists. "You've put her in a position she wasn't ready for. You've hurt her."

"I didn't—"

"Enough!" Tavish's voice rang out, cutting through the tension like a blade. He stepped between them, his usual calm demeanor now replaced with something harder, a quiet fury that silenced them. "You've both made your point. But we're not going to tear each other apart over this. Rhys, you've crossed a line. Callum, you're angry. But we need to focus on her."

The words seemed to land with force, making Izzie's heart lurch in her chest. Tavish's gaze turned to her, his expression softening, but the weight of his words felt like a verdict. "Izzie, you've been through more than any of us can imagine. But you need to face what you're becoming. You need to choose who you want to be in this family, what you're willing to accept and what you're not."

Izzie's breath caught in her throat. The weight of Tavish's words was heavier than anything she had felt. The magic inside her was no longer just a gift—it was a force, a power she couldn't control, and it was pulling her into dangerous territory. The brothers, the bond, the desire—it was all spiraling out of control.

"I don't know who I am anymore." Her voice was barely audible. "Everything feels so…intense. I can't keep up."

Tavish's eyes softened. "You're not alone in this, Izzie. We're here for you. But you need to take control. Don't let this power control you." He glanced at Callum, then Rhys. "And none of you can protect her if you're too busy fighting among yourselves."

Callum nodded, his jaw tight. "We'll talk. All of us. But first, Izzie needs space. We all do."

Rhys remained silent, but his eyes never left Izzie. There was guilt there now, but also something else—a quiet, stubborn refusal to back down. He wasn't going anywhere. And neither, it seemed, was she.

Chapter Forty

The river had long since fallen silent. No birds called, no insects hummed. Even the wind had stilled, leaving only the sound of their own footsteps crunching over damp earth and tangled roots. Shadows stretched long as twilight crept over the land, the last slivers of light filtering through the dense canopy.

The Silent Watcher's words had led them here. *"Follow the river as it winds eastward until the waters turn silent — where no bird sings and no beast stirs. When you reach the hollowed yew, step between its roots at twilight."*

Izzie ran her fingers over the ancient yew's hollowed trunk, its gnarled bark rough beneath her touch. This was the place. The Silent Watcher's words echoed in her mind — *"Step between its roots at twilight. Only then will the glen reveal itself to you."*

Her dragons waited at her back, their presence a steady force. Rhys, Callum, Tavish, Lorcan, and Finn — her family. The magic between them thrummed, pulsing in time with her heartbeat.

"This is it," she murmured.

No one questioned her. They had followed the river eastward, watched the world grow unnaturally still, and now stood before the threshold of something ancient, something forgotten.

Izzie took a breath and stepped forward.

The moment her foot crossed the twisted roots, the world shifted. A soundless ripple passed through the air, bending time itself. The yew's hollow deepened, stretching into darkness, and beyond it — something waited. A glen bathed in silver mist, untouched by time, hidden in the heart of the oldest forest.

And in the center, standing motionless, was the Harp's keeper.

His gaze met hers, unreadable and unyielding. The Silent Watcher had warned them — *"The Harp is not unguarded."*

Izzie's fingers curled into fists.

She was ready.

The mist curled around Izzie's ankles as she stepped fully into the glen, her dragon shifters following across the threshold, the air thick with an ancient hush. Trees loomed high, their trunks twisted and gnarled with the weight of centuries. The figure in the heart of the clearing was draped in a cloak of deep green, his long hair streaked with silver, his face carved with lines of wisdom and time.

The Harp of Ceòthach Glen's Keeper.

His eyes, the color of storm-touched steel, settled on them with knowing.

"You have come," he said, his voice quiet but carrying through the stillness like the whisper of wind through leaves. "Few find their way to this place. Fewer still are meant to."

Rhys and the others stepped close at Izzie's back, their instincts sharp, their magic stirring just beneath the surface of their skin.

"We were sent by the Silent Watcher," Izzie said. "She told us the Harp lies here, in your care."

The Keeper inclined his head. "It does." He turned, stepping aside to reveal the Harp resting upon an ancient stone altar. It was unlike any instrument Izzie had ever seen — its frame was carved from living wood, inlaid with silver, its strings shimmering with a faint, ethereal glow. It pulsed, alive with the heartbeat of the land itself.

"The Harp of Ceòthach Glen," the Keeper murmured, reverence in his tone. "It carries the songs of the first dragons, woven into its strings by the gods themselves. It cannot be taken by force. Only those deemed worthy may claim it."

Izzie felt the weight of his words settle deep in her bones. "And how do we prove our worth?"

The Keeper studied her, then turned his gaze to the five men standing at her back. "The Harp recognizes strength of spirit, the bond of trust. But it also demands sacrifice." His eyes darkened, unreadable. "One of you must relinquish something of great value — something that cannot be reclaimed."

Silence stretched between them, thick with unspoken thoughts.

Then, before any of them could speak —

The air cracked open like shattering glass.

A gust of dark energy swept through the glen, scattering the mist, rattling the branches overhead. The portal in the hollowed yew flared with unnatural light, and from its depths, a figure stepped forward, his presence twisting the air with malevolent intent.

Thorne, and with him, his loyal fixer.

Thorne's long black coat billowed as he strode into the clearing, his sharp features carved with triumph. "Well, well," he drawled, his voice thick with amusement. "I knew if I followed your trail long enough, you'd lead me to something worth taking."

Dario took up a position at his shoulder, ever loyal.

The brothers tensed, magic crackling around them. Izzie felt Rhys' presence just at her side, solid and steady.

The Keeper's expression remained unreadable, but a shift in the glen's energy told her he recognized the intrusion for what it was — an affront to the balance of this place.

Thorne's gaze flickered to the Harp, and his lips curved into a slow, knowing smile.

"That," he said, eyes gleaming, "belongs to me."

The air in the glen thickened, charged with an unnatural force as Thorne strode forward, his gaze fixed on the Harp. The smirk on his lips sent a shiver through Izzie, but she stood her ground. Rhys and the others formed a barrier between Thorne and the altar.

"I'd advise you to step aside," Dario said, his voice smooth, mocking. "This isn't a fight you want to start."

Izzie ignored him. "The Harp isn't yours to claim," she said to Thorne, her voice firm. "It belongs to the land, to the Keeper."

Thorne chuckled. "And yet, here you are, trying to take it." He tilted his head, eyes glinting with dark amusement. "Why shouldn't I do the same?"

Without warning, he raised a hand, fingers curling as a pulse of dark magic crackled to life. Shadows twisted around his wrist, coiling like snakes before surging forward in a jagged arc of energy.

Izzie barely had time to react before Rhys pulled her back. The shadows struck the ground where she'd stood, leaving a patch of blackened earth that sizzled and cracked.

The Keeper did not move.

His eyes, sharp as flint, remained locked on Thorne.

"You were not invited here," he said, his voice as steady as the roots beneath their feet. "You are not worthy."

Thorne sneered. "I don't need your permission." He took another step forward, reaching toward the Harp. His fingers hovered inches from the glowing strings —

The moment he touched it, the air around him convulsed.

A sound like a thousand voices crying out in unison filled the glen, reverberating through bone and soul. Thorne's smirk faltered, his fingers jerking away as if burned. But it was too late.

The Harp had judged him.

Golden light erupted from its strings, the magic rippling outward in a wave that swept over Thorne and Dario. They both recoiled, eyes widening in terror as the power of the glen surged through them. They staggered backward, unable to escape the pull of the Harp's judgment. Thorne's breath hitched in his throat, his limbs trembling as ancient magic wrapped around him, an oppressive force that dragged at his very soul. Dario struggled but it was impossible —

The Keeper raised a hand, his voice ringing out with a single, commanding word.

"Begone."

The earth trembled beneath their feet. With a violent jerk, Thorne was lifted from the ground, followed by his henchman, the magic of the glen binding them in place. A heavy force, the weight of centuries, pressed down on them, and they could do nothing but struggle in vain. Their bodies twisted and contorted, as if the very land rejected them. The air around them hummed with ancient energy, thick and suffocating.

Thorne's body lurched forward, followed by Dario's, flailing as if the very ground beneath them had given way. Then, with a final, forceful motion, the magic wrenched them both from the glen entirely. The Harp's light flickered once more before fading, the hum of magic dissipating into the quiet.

They were gone.

The glen seemed to breathe a collective sigh of relief, the tension that had hung heavy in the air now lifting. The trees rustled softly, their branches swaying as if in approval. The oppressive darkness that had accompanied Thorne's presence melted away, leaving only the quiet, timeless beauty of the sacred place.

Izzie's breath returned to her lungs, her heart still racing from the intensity of the moment. She glanced at the brothers, their faces reflecting the same shock and disbelief.

It was over. For now.

The Keeper stood in silence, his eyes fixed on the space where Thorne had been, as though ensuring that the glen's judgment had been fulfilled. Slowly, his gaze turned to Izzie, and he nodded once, solemnly.

"The glen does not suffer those who would desecrate it," the Keeper said, his voice deep and steady. "Nor does it tolerate the poison of those who seek to control its power."

Izzie nodded, a wave of exhaustion sweeping over her. She had never felt such relief. Thorne had been cast out. The glen had been protected. She swallowed hard, staring at the spot where Thorne had stood.

"He was unworthy," the Keeper said simply, as if nothing of consequence had happened. His expression remained unreadable. "And now, the Harp's choice remains."

He looked to them expectantly, waiting for the sacrifice that would prove their worth.

Cold realization settled over her like a weight pressing against her ribs. *The geas.* The bond that tied her to the brothers, to her dragons – the magic that ran through her veins, weaving their fates together. The very force that had brought them here, to this moment.

What greater sacrifice could she make?

Her hands trembled, and she glanced toward the brothers. They were watching her, their faces a mixture of uncertainty, concern and love. Rhys stood closest, his eyes filled with a deep, unspoken question, and she could feel his gaze pressing down on her.

The Keeper's presence filled the space around her, waiting for her to make her choice. The land itself seemed to be holding its breath. Izzie knew what the sacrifice must be.

Taking a slow, deliberate breath, she stepped forward, her heart heavy with the decision she had already made. "The geas," she said, her voice hoarse. "The bond that ties me to the Sìol Dòmhnaill brothers-of-the-egg. I offer it willingly."

The Keeper's gaze flickered, unreadable, but he did not speak. Izzie reached out for them with trembling fingers, feeling the magic that tied her to them, woven like threads of gold through her heart. Each of the brothers, each of the men she loved. She had never truly understood the cost of the geas until now, never truly known what it meant to carry such a weight.

Tears burned at the corners of her eyes as she closed her hands into fists, holding the bond as though she could grasp it physically. The magic that connected her to them felt like an extension of herself — something so deeply entwined with who she was that the thought of breaking it threatened to break her as well.

"I offer it," she whispered, her voice shaking. "To free them. To free myself. And to prove my heart is pure."

The moment the words left her lips, the air around Izzie seemed to shift. The ground beneath her feet rumbled, a surge of power flooding her body, making her tremble. Her legs buckled, and she dropped to her knees, struggling to catch her breath as the weight of what she had offered pressed down on her. The geas — her bond to the five brothers, the magic that had tethered her to them — was a sacrifice so deep it was as though she were being torn in two.

But then, through the dizzying rush of energy, she saw the Keeper step forward. His eyes were unwavering, his presence both ancient and calming. "You have proven your heart, Izzie," he said, his voice deep but gentler now. "The sacrifice you offer is great, but your sincerity is greater still. Your heart is pure."

Izzie blinked, stunned by his words. She had expected him to demand the sacrifice — to take it from her, to sever the bond completely. But instead, the Keeper's gaze softened, and with a slow, deliberate motion, he placed the Harp in her hands.

"It is yours," he said, his voice full of reverence. "You have earned it."

Her hands shook as she wrapped her fingers around the Harp's delicate frame. It was lighter than she had imagined, but the weight of the moment — of what she had just given up — pressed on her chest. Yet the geas that bound her to her dragons remained locked inside her. The love she had for them remained. It was a love that had been tested and shaped in the fires of sacrifice, living deep within her. The bond of magic was unbroken, stronger than ever.

Tears welled in her eyes as she pressed the Harp to her chest, feeling the pulse of magic within it, the echoes of the ancient power it held. A wave of relief swept over her.

Callum moved toward her, kneeling beside her and placing a hand on her shoulder. His expression was unreadable, but his touch was warm, grounding.

"You did it," he whispered, his voice rough, emotion thick in the words. "You've claimed the Harp."

Izzie nodded, her chest tight with hope. The brothers were everything to her, and now, despite her betraying them — offering to break her geas — they didn't move away. The love between them remained. It wasn't the same, but it was real, pure, and enduring.

The Keeper turned, his form beginning to fade into the mist rising from the earth. His presence was no longer needed, and the glen was quiet once more. But in that silence, Izzie felt the warmth of the brothers around her, a quiet strength, their presence wrapping around her like a shield.

They had come to find the Harp, to seek the power it could offer. But in the end, it was Izzie who had found herself. And in doing so, she had found the heart of what truly mattered.

Chapter Forty-One

The journey through the night from the Glen to the cliff above the sea had been long and quiet, a steady hike across the rolling, rugged Highlands. After the confrontation with Thorne and the solemn exchange with the Keeper, the group moved in a reflective silence, their minds still heavy with the weight of the moment. They followed a narrow, winding trail that led them away from the sacred woods, the mist swirling around their feet as the trees gradually thinned, giving way to the wide-open spaces of the Highlands. Rugged mountains loomed to the east, Ben Hope's jagged peaks cutting into the pale blue sky, while the westward path seemed endless, stretching toward the horizon where the sea awaited them.

Each step seemed to carry them further from the mystical magic of the glen, grounding them in the harsh but familiar reality of the world outside. The air here was raw and biting, the scent of wet earth and heather filling their lungs as they walked. The brothers kept a steady pace, each lost in his own thoughts, though they occasionally exchanged quiet glances, checking on Izzie without needing to speak. Callum walked beside her, his presence comforting in its steadiness, but even he seemed distant, as if his thoughts were also somewhere far away.

As the day wore on, they came to a high ridge, the land sloping gently downward toward the sea. The path had become more treacherous, the rocky terrain demanding careful footing. But with each step, the promise of the ocean grew nearer, the salt in the air mingling with the scent of the wildflowers and grasses around them. Izzie could sense the change in the landscape — a tangible shift in the world around her, as if they were crossing into a realm that belonged to the sea, where magic and earth met in a harmony all their own.

Finally, as the sun began to dip low in the sky, casting the world in a warm, golden light, the trail narrowed, winding through a cluster of ancient stones. From there, they could see the cliffs ahead, jagged and wild, plunging into the churning waters of the ocean below. The sea breeze tugged at their clothes, and the sound of the waves crashing against the rocks echoed in the distance.

Izzie stopped for a moment, her gaze fixed on the horizon, her heart heavy and conflicted. They had come so far, crossed so many boundaries — both magical and emotional — but she still carried the echo of the glen deep inside her. It was as if the land itself had marked her in ways she couldn't fully comprehend. Yet, in this moment, standing at the edge of the world, she sensed the connection between herself and the brothers more strongly than ever.

"Is this it?" Rhys asked, his voice carrying on the wind as he came to stand beside her.

Izzie nodded, her gaze still fixed on the sea. "For now."

The others gathered around her, the weight of their shared journey settling between them. And as the final rays of sunlight bathed the world in a soft, amber glow, they knew that they had reached the end of one path and the beginning of another — one where the sea and the sky would meet, where the mysteries of their past could finally be left behind, and where their future awaited.

* * * *

Izzie knelt on the edge of a cliff, her hands gripping the rough stone beneath her, the cool wind whipping through her hair. Below, the sea crashed against the rocks, each wave seeming to mirror the turmoil inside her. The confrontation with Thorne, the sacrifice she had made — and that had been rejected by the Keeper, out of compassion — nothing seemed as it should.

She should experience relief. Should embrace the safety that Callum and the brothers promised, but all she carried was the raw, lingering energy of the confrontation. The weight of it had settled deep inside her, and she couldn't shake it.

"Callum?" Her voice was a breath, barely carried by the wind, but he heard it. Always.

He stepped beside her, his presence a constant force of stability. His hand brushed lightly against her back, a touch so gentle, but it sent a current of warmth through her.

"I'm here, Izzie." His voice was soft, but there was something in it, an unspoken understanding of the heaviness between them. Behind him, Tavish held the Harp in his arms, secure against the coming of night.

Izzie turned to face Callum, sensing the electric pull between them — stronger than ever, and deeper than she ever could've imagined. It was no longer just about the geas or the bond — it was something far more profound. The connection between them wasn't simply magic — it was *everything*.

"I'm not sure how to process any of this anymore," she confessed, her voice barely audible, but her heart lay open to him. "It's like...I don't even know where I end and you begin."

Callum's gaze softened, and he reached for her, his hand cupping her cheek, his thumb brushing along her skin. The familiar fire in her chest sparked, but there was something else, too — something deeper.

"Izzie, this bond..." He paused, searching for the right words, his eyes searching hers with such intensity it almost overwhelmed her. "This isn't just magic. It's fate. It's destiny. We've always been meant to be. All of us."

Izzie absorbed the weight of those words. There was truth in them, a truth that rang louder than any warning or fear. But it was a truth that she wasn't ready to fully understand, not yet. She closed her eyes, leaning into his touch, the warmth of his hand grounding her, even as the storm of emotions threatened to sweep her away.

"But...we can't ignore what's happening to us," she whispered. "To me. To each of you."

Callum's gaze darkened, his jaw tightening. He stepped closer, his other hand coming to rest on her waist, pulling her even closer. "We won't let anything tear us apart. Not now, not ever."

He had the good grace not to bring up her willingness to sacrifice their geas for the Harp. None of them would. They knew it was the most valuable thing she possessed.

Then, without another word, he lowered his lips to hers.

Izzie's breath hitched as his kiss deepened, searing her with a heat that was unmistakably their own. The connection between them flared like a wildfire, consuming everything in its path. She kissed him back with a fierceness that matched his, her hands threading through his hair, pulling him closer.

In that moment, there was no Thorne. No fear. No uncertainty. Only Callum and his brothers, standing beside her on the cliff above the sea, the bond between them crackling like lightning in the air. The energy between them was a force that seemed to hum with life, growing stronger with each heartbeat. Izzie experienced it deep within her, a pulse that connected them all, binding them together in a way she couldn't fully explain, but could undeniably sense.

The eldest of the Sìol Dòmhnaill brothers held Izzie close, his arms wrapping around her as the wind tugged at their clothes, but neither of them cared. She could sense his heartbeat beneath her palms, strong and steady, and the raw, unspoken desire that pulsed between them. But it was more than just passion. It was something deeper, beyond the magic that held her to them.

They weren't just bound by magic anymore. They were more than that. They were one.

The others moved closer, the presence of the brothers surrounding her, filling the space with quiet intensity. Rhys, Lorcan, Tavish, and Finn — all of them there, their silent support as palpable as the wind on the cliffside. Izzie could sense them all, each one a part of this connection, a part of her.

When Callum finally pulled back, breathless and trembling, Izzie leaned her forehead against his, trying to steady the racing of her heart. The sea stretched out before them, its waves crashing against the rocks below, but the world seemed still, as though everything had paused in that moment.

"I'm yours," she whispered, her voice barely audible over the roar of the ocean, but it was enough. In that instant, she knew it was true. The words didn't just belong to her — they belonged to all of them. Whatever came next, they would face it together, bound by more than just magic. More than fate.

They were bound by something deeper, something stronger.

She turned to face them — Callum, Rhys, Finn, Tavish and Lorcan. Their eyes were full of longing, desire, but also something more — something unspoken. They weren't just waiting for her to make a choice. They were offering themselves, offering their trust, their bond. It was up to her to decide how far she was willing to go.

Callum, the steady and protective one, spoke first. His gaze was soft but filled with a heat that matched Izzie's growing desire. "Izzie," he said, his voice a low murmur that sent shivers through her. "We've always been connected. But now...now we're something more. We don't have to fight it anymore. We can be what we were meant to be."

His words pulled at something deep within her, a yearning she hadn't fully understood until now. She wanted this—wanted them.

Finn, ever the calming force, stepped beside Callum. His smile was understanding, but when his touch brushed her arm, it was like an electric spark. "We're not asking you to surrender, Izzie. We're asking you to embrace this with us. To accept that you are not just with us—you are part of us. Don't hold back."

Her breath hitched as Tavish moved closer. His eyes, full of intensity, bore into hers, but there was a gentleness there she'd come to expect from him. "You're not just a part of this family, Izzie. You are the heart of it. The magic that flows through you, the power you hold—it's a part of who we are now. Let us show you."

Lorcan, ever the impulsive one, leaned in, his voice barely a whisper. "You've already come so far, Izzie. Trust us. Trust yourself."

But it was Rhys, the dominant one, who had stayed a step back until now, who finally spoke, his voice low but filled with a depth that seemed to echo from within him. "Izzie...we've all been waiting for this moment. Waiting for you to see what we've always known—that you're ours, and we're yours. Together. Not just bound by a geas, but by something that goes beyond magic."

His words hung in the air between them, and Izzie experienced her heart racing, the weight of the moment pressing down on her. The bond they shared was like a thread, delicate but unbreakable, woven between them with each word, each touch, each glance.

The air was thick with unspoken promises, the pull between them undeniable. Izzie sensed it—every part of her. Her magic surged, not just from the geas, but from something deeper, something ancient. It wasn't just the brothers' magic — it was hers too, born from the bond they had forged, that had become a part of her.

Together, all of them — the five brothers and Izzie — stood as one, the world around them fading into nothing but the crackling energy that pulsed between their hearts.

With a final breath, Izzie let go. She allowed herself to be pulled into them, into the connection they shared, into the magic that bound them all together. And as they came together, all five of them, the world outside ceased to exist. There was nothing but them — their magic, their desires and the unity that had always been meant to be.

She wasn't just Izzie anymore. She was theirs — and they were hers.

Chapter Forty-Two

Izzie awoke to the soft caress of morning light, filtering through heavy velvet curtains. Her bedroom, quiet and still, pulsed with an energy that carried both familiar and new. The air around her was thick with the weight of days spent rebuilding, followed by evening hours spent in the quiet solitude of the Dower House on the Isle of Skye. The damage to the manor had been extensive, but after weeks of hard work alongside the brothers, they had made significant progress. The house was beginning to take shape again, but more than that — there was something in the very bones of the estate that hummed with a renewed life.

Her fingers brushed against the soft sheets, and she sensed it — something different in the air, a charged hum that sent a ripple of awareness through every nerve. Her skin tingled with the lingering magic from the night before. A union unlike any she had ever known, binding her to the brothers in ways she couldn't fully grasp but could certainly experience. It was deep, visceral—a connection that had fused her body, her heart and her very essence with theirs.

She blinked, her eyes adjusting to the early morning light, and inhaled sharply. Magic, raw and untamed, thrummed inside her, a living thing beneath her ribs. It had always been there, a quiet undercurrent, but now it was something more—a storm that coiled within, waiting for release. The connection had deepened, and with it came a flood of realization. The power that pulsed in her veins was not just a bond—it was a force that surged through her, stronger than before. She could sense its untapped potential, the swirls of energy that danced just below her skin, ready to be wielded.

Her breath caught in her throat as she sat up, pulling the blankets around her, absorbing the sharp pulse of magic that now defined her. Her memories of the night still clung to her, and of all that her dragon shifters had made her experience in their arms, a reminder of how far she had come—and how far she was yet to go. The storm within her, though still wild and untamed, seemed like something she could control, if only she understood it fully.

The quiet of the Dower House was different now. The house itself carried a sense of temporary refuge, a place to rebuild the remnants of the past, but now, it held more like a home—one that echoed with the promise of what was to come.

The geas was no longer just a binding force. It was a living, breathing entity, woven into her very soul. And with it, she was stronger—so much stronger. The power she held was no longer confined, no longer just magic bound by ancient rules. It was wild. Free. Unyielding. She could sense it in her bones, coursing through her blood like molten fire. And as she moved, her power seemed to flow with every motion, weaving through her fingertips and wrapping around her thoughts.

But even as her senses flared with this new strength, a cold, gnawing presence lingered at the edges of her consciousness. Thorne's warning echoed through her mind like a distant storm on the horizon, dark clouds swirling in the distance.

"You think you've won, but this is far from over. The power you hold…it belongs to me. And I will have it, Izzie."

The words were a shadow, a whispered threat carried on the wind of her thoughts. The reality of them struck her like a sudden gust, making her pulse quicken. She had barely begun to understand the power she had now — yet, Thorne's obsession with it was far from finished. His presence loomed like an ever-encroaching storm, and she could sense its weight pressing down on her chest, as if the very air was thick with it.

Izzie rose from the bed, the cool stone of the floor sending a shiver up her spine. She reached for her reflection in the mirror, her fingers tracing the line of her neck, absorbing the hum of magic beneath her skin. Her eyes — bright, glowing and more alive than ever before — met her own gaze. There was no denying it — she had changed. And not just in the way the brothers had made her…*whole*. She was something else now, something she wasn't sure she could control.

The brothers, she knew, would sense it too. They'd seen it in her before, that spark of something greater. But now it was undeniable. She wasn't just bonded to them — she was entwined in a destiny she hadn't asked for, and one that she could sense pulling at her, relentlessly.

Her hand dropped from the mirror's surface as a distant rumble of thunder echoed across the sky. The storm was still out there, gathering strength, waiting to descend.

Thorne's storm.

And she wasn't sure if she was ready for it.

Chapter Forty-Three

The Scottish highlands were colder than she'd expected in the autumn, but then again, she had changed. Everything had changed. Her body no longer felt like her own. She stood in the grand hall of the brothers' ancestral estate, a fire roaring in the fireplace behind her, facing Margaret, who had flown in from North Carolina to find out what the hell had happened to her.

Margaret's sharp gaze swept over Izzie, taking in the changes. Her stance, her confidence, the faint glow beneath her skin—subtle, but unmistakable. The geas had transformed her.

"You have two choices," Margaret said, her voice even but firm. "Come back with me. Return to your life, your career. Or stay here."

Izzie placed a hand over her abdomen, where a strange warmth had settled days ago, a presence she hadn't fully understood until now.

She wasn't just staying because of the brothers. She was staying because...

"I'm pregnant."

Rhys shifted beside her, his golden eyes narrowing. "You're sure?"

Callum was tense, as if he already knew the answer.

Margaret sighed, rubbing her temple. "Fine. We'll confirm it." She reached into her satchel and pulled out a small silver vial filled with an iridescent liquid. "A magical determination spell. Standard procedure for supernatural pregnancies."

Izzie swallowed, a mixture of nerves and excitement curling through her. She wasn't afraid — but she had to know.

Margaret uncorked the vial. The liquid shimmered, swirling into the air, tendrils of glowing mist curling toward Izzie's stomach. It hovered, pulsing, as if tasting the truth.

Then, the magic changed.

The glow expanded — splitting into five distinct strands. Each thread linked itself to one of the brothers, weaving around them like living fire.

Margaret's breath caught. "That's...not possible."

Callum exhaled slowly, his expression unreadable. Rhys, however, laughed — dark and pleased.

"Looks like we all share more than blood," he murmured.

Izzie stared at the swirling magic, realization crashing over her. Their essence had mingled. Their sperm had fused into something more.

She wasn't carrying one child. She was carrying a clutch of eggs.

A deep warmth unfurled inside her — not fear, but acceptance.

The dragons had chosen her. All of them.

Margaret stared at the results, pressing her lips into a thin line before she sighed. "Then I suppose you've already made your choice."

Izzie turned to face the brothers. Callum, Rhys and the others — her mates.

She smiled. "I stay."

Margaret left Scotland that night.

Izzie, however, remained — to carry, to protect, and eventually, to hatch the next generation of dragons.

And she would never be alone again.

* * * *

Izzie lay on the examination table, the cool gel on her stomach a stark contrast to the warmth radiating from Callum's grip on her hand. His expression was unreadable, though his storm-gray eyes flickered with barely restrained emotion. Excitement? Worry? Possessiveness? Probably all three.

The doctor — an older dragon shifter with silver-streaked hair and an air of quiet authority — studied the screen as he moved the ultrasound wand over Izzie's lower belly. The monitor flickered to life, revealing a series of perfect, oblong shapes nestled deep within her womb.

Eight of them.

Izzie swallowed hard. "Those are…the eggs?"

Dr. Alaric nodded, his mouth twitching slightly in amusement. "Indeed. Eight healthy dragon hybrids. Congratulations, Callum."

Callum exhaled slowly, but his grip on Izzie's hand tightened. He ran his other hand through his dark hair as if he still couldn't quite believe this was happening.

"How big are they?" Izzie asked, her pulse quickening.

Dr. Alaric adjusted the screen. "Right now, each egg is about the size of a walnut. That's perfectly normal for the first trimester. Your body is adapting well — your womb is already reinforcing itself with a denser lining, thanks to the magic in your system."

Izzie blinked. "You mean...my body is changing to accommodate them?"

"Yes. Dragon pregnancies work differently from human ones." He tapped the monitor. "By your third month, the eggs will be closer to the size of a grapefruit. By month five, they'll be as large as ostrich eggs. That's when you'll require full bed rest."

Izzie's breath hitched. "Bed rest?"

Callum spoke for the first time. "That means you'll be protected. You won't have to do anything but focus on carrying them." His voice was steady, but his thumb stroked over her knuckles — a silent reassurance.

Izzie turned back to Dr. Alaric. "And after that?"

The doctor's expression became more serious. "By the seventh month, each egg will reach the equivalent size of a full-term human fetus. At that point, you won't be able to carry them naturally anymore."

Her stomach twisted. "Meaning?"

Alaric met her gaze evenly. "You'll need a C-section to remove them from your uterus. The eggs will be transferred to an incubation chamber, where they'll continue to develop externally for the final weeks."

Izzie felt the blood drain from her face. "So I won't...give birth, in the traditional sense?"

The doctor shook his head. "No. Dragons don't give live birth. The incubation period is necessary to ensure their shifter forms develop properly. They'll hatch when they're ready — fully formed, with their dragon instincts intact."

Izzie exhaled sharply, trying to wrap her mind around it. "How long is the incubation period?"

"Typically another two to three months post-extraction. But don't worry — the process is natural, and they'll be monitored every step of the way."

Callum finally spoke again, his voice low but firm. "You won't go through this alone, Izzie. We'll be with you."

Izzie searched his face, taking in the quiet protectiveness behind his words. She felt the bond between them settle deeper into her bones. Whatever was coming — however impossible it seemed — she wasn't facing it alone.

She smiled, albeit shakily. "Well...at least I don't have to push out eight baby dragons."

Callum let out a breath of laughter, but his eyes still burned with something deeper.

Dr. Alaric smirked. "No, but you do have to carry them to the extraction phase. And trust me, by month seven, you'll be begging to get them out."

Izzie groaned. "Great. Can't wait."

Callum leaned down and kissed her forehead. "You're strong. You can handle this."

Izzie wasn't sure, but looking at the monitor — at the eight eggs nestled inside her — she realized something.

She already loved them.

Izzie stared at the monitor, her mind struggling to process everything. Eight eggs. Growing inside her. And soon, they'd be the size of ostrich eggs. She swallowed hard, turning back to Dr. Alaric.

"So...when they hatch," she began slowly, "will they look like dragons? Or...like human babies?"

Callum's grip on her hand tightened slightly, as if the question unsettled him. Dr. Alaric, however, seemed unfazed. He leaned back against the counter, arms crossed, clearly anticipating the question.

"A fair question," he said. "And one without a simple answer."

Izzie narrowed her eyes. "Try me."

The doctor chuckled. "Dragon hybrid infants are unique. They hatch in their most instinctual form, which means their first moments will be as dragons. Their bodies will be small—about the size of a housecat—but fully functional. Wings, claws, fangs, everything. It's their natural defense mechanism. The world is dangerous for hatchlings, and they need to be able to protect themselves immediately."

Izzie blinked. "So...I'll be the mother of eight tiny dragons."

Callum finally spoke, his voice calm but tinged with something unreadable. "For a short time, yes."

She turned to him. "What do you mean 'for a short time'?"

Dr. Alaric stepped in again. "Dragon shifter infants instinctively shift between forms within a few hours of hatching. Their human side emerges as soon as they bond with their parents. It's an imprinting process— once they feel safe, they'll take human form, and from that point forward, they'll shift at will."

Izzie let out a slow breath. "So I won't be raising a nest of dragons?"

Callum smirked. "Not unless you want to."

She shot him a glare, but her mind was already racing. "And they'll look...normal? Like human babies?"

Dr. Alaric nodded. "Mostly. Their eyes may retain a bit of their dragon form—pupils that shift in certain lighting, or an unusual glow. And they'll be stronger than human infants. More aware, more coordinated. Dragon babies don't flail helplessly—they grasp, they climb, they test their limits quickly. You'll need to be prepared."

Izzie exhaled. "No pressure or anything."

Callum brushed his thumb over her knuckles. "You'll do fine."

She wasn't sure about that. Eight tiny dragons, shifting between forms, imprinting on her, on the brothers, learning to navigate two worlds before they could even walk?

Her heart pounded. This was real.

This was happening.

And despite the sheer terror of it all…

She couldn't wait to meet them.

Sign up for our newsletter and find out about all our romance book releases, eBook sales and promotions, sneak peeks and FREE romance books!

Want to see more from this author? Here's a taster for you to enjoy!

Eldritch Curiosities: Embers of the Emerald Isle
Kiera McKenna

Excerpt

The Cairn in the Rain

Rain slashed across the bog like a living thing with teeth. Emily Nicolson bent her head against the wind, boots squelching through heather and moss that tried to claim her ankles with every step. The compass needle in her palm spun lazily between magnetic north and something else entirely. *"Ley line interference,"* Margaret's voice echoed in her mind. *"When the needle dances, you're close."*

Three days of hiking through Connemara's wild heart had left Emily's jacket sodden, her hair escaping its braid in dark tendrils that whipped across her face. She paused to wipe rain from her eyes, scanning the terrain ahead. The tor-stone burial mound rose from the landscape like a sleeping giant's shoulder, its ancient cairn wreathed in mist.

This was it. The coordinates matched Margaret Alden's careful notations.

Emily shifted the artifact bag against her hip. The leather grew heavier with each step. Inside, wrapped in oiled cloth and warded silk, lay detection crystals that had remained stubbornly dormant for seventy-two hours. Six months ago, she would have dismissed such objects as elaborate props for an academic hoax. That was before Margaret had recruited her from her position at the University of Pennsylvania, before two months of intensive training at the Eldritch Curiosities facility in Wilmington, North Carolina, and before she'd learned that the supernatural world existed parallel to everything she'd thought she knew.

"*Dragon relics respond to proximity and intent,*" Margaret's training kicked in automatically. "*Approach with respect, not hunger.*"

The older woman's lessons had become a litany during the long trudge across sodden Irish countryside. "*Ley line resonance follows water and stone. Dragonkind masking glamours shimmer like heat mirages. Never assume you're alone.*" Most importantly, she had said, "*You're not just an archaeologist anymore, Emily. You're a liaison between species that have coexisted in secrecy for millennia.*"

Emily had thought Margaret was being dramatic during those first briefings in the Society's headquarters. The elegant building in Wilmington's historic district looked like any other antiquities firm, complete with glass cases displaying ancient artifacts and scholarly texts lining the walls. It wasn't until Margaret introduced her to their first "client" — a man whose eyes held flecks of gold that moved like living flame — that Emily understood she'd stepped into a world where legends walked among humans.

"*Dragons integrate into human society more easily than you might expect,*" Margaret had explained during one of their evening sessions. "*They've had centuries of practice. But they need partners who understand their true nature, who can help them navigate the complexities of their dual existence.*"

Partners. Emily still wasn't comfortable with the implications of that word. Margaret's briefings had been remarkably thorough about the intimate aspects of dragon-human relationships, complete with clinical discussions of biological compatibility and bonding rituals that made Emily's academic background in ancient cultures seem quaint by comparison. But the thought of bonding for life with a clutch of dragon-shifter brothers…

The very thought made her shudder.

A gust of wind almost knocked Emily sideways. She braced herself against a weathered stone marker, squinting up at the cairn. The burial mound was older than recorded history, its stones fitted together with the kind of patient craft that spoke of reverence rather than mere construction. Celtic spirals carved into the granite caught rainwater, creating temporary rivers that traced ancient symbols.

This was her first solo mission for the Society — a test of everything she'd learned about artifact recovery and supernatural diplomacy. Margaret had been characteristically cryptic about the details — "*Ancient dragon torc, likely pre-Roman. Last documented in Irish territorial records from the 1800s. Approach with caution — the local bloodline has a complicated relationship with outsiders.*"

What Margaret hadn't mentioned was how complicated that relationship might be, or why Emily's enhanced senses training would be necessary for what seemed like a straightforward recovery mission.

Emily approached the cairn's base and froze.

Her artifact bag pulsed.

Not the steady thrum of ley-line energy she'd grown accustomed to during training exercises, but something else that made her bones ache and her pulse quicken.

The leather grew warm against her hip, then hot enough that she hissed and stepped back.

The torc was near. Close.

Emily fumbled for her field journal, trying to keep the pages dry as she sketched the cairn's configuration. Margaret would want detailed documentation of the site before any retrieval attempts. The protocols drilled into her during those intensive weeks in Wilmington were clear—"*Document everything. Assume nothing. Remember that dragon artifacts have been known to test those who approach them.*"

But the bag pulsed again, more insistent this time, and Emily found herself taking another step toward the stones. The sensation reminded her of her final assessment at the Society—being led into her bedroom while Margaret observed from recessed cameras, testing Emily's ability to remain composed in the presence of sexually aroused dragon shifter men. She'd passed, barely, though she still didn't understand why the ability to mate with dragons was a job requirement.

"*The torc sings with old power.*"

Margaret's words felt prophetic as a sound reached Emily's ears—not quite music, not quite crying. It seemed to rise from the stones themselves, a harmony that bypassed her hearing entirely and resonated in her chest cavity. The melody was alien and achingly familiar at once, like a half-remembered lullaby sung in a language she'd never learned.

During her training, Emily had experienced controlled exposure to dragon magic—carefully regulated demonstrations designed to acclimate human senses to supernatural energies. This felt similar but amplified beyond anything she'd encountered in the safe confines of the Wilmington facility.

Emily's vision blurred. The rain turned to silver threads, the cairn's stones glowing with inner fire. She saw wings spanning impossible distances, eyes like molten gold, flames that burned without consuming—

The world tilted.

Emily's knees struck wet moss, her field journal scattering pages across the bog. The singing stopped abruptly, leaving only the wind's hollow moan and her own ragged breathing. Her hands shook as she pressed them to the ground, trying to anchor herself to something solid.

What the hell was that?

"Well, well." A man's voice cut through the rain, low and edged with something that might have been amusement. "What have we here?"

She snapped her head up. A figure stood between her and the cairn—tall, broad-shouldered, moving with the kind of fluid grace that suggested either dancer or predator. Rain streamed from dark hair that fell past his collar, and even through the downpour, she could see the sharp angles of his face—high cheekbones, a jaw that could have been carved from the stones around them.

He studied her with eyes that seemed to catch and hold the gray light. "You're on private land, girl."

Scrambling to her feet, she grabbed for her scattered notes. "I have permission—"

"From whom?" The stranger stepped closer, and Emily felt the hair on her arms rise. There was something about him that made her instincts scream *danger*, even as her rational mind noted that he wore ordinary clothes—wool sweater, worn jeans, boots that had seen serious use.

"The Irish Heritage Society." Emily straightened, trying to project confidence despite the mud on her knees and the way her hands still trembled. "I'm conducting archaeological research on pre-Christian burial sites."

The man's laugh was winter wind over stone. "Are you now?"

Emily's fingers found the emergency ward-sigil Margaret had given her, a small pewter disk warm against her palm. The older woman's voice echoed in her memory. *If you encounter hostility, show them this. Most dragonkind will recognize Council authority.* It was one of the few concrete tools Emily had been given for field work, along with protocols that seemed increasingly inadequate for the reality she was facing.

During her training, Margaret had emphasized the importance of proper introductions and diplomatic courtesy when dealing with dragon territorial claims. Emily had practiced the scripts dozens of times in role-playing exercises with Society staff. None of those controlled scenarios had prepared her for a confrontation in a storm-lashed bog with someone whose very presence made her primitive brain scream warnings.

She held up the sigil, hoping the rain hadn't obscured its carefully etched symbols. "I'm here under official sanction."

The stranger's eyes flicked to the disk, and for a moment, Emily thought she saw something flicker across his features — surprise, perhaps, or recognition. But when he spoke, his tone held only contempt.

"Official sanction." He shook his head, rain drops scattering from his hair. "Let me guess — you're one of Margaret Alden's little archaeologists."

Emily's blood went cold. He knew Margaret's name. That meant —

"Ronan O'Ceallaigh." The man's smile showed too many teeth. "And you, girl, are trespassing on O'Ceallaigh land."

O'Ceallaigh. The name from Margaret's briefing files, marked with red ink and warnings about territorial disputes. The last of an ancient bloodline, guardians of sacred sites, descended from dragons who'd ruled Irish skies when Rome was still a collection of mud huts.

"I'm Emily Nicolson." She forced her voice steady, professional. "I'm here to retrieve a dangerous artifact. If you'll just let me complete my work—"

"Your work." Ronan's eyes flashed, and for a split second, Emily could have sworn she saw gold fire where human irises should be. "You mean grave robbing."

The artifact bag pulsed again, so violently that she gasped and pressed her hand to her side. Ronan's gaze dropped to the leather satchel, and his expression went deadly still.

"What," he said with quiet menace, "is in that bag?"

As Emily backed toward the cairn, her mind raced. Margaret's protocols were clear—if she was discovered by dragonkind, she should reveal nothing about the artifacts until safe at headquarters. But Ronan was moving toward her with predatory focus, and she realized with sick certainty that running wasn't an option.

"Research equipment," she managed. "Compass, measuring tools, documentation—"

"Liar."

The word hit her like a physical blow. Ronan closed the distance between them in three swift strides, his hand shooting out to grasp her wrist. Power flowed between them as his fingers closed around her wrist—

furnace-hot against her rain-chilled skin, and so alien that her knees nearly buckled.

"You reek of magic," Ronan said softly. "Old magic. The kind that calls to things better left sleeping."

She tried to pull away, but his grip was iron. "I don't know what you're talking about."

"Don't you?" Ronan moved his free hand toward her bag, and panic shot through her.

"Don't touch that!"

The words came out sharper than she'd intended, laced with authority she didn't know she possessed. Ronan stopped his hand inches from the leather, narrowing his eyes.

"Interesting." He tightened his grip on her wrist tightened. "What exactly are you carrying that has you so protective?"

Emily's mind scrambled for a plausible lie, but the artifact bag chose that moment to pulse again — bright enough that light leaked around the leather edges, impossible to ignore.

Ronan's expression went from suspicious to furious in the space of a heartbeat.

"You're a tether," he breathed, and the words carried such venom that Emily flinched. "Margaret sent a bloody tether to my cairn."

Emily had no idea what a tether was, but the way Ronan said it made her skin crawl. The term hadn't appeared in any of her training materials — not in the extensive briefings about dragon culture, not in the clinical discussions of bonding rituals, not even in the comprehensive field manuals Margaret had made her memorize. If tethers were important enough to inspire this level of hostility, why hadn't she been warned?

She reached for the ward-sigil again, channeling every scrap of Margaret's training into the gesture.

"I am under Council protection," she said, holding the pewter disk between them like a shield. "You have no right to—"

Power flared from the sigil—or tried to. Instead of the protective barrier Margaret had described during countless training sessions, Emily felt the magic sputter and die like a candle in a hurricane. The disk grew cold against her palm, useless metal.

This wasn't supposed to happen. During her training, the ward-sigils had functioned flawlessly in controlled demonstrations. Margaret had assured her that Council authority was universally recognized, that the sigils would provide protection in any legitimate dispute. But nothing about Emily's current situation felt legitimate, and she was beginning to suspect that Margaret's curated training scenarios had prepared her for diplomacy, not whatever this was.

Ronan smiled, and there was nothing human in the expression.

"Your little ward doesn't work here, girl." He released her wrist only to grasp her shoulder, fingers digging in hard enough to bruise. "This is O'Ceallaigh land, under O'Ceallaigh law. And tethers aren't welcome."

"I'm not—I don't even know what that means!"

"It means," Ronan said, leaning close enough that she could see the unnatural gold flecks in his dark eyes, "that you're exactly the kind of trouble Margaret specializes in sending into the world."

Thunder cracked overhead, and the rain intensified until Emily could barely see beyond the cairn's stones. She tried once more to break free, but Ronan's grip was immovable.

"Let me go," she said, hating how small her voice sounded. "I'll leave. I'll tell Margaret the site was empty."

"Oh, you'll tell Margaret a great many things." Ronan's tone was conversational, which somehow made it more frightening. "But first, you're going to explain exactly what you've awakened."

As if summoned by his words, the torc's song rose again from somewhere within the cairn—fainter this time, but unmistakably present. Emily felt it in her bones, a harmony that made her teeth ache and her vision blur at the edges. The artifact bag grew hot against her hip in response, and she could swear the resonance crystal inside was pulsing in rhythm with the ancient melody.

Ronan went very still. His grip on her shoulder tightened until Emily bit back a cry of pain.

"How long?" he demanded.

"How long what?"

"How long have you been carrying that cursed thing?"

Emily's mouth went dry. "I don't—"

"Answer me!" The words came out as a roar that seemed to shake the very stones of the cairn. For a moment, Ronan's face was different—sharper, inhuman, with teeth that belonged in a predator's skull.

"Three days," Emily whispered. "It's been quiet until now, I swear."

Ronan stared at her for a long moment, his expression unreadable. When he spoke again, his voice was deadly calm.

"Three days," he repeated. "Three days you've been walking across Ireland with a tether stone singing in your bag, and you thought you could just waltz onto sacred ground and wake what sleeps here."

Her heart hammered against her ribs. "How did you—"

"Because, you little fool, that stone has been calling to every dragon within a hundred miles." Ronan shifted his grip to her upper arm, and he began pulling her away from the cairn with inexorable force. "Including some who'd rather see you dead than let you carry it another step."

Heels digging into the soggy ground did nothing to slow his pace—she might as well have tried to resist a landslide. "Where are you taking me?"

"Somewhere safe." Ronan didn't slow his pace, dragging her through heather that caught at her legs and tried to trip her. "Whether you survive the experience depends entirely on how honest you're willing to be."

The rain lashed them both as they descended from the cairn toward a valley Emily hadn't noticed before. Through the downpour, she could make out the dark bulk of a building—stone walls, slate roof, windows that glowed with warm light. Smoke rose from multiple chimneys, and Emily caught the scent of peat fires and something else—a metallic tang that made her think of lightning strikes.

"My research," she said desperately, glancing back toward the scattered pages of her field journal. "I need—"

"You need to start worrying about staying alive," Ronan cut her off. "The stone isn't the only thing that's been awakened today."

As if to underscore his point, Emily heard something in the distance—a sound like massive wings beating against storm-heavy air. She craned her neck skyward, but saw only gray clouds and driving rain.

Ronan heard it too. His pace quickened, and Emily stumbled to keep up.

"What was that?"

"Trouble," Ronan said grimly. "The kind that follows tethers like sharks follow blood."

The longhouse loomed ahead of them, its windows casting golden rectangles across rain-darkened stone. Emily could see figures moving inside — tall shapes that moved with the same predatory grace as the man dragging her forward.

"Please," she said, hating the desperation in her voice. "I just want to complete my mission and go home."

Ronan paused at the threshold, his hand on the heavy wooden door. When he looked at her, his expression held something that might have been pity.

"Girl," he said, "if you've woken the torc, you don't have a home anymore."

He pulled open the door, releasing a wash of warm air scented with woodsmoke and something indefinably wild. Light spilled across Emily's face, and she heard voices inside — male voices, speaking in what sounded like Irish Gaelic punctuated by laughter.

The conversation stopped the moment Ronan appeared in the doorway.

"Brothers," he called into the sudden silence, his voice carrying grim satisfaction. "Come meet our uninvited guest."

Emily tried once more to pull free, but Ronan's grip was unbreakable. He stepped across the threshold, dragging her with him into warmth and light and the predatory attention of eyes that held far too much intelligence.

The door slammed shut behind them with the finality of a tomb sealing.

Ronan released her arm and turned to face the room's other occupants—two men who rose from chairs near the fire with fluid grace that made Emily's skin prickle. They were clearly related—the same dark hair, sharp bone structure and unsettling golden gleam in their eyes when the firelight caught them.

"If your stone has woken the torc, girl," Ronan said without taking his gaze from his brothers, "you'll answer to more than me."

About the Author

Kiera McKenna writes darkly lyrical fantasy where strange magic stirs in the margins and forgotten things refuse to stay buried. Her debut, The Dragon's Harp, is the first installment in the Eldritch Curiosities series — a shadow-laced blend of myth, mystery, and slow-burn attraction set in a world where the magical and mundane bleed together.

With a love for gothic atmosphere, twisted folklore, and characters who carry both secrets and scars, Kiera crafts immersive tales that linger like candle smoke and stormlight. When she's not writing, she's likely haunting antique shops, reading about curses, or dreaming up her next endowed object.

Kiera loves to hear from readers. You can find her contact information, website details and author profile page at https://www.firstforromance.com

ENTWINED PUBLISHING